I0546065

Season of the Witch

Connal's Eternal Love
Christine Young

Sorceress' Secret
C.L. Kraemer

Thirteen Magic Pumpkin Seeds
Genie Gabriel

Published by Rogue Phoenix Press
Copyright © 2020
ISBN: 978-1-62420-593-4

Cover by Designs by Ms G

Connal's Eternal Love
Christine Young

Chapter One

1720
Highlands of Scotland

Connal McKenna paced the tower overlooking the Scottish countryside. Something was wrong tonight, verra wrong. He felt it deep in his soul, the darkest part of his being. It seemed the wind whispered the evil that was close, too close to ignore the feelings in his gut. Running his hands through his hair he decided not to speculate and also not to ignore the sensations that were quickly becoming something he could not disregard.

"What is it?" Brenna, his sister, stood by his side, her hand resting on his back as if attempting to reassure him. "I ken you're not of a mind as we are verging on All Hallows' Eve to enjoy yourself.

"You don't feel it? There are whispers in the air, wicked sounds, and deepest, blackest evil. You are usually more in tune to the wind's undertones than I am," Connal said, turning toward her. "Something in the wind doesn't bode well."

"I ken there is something afoot, but most of it is in your imagination, big brother. Ever since our mother and father died, you have seen shadows where there are none, darkness where there is light. You brood, Connal, and it is not well done of you." She pointed to the hill just a wee bit north. "Bonfires are lit, celebrations are at hand. What will it take to cheer you up?"

"It is not just the death of our parents." He didn't want to acknowledge how Maurina crushed his heart. He felt injured and broken. He'd thought she was his mate. When he discovered the truth, the pain had been unbearable.

"Maurina then, she has done this to you?"

Not wishing to speak of the woman, his once fiancée, he ignored his sister's question. Sympathy was not needed, as he was better off without her. He had been taken in by her beauty not realizing how self-centered and pretentious she was.

"I'm not wrong about this. There is evil in the air tonight. Something desperate and depraved that will change our lives forever is traveling our way," he paused then looking skyward, "At least it will change my life. I ken it but don't know if the change is for good or evil. When the wind murmurs, I shiver and the sensations deepen."

"I've never known you to be so superstitious or bothered by the undertones soaring with the ever-changing wind," Brenna said, and Connal did not miss the worry in her voice. Yet with an indulgent smile, he said, "You would ken it too, if you weren't constantly stealing glances at the lads in the hall."

This time he was right. They were on the verge of All Hallows' Eve and, in the highlands, everyone acted strange and the nights were eerie but this was singular. The villagers already set fires on the hilltops, already slaughtered cattle for sacrifice. Usually none of this was done until the night itself. He was not the only one who sensed the evil.

"I'm not mired in fantasy, and this has nothing to do with superstition or the occult. My feelings are based in fact. If you cannot see what is happening right in front of you, you should try opening your eyes, Brenna."

"Just because I've a different opinion does not mean I'm not seeing clearly. My eyes are wide open, Connal McKenna." She turned toward the steps seemingly intent on removing herself. Her back was stiff as she marched away, leaving him to brood even more. She must have changed her mind because she was suddenly beside him again, her hand resting on his back.

A hawk swept by touching Connal on the shoulder then flew upward. The nearly full moon highlighted the bird's silhouette. A shiver swept down his spine as he watched the sky and listened to the sounds of the earth. This evening every shadow of a noise beckoned to him. He meant to discover the truth, tonight.

The dark silence touched him in ways he couldn't explain to Brenna let alone himself, the world so different now. He believed in the powers of nature, believed that in time people would come to accept who he really was.

"Would you like to go for a run with me?" he asked Brenna, knowing she did not leave the turrets although a few moments ago that had obviously been her intent. "We could swim in the loch when we are finished."

"You want me, a woman, to go for a run with you so close to Samhaim?" She sounded incredulous. "Just as with your fiancée, the good villagers will take exception to who you are if caught. You cannot let yourself become so vulnerable it might cost you your life. I weel nay risk mine."

He almost chuckled but thought better of it when he saw the expression on her face emphasized by shadows created by the light from the torches. If he didn't understand her so well, he knew she was angry and frustrated at him.

"No, I suppose it might not be a good idea. If you were caught..." he let the thought hang unsaid but she finished for him.

"I would be burned as a witch before having a trial, vigilante justice." Her voice shook with raw passion, the emotion emanating from her savage and primal. "Even now more and more people fill our tiny part of Scotland. The chance to roam free and be ourselves is disappearing. The clan is growing restless. Some talk of moving where there is more room."

He was not afraid of these people, those living in the highlands. He didn't feel the need to leave his country. The clan Chattan were different, and they would not be caught, had never been, but he did have to admit the spaces were growing smaller. There was less land to roam free. He understood the need for that freedom.

"We would not have to shift back if we saw anyone. You could stay in your cat form." For some reason, he didn't want to go alone. He tried one more time to convince her. "If someone saw us, I would protect you."

"How? If either of us was captured, we'd be held as a prize to be shown off and would not be able to shift back to human form. Black panthers do not exist naturally in any part of Scotland as you well ken. Don't take any chances."

"I would find a way," he told her but knew in his heart a rescue might not be possible and might result in his capture also. Long ago, the clan Chattan made a pact addressing this very thing. If caught, there would be no rescue from the others. One would need to fend for themselves and find their own way, whatever that might be.

"You should take a couple of the cousins with you and maybe Alistair too. They are all shifters, and you can take care of yourselves, defend each other if the need arises. The four of you together are an impressive force, one to be reckoned with." She hung back from him seemingly afraid his arguments could not be denied much longer.

"Perhaps you are right. I will see what they think. This restlessness is eating at my heart. Pacing the turrets does nothing to ease the feelings in the deepest part of my soul." He leaned against the wall, his forearms on the cold stone, searching the countryside for anything that was tangible or would present danger. He saw nothing, only heard the rumors of the wind.

Moonlight glinted on the nearby lock, the water shimmering and bright. A cold swim might be good for the soul as well as the ache in his heart. He laughed, knowing the water would be frigid and would serve only to numb him for a few hours.

"The lot of you can be as foolish or as daring as you want and," she paused, smiling at him for the first time tonight, "maybe you will work some of this brooding monster from your soul. Perhaps when you return, you will be easier to talk to and live with. You should find a willing woman."

"I'm not brooding nor am I a monster," he grumbled, giving credence to her words. His gut churned and his mind ached. Good sex would serve to ease him for a little while then all the black feelings would return with a vengeance.

She sighed long and deep, seeming to expect something from him he could not give to her. "You don't have to live with you. You chastised the sweet maid when she spilled a tiny bit of wine on the table this evening. You've spilled more when you were in your cups." She reprimanded him yet the grin on her face told him she was indulging him. "You knew it was an accident. The poor girl tripped on the edge of the rug."

He raked his hands through his hair, the ends flying around his face, coming unleashed from the leather thong he held it with. The dark ends dipped rakishly below his collar. "I wasn't angry. I just wanted to make sure she understood her behavior wasn't acceptable."

"What does have you brooding more than usual? Really. You need to come to terms with the facts and deal with them logically. Only then will you become a suitable person to live with."

"It's this damn feeling that has settled in my heart. I cannot fight it nor do I understand why the deep weight on my shoulders doesn't go away. It is as if I'm just waiting for something to happen, and I can't do anything about what is coming my way until it presents itself." Years ago, he learned how much he detested surprises. He leaned on the wall once again, his mind wandering, drifting to thoughts of the woman he once believed was his mate. Reflections of Maurina in his head and the words she spoke when she left.

You're a freak of nature.

He recalled the words as well as the inflection in her voice when she spoke them. *Freak of nature.* Because of her knowledge, and the possibility she would divulge the clans' secrets, she was sent away, far away where she could do no damage to clan Chattan. Her whereabouts was never divulged to him. He supposed that was good. But he also kenned she was sent to the Kinnell stones.

Brenna sighed softly, placing a hand on his back, "You should go now, go run, see if Angus and Fergus will shift and run with you until all these black brooding feelings leave your heart and soul. Perhaps Alistair will be there also. Seems he has the same thoughts as you. He paces and frets, his face grim as he acts as if things plague him over what seems like nothing to me. He cannot find his mate and is questioning now if they exist. I think you will find all three of them in the kitchen flirting with the cook. They are all incorrigible," Brenna laughed, rolling her eyes as if she

5

was thinking of some of their exploits.

Perhaps all that Brenna said was true but a black brooding monster? He was not that bad. Was he? It seemed he did look at everything with a jaundiced and cynical eye. Mayhap he did frown more than he smiled.

Striding down the steps he thought on where they should go. Brenna was right about one thing. They should not run close to any of the villages. There were a few inhabitants who would question seeing three or perhaps four black panthers in this part of the world.

As predicted by his sisters, the three young men were indeed in the kitchen flirting with the cook. When Alistair saw him, he looked up frowning then it seemed Angus and Fergus noticed his arrival as well.

"What are you doing darkening the kitchen?" Angus asked with a chuckle. "Are you going to leave everyone here depressed and moody?"

If that was meant as a joke, the words did not sit well with him. "Wanted to shift, run with the wind. Anyone interested?"

"You would leave the cozy fire at the hearth and a willing woman in your bed to wear yourself out?" Angus asked, laughing, his eyes twinkling with mischief. "Would rather spend the night with a high spirited and eager woman, one who wants to be in my arms as well as my bed."

"Don't have a willing woman, eager or high spirited," Connal muttered, feeling sorry for himself and alone in this world, at least where female companionship was important. "Need to do something tonight. Feel the need deep in my bones. If no one is interested, I'll go by myself."

"Not safe to go alone," Fergus said with a grumble. "Suppose we'll have to leave the warmth of the kitchen and the willing maid," he said as he winked at the lass.

"I've the same need as you," Alistair spoke up, heading to the door. "Where do want to go?"

"I plan on riding north a few miles and away from any hamlets. Looking for privacy and perhaps a way to vanquish the restlessness I feel."

"Dangerous for just the two of you. We'll both go," Angus said, sending his brother a look.

"Then grab a coat and I'll meet you in the stables."

Second thoughts assailed him as he thought about the myriad of things that could go wrong. Two evenings away from All Hallows' Eve and the strange happenings on that night. He inhaled a long deep breath wondering if he should leave his cousins and friend behind, not feeling any danger in his gut, just the bleakness as well as the evil.

He wasn't given the chance of leaving them behind when Alistair arrived seconds behind him with the cousins. Mounted and heading into the darkness accompanied by the murky fluttering shadows, they road at a gallop for a few miles then slowed.

Connal turned his horse down a narrow animal trail, branches hitting him in the face, spider webs clinging to him. He brushed them away with a curse knowing he could be in the warmth of the castle. The trail twisted and turned, going ever deeper into the forest until the only light from the moon was so dim one could barely see his hand in front of his face.

"Think we've gone far enough?" Fergus asked. "Don't see anyone around, don't expect to see anyone but, in this gloom, who would know? One would have to hear or smell them."

"Looks like the best place to me," Angus seemed to agree with his brother. "The only question is can we see to run?"

Connal stopped, sliding off his horse, the other men following. They all disrobed and shifted then ran despite the darkness. Their cat eyes easily adjusting to the blackness surrounding them, they ran. He raced the night and the wind. The big cats were made for speed not endurance so it was not long before they all became winded. Connal sat on his haunches staring at the loch and wondering if the others would follow if he went for a midnight swim. They probably would because none wanted to be left alone this evening as they shared an unbreakable bond.

By the time the men cooled themselves in the frigid loch, a few clouds hung in the sky and a brisk wind picked up. With silent acknowledgement, the men headed for their mounts as well as their clothing. Connal knew the edginess had not vanished, but the night didn't seem quite so bleak or desperate. For a timeless moment, the sounds of evil were slowly being replaced by light and goodness.

"Do you feel better now?" Alistair asked laughing. "I don't. Now I'm cold and tired, ready for my bed. We'll be back late enough there will be no willing women about to warm us."

"Well, suppose I feel the same," Connal admitted chuckling, "but at least now I'll be able to sleep."

"Think so?" Fergus asked, lifting one eyebrow. "For a while this evening I did believe the cook would be in my bed, now I'm sure she's found someone else or she's alone for the night too."

"She likes me better," Angus said, "as well you ken."

"Perhaps she would have enjoyed both of us," Fergus said, shooting his brother a look, his voice gruff with raw passion. "We've never shared but there is always a first time."

"Then neither of us would have slept," Angus said, laughing and throwing a shirt at his sibling.

"It's after midnight now. We should get back and still I feel something is about to happen, something that will change my life," Connal muttered, wishing that whatever was about would do it now and end the suspense.

"Then nothing was solved by this midnight romp?" Alistair asked quirking one eyebrow skyward.

Connal was shaking his head while he pulled on his boots. "Nothing so far."

On the trails back, the night seemed to darken even more. Clouds passing across the moon dimmed the already meager light. Everything Connal felt earlier intensified. When they reached the main road, he pulled up, searching both directions. The sensations no longer felt evil but desperate, fraught with pain. He sensed fear, sheer terror, but it wasn't his.

"Do any of you feel that?" he asked, turning the horse to look away from the McKenna land.

"The wind has shifted," Alistair said, his voice stern. "Perhaps your intuition is better than we thought."

Connal's hand settled on his sword, his heart beating hard. "Be prepared. I sense a fight of some sort. Man or beast, whatever it is, it is coming closer."

He heard the pounding of the hooves, a single horse, but racing down the darkened road, shadows hiding the horse and rider. Suddenly, the silhouetted form raced around the bend in the road, cape and brilliant hair flying behind. Moonlight caught the vibrant strands for a brief moment sending slivers of color to greet his gaze. Connal's heartbeat stopped then slowly began to beat again, the brilliance or the color, shimmering a deep red catching all the meager light until the elements appeared on fire.

Connal's breath caught in his throat, captivated by the site as the woman drew closer. She didn't seem to see them, continuing on her wild ride toward him. Yet to Connal, she seemed remarkably skilled for a woman, vulnerable as well. He only knew of one other woman who could ride that well and that heedlessly without injury. His sister.

When the woman was too close to turn around and race in the opposite direction, "Hold!" Connal raised his sword, moonlight glinting off the steel. Behind him, his men did the same.

She pulled on the reins to stop the stallion's mad dash down the road before she would run into him. The horse reared its front legs rising high, pawing in the air as she clung to him, desperately hanging on.

"No," her whispered word did not escape Connal. The single word sounded and felt like a cry for help.

Yet perhaps he was mistaken. As soon as the young woman controlled the horse, she dashed through the woods away from them. A moment of breathless silence followed before Connal regained his wits, pushing the cobwebs from his brain.

"Stay here and wait for me," he ordered then followed the woman into the trees, hell bent on catching up with her. He suddenly felt alive and whole, all instincts driving him forward to claim the prize that had suddenly appeared in front of him.

He couldn't see or hear her. Pulling to a stop he listened and the silence was foreboding, unnerving. The wind's murmurs no longer sounded evil to him, just fearful. She must have done the same. With nothing to lose, he would wait for her to make her move and when she did, he would have her and discover what caused her frantic and wild race this evening. He would ascertain what motivated her to put herself in such danger.

It did not take long. A few minutes later he heard the swish of movement through the bushes. He smiled; his keen hearing would pay off. She must not realize it, but she was slowly moving toward him. When she was close, he spurred his horse, capturing the reins of hers before she could flee again.

"You are mine now." And he understood his words were true despite the fact she would gainsay him at every turn. His heart beat stronger suddenly and his mind cleared.

"No!" This time her cry was of alarm and horror. "Leave me alone." She tried to push his hand away, swatting at him but to no avail. "I weel nay go back."

"I won't hurt you, lass," he said as her fist hit his jaw. Then needing to laugh, "I suppose I didn't see that coming."

"I've heard that before," she grit out, still pushing at his hands, struggling away from him. "You've no right."

"Which part? I won't hurt you or I didn't see it coming."

"Let me go." She jerked on the reins to no avail.

"Stop it." He tried to grab her around the waist to lift her onto his horse, hoping to control her struggles and subdue her in the process yet he realized that would not be an easy feat.

"Never," she said, still hitting at him, her fingernails raking across his face, drawing rivulets of blood. This time she pushed so hard, she fell from her horse.

For a moment, she lay stunned on the ground, gasping for air. That tiny second gave him time to dismount and reach for her. He held her now, once again her arms and legs flying through the air, her efforts directed at him. He wanted to shake some sense into her and tell her she didn't need to fight him. He meant her no harm, but he also understood she wouldn't believe him.

He didn't know what to tell her. She needed to stop this foolishness before one of them got hurt. At this moment, he suspected it would be him who took the brunt of her blows.

"Let me go. You've no right." Her words were short and pained. She was very nearly breathless, exhausted by her desperate thrashing.

10

The pounding on his chest weakened her until she fell limp in his arms, her head resting against his chest. He heard the long raspy attempts for air, felt the rapid beat of her heart against him. In her gasp for air, a sob rumbled forth. A moment of sympathy or perhaps it was empathy that filled his soul for this lass.

"Now are you going to stop fighting me?" he asked, even as she pulled back, hitting him in the chest with her head then with one last and very weak punch she quit for the moment.

He didn't trust the slender bliss filled moment of peace. "Blessed hell." He'd had enough of this, would take no more this night. He swung her onto his shoulder before whistling for his horse. Interestingly, her steed came as well, but he wasn't about to put her on the mare. There was no trust involved here. If he let her go, she would run and whatever demons were chasing her would catch her. He prayed not before he did. Another chase tonight was not going to happen if he could help it. Meaning to protect her, he intended to keep her close until he understood who she was and what she was about. Why she fought him so hard.

He returned to the road and to a roar of applause from his friends. It appeared at least for the time being she quit fighting him. "A tiny little slip of a woman almost bested you," Angus laughed, chortling with glee. "I can hardly wait to see what comes of this strange union."

"Tis no union, strange or otherwise." But he suspected there might be more truth to Angus' words than he was willing to admit at this moment. He didn't understand why, but this tiny female intrigued and fascinated him. Perhaps it was just because she fought him so desperately. No other lass had ever dared to fight or disagree with him, the laird. All knew that he was the head of the clan.

"Are those scratch marks on your face?" Alistair asked with a chuckle. "Was she trying to mark you or is it just a coincidence?"

Men marked their mate, not the other way around. "Get off your horse and help me. Be careful." Connal handed the girl over to Alistair then pulled the thong from his hair.

"Be glad to," he said, still laughing and finding this situation Connal was in too amusing to ignore.

When he sat his horse, Alistair placed her in front of him, "Tie her hands for me." He was angry now and in almost any other time, he would have explained his actions, but not tonight. His friends could wonder what had gotten into him.

~ * ~

Wynnie understood she'd just hopped from the boiling pot into the fire. Now she leaned against this man's broad chest, pressed so hard against him she felt each breath, her hands useless. She could not fight. Truth be told, she didn't have the energy to struggle let alone voice another protest. Waiting for an additional moment might be prudent, but she was pretty sure she would not get the chance.

"What's your name?"

His voice rumbled against her back reverberating, pulsing. The sound was low and deep, somehow soothing in this turbulent time. This was a man who was used to getting his way in everything. She closed her eyes, praying the leather tying her hands would come undone, wishing she would have seen these men and gone the other way before it was too late.

Resting against him, she tried to draw some energy into her body but she'd been running for days now, sleeping with one eye open. She had barely eaten, finding a few mushrooms on the ground, digging for wild potatoes. Exhaustion tried to steal inside.

"Mine is Connal, Connal McKenna. You can call me Connal. What's yours?" he repeated the question. He held his breath, as if hoping she would answer and he would hear.

She gasped, startled by his voice. She must have dozed for a second, her lashes heavy. Then in a whisper thin voice, "None of your business."

She felt the masculine lift of his shoulders. "Have it your way but I can guarantee I'll be a lot nicer to you if you answer my questions." He chuckled as if he didn't just claim her as a prisoner, as if this was just another day in his life.

Well it wasn't just another day in her life. He was trying to be nice. How dare he, when she knew he had other motives? All men had motives other than what they presented to a woman.

"Where were you in such a hurry to get to?" His probing question was not going to be answered.

"Not here," she told him begrudgingly.

He laughed and that just didn't sit well with her. She tugged on her bindings until her skin was raw.

"You should stop that. You're hurting yourself." His voice was low and smooth reminding her of warm whiskey.

He sounded concerned but she knew she was imagining the tone of his voice. He was just like all the other men she'd known; self-centered, egotistical and filled with himself as well as the masculine arrogance that seemed to ooze from every pore. He would take what he wanted from her as long as he wanted. Understood she would have no say. He would hurt her just as the others had done.

"You could untie me." She tried to add a sugary tone to her voice but that just wasn't her and the words came out more like a command than a flirtatious request.

"Then you'd be hurting me," he laughed again as if something was funny. "I've scratch marks on my face as well as a bruise on my jaw to prove my claim to that fact."

"You afraid of a mere girl?" she asked before realizing she was challenging him instead of giving him what he wanted, sympathy and her compliance.

"There is nothing mere about you." He tossed back at her.

"You should untie her and see what happens. She might warm your bed if you're nicer. Lately, you seem to be lacking in that quality where women are concerned," Angus said appearing to have a good time at his expense.

"No female wants to be in your bed, not one. You're too gloomy and brooding," Fergus jabbed at him. Then to finish the insult, "And menacing."

"What do you think, little lady? Do you want to be in my bed?" He was playing her, his voice assuming a kind gentle tone. She detested the tenor as well as the meaning.

While she did not find him repulsive as she did other men of his ilk, she didn't want to be forced into any man's bed. Somehow, she didn't think he would force her. "No."

"Then you'd rather I put you in the tower prison? You like mice better than men?" he queried. "I can guarantee you the tower is full of mice."

"No." She cringed against his back and was sure he felt the tension in her arms when he mentioned the rodents. Mice weren't as bad as rats. Then it seemed he read her mind.

"She does speak. I've heard there are also rats in the tower though I haven't seen one myself."

She wasn't going to say anything more. He was baiting her and she fell right into the trap. Without saying much at all, he read her body language, the way she reacted to his words. Tears formed in her eyes. She fought them, fought them with everything she could. Yet the last weeks...

"What's your name, lass? I'd like to start over if you don't mind." He wrapped one of his hands around hers.

She discovered her fingers were numb with the cold and the tightly bound leather stopping the flow of blood. Stifling the groan of pain was impossible. He stroked them, perhaps trying to warm her hands but the blood wasn't cooperating.

Wynnie didn't want to give in to the exhaustion and the horror of the last weeks, but her body had different intentions. She slumped against him, her mind hazy. Yet she still heard the words floating around her and about her, teasing words about mice and beds, men as well.

"I'm worried about the lass," Connal said. "Her hands are freezing. She might even now be falling asleep. We all ken, she needs to stay awake. Don't want her succumbing to the cold night air."

"We should be home soon and you can warm her up," Angus said, his words filled with humor.

"If I didn't fear for my life when she is not bound, I might be more amenable to a little coaxing or verbal persuasion in order to see her softer side," Connal said, feeling as if this woman was beginning to touch his heart in some strange way.

"Perhaps she's as feisty in bed as she is on the battlefield," Alistair mused. "Think she could be your mate?"

14

"Not a chance. I would have felt something, wouldn't I?"

A mate?

"Suppose so. Bed her then and send her on her way. She obviously is running from someone or something," Angus seemed to be encouraging. "If perhaps you protected her, she might be eternally grateful and you will be much more biddable."

"The only way she'd bed me would be to force her," Connal said. "I won't do that or seduce her so she thinks she wants me when she really doesn't. Had enough of that ridiculousness with Maurina. The next woman I take to my bed will understand who I am and will want me for those same reasons."

"Then you might be an old man before you get any sex. There are a lot of willing women in the village. You should try one or two for the duration. It will ease your needs and no one will be calling you morose and brooding," Alistair said seeming to watch him as he gave his opinion.

"We're home," Connal said the obvious as he turned his horse into the stables. "Help me with her." He slit the bindings holding her hands and she started to slip from the horse.

"Catch her," Angus said, rushing to reach her before she hit the stable floor.

She landed with a thud, groaning and opening her eyes. "What happened?"

Connal was beside her, stroking her hair away from her face. "Your hair looks as if it's on fire." He murmured so very intrigued. "You must have fallen asleep. When I cut the bindings, you fell. Guess they were all that was keeping you on the horse."

She didn't move, just stared at the dark brown eyes looking back at her as well as the row of even white teeth he was showing her. Her breath caught. She swallowed as he slowly set a strand of hair behind her ear. The touch was gentle, not like the ones she endured at the hands of other men. Even when she was running from him, struggling against his brute strength, he'd been gentle with her. She reached up and touched one of the scratches on his cheek.

"Are you going to walk by yourself or do I need to toss you over my shoulder again?" he asked, his voice deep yet also held a hint of humor. "You do know I won't let you get away from me."

She nodded thinking over his words and while she looked around, his men surrounded her.

"I'll walk." She tried to stand but the coldness seemed to have penetrated every muscle she possessed. He extended his hand. She reached out to accept the offer but groaned instead.

"Are you hurt?"

She was shaking her head, "No, no I don't think so. Just cold and stiff, my feet dinna want to work."

"But you can't stand or take my hand." His voice was calm, seemed to calm.

"You're right, of course."

He swept her into his arms, striding through the stable to the castle doors then up the steps and more steps and more then it seemed an eternity before he kicked a door open with his foot and set her on the paltry bed in the single room.

The mattress was lumpy. Straw poked out of the seams. She looked up at him and knew horror was painted on her face. Eyeing the open door, she was tempted to flee but understood she would not make it to the door before he caught her again.

"You can't mean to have me sleep here." This was horrible, more than horrible. "Am I a prisoner then? What did I do besides run from you?" *Please dear God don't let him touch me. I could not bear the thought of another man taking me against my will.*

"Yes, yes and yes," he smiled at her. "What is wrong with the bed?"

"It's nasty." Despite her circumstance these last few weeks, she was not used to such places.

"Aw, you must be a princess. Prisoners are not usually that picky. But these are your accommodations."

"No." She stood too quickly, falling back to the bed almost at the same time. "Do I get a blanket or water? Food perhaps." Heat rose to her cheeks as her stomach rumbled in protest.

He stood over her, a small grin on his too handsome face. The smile was almost a smirk yet if she wasn't mistaken, it turned hesitant, almost apologetic. "Perhaps if you tell me your name and answer a few questions I would consider your requests. I wouldn't want to stay here either, but you need to tell me who you are and if I should expect someone to be coming for you."

She looked away then back, her eyes appearing to cross with fear, "Wynnie."

"Well, that wasn't too hard now was it? What is your surname?" He held a strand of her hair in his fingers seemingly mesmerized.

She didn't want him to know her last name or where she was from. He would turn her in if he learned anything. Her father and her intended would be searching for her. A few hours before she met Connal on the road she was sure they picked up the trail. She would die before she would let either of those men lay another hand on her.

The wind changed and she heard things whispered through the branches on the trees then through the tiny window in the room. Animals chattered about the events. Evil seemed to find her and settle deep in her soul. They were coming for her. She knew it as the darkness entered her heart. This place was her only chance of escaping them; this man her only protection.

She moistened her lips, looking at him and trying to plead with her eyes. "I can't." she let out a long whoosh of air.

"And why is that?" He sat down beside her. "You in trouble somewhere?" He bounced on the mattress a few times then adjusted his weight. "This bed is lumpy. There is another choice you know." He flashed a brilliant smile, placing her hand in his large one.

"What's the other choice?" She knew what he was thinking, understood the way a man's mind worked.

"Why can't you tell me your last name?" He persisted, moving his leg so it touched hers.

Heat welled up inside her, a burning warmth, something she'd never felt before. She shook it off as her imagination and jerked away. "What's the other choice?"

"We've reached a stalemate," he laughed, his grin broadening. "You're a formidable opponent, Wynnie with no last name. Shall we continue this tomorrow?"

"No, I need a blanket and water, a place to..."

"A prisoner who wants comforts of home. How ironic."

"You never told me why I'm your prisoner."

He shrugged standing then walked around the room, stopping at the window. "You have a pleasant view of the lake. I think you will enjoy watching the moonlight glimmer on the water. Except for the mattress there is really nothing wrong with this room."

"It's drafty. I would also request something to cover the opening."

"When you're honest with me, I'll give you whatever you ask for."

She was fuming now, her eyes blazing, irritated with him and his strange behavior. Men were all the same. She could not tell him her last name. "If there is a second choice, I'll take it. It can't be worse than here."

Wynnie couldn't help herself, she squealed then screamed when a mouse ran from beneath the bed.

"What's wrong," He turned, pistol in hand, searching the entrance to the room for the object of her fear.

"No-nothing," Her hand at her throat, she gulped in air, her pulse speeding.

"You always scream at nothing?" His voice held contempt and perhaps a huge amount of annoyance. "If you are going to deal well with me, you need to speak the truth."

"So should you." Unwisely she stood up to him. Her voice shook with the realization while expecting the blow. When it didn't come, "You haven't told me why I'm here. You haven't been straight with me about your intentions." She moved closer to him, pressing herself against him as the mouse poked its head from behind an old ragged chair.

"You're haughty for someone who has no rights or friends. Tells me you are used to getting everything your way."

She pointed in the direction of the creature then, "I'll jump out that window."

"The scream was because of the mouse?" He sounded incredulous even while he wrapped an arm around her and pulled her closer to him.

She shivered, pushing against him although she knew she shouldn't. "The mouse..."

18

"It won't hurt you. Indeed, I do believe it's more scared of you," He laughed outright, continuing to chuckle as the tiny creature scurried from the room. "So you want to try the second choice. You might not like it any better than this one."

"Does it have mice?" She closed her eyes praying for the strength to endure this nightmare of a man. Who did he think he was?

"Not that I've seen." He was still laughing, running his large hand up and down her arm as if he was trying to warm her and soothe her rattled nerves.

"I'll try it."

"No, make the commitment now. I won't be climbing up these steps again tonight. If you choose the second option, that is where you will sleep."

"Will you tell me something about it then?" He was being straight with her. She didn't want to take him up on that option but she couldn't stay here.

"If you tell me your surname."

"Are we back to that?" she asked, realizing he was like a dog with a bone, and he wasn't going to let go but worry it to death. Well, she could be just as stubborn. "Very well, I'm ready to go and I'd like to try to navigate the steps on my own if it's all right with his highness."

"I'm glad you are understanding my status in the castle." He helped her to stand, and this time she could manage, then he offered his arm. "There are a lot of steps. Just say the word if you'd like me to help you more, I am getting used to holding you in my arms."

"I'm sure I'll do well enough. My feet and hands are no longer numb." She spoke primly, she knew. If he could be king of the castle, she could match him and act the queen.

"Shall we then?" he asked, still grinning, his all-knowing expression infuriating.

Immediate misgiving swept through her. He knew more than he let on, obviously, and she was sure now she might regret this hasty decision and the room he was leading her to more than the first one.

They stepped down two levels then turned right. The door they stopped in front of was huge and foreboding. The meaning of its size implicit to anyone who ever lived in a castle. This was the master's chamber, and this was where he was leading her.

His men spoke of his bedding her, but he told them he wouldn't force her nor would he seduce her to the point where she didn't understand or know her mind. Obviously, he lied. Why else would they enter his bedroom, his domain?

"I see by the look on your face, you understand the choice you made." He ushered her inside. Standing back, his arms crossed in front of him it seemed he waited for something.

The room was warm and a fire crackled in the fireplace. Candles lit the chamber, casting shadows along the floor and the walls. The tapestries hanging from ceiling to floor were thick and told a story of panthers and people with the title clan Chattan woven into the fabric.

Clan of the cats.

She looked at him then, really looked at him, her eyes wide with shock or fear she wasn't sure. Then the bed caught her attention. It was huge, obviously made for him as well as room for a partner.

She understood now how so very far out of her element she was. He was the laird here, and his clan were shifters. Knowing the truth left her with ominous and dark sensations. The rumors abounded about these people; some good, some bad but nothing she'd heard was fact, only speculations.

She supposed she would know soon enough what he expected of her. Defiantly, her arms crossed in front of her. She rubbed them, trying to ward off the sudden chill sweeping through her.

One of the other men talked about his mate. She was shaking her head, backing up. She could not be this man's mate. Still behind her he blocked her way as she collided with his chest.

"Not so sure this is where you want to be. Perhaps I can change your mind though." One hand rested gently yet intimidating on her neck, his thumb rubbing tiny circles at the base seeming to warm her from the inside out. His other hand was on her waist.

She was sure he could feel the rapid beating of her pulse, smell her terror, still there was something about this man that fascinated and intrigued her. Raw power emanated from his muscular frame, yet he wore gentleness in his soul. His broad shoulders and long slim torso intrigued her, left her wanting to discover more of him.

Then she reminded herself. He was a man and he would take what he wanted with no regard to her or her wishes or even her pain.

Her voice shaking, "You said you would not force or seduce anyone into your bed." She challenged, hoping he would stand by his words.

"Thought you were asleep when I said that. Guess you weren't. What else did you hear?" Still he didn't remove his hands from her or stop the gentle stroking that seemed to be heating her from the inside out.

"I don't remember." She saw her saddlebag on his bed. "You knew I would agree to this, knew I would not want to be left in the tower room." Anger threatened to explode within even while the unknown had her trembling so hard she thought her knees would buckle.

The door was closed and locked behind her. He was now sitting on his bed pulling items from the satchel. "I need to know more about you as I've a clan to protect and you willingly tell me nothing, Wynnie. Perhaps you are a spy, an enemy of my people. It's my job to safeguard all of them."

Hand shaking, rushing to him, to the bedside, "Stop. You've no right to go through my things." He would find out the truth, learn her last name. She couldn't risk that but knew her meager strength was no match for his.

He would have his way in this. There was naught she could do to prevent it from happening.

"I would do anything," she blurted before she could possibly understand what the word anything might mean to a man such as Connal McKenna, laird of clan Chattan. But the grin on his face told her she might be in deep and very dark trouble.

~ * ~

Unable to sleep Brenna was sitting by the hearth when the cousins and Alistair entered the room, laughing and talking about Connal and the feisty woman he found quite by accident along the road. Deciding she needed to find out more, at least from these very biased friends, she stood and smoothed her skirts before she walked to where they were sitting.

They already had tankards of ale in hand as well as a plate of bread in front of them. She sat down, pouring herself a glass of mulled wine.

"I see something happened. Was it as dark and as dangerous as Connal thought it would be?" She tilted her head, flirtatiously understanding that with a smile and a toss of her hair, she could get all of these men, especially Alistair, to spill whatever they were keeping to themselves as well as sworn secrets.

"Ah, he found a pantheress to meet his needs, we've been thinking." Angus said before he tossed back his head and drank long and deep then set the metal cup on the table with a resounding thud.

Alistair stared at her then. She felt a sudden rush of heat sweep through her, his gaze resting on her mouth then dropping to her bosom. Sensations she'd never known before. Her breath caught deep in the back of her throat as her heart double-timed. What was this?

"We're hoping he'll come down to breakfast in the morning with a smile on his face instead of the frown we usually see," Fergus added to what his brother was saying. "Probably not going to be able to tame her in one night though. She's a feisty lass."

"Don't like the sound of that. Tame her?" Brenna queried, still curious. Yet, Alistair's gaze was still fixed on her almost as if he'd never seen her before. She smiled at him then tossed her hair over her shoulder flirtatiously. His eyes darkened until they were very nearly black. Butterflies flitted in her stomach.

"Ah, we don't mean anything by that. She is high spirited and she won't fall into his arms easily," Fergus said.

"Connal found his mate?" Brenna's spirits lifted. She decided she would intrude on her brother and this woman just to find out a tiny bit more than the men were willing to share.

"Don't know about that but she's beautiful and secretive," Alistair mused stroking his red beard a few times, his concentration still focused on her. "She marked him in a way. Left a set of four tiny scratch marks on his cheek. He could have let her go but for some reason he chased her down and acted as if she was his prisoner. Strange as that sounds, she did nothing to warrant that kind of treatment."

That didn't sound like her brother. "How so?" She leaned forward intent on discovering more about the incident.

"Tied her up, made her ride in front him."

"Really?" This story was growing more intriguing by the second. "Where are they now?"

"Took her to the tower room, but I'll bet they're now in his bedchamber. Tower's not a place for a lady and a laird who has had his share of bad luck with the women in his life."

"A lady? Do you think they will want food and drink? A bath perhaps?" Brenna stood, heading for the kitchen before hearing the answer. It was, after all, her sisterly duty to find out what was happening with her brother.

In the kitchen and directing two servants, she discovered her brother had ordered a bath, for two. She thought over everything her cousins and Alistair told her. The woman wasn't willing, yet she was now in the master chamber alone with Connal. This was just not like him. She felt a sudden and urgent need to interfere or at least make sure the woman was indeed accepting of her lodging.

Alistair was suddenly behind her, his hands on her waist, stroking her. "You shouldn't interfere, lass. This is bigger than you can imagine." His breath whispered along her neck, sending a wave of flames searing through her body. The touch of his tongue where her blood pulsed sent a wealth of never before felt sensations coursing inside. Good god, but she'd known this man her entire life and never experienced anything like this.

She turned, and with a gasp, confused and curious as well, "What are you doing?"

For a moment, he looked just as baffled as she felt. His voice raw and different, "Believe I'm going to kiss you, lass, that is if you won't scratch my cheek. Make you forget your mission upstairs and perhaps find a mission together, possibly in my chamber."

"Alistair, you're a friend." She chastised him but when his warm lips settled over hers and her fingers touched the softness of his beard. She couldn't help but give in to him as well as what he offered. Tiny sounds rippled from her throat as he deepened the kiss.

"Perhaps we should take this someplace more private," he repeated and this time he seemed more sincere.

"No." She backed away, running her tongue along her lips. "You would have me in your bed and beneath you, and just because you dinna find your mate when you thought you had." Her breath whooshed in and out in short little pants. "I can't allow that to happen. I'll only give my virginity to my mate."

He smiled then his teeth gleaming white behind the red of his beard. "Are you afraid of me, lass? What harm could a little fun be? Besides, I suddenly believe there is more between us than friendship. I'd like to pursue the possibilities."

"If you bed me, you should be afraid of Connal." She left then, wondering why the sudden attention Alistair was giving her. He'd never hinted at a kiss before this night, had searched for his mate diligently. She touched her lips with a fingertip, remembering the kiss and the warmth as well as the heat.

She gulped air, her heart in her throat. When she closed her eyes for that one moment, she saw them together naked in his bed. She was his mate.

Chapter Two

"Anything?" Connal looked up, a slow purely masculine smile forming as he studied her intensely. Then he pulled out a silken chemise, caressed it with his fingers and brought it to his face to smell. "Lemons. Where do you come from? Will the contents of this bag tell me more about you than you want me to know?"

"If you hand that over, anything. I'm willing to do anything. You would nay be askin' me to do anything I was nay forced to do before." He watched her as she swallowed hard, understanding this was far more difficult for her than he'd ever imagined.

Yet the more she kept secrets the more he needed to understand, the more compelled he was to discover all her truths. He held the satchel up for her, realizing he wanted her to tell her story. The truth as well as trust was too important to him to let this go. "Anything you want to give me."

She grabbed the bag from his hands then quickly stuffed the items back into the satchel. Her face red with embarrassment, "I don't want to give you anything."

"So be it." He leaned against the headboard of the bed and patting the opposite side, "Perhaps in time you will trust me enough to confide your secrets and perhaps in time you will give me something in return for the roof over your head and the food to feed your belly."

"Am I to be a prisoner in this room?" She found a chair to sit in that was located on the far side of the room. Then petulantly, "I've seen no food."

Her ploy, the small act of defiance, made him smile. "Only until I can trust you. How long that is, is up to you." He patted the bed again.

Then said pleasantly. "Unlike you, I won't bite or scratch or punch and I will see you fed."

"But I would do it again." She paused a few seconds then with a huge breath and indignantly she said, "I didn't bite you."

She was sitting straight and stiff, her hands on the bag visibly quivering. Lord but he would give just about anything to see what she hid from him but then once more he reminded himself he wanted to hear it from her lips. Only then could he trust her.

So intent on answers the knock on the door startled him even though he ordered a bath for her then for him. "Come in."

He was surprised once more when his sister entered behind the servants with the hot water. "What are you doing here?"

"Came to meet our guest. We do have other rooms, you know." Brenna looked at him a frown of disapproval marring her lovely face.

"Not that she can stay in." Connal knew his voice was harsh, needing to press home to his sister none of this was her business and she was to keep her opinions to herself. He would deal with Wynnie the way he saw fit even if his sister disapproved.

"I see." She smiled walking to Wynnie and holding out her hand. Then shooting him a black look, "I'm Brenna, Connal's sister. If you need anything, make sure you let him know. I'll be happy to get it for you if it's within my power."

"I'd like that room you're talking about." Wynnie said so softly spoken Connal had to lean forward to hear her. For some reason he couldn't fathom, he didn't want her out of his sight.

Brenna looked to her brother, the scowl on his face, all-consuming. "That's up to the laird. Do you need clothing? I've food and drink on the way. What did you say your name was?"

"Wynnie..."

"Nice name." Brenna strode to a corner of the room then directing her attention toward her brother. "Help me with this."

He did her bidding, lifting the privacy screen and setting it between the room and the tub. His anger seemed to boil over. "You know, little sister, that it will take more than a screen to stop me from doing what I want."

"You mean watching her bathe. Thought you had more respect for women than that, dear brother." She touched her lips before looking at him. "What has happened to you this dark night? You go for a run and return a different man."

It was a guilty look she slanted him and Connal wondered who kissed her. When he got the opportunity, he'd have to sit down with his little sister and discover that truth, the fact she meant to keep from him. She opened the door for the servants bringing food and drink.

"I never intended to watch," he muttered, wishing his sister would leave as he would have when Wynnie bathed but now that he thought on it, he wasn't sure what he was going to do. If he left, she might try to escape but not if he took her clothing to get them washed.

"You would leave her alone?" One eyebrow rose in speculation. "Really? The way you are acting right now? I'm having a difficult time believing that."

So far tonight he'd been the brunt of his cousins and friends jokes and now disproval from his sister. He'd had enough censure for the time being. Striding to the door he opened it, waiting for both his sister and servants to vacate his chamber.

The servants left but Brenna stopped at the door, "Have a nice evening, Wynnie. Tell Connal about yourself he puts all his respect into two things, trust and truth. You won't go wrong and you won't remain a prisoner. If you need help, he will give aide to you." With that said she turned to leave, her skirts swirling around her feet.

"Brenna is right, you know." He didn't wait for her to answer, suspecting Wynnie would remain silent. "The bath is ready for you. I will respect your privacy. Don't wait too long or the water will be cold. If you need any help, just ask." He sat back on the bed and watched as she slowly walked behind the screen.

The silhouette was intriguing, fascinating and so sensual he nearly left the bed to join her. He'd never watched a woman disrobe quite like this. The sight was physical and erotic. His body tightened, inflamed would better define his mood as well as his body when he thought of claiming her, wondering then if she was a virgin, not that it mattered to him.

As the minutes passed, he became too captivated and infatuated with the idea of seeing her naked. He would eventually, but this time he would show her his cat form and see how she responded. If she was anything like Maurina, he would let her go and she could fend for herself. When they first entered the room, her gaze had been fixed on the tapestry. It would be better for her to know from the beginning who he was, who his people were.

No secrets.

He disrobed and quickly changed to his animal form then slowly walked around the screen and sat down in front of her, watching and waiting for a reaction. In the back of his throat, he purred softly.

There was no response and that amazed him. Actually, he wasn't sure what he'd expected from her but not this calm reserve. Her eyes were wide and a dark shade of blue, midnight blue. Her skin was white. her breast tipped with tight coral buds. She moistened her lips, still gazing into his eyes. He wanted her.

"This is not well done of you, Connal McKenna, and no I'm not a shifter. You told me you would respect my privacy." She tried to cover herself with her hands, but from one second to another he saw every beautiful curve she possessed. He yearned for her in a way he'd never felt before, not even with his once fiancée.

He smiled, thinking of grabbing the huge bath sheet that had been left there and taking it away. If he did that, he'd be deprived of viewing her rising from the water.

Patience was one of his stronger characteristics but he was going to have to call out every iota of it, if he was to best her. Yes, he could wait her out, especially since the water would be taking on a decided chill soon. Moving closer, his head resting on the lip of the tub, he hoped she would take a chance and touch him. She didn't though. Instead she scooted farther away.

Not wanting to terrify her, he wasn't sure what to do so he backed up and sat on his haunches again. Perhaps he should shift back to his human form so at least they could talk about his revelation, a revelation to his surprise that failed to shock her or even amaze her, neither did it seem to disgust her.

If he did, they would be on equal footing. He grinned and wondered if she could tell what he was thinking. Perhaps she was a witch come to torment him before Samhaim. That, at least, would explain the evil murmurs of the wind, yet he didn't think there was anything evil about this delicate lady.

They would both be naked. He liked that idea but he was sure she would not. Intimidation was not what he meant for tonight. Trust was the issue and at this point in time he wasn't really sure how to go about gaining her confidence and was thinking now that what he did impulsively was wrong and worked against the very thing he sought.

Blessed hell, he was never impulsive. She must have cast a spell on him.

"Are you going to go away before I turn into a prune?" Her soft voice enticed and tempted him, made him want to remain in this spot and see what she would do next.

He shook his head, the only answer he could give in this form. Yet he understood he would have to be equal with her. Backing farther away, he shifted again. Now he was also naked.

"I'd like a bath so if you are not getting out, I'll join you. We could share the water. The tub is big enough." One perfectly shaped eyebrow rose in speculation. Indeed, he put her in a predicament. He handed her one of the towels left for them, holding it out in front of him. Goddess like, she emerged from the water.

He caught a glimpse of her breasts and the sweet curve of her hips as well as her long slim legs before she wrapped herself in the bath sheet, effectively stopping his slow and very male perusal.

Their encounter this evening seemed a coincidence at first, however now he realized the meeting must have been written in the stars. Fate stepped in and brought her to him. All shifters were meant to find their mate and she was his. There wasn't a doubt in his mind. The problem here was how to convince her of the fact.

He slipped into the water, quickly washing sweat and the fine layer of dust from his body. The soap and water stung when it touched the scratches, reminding him she was a woman to be reckoned with. Without thought, he rose, water sluicing from him, turning so she could see him. He paused for a moment before reaching for the towel and drying off.

He wrapped the bath sheet around his waist and joined her on the fur rug in front of the hearth. She was combing her hair. When dry it was wild and free, full of brilliant sun kissed flames, curling sweetly around her face, enhancing every feature.

"I've nothing to wear," she murmured, "Someone took my dress and underclothing. Your sister said she would help me if she could. I take that to mean if you allow it."

"Only because they needed washing. In case you forgot there was blood, my blood, on the bodice of your gown."

She visibly cringed at his words, reaching up to touch his scratches. Her fingers were gentle. "I'm truly sorry. I was frightened, nay terrified of what you would do to me."

"Are you still terrified?"

"Worried and nervous I suppose, but not terrified."

He took the comb from her shaking hands and began running it through her hair. "Your hair is beautiful. It feels like the finest silk and the color matches that of a sunset, no, a deep claret with gold and lighter threads of red running through." He spread the length around her shoulders. "How long does it take to dry?"

"More time than you have," she spoke softly and he wondered what she was thinking now.

Was she still trying to find a way to run, flee from the safety of McKenna hall? "I've patience where you are concerned. Are you tired? Perhaps tomorrow you will tell me something about yourself, other than your name." Now was not the time to regale her with the truth about clan Chattan.

"Truly I would be forever in your debt if you found me something to wear tonight besides this towel." She touched it, making sure it remained secure. "It's damp now and I would most likely take a chill."

"You are already forever in my debt. I've the distinct feeling that my capture of you has saved you from something worse than me. Although I don't like to think of me as someone you would rather avoid." Continuing to run his fingers through the length of her hair, he paused then rose from the floor.

He strode to the armoire and from there he pulled out a white shirt. Tossing it to her, he waited for her to put it on. She closed her eyes, her fingers gripping the fabric as if it were a lifeline.

Moistening her lips, she stared at him but didn't say anything.

"Go ahead, put it on. It's all I have. It won't fit but the shirt will probably cover you to your knees." He grinned, wanting to add that he slept naked, as did everyone who shared his bed, but restrained himself.

She slipped it over her head, letting the towel pool around her ankles. Even with the faint light of the room, the garment showed off her curves more than hid them.

"Where am I going to sleep?" Inadvertently she tugged on the fine Holland linen, her nipples dark circles visible beneath the fabric.

"What are you going to tell me about yourself?" He poured them each a glass of wine before sitting beside her again. She stiffened but didn't move away.

"Not my last name," she hesitated. "You're right. I am running from someone and yes, I believe you are the lesser of two evils."

"Who? I'd like to know." He watched her drink the wine then pick at some of the food on the tray. She looked hungry and he wondered how long she'd been running and when was the last time she ate.

She looked at him then down, her fingers tightening around the stem of her glass until her knuckles turned white. After a huge gulp of air, "You won't hand me over to either man? Promise?"

"I would not, not if you didn't want them to find you." Unable to resist, he held a strand of hair in his fingers again. "My sweet fire. Can you tell me what has happened between you and these men that is so horrific you put your life in danger without thought?"

"What I've done?" she queried.

"I didn't mean my words to sound accusatory." He was rubbing the strand between his fingers.

She closed her eyes and the slight quiver of her shoulders along with another gulp of air told a story all its own. Wynnie was terrified of someone and most likely in fear for her life.

Her voice a tiny whisper, "I don't really want to tell you. You are nothing to me and would judge my actions. Men always do." Clearly disturbed she set aside the food she'd been eating.

"I can't promise not to judge but I can try to understand." He leaned against the hearth, wrapping an arm around her and drawing her close to him only to find her shuddering before pushing away. He let her go, wondering. Then she turned to him, courageously, he thought, "A few years ago I met a woman, a very pretty woman who stole my heart. And for a time, I thought she was my mate. If I'd had certain facts at my disposal the first time we made love, I would have known the truth."

"So she wasn't?"

"No, you are." He expected her to deny the fact but she didn't. She seemed to be content with listening to his story. "You're not shocked? I thought you would be, at the very least, tell me I was crazy or perhaps that there was no such thing."

"You looked at me a certain way and I saw it in your eyes. You cannot be sure and truly I don't see how it can be true. I'm neither a shifter nor a witch as you mentioned earlier. I cannot cast spells. If I could I would not be in this predicament that I find myself in now."

He laughed, a gritty sound, harsh in the back of his throat. "You have cast a spell over me whether you ken the fact or not. I'm infatuated with you. If you'd allow it, I would take you to my bed this very instant and claim you."

"Why would I cast a spell such as that? I don't want you or any man. Men only hurt women." Her hands were folded in her lap, her eyes downcast for a moment before looking back to him, a challenge perhaps.

He waved a hand in the air, dismissing her questions while at the same time wondering what prompted her comment. In any case he didn't have a logical answer for her. "Needless to say, we'll discover the real truth sooner than later. I know I want you and I don't think you'll refuse me when the time is right."

"Not tonight though?" she asked, turning toward him, her eyes wide, midnight blue pools of incredible passion just waiting for him. "Because you need answers."

"Only because it's too soon. We are just getting to know each other. So, tell me, why do you run from two men and who are they?"

She looked away, plucking at his shirt then with a huge sigh. "When I was fourteen my father started giving me to men for money. My intended was one of those men. In fact, he was the first." She was talking quickly, her words coming out in a mindless scatter that was hard to follow. "The men paid my father to have me anyway they pleased. From that moment on, I tried to stay away from the house. I would slip into the woods and hide. There was a woman, an elderly woman, who would help me and she showed me a cave where they never found me. But I wasn't always successful in avoiding them."

His gut churned at her words, fists clenching. "Yet you stayed with your father, remained in his home and allowed that to happen."

Tears were falling from her eyes, sobs wracking her slender body as her story began to meld together into a horrific scenario of lust and greed. Then her shoulders lifted. Her chin tilted up in moment of defiance. "Where would I go? Over the years, I saved money, kept the coins hidden until I felt the confidence I needed to leave. Remember, I was only fourteen when all this started."

"When was it you left?" He tried to warm the chill that seemed to encompass her, rubbing his hands up then down her arms even while she tried to distance herself from him.

"A few months ago. Then I ran out of money. I've been sleeping in the forest and eating whatever I could find that was edible. This time of year, there is not much to be found."

"I don't judge you, lass. The judgment is on the men who abused you and your father who sold you." Moisture filled his eyes as she finished her story. All he could do was pray that he would be able to keep her safe and, in the process, change her opinions about men in general, specifically himself.

~ * ~

Wynnie didn't understand why but she was suddenly breaking down and speaking in a rush. Her fear of him had vanished sometime in the last few hours. He would never want her for his mate now that he knew about her past life. She wasn't a virgin and men of his ilk wanted innocent, untried women to marry. They needed to be their first as well as their last.

"So, you see. I can't possibly be your mate." She was plucking at the shirt again, wishing it fell past her knees. Her toes were cold. While she still sat, the length didn't matter but as soon as she stood, he would see her legs and probably all of the rest of her. She reminded herself he'd already seen all of her naked. All that and he didn't force her.

Not yet.

"No," he spoke slowly. "I don't see anything of the sort." He touched a finger to her cheek, absorbing the salty tears onto his flesh. "No matter what has happened to you, you are still my soul mate."

"Now you're just being kind and perhaps foolish as well." She stood then tugging at the fabric of his shirt, "I'd like to go to bed now."

"Not until you finish eating." He reached for her hand but she sidestepped him. "I don't mind sleeping on that large chair over there if you lend me a blanket and perhaps a pillow if you're feeling generous. I will be comfortable there, more comfortable than sleeping on the ground which has been my bed for many weeks."

His brows furrowed together and she wasn't sure why. "You should eat. You will waste away to nothing."

"I'm no longer hungry. The food seems to turn to dust in my mouth and my belly seems all a flutter."

"You can wash it down with more wine."

"I don't want to drink too much." No, she needed her wits about her. This man had the ability to wheedle the truth from her when she didn't want to speak it.

"Very well, sleep it is." He walked to the bed, pulling back the covers. "This should do just fine, much more comfortable than the chair."

She remained in one place, her breath catching in her throat. "I won't take your bed and I won't sleep with you tonight. In any case, you don't want me."

"I never said that. Rest assured I want you more than each breath I take. Every second I look at you seems an eternity before you will allow me to claim what is rightfully mine."

She gasped then, startled by his comment and began shaking her head. "I'm not a virgin."

"Don't fash yourself. That fact matters not to me except that I wish I could have met you before. Go to bed now and don't fear me. I will never hurt you."

"You cannot promise that."

"I've things still to do. Perhaps when I return, I'll join you, perhaps I'll take the chair. Funny, you don't look sleepy at all. Would you like me to send Brenna here? The two of you can talk. I believe she has some secrets too. Perhaps she will enlighten you as to who kissed her today and you will in turn pass on the information to me. It is something a big brother needs to know."

She nodded but refused to give in to his wishes. Just because men used her for their selfish lust, she would not give of herself to a man anytime that man snapped his fingers or proclaimed her his mate.

He sighed heavily then, "You're still fighting me and while you've told me a small bit about yourself, I cannot trust you to stay put. There will be a guard at the door. I trust then you will not flee from this room. If the men you spoke of were close on your heels this evening, the best way to avoid them is to remain inside this chamber."

"You don't have to do this, to protect me at the cost of your life." She sat down on the edge of the bed. "Where would I go wearing only your shirt and nothing else?"

"I've no idea, lass, but I take you for a woman of creativity. Left to your own devices, who knows what you might be able to figure out. I was going to have Brenna come upstairs to keep you company as it is still not time to retire but now, well, the two of you putting your minds together, I'm not at all sure a visit would be wise."

She watched him slip on a shirt and his kilt then the rest of his clothing. He was handsome and strong, she thought, as she found herself staring at him. She couldn't help but admire him. What would it hurt if she gave into him and slept with him? What did it matter if she let him pleasure himself with her body? She didn't believe he would hurt her as the others had.

Wynnie realized she trusted Connal McKenna. She told him so much about her that no one else except the men involved knew. Still, she didn't speak of everything, didn't mention the child she lost or the trauma when the men penetrated her. A man wouldn't understand any of those emotions and terror.

The locked door bothered her even though she understood why he would consider it necessary. She tried to believe the guard was to protect her not keep her inside. If she told him her surname, he would not have believed her story. As it was, she was pretty sure he thought she told the truth, but with men one never really knew.

She sat on the hearth then poured herself another glass of wine. He was right, she was hungry but her stomach, over the last few weeks, had shrunk and she couldn't hold very much.

The huge door creaked open, "Wynnie, it's me, Brenna. Do you want some company?"

"If you can shed some light on your brother, yes." She almost laughed yet didn't dare. While she liked Brenna, she didn't know anything about her and understood she needed to be cautious.

Brenna stepped through the door holding a bag. "And if I cannot?" Brenna asked. "I've been sworn to secrecy where my brother is concerned. I've also vowed not to help you escape for any reason you might give. 'Tis dangerous out there as well you ken. Anything can happen in the highlands."

"I don't want to escape. At least for now this is the most pleasant and safe place I've encountered in a very long time. Your brother wants me in his bed, says I'm his mate but I can't be. It's just not possible." She felt as if she was rambling, her words a blur, some things she told Connal some she couldn't remember.

"Why can't you be his mate?" Brenna pulled clothing from the bag, including a long white nightdress, one that would reach from her neck to her toes, possibly farther. She was not as tall as Brenna.

"Are those for me?" Wynnie ran to the bed, going through the items Brenna brought for her. "You are such a dear, thank you. I'm not sure I deserve your kindness. I might be bringing danger and evil to your door. There are bad men who want me."

Brenna sat down, a glass of wine in hand, joining Wynnie. Then, "The evil I believe is here now. It is if you are Wynnie Adair."

36

The tiny sip of wine spewed from Wynnie's lips. She wiped some of the droplets with the back of her hand. "You know who I am? Connal knows who I am? You've got to help me leave." She was frantic with worry, understanding danger hovered over everyone in the castle.

"I won't do that simply because leaving is not in your best interest. Where would you go? If you dinna want the men to find you, the best way to keep that from happening is to remain here, in the laird's chamber. Everyone will believe you are his and that fact alone will keep you safe."

"Anywhere my presence wouldn't be detrimental to the McKenna's." Her hand on her chest she tried to breathe and calm her rattled nerves. "They will seek revenge against the clan."

"The McKenna's thrive and prosper here. That man won't be allowed to harm you in any way or the clan."

"My father has a lot of power, and he wants me to wed that awful man who has raped me more times than I can count. If we wed, he will continue to do the same as well as give me to his friends for profit and entertainment. I'm naught to them save a plaything. If I ever have baby, a girl, they will do the same to her."

"If you leave here, they will catch you and few in this part of the highlands have as much power as Connal McKenna, laird of clan Chattan. Our people will rally in your defense, particularly if you agree to marry my brother. Will you do that? Become Wynnie McKenna?"

"Marry Connal? I told you I cannot. I'm not a virgin. A man like Connal deserves a wife who has not been brutally used."

"Connal only wants his mate, and he believes he has finally found her," Brenna said. "It's funny." A smile on her face, she paused, "I believe I found my mate tonight also. Connal will not like it at first, but he will have to come to terms with the fact the man is one of his friends, his best friend."

"You found your mate? Is that the man who Connal says kissed you? I dinna ken any of this although I've heard things, rumors."

"With the shifters, your mate follows you through time. When both die, they will find each other in the next rebirth. When Alistair kissed me, I saw our other lives together. I was running with him in the fields, both in our cat form and as humans."

"You truly believe all that? Connal hasn't kissed me. Just looked at me naked when I was bathing." Wynnie grimaced at the thought until she recalled the way he looked naked and stepping from the tub, water sluicing down his hard, lean body; a god, rising from the water.

"He promised me he would not watch you," Brenna muttered, holding up a gown made from the McKenna clan tartan. "So much for promises and big brothers. They will do what they want when they want. Now, would you like to put on this dress?"

"I thought to dress in that nightgown and go to sleep soon." Wynnie tried to figure out Brenna's expression. "It's been a long day and a long couple of weeks and I'm exhausted."

"I'm afraid that would not be wise, at least not until after the wedding ceremony. I was not joking. You need to wed now, tonight, before your father can lay claim to you and drag you from here."

"Wedding?" she squeaked, alarmed at what Brenna was saying. "In order for Connal to protect you from your father, you must wed him."

"Connal has sent for father Michael. If you are agreeable, the two of you will wed in about a half hour. It is the only way to keep you safe from your fiancé. You do have to agree to this. If you do, I'll help you get dressed and ready. If you don't, Connal will be obligated to hand you over to your father."

She couldn't breathe, couldn't believe what Brenna was telling her. This was all happening and she wasn't prepared. Marry Connal McKenna? "They will protest. You said my father and Perkins were downstairs." Everything was happening too fast. She couldn't think and knew she shouldn't protest. All that Brenna said was true but wouldn't they also have to consummate the marriage.

"They won't know anything about what is going on in Connal's private chamber until all is finished then the men will allow them to see for themselves that Wynnie, you are no longer under their control." Brenna shook out the dress. "It's lovely isn't it? Our mother wore it on her wedding day. It should fit you fine. The gown is too small for me so it's only right and proper that the dress goes to my brother's wife."

"Why?"

"It is necessary. I suppose for your protection."

Connal strode through the door then, "We've ten minutes to get you clothed properly. The minister will be here then and we will wed whether or not you are wearing only my shirt, although it is fetching on you, or the gown Brenna brought." With that said he turned his attention to putting on his dress plaid and white linen shirt with ruffles down the front, his cravat tied immaculately. Then with a quick nod to Brenna, he left.

"Hurry, we don't have much time," Brenna said, her words sounding frantic and breathless. "Connal and all the rest of them will be here before we can blink. You don't want to be naked when they arrive."

True to his word, ten minutes later Connal, the cousins as well as Alistair and the minister strode into the room. He placed Wynnie's hands in his then bending close, "When all the danger has passed, we can have a proper wedding if you would like."

She didn't know what to say or what to expect next. They were standing beside each other, the minister behind them reading from the scriptures. She was terrified. She wasn't really his mate. When he discovered that, he would toss her out. There had been no pretense on her part, but what he would do when the truth was revealed she had no idea. After all, he'd been wrong once before.

Then the minister was announcing their marriage was done and that he could kiss his bride. When his lips found hers, she nearly swooned from the sensations coursing through her. She'd never heated from the inside out, but she'd never really been kissed and so intensely. She never felt so exhilarated even when she was racing her mare across a field. With her hand on his chest, she tried to steady herself, but it seemed all that kept her standing was his hands on her waist.

When he drew away, he grinned, satisfied by the kiss she supposed. She realized she didn't have any visions of the two of them in another life, running in fields or anything else. Disappointment filled her heart and soul. She had been right about the one thing she didn't want to be right about. She wasn't his mate.

When he turned her to face the witnesses, there was applause and cheers. The minister closed the bible with a tiny thud and a grin on his face. "It's about time, Connal McKenna. I was pleased to be the man who married you to this beautiful woman."

"A toast to the newly wedded couple, Wynnie and Connal," Alistair's glass was raised high and he was gazing at Brenna, passion filling his glittering green eyes.

"Perhaps Alistair and Brenna should wed tonight as well," Wynnie spoke softly but it seemed everyone heard and a hush settled around the room.

"What did you say?" Connal sounded surprised as his gaze settled on his sister then Alistair.

Brenna's cheeks burned a bright shade of red her hands on her cheeks as if she tried to cool them. "No, tonight is for the two of you."

"Explain yourself." Connal sounded angry as he spoke to Alistair. "Why would Wynnie say such a thing?"

Alistair looked from one McKenna to the other. "It was earlier this evening that we discovered the truth about ourselves. We are each other's mate. But this is not the time for us. We still have to show ourselves downstairs and convince our guests we know nothing about Wynnie while Connal does his best to consummate the marriage or at least give the impression that he has."

"I apologize for mentioning it," Wynnie said, her voice thin and seemed to be held together by nothing more than a single breath of air, nothing more. "I should not have given anything so important away."

"We will deal with this new revelation later," Brenna said. "All weel be fine."

She watched as Connal directed his family from the room. They were alone now and she was fidgeting with her dress, unsure of herself or what she should do.

"What now?"

"If I'm right, we have about five minutes to undress and get into bed together before your father and intended are in this room. My men are permitting this but they will only be here a moment, just long enough for them to see and understand that you are mine now."

She gasped, startled. She'd thought there would be time to get to know him before she'd be in his bed. Thought there would be more daylight hours between them as well. By the time she caught her breath, his shirt was off, along with his shoes and stockings. Then he was naked and striding toward her.

He must have experience with women's clothing because in a matter of only seconds her dress and underthings were on the floor near his clothing. He swept her into his arms and with only a few strides they landed on the bed and beneath the covers.

"Connal, no, don't do this." She closed her eyes, realizing that once again she would have to go to that place in her mind where she could escape the pain and humiliation.

"Just kiss me lass." He was between her legs, his rod pressing against her belly and she knew what would happen next. He was hard and all male, terrifying.

Tears slipped from her eyes, and she heard his curse, sure the words were directed at her. "You cannot mean to..."

"I cannot," he agreed. "Nor will I. Just kiss me, trust me and everything will be fine. Open your sweet lips for me and I promise you will feel no pain just pleasure."

She heard boots pounding down the hall and shouts.

"Blessed hell. Too soon, way too soon." He reached for his knife. She gasped for air, thinking he was going to kill her. Didn't understand what she saw next.

He pricked two of his fingers. "Now I know there will be no virgin's blood, but I want to make this look real from your father's perspective." He spread the blood on the sheets then his seed. "Pretend, as I'm sure you have every other time that they forced you. Tears are fine. Cry and make sure they believe the pain is real."

"I never cried." She turned her face away. "And the pain is always real."

Her father was first as he burst into the master chamber, Perkins and his guard behind him. "What is the meaning of this?" Connal rose, blood on his rod his seed obvious on the sheets and her legs."

She cringed, curling herself into a silent tiny ball, wishing everyone away.

"She is promised to me," Perkins said with a furious growl. "How dare you take what is mine?"

From behind her Connal's voice boomed with contempt. "You're too late. All the papers are signed and as you can see the marriage has been consummated."

"There should be no blood. She has been well used before this night."

"I suppose I was a little rough. She'll recover." Connal said with an air of indifference.

~ * ~

"What are you going to do about this travesty?" Perkins asked, his voice filled with rage. "They lied to us and it's obvious they were wed only moments before we broke into the room."

"Nothing we can do about it at the moment. No reason we can't find a way to discredit Connal McKenna. When we do, she'll be yours again," Oscar Adair said, feeling the malice for his daughter all the way to his toes. "She will regret this day."

"I don't want to stay in this god forsaken part of Scotland until you figure out what to do," Perkins said. "There are other women who can do my bidding. Wynnie is no longer mine to do with as I please nor do I care."

"She doesn't deserve happiness," Oscar grit out, thinking of his late wife. She abandoned him, leaving him with a daughter he detested. Blessed hell, but he didn't even know if she was his daughter and not some bastard's that his wife dallied with when she should have been in his bed.

When Wynnie turned fourteen, he enjoyed giving her to his friends and watching the pain slash across her eyes. He never expected her to assert herself and run away. She surprised him. It was not well done of her.

Alistair escorted the two men downstairs, offered them food and drink, all the while listening to their complaints. The men would not give up, he was sure. Oscar could go to the law, claim he had not given his consent to the marriage. There were myriad ploys the father could enlist to get her back. Connal would have to be watchful. He was concerned now for Brenna. He had no idea what Perkins might try while in this frame of mind. Using Brenna could be his revenge. She should not be alone this evening and he didn't intend to let her out of his sight.

"If you've had your fill, I'll show you to your rooms. I expect you to be gone in the morning," Alistair said, understanding that at some time they would be back. Wynnie was a prize neither would want to give up. Even Perkins though would think a second time when it came to possessing Wynnie. To exact his revenge, he would pick someone else, someone important to Connal.

"Any willing women?" Perkins asked, looking around the hall, which except for Brenna was filled with men.

Alistair followed the direction of Perkins glare. "No, not tonight, not in the hall. The hour is late, I'm sure all have sought their beds. We expect you gone in the morning."

"What about that one?" Perkins nodded toward Brenna, his eyes fixated on her.

Alistair, his gut rolling, strode to her then placed an arm around her, his hand curling around her breast. He grimaced when he heard her tiny gasp of surprise but she seemed to understand and leaned into him, giving his words and actions credence to everyone who watched.

"She is my plaything. Aren't you?" He squeezed her breast and understood from the way her back stiffened he would pay for those words as well as his actions. He would have a great deal of explaining to do. "Come, I'll show you to your rooms." Then to Brenna, "Go on to ours." He nodded to Angus and Fergus before giving her a tiny swat on her backside, something else he would pay for when they were alone. Needing to laugh though, he wanted to see her expression. The confrontation between them was only minutes away and he looked forward to it, enjoyed a feisty woman, one who would let him know how she felt. He wanted no secrets between them.

After showing the two men to rooms in the opposite end of the castle, he strode quickly to his solar, anticipating a night of loving with Brenna. Angus and Fergus stood outside guarding the door.

"She is not in good humor," Angus warned, a smug expression on his face.

"You took advantage of the situation and she was the recipient," Fergus added to Angus' warnings. "But I'm sure in the end you two will find common ground. "Enjoy your evening."

"I believe I can persuade her to my way of thinking," Alistair grinned confidently, knowing he would relish the delicious raw passion that was Brenna McKenna.

He couldn't believe his good fortune in discovering the truth about the two of them. For years he watched her grow up, knew she'd be stunning but never expected her to be his mate. If she were willing, he would claim her tonight. They would wed once the Samhaim was over and the goings on in the castle returned to normal.

When he opened the door, he was barraged with a series of objects: books, candle holders then the pillows. And with each object a new swear word. He laughed, dodging the missals while he slowly made his way to Brenna.

"Blessed hell, jerkoff, damn you, Alistair!" Then she repeated each word throwing one more item his way. A book nicked his head. He tried to duck as he moved forward, but Brenna had a good aim and she hit him as often as she missed.

Grinning and appreciating the skirmish, he closed in on her. She was breathing hard, her breasts enticing him, still holding a pillow in her hand she hit him then hit him again. He tossed his head back laughing and pulling the weapon from her hands.

"Kiss me, lass. I know you want to." He held her hands behind her back while his mouth descended to meet her sweet parted lips. It was a short kiss before he said, "I'm sorry I offended you. You can make it up to me." His breath whispered so close to her lips. Then his teeth closed on her bottom lip, tugging slightly as he kissed her, enticed and heated her to a point he hoped she wouldn't refuse more intimate advances.

She squeaked when he slipped his tongue inside her open mouth, traced her teeth and her soft upper lip with his tongue and was delighted when she responded in kind. He swept her into his arms, striding to a huge chair near the fireplace, hoping she would continue willingly.

When he sat down, he kept her on his lap and kissed her again and again. When he stopped, she drew his head closer to her. "You are an asshole," she told him but then she kissed him, swept her tongue across his teeth, dueled with his tongue, played and danced. She didn't seem to notice when he slowly began to remove a few layers of her clothing from her body. Thank goodness she was a sensible lass and tonight wore only her dress and chemise.

He explored, finding the warmth of her leg and moving higher until she gasped at the familiarity he claimed. His fingers found intimate soft female flesh, hot and moist for him. His mouth touched upon a veiled nipple.

"Alistair." she breathed in a ragged lungful of air, her pulse beating rapidly at the base of her throat. "We cannot."

"Of course we can. You are my mate. I want to claim you tonight."

"No." She tried to tug her gown up and refasten it, but his questing fingers would not allow such a thing. "You are touching me." She closed her eyes, "You—I never, Alistair." Her voice was a thin wail as he probed her deeply, hoping she would accept him.

"You are hot, and so very wet, your women's flesh is swollen, the petals begging for me, begging for my rod to come inside you. Let me claim you and mark you as mine. Forget everyone else, just live in the moment."

"Not tonight, Alistair. Not before we talk to Connal and receive his blessing. Oh..." I cannot think."

"Don't think, just feel," With his teeth he tugged on her lip again and she moved her legs apart, opening further for his exploration. Her hands slipped through his hair as she arched against him, giving him more flesh to stroke.

"You are delicious. Wickedly, delicious," he whispered while he struggled from his shirt. He didn't want to take his hands away, didn't want to give her a chance to think.

"Alistair," she sighed into his mouth when he kissed her again.

"Yes..."

"We should nay do this." But this time her protest was weak as her fingers slid into his hair, tugging and pulling him closer.

"But you want to." His kilt dropped from his waist to the floor then her dress followed along with the rest of her clothing. This time he carried her to his bed.

"I do," she said, her voice soft yet he heard the conviction in her words. "Teach me, Alistair."

"Then tonight you are mine and for every night for as long as we live. I vow I will find you again after we are separated by death."

Chapter Three

"I'm sorry, lass. It was the only way I could think of to convince them of your bedding. Thinking the way they do, they understood what I was showing them and that I had consummated our marriage. They have no recourse now but to leave." He did regret the moment, had yearned for something sweet and wonderful between them. At this time, he would have to figure out a way for her to come to terms with this hasty marriage.

Wynnie turned, pulling the bed sheet to cover her breasts. It didn't seem she wanted to talk, just dissolve into the mattress. She was shaking her head now, tears flowing, her back slumped over.

Connal strode to the basin of water then dipping a cloth in it, he walked back to the bed. For a few seconds he watched her, his heart breaking for her. Yet he couldn't allow her to remove herself from the reality of the moment. He tugged on the sheet she was desperately clinging to. "Let me clean you then we can talk."

"There is nothing to talk about and I can clean myself. I've done so many times before. You don't owe me an explanation. I ken what this was all about. Though I was humiliated once more by men, always men."

Always men, men humiliated her and hurt her and I just did the same. Unable to control the emotions pulling through him, he shuddered, trying to understand the turmoil that was enveloping him, swamping him. Yet he kenned it was nothing like she was feeling.

"Maybe not but I want to explain and ask your forgiveness. This is something I feel you deserve." He handed her the cloth before sitting on the bed with her. "I'm not going away. You are my wife now as well as my mate. We will find a way to make this life a good one."

"I don't want to be naked in front of you." Her words were

47

clipped, her voice weak.

"I've already seen all of you." This was something he could not give her, would not bow down to this wish. If he backed away from her now, that action would set the tone for the rest of their lives. He didn't intend to live a celibate life.

"It doesn't mean there has to be a second time," she said as she turned her back to him, once more opening the sheet so she could wash his seed and blood from her legs.

Wynnie was right of course but, he paused thoughtfully, "They will return you know. Those two men won't give up." He needed to find some way to convince her that he wouldn't hurt her. He just didn't have the words.

He cursed then, running his hands through his hair, needing to leave but understanding he would send the wrong message if he vacated the room, leaving them both alone with their thoughts, his still brooding. What he wanted so badly was his, but he could not have her. He felt as if their lives had been ripped apart. He would not be whole again until she accepted him as her husband.

If Perkins and her father had not shown up tonight...

Pacing the room, he went over every possible argument to convince her, yet he understood any words he could think of would not undo what had been done to Wynnie in her past. They both needed to look to their future together and figure out a way to live their lives whole.

Connal sat down on the chair, head in his hands, wondering still how he could fix this mess.

"You can do what men do. I'll be fine." Her voice and words surprised him. "I won't break, at least so far I haven't."

Do what men do?

She was resigned that any sexual encounter would cause pain. He was determined to show her the difference. Yet, so much had happened that tonight just didn't seem right.

"Go to sleep, Wynnie." His voice was guttural and curt yet he couldn't help the barrage of emotions from showing in his tone.

"I don't want to and I ken you're upset with me." Her voice was shaking. "I do want to be a good wife. You can have me, do what you will."

"You will be a good wife, I ken it. This isn't the time though and I couldn't handle the situation if you're eyes crossed and went dim again. I'm sorry for all you've lost and the fears simmering deep inside. In time you will trust me with your body and your pleasure. But not tonight, Wynnie."

He heard her stifled sob and almost gave in to her dishonest wish. If she told the truth, what she wanted was to be left alone and for him to leave and never return. He decided though he was going to sleep in their bed and he was going to hold her through the night, through her tears and nightmares if she had any.

Perhaps that could be a new beginning.

"Can I have the nightgown Brenna brought to me?" she asked, sitting up, her wild hair flying around her shoulders, her eyes wide.

"No." Blessed hell but he needed to run his fingers through the long strands, feel the silken burn touch his soul and make him whole again. It had been so long since he felt complete. The woman who could give that to him, denied him.

Climbing into bed with her, he pulled her close, her back to his chest. She rested her head on his arm and he knew in a short time it would be numb, but he meant to carry through with this.

"Go to sleep," he murmured, wishing her past away. "I won't make love to you but I do intend to hold you until dawn and the morning light filters through the window."

He did close his eyes and he must have slept. When he opened them, the chamber was lighter. He smiled, though, she must trust him at least in her subconscious. Her hand rested on his chest and she was nestled against him, her breast touching upon him.

Perhaps it was just for the warmth.

He smoothed her hair away from her face, her eyes slowly opening. She didn't appear surprised or shocked that she was in his bed and his arms. "My god you are beautiful. Did you sleep well?"

"I was warm." She smiled at him, moistening her lips with her tongue. She pushed away sitting up then seemed to realize she was naked beneath the sheets as was he.

Wynnie surprised him, looking at him then herself, lines furrowing across her forehead.

"You didn't put your rod inside me. While I don't understand why, I'm grateful. I also understand you will." She was still smiling, her hand still resting on his chest. "It is something men do, seem to need. Thank you for waiting for me to get used to you."

Connal needed to see inside her head as well as her heart. He would wait as long as she needed. She was slowly giving him glimpses of herself. "Yes, you're right. I will when you trust me to treat you gently and not cause you pain. I promise someday you will know a woman's pleasure."

"You've said that before but it's not possible. Men cause pain and there is no pleasure for a woman." She shrugged, still naked and delightful, her breasts swaying with each tiny movement.

"You are sure of that." He wanted to dissuade her this moment. Inhaling a deep breath of air for strength, he set his hand on her shoulder.

Then, he ran his finger across her collarbone, then lower between her breasts. Looking up he saw the slight crossing of her eyes. "Don't look down and cross your eyes, don't disappear into some distant place where I can't find you. Look at me Wynnie, at my finger and where it is travelling. Tell yourself this is Connal, say my name and remember everything I've told you about myself." His fingertip lingered on the tight bud, which grew harder with his caress then he moved to the other breast.

She gasped at the sensations he knew he created, staring at him, her eyes wide with seeming wonder, disbelief as well.

"Does this hurt?" he asked as he continued the gentle caress. "You must tell me if it does."

"No..."

"How does it make you feel?" His fingers journeyed down her leg, her inner thigh to her knee then back up. He felt the quivering of her muscles, knew she would feel a sensual ache between her legs, yearned to caress the tiny nubbin hidden within her feminine folds.

"Hot."

"Anything else?" His voice was soft and he hoped seductive, prayed also she would realize he would never bring harm to her.

"I don't know?" Her voice thinned to a tiny mew. "I'm embarrassed. Wet, I suppose."

"No need to feel embarrassed or ashamed. Your feelings are good. Your first lesson is complete. All the things you've mentioned means I won't hurt you when I come inside you. Now, let's get up and dress then see what our first day as man and wife has in store for us." He was eager to pursue the day and discover more about Wynnie Adair, now a McKenna of clan Chattan.

She sighed softly, her gaze searching his face for something he couldn't define. "Hopefully my father and Perkins will have left the castle. I couldn't bear to see them again."

"One can always hope." He smiled at her, wishing for one more lesson, but deciding time and seduction was on his side in this journey between them. Extending his hand to help her from the bed, she accepted and he was pleased.

A few minutes later, he was dressed and it seemed she wanted to linger. "I'll meet you downstairs. Don't take too long. Would you like me to send up Brenna for you to talk to?"

She still wore just her chemise and stockings. He loved the way she looked half naked, her hair wild and curling around her face. She could be his heaven on earth. Inhaling a deep breath, he strode to her, touched her cheek with the back of his hand.

"I'd like to see Brenna. She listens to me and helps me understand." Her voice was soft yet there was a unique tone to it. She was somehow different today, more relaxed if he had to guess.

So tempting, the smile on her face couldn't be resisted. He made a small kiss to her lips, simple and undemanding but her taste was sweet, intoxicating. Waiting for tonight might be his undoing. He thought of all the private spots in the castle where no one would dare interrupt a tryst then tucked them away for future visits.

He strode out the door and up to the tower where he could see the countryside. The day was gloomy, covered in clouds and threatening rain, matching his inner thoughts, yet for the first time in so long there was also hope in his heart. He turned at the sound of footsteps.

Brenna and Alistair walked towards him. One sight of the couple and the expressions on their faces told a tale he didn't want to hear. His fists tightened and he wondered if he'd have to call his best friend out for sleeping with his sister. Alistair new better as did Brenna. She should have waited for her soul mate.

"Good morning," Brenna stepped forward but Alistair reached out a hand to stop her.

"No, Brenna this explanation is up to me." His voice was gruff while he looked from Brenna to him.

She glared at him but stayed quiet, bowing to his wish. Alistair wrapped an arm around her, drawing her close. Then he began, cautiously at first, "Connal, how was your night?"

"Not, it seems, as good as yours." Connal looked at the happy couple then gritted out. "You slept with my sister. That was not well done of you."

"I did and don't regret a moment. We will wed as soon as it's appropriate, but she will sleep with me every night from now on." Alistair braced his feet apart, clearly ready for the blow that should be coming his way.

"I'm not going to hit you although the thought crossed my mind. Seems I've known you all of my life. You've never been dishonorable with my sister until now. Why?" His demand sounded harsh, but he was the laird and she was his family.

"She's my mate. I've marked her, last night to be exact. I would have waited but Perkins was eyeing Brenna as if she was a delicious morsel just waiting to be tasted. I could nay allow that."

Connal understood a need to talk this out with his friend without his sister hearing every word. "Brenna, will you please see to Wynnie. She's, well, confused I think yet still terrified of me. Perhaps now that you know things..." He wasn't sure exactly what to say to her. "You have a woman's understanding of what goes on between a man and a woman now. Maybe you can ease Wynnie's fears."

"I was willing, Connal. Alistair didn't take anything I didn't want to give. He isn't lying. He is my mate. We would have slept together sooner than later." With that said, she turned and picking up her skirts left the area as if it was on fire.

Connal leaned against the wall, arms crossed in front of him, waiting for his friend to speak. Myriads of thoughts scattered through his head overpowering anything rational. His sister ignored him but he was sure she would see to Wynnie. It wasn't like Brenna to act that way.

Alistair cleared his throat, seeming to look for time and maybe the right words to approach the subject. "I've watched Brenna grow up. She always held a unique place in my heart, but I thought it was because she was your sister. I never believed..." He cleared his throat again, standing beside him at the wall. "Until she came of age, I never looked at her except as a little girl then your sister. Last night was different and when I kissed her, tasted her essence, I knew the truth as did she."

"That's supposed to make me feel better?" Connal asked, one eyebrow lifted. "I suppose you treated her right and will from this day forth. That's all a brother can ask. I would have appreciated some time to adjust to the new situation between the two of you."

"With Perkins here there was no time. You were dealing with issues too. I pledged my life to her last night when we claimed each other. As long as I'm alive, I'll give up my own for her."

"I have to accept this." Understanding swept through him, "I should be pleased it's you and not some man I despise."

"Would you want anyone else for a brother in law?" Alistair laughed, looking to the stairs as if he needed to follow Brenna. "We are best friends."

"No, if I was to handpick a husband you would be at the top of my list as long as I knew you'd given up all your other women for Brenna. Have you done that? I know the list was long."

"No longer than yours. I have given them all up, but I haven't spoken to them yet. No one else intrigues me. She is the only woman I want to be with for the rest of my life. I understand you must feel the same about Wynnie."

"Yes, but our night was not so pleasant. We've a long ways to go before she will give herself willingly to me. I take it Perkins and Wynnie's father have left the castle."

"You can just see their dust right now." Alistair pointed down the road. "I feel a sigh of relief sweeping through the castle walls."

Connal let out a long slow breath of air. "They will be back and at the moment I've no hopes that Wynnie will be with child by the time they return, looking to steal her away."

"She is your wife and your mate, with child or without should make no difference in the eyes of the law," Alistair said.

"They will say I'm a thief stealing her away and will have righteousness on their side. How do I go about bedding my wife who is terrified of men?" And with good reason.

Alistair turned toward him, "Slowly very slowly, one small step at a time and she will eventually give you her heart."

~ * ~

Moisture in her eyes, Wynnie sat on the sofa, staring at the door and remembering the way Connal left. He wasn't angry exactly, just perhaps frustrated and wanting more. Brooding might be a good word to describe him. She knew he wanted more of her. She'd offered but he refused because he understood she was terrified.

She didn't know what to do or how to fix the problem.

The door squeaked open. Brenna poked her head around the corner, "Hello? Would you like company? Connal and Alistair sent me away, and Connal made the suggestion you might want to talk."

"I'm not really fit for company but yes, if you can stand the tears and self-pity, I'd love to have someone to speak with." Wynnie didn't know how talking to Brenna could help, but she was eager to try everything.

"I'm a willing listener and I happen to comprehend the cause of those tears and self-pity very well. Connal is a gentle man, big but gentle. He is even loathe to kill flies." Brenna laughed softly seeming to think about her words. "Well, maybe not flies."

Wynnie fiddled with the lace on her gown, one Brenna had given her. She didn't like feeling beholding, but Brenna was sweet and generous. "Connal is not the cause. It's my father, and Perkins too. I told Connal last night he could have me and he told me to stop crossing my eyes."

Brenna laughed softly, "Only my brother would say something like that. Do you cross your eyes when a man kisses you?"

She shrugged wondering about kisses. "Don't know, never been kissed before yesterday, but I do cross my eyes and go to someplace where I can't feel or see anything when..." Wynnie said with a long sigh not wanting to finish. Brenna didn't need to hear her story. "I want to please him but I don't know how. Can you help?"

"I don't know much about lovemaking and pleasing men," Brenna said. "Just what I learned last night."

"We are both ignorant then." Wynnie turned away, more moisture welling in her eyes and threatening to fall. "I just don't know what to do. If I keep this up, my face will be puffy and eyes swollen. He won't want anything to do with me."

"You will most likely still be beautiful to him."

"Even with red swollen eyes? Perkins says I'm ugly when I look like that, but it kept him away from me sometimes, not the other men though, never anyone else."

"I'm not entirely ignorant," Brenna volunteered. "I slept with Alistair last night. We made love but... I don't think I can give you any advice. It was all so new."

"I understand," Wynnie said, looking down, sure now she would never figure out how to please Connal.

Brenna turned toward her, a smile on her face. "No, listen. I think you should put this in the hands of your mate. He will figure it out for the both of you. Trust him and I'm sure this will all turn out the way you want."

"You make it sound so easy." She was shaking her head, wishing she felt a bit more eager to see Connal again. "It's impossible and now he's so busy with everything. You know he left this morning without me right after he said we should see what the day has in store for us."

"I'm sure you misunderstood. He will be pleased to see you and you cannot deny the fact he married you knowing about your past."

"He just felt obligated and sorry for me," Wynnie said, walking to the window, still feeling sorry for herself when she should be feeling ecstatic that she was no longer on the run from her father.

"A man like my brother would never marry anyone if all he felt for her was obligation or pity. Connal would have found a means to help you in some other way."

"I want to believe you, it's just that..."

"Stop that, we're going downstairs and see what is happening. You'll be surprised to see the smile on Connal's face, but I won't."

She was hesitant but the huge grin on Brenna's face gave her a small measure of hope. Wynnie was nodding her head in agreement even while Brenna stood at the door, waiting for her.

"Let's try the tower first," Brenna said, opening the door for her.

Wynnie waited outside, unsure of where to go. If left alone, she wouldn't know which hallway to go down or what stairs to take. Brenna nodded towards the left, which brought them to the stairs leading upwards. She lifted her skirts, taking each step with hesitation.

At the top, Alistair stood next to Connal. They appeared to be deep in conversation and Wynnie started to turn, changing her mind about the prudence of meeting him.

"No, you don't," Brenna said, softly the hint of laughter in her voice. "If you ask me, which of course you haven't, there is no better time than the present."

Wynnie held back, watching as Brenna walked towards the men, her back straight, confident. She wished she could feel so poised and sure of herself. Wrapping her arms around her waist, she stared as both men slowly turned towards them.

Connal's face lit in a wide grin as did Alistair's, but Wynnie couldn't be sure if Connal was pleased to see her or his sister. Her mind was changed when Connal stepped past his sister, his arms open wide, she assumed for her. To make sure she glanced behind her.

"Wynnie." He embraced her, drawing her close.

He was warm and strong. In his arms she felt protected and safe. She rested her head against his chest hearing his strong, steady heartbeat.

"I've missed you. Did you enjoy your talk with Brenna?" he asked, still holding her with one hand but running his fingers through her hair with the other.

"Think we'll leave the two of you alone," Alistair said, his voice gruff with passion as his gaze remained fixed on Brenna. He extended his arm, Brenna accepting. "Would you like to go somewhere private?"

Brenna nodded, leaning into Alistair. Their relationship seemed to be one of love as well as ease. It appeared to Wynnie they loved each other very much. She turned to Connal, wondering if there would ever be love between them.

He was holding his hand out to her. She stared at him a few seconds then placed her hand in his. Pulling her towards him, he wrapped his arms around her. "Ah, lass, I'm glad to see you came up here. But it must have been Brenna's idea. She knew we were on the parapets when she left us."

Wynnie rested her head on his chest, afraid to meet his gaze then inhaled deeply, hoping the new air in her lungs would fill her with enough courage to proceed.

"Yes, Brenna thought you would be here," Wynnie said as she pushed slightly away, looking up and into his eyes which seemed to be filled with raw passion. She gasped and tried to push away but he was too strong, just as Perkins and the other men had been.

Then to her surprise, he let go. "I will never hold you against your will." But there was a deep undercurrent of sorrow in his voice.

"No," she stepped closer. "You are not Perkins. It's just that my reactions come from ghosts of the past, which haunt my days as well as my nights. I would have your help in vanquishing these demons of mine."

"Kiss me." Connal's gentle smile warmed her heart.

"I..."

"'Tis just a kiss, lass" he prompted, his hands behind his back. "I want nothing more from you."

She sucked her bottom lip between her teeth before blurting. "I dinna ken how to kiss."

"Certainly..." he stopped, rubbing his chin as if thinking. "No one, not one of the men... Should I kiss you, Wynnie? Would you like that? Then, if you want to kiss me, you'll know what to do."

"Brenna told me she liked Alistair's kisses." She hoped Connal would not be put off for what she said and what she didn't know how to do. "Don't most men like to be kissed too?"

"I would laugh because you are so very sweet and gentle and despite your past, you are innocent beyond belief, but you might take offense. Aye, most men loved to be kissed by pretty girls and I'm no different. I also take great delight in kissing pretty girls."

"Father says I'm passable but my breasts are too small. He told me men would enjoy me more if parts of me were larger." Wynnie wasn't sure why she told Connal that, but she was terrified when rage seemed to possess his expression.

"How I feel about you is all that matters. Your father is an idiot and a horrible man," Connal said in an outburst. "Now let's see about kissing. It's a very good idea you have."

"I've seen people kissing," she said.

"Good then you've some idea as to how it goes."

"Perhaps if I'm to kiss you I could use a footstool." She smiled at him then, thinking she would have to jump up and down to reach him.

He did laugh then, touched her lips with his finger. "I will not make this difficult, and since I'm to kiss you first, well, then I will bend down close to you."

With his hand around her waist, he pulled her closer. She felt his hard body against hers and remembered the way he looked just this morning when he rose naked from their bed. She swallowed, wondering what would come next, but his lips hovered close to hers without touching.

She ran her tongue across her lips and touched his mouth. A startled gasp escaped her. He chuckled softly. "That was a start." Then his lips found hers so very gently she wasn't at all sure he was kissing her. He drew away then and smiled at her.

"Is that all there is?" she asked as he put some distance between them. "I thought there was more."

"You're right, of course. It's your turn now." Once again, he bent close to her, his lips only a fraction from hers, waiting.

Wynnie ran her hands through his hair, enjoying the softness before touching his lips with hers. She touched then pulled back then touched him again. He slid his tongue across the seam and she gasped again, startled by the simple yet mercuric sensations the contact summoned.

"That was good, very good," he told her, taking her arm in his. "Shall we go downstairs and I'll introduce you to some of our people?"

"That's it? I expected something more."

"I enjoyed your kiss very much. Did you want a third kiss? Greedy girl," he laughed seeming pleased with himself. "Perhaps tonight I'll let you kiss me again.

~ * ~

Adair and Perkins stopped at the first inn they came across that morning. They were only a few miles from the McKenna castle. Perkins wanted to stay on McKenna land, but Oscar thought it would be best to wait a few months before returning, lull Wynnie and the laird into a sense of comfort and leave them unsuspecting.

"Wynnie won't be able to stay in the confines of the castle for more than a few days," Perkins argued his case, thinking if they stayed here, they would find her alone and vulnerable sooner than later.

"She has someone to keep her tied up if she tries to leave. I wouldn't put it past Connal McKenna to do just that if she acted foolishly," Oscar said. "I've the strange feeling he'll be the first man she obeys.

"Well, in any case, I'm not all that sure I want used goods." Perkins laughed at himself. "Used by other than those I've hand picked. What if he does get her pregnant?"

Oscar shrugged. "McKenna will fight all the harder to keep her close. What you have to decide is if it's your pride that wants her or if you really do like to have her beneath you and at your whim."

"Both," Perkins said quickly, rubbing his crotch, remembering the way he felt when he forced her and was deep inside her. "I want both. She was always such a willful lass and full of her self worth. She looked down her nose at me too many times, and it was fun to tame her. I need to keep making her pay."

"You've always needed everything." Oscar smiled, "That's why I picked you first."

"We'll do this your way. Go home, figure out what we have on our side and bring the necessary witnesses. We could claim I married Wynnie before she fled."

"I know just the person to forge the proper documents," Oscar said. "This won't be too difficult. Your marriage to Wynnie should prevail, don't you think?"

Chapter Four

Connal wasn't sure where to go from here, his body tense with barely controlled agony. He needed release and there were only a few ways to gain it. Two were not possible at the moment.

He watched Alistair, relaxed and at ease, chatting with Brenna in the hall. His fists clenched. His best friend's relationship with his sister still left him with misgivings, understanding the reasons he claimed her without benefit of marriage but the act still left distaste in his mouth.

With Wynnie by his side, he strode to his sister and his friend. The need still encapsulating him, "Let's takes this outside." He addressed his statement to Alistair.

"Fists or steel?" Alistair laughed, seeming to understand what was driving him and the need to hit something.

"Swords first," Connal gritted out, then to Wynnie, "Stay here with Brenna. The two of you can get to know each other better."

Wynnie looked to him, her forehead creased between her eyes then to Brenna. "If Brenna has nothing better to do. I suppose." She seemed to hesitate. "I do have things I would like to ask her."

Brenna reached out to her. "Please sit. You must want something to eat and drink. We will watch them later. They will work out whatever is bothering them then they'll want some solace from us. Our men folk tend to beat themselves to a bloody pulp under the guise of feeling better then they want their woman to tend to and heal their wounds."

Wynnie looked to him again. He tried to smile, "Go on, Brenna is right in all she has said." It seemed once again he was abandoning Wynnie to his sister so she could make things right between them. He ran both hands through his hair, wishing he had some way to make things right with Wynnie. A short talk with his sister would not break down the barrier between them.

But he had no ideas.

In the yard, the two men met, steel meeting steel, ducking and parrying, the pair seemed to enjoy the fight. Clashing steel rang out in the courtyard and with each jarring noise, the grunts of the men were heard as they put all possible effort into their blows.

Seconds ticked by turning into minutes. Sweat dripped into Connal's eyes, his muscles strained with each blow. The metal met above their heads as they pushed to gain supremacy.

The men were equally matched in many ways. Connal was quicker, faster on his feet, but Alistair bested him with brute strength and bulk. They shoved against each other, both men falling back and tossing their swords to the side.

Alistair roared, lunging at him while Connal met him head on, the two men grappling together trying to best the other. Rolling on the ground in the mud and the dirt the grunts seemed to be one with each punch. Somehow Connal slipped from Alistair's grip.

Bent, feet dancing, they circled each other, looking for a weakness. Alistair lashed out and Connal ducked and whirled landing a kick to Alistair's side, eliciting another grunt. Connal guarded his face and upper torso to block the ferocious blows his opponent rained down upon him. He spun and ducked again. Alistair fought, countered the attack, but this time he did not move fast enough. Connal's next punch was so fast and so hard Alistair didn't block the punch. He staggered backwards, blood running from his nose. The crowd that gathered around them yelled and cheered for the two combatants. Alistair roared and bent over attacked Connal around the waist and they fell to the ground again, rolling on the earth as each tried to win.

Then they were both sprawled on their back, laughing. "You didn't have to hit me so hard." Alistair moaned. "Thought we were friends."

"Seems to me you could have been a wee bit gentler," Connal shot back. "With me and my sister."

"And what good would that have done?" Alistair asked, rising from the ground and extending a hand to help Connal stand. "Neither one of us would feel better. As soon as I see Brenna all sensation will coming rushing back."

"Not sure I feel better anyway," he said, breathing heavily, winded by the conflict with his friend. "Still have to face another night with Wynnie and figure out just how I'm going to ease her mind about me."

"Know only one thing that will make either of us feel better," Alistair said, looking through the crowd.

Connal followed the direction of Alistair's gaze to see Brenna and Wynnie standing on the sidelines watching. Wynnie's eyes were huge pools of dark blue. He didn't have any idea what she was thinking but she appeared horrified. This was not the way he wanted to deal with her.

One small intimacy at a time was prudent. If he terrified her, he would be taking steps backwards in their tenuous relationship. He stood then arms spread wide as his men dumped a bucket of water over his head, intended to wash most of the dirt and sweat from his body before he entered into the main hall.

Trying to catch Wynnie's attention, he smiled at her. The thought that she was afraid for him crossed his mind, but he set the notion aside as being ridiculous. She probably hoped for his demise... no, that would not be wise and he thought of Wynnie as an intelligent woman who would understand he protected her from a worse fate than himself.

He exhaled a long slow breath of air, wishing for a different relationship with her. While he never believed in undying romantic love, he did acknowledge she was his mate for life. He didn't know how to win her over to his way of thinking or his bed though. Alistair told him one sweet kiss at a time, but she barely allowed a touch between them let alone a kiss. What few intimacies they shared had been forced upon them by circumstances.

"All you need do is court her as if she was a virgin. She is in a way," Brenna stood by his side while Alistair seemed to be glowering at her. "Pretend you are just as afraid of touching her as she is of you."

He shook his head, watching as water droplets littered the air around him and Brenna stepped back, grimacing at him. "Don't know how to court a lady. Don't know anything about the gentler side of women. Never was afraid to touch a woman or a girl even when I was younger for that matter. She would never believe it if I tried."

"You didn't court Maurina?" Brenna asked, puzzled by his announcement. "There must have been some hesitancy with the first kiss."

"Don't remember," he muttered. "Doubt it. I wasnae her first lover."

"Come." Alistair was by her side, his hand resting possessively on her shoulder. "We need some time to talk about us and plan our future. You must stop hounding your brother. He will figure it out."

"Go on with him." Connal seemed to be shooing them away. "I'd like some time with Wynnie if she'll allow it."

"You cannot treat her as if she has always known you and kens that you would never hurt her. Wynnie is fragile, along with her heart and soul. I suspect she will give herself to you completely when she comes to love you. But you've got a long road ahead of you. She has only been treated badly by men. In her mind, why should you be any different?" Brenna said as she left with Alistair, his arm wrapped possessively around her shoulder.

Connal inhaled several long breaths of air then seemed to hold it inside before he turned once more to cast his gaze on Wynnie, his wife. Last night seemed to have passed in front of him in a blur, everything happening too fast to comprehend. For the time being the title of wife was in name only and most likely would be for some months to come.

She stood in front of him, her hands clasped tightly in front of her. Her eyes still huge wide terrified pools of blue. "Would you like me to order a bath and food for you?"

"Will you join me in the solar?" he asked, wishing he dared wrap his arm around her as Alistair did his sister. "I would relish more time with you."

"Not for your bath." And he was surprised when she smiled. It seemed genuine and from the heart.

"Are you teasing a bit?" he asked, hoping some time in their not too distant future she would truly share a bath with him and so much more. For now, he would settle for what was right in front of him

For a brief moment, she looked down then decided to meet his gaze. "I was thinking of yesterday when you changed to your cat when I was in the tub. I thought you would jump into the water with me. Didn't think cats liked water but I'm infinitely more comfortable with you in your other form."

He roared with laughter and he stifled it as soon as he noticed the changing expression on her face. "Sorry, lass, that's a misnomer. Big cats love water but I was laughing at the fact you are more at ease with cats than humans. What about you? Do you like to swim? The loch is cold this time of year but invigorating for a short swim. We could go now."

She started walking toward the main hall. He joined her, wondering once more if he said something wrong. He kept his hands at his sides, looking straight ahead.

"I can swim well enough but don't relish freezing water. Don't find anything invigorating about it. Should I wait downstairs until you are through bathing?" She stopped at the steps, looking over her shoulder at the room behind her as if longing to hide there.

"Do you want to remain here?" It seemed to Connal once again she was caught between two things she didn't want to do.

"No, I wouldn't feel at ease. The only person I know besides you is Brenna and she has gone to be with Alistair." Once again, she clasped her hands in front of her while she stared at her feet.

"And you would feel more at ease observing me in my bath?" He wanted to laugh but wisely held the merriment inside. She loathed men but... but what, he wondered. Perhaps she did feel a tiny element of trust when she thought of him. He was fairly confident she enjoyed the kiss they shared a couple of hours ago.

"Yesterday I would have said nay but today..." She lifted small shoulders, ones that seemed to have carried the weight of the world on them for too many years. He would like nothing more than to take that weight from her shoulders. "Today I would feel more at ease with you," she hesitated then, "even seeing you naked. So far you have not harmed me."

He grinned, pleased with her honesty as well as the slender thread of trust she held out to him. Perhaps there was hope for them. "I will set up the privacy screen so you don't have to look upon me."

For a moment she turned away. He would have sworn she was about to object. "That would be nice."

"Only if you don't want to enjoy... my nakedness. It matters not to me." Yet he acknowledged it did matter more than he cared to admit right now.

She moistened her lips before looking down then back to him, seeming to hesitate before saying, "I do like..."

"Your bath is ready." A servant interrupted the conversation. "When we saw you and Alistair fighting in the yard, we anticipated your needs."

"You do that often? Fight?"

"When the mood hits. Fighting each other helps hone our skills." He gave a quick lift to his broad shoulders. "Other things as well."

Connal imagined Wynnie was thankful for the disruption. He was having a hard time picturing her breaking out of her shell quite so quickly as to admit she liked the way he looked naked. Maybe he was wrong. Perhaps that was not what she was going to say.

In silence they walked the rest of the way. He opened the door to his solar and waited for her to pass through. Near the fireplace a huge tub waited for him with steaming water. Clean clothing had been set on the bed for him. For the moment he had just about everything he needed.

"Connal," her voice was whisper thin. "I was going to say you are the most pleasant man to look upon I have ever seen. Perhaps it is because you are not forcing me to have sex with you or mayhap it's because you..." she swallowed hard, "You do not seem to possess any fat."

Then as if totally embarrassed, she walked to the big chair near the fireplace and sat down, her gaze riveted on the floor. He needed her to look at him. Her words brought awe to him.

He appreciated her candid assessment even though it seemed to have embarrassed her. At least he hoped it was honesty unsure of what else it might be. Briefly last night he'd seen her naked. She was slender and possessed beautiful curves. Her breasts would easily fill his hands, if she ever allowed him the closeness. She was willow thin though but her muscles seemed tight. Perhaps some of that came from hiding in the woods and riding. She handled her horse with skill and expertise.

One small touch at a time.

Slipping into the hot liquid he closed his eyes, dreaming dreams of Wynnie and himself lost in the throes of passion. He imagined claiming her and truly making her his, marking her. He wanted her in the most elemental ways, primal and mercurial in nature.

If her father had thoughts that this marriage wasn't valid or real, he was right, but it was much more real than anything that would ever exist between Wynnie and Perkins. If she had not run, Perkins most likely would have never wed her yet he would have continued to use her.

Servants entered with food and drink. He wasn't sure if she wanted to stay ensconced in this room or meet more of their people. Brenna must have introduced her to at least a few of the clan when he and Alistair first began to fight.

He jerked slightly when she stood beside the tub, a glass of ale in her hand, offering the drink to him. She set a table nearby so he had some place to put it.

"Thank you. Did you serve yourself?" he asked, amazed at her actions and wondered why when she was so clearly frightened.

"Thought I should wash your back if you'd like," she murmured, seeming to try to smile. "It is not foreign to me. Was asked to do that numerous times. Every time..."

"I would but I've the feeling it's the last thing you want to do. Why do you ask?" He touched her hand with his, holding her fingers for a second before letting them go.

"I thought you would like me to do it." She soaped a sponge. "You will have to lean forward though. I'll try to be gentle."

"Not until you tell me why. Tell me again so I can fully understand." He studied her expression and could see nothing in her eyes that would tell him anything. They were blank and distant, a place where she must have gone in the past. He didn't want to continue on in this vein. His guess was that she'd been forced to wash the men who forced her.

She sat back then, seeming to focus a bit more on him. "Because they wanted me to and if I did something as simple as washing the man's back after..." she swallowed again, "then..."

"Then what?" he felt a deep and very dark anger begin to simmer inside when he thought of all that happened to her before she fled her home, risking her life.

"Then father wouldnae beat me." The words were quick and staccato like as she said them. She closed her eyes as if remembering those times but trying to force them from her head.

"I would rather you tended to me because you wanted to rather than from fear that I would beat you. I won't ever do that, Wynnie."

"So you say. You are a man and men cause pain." She still held the sponge in her hand, but her eyes were no longer hazy.

"Go relax, enjoy something to drink and whatever snack cook sent up. I will be out in a few minutes and dressed. After that we can walk along the parapets. It is my favorite place and you can tell me more about yourself."

"There is not much to tell that you don't already ken," she murmured, her head down once again.

He heard the underlying tone that told him what she said wasn't entirely true. She was holding something back, perhaps her hopes and goals, things she had never thought to have. He would love to uncover the truths she didn't want to believe in and teach her that now there was hope.

Ducking beneath the water then standing he poured the bucket of rinse water over him. The tiny amount of water had cooled and he shuddered when the liquid hit his flesh. Surprising him, she was in front of him, a bath towel in hand, giving it to him.

"You don't have to wait on me, lass. I understand that I make you uncomfortable," he said, his voice husky with a growing passion for her he was having a devilishly hard time concealing. He would have to school his baser needs.

"I..." She stepped backwards a few steps, her voice shaking. "Don't want to displease you. You are my husband and important to me."

Guessing the truth of her behavior, "I will not hit you, ever. If nothing else, you need to understand that one fact." Truly he didn't ken what it was he needed to do to prove that to her. Time perhaps or would she ever trust him, ever give her heart and soul over to his safekeeping?

Hopefully in time she would do just that.

Quickly he dried off and dressed then extended his arm to her, hoping she would accept. "Shall we go to the battlements? You can look over your land, the land of our clan."

For several moments she held back then seeming to understand this was something he wanted her to do, she hesitantly placed her hand on his arm. He felt the touch all the way to his toes, his body responding.

"My being your wife does not make the land mine. The people will have to accept me first for that to be true." She walked beside him, up the steps until they reached the top. "You dinna ken if they will do that."

He led her to the wall where she'd found him early this morning. Where she'd come with Brenna. He'd left her with dangerous and dark frustrations eating at him.

The view of his land always caused his smile to grow. Most of these lands were treeless yet rugged. Mountains pushed to the sky while streams flowed quickly downward in places creating beautiful waterfalls. Cliffs protruded from the hills and heather covered the ground. In some places the soil and the weather were not good for growing plants, but it was good for the clan Chattan.

"Clan Chattan will accept you simply because you are my mate. I ken you are sweet and kind. For that reason alone, they will come to love you." He realized the truth of his words as he spoke them, even knowing so little about her.

"You can't possibly know that," she murmured, a small smile on her face seeming to form. "We've known each other less than a full day. I could be wickedly evil for all you know."

He chuckled softly, one eyebrow above the other, "Wickedly evil?"

"Yes, what do you know of me except what Perkins and my father told you. I'm sure their words were not laced with honey. They've told others that I was a wild child and needed taming. That sex with me would help me behave and bow down to the ways of men. Sex would teach me how a man wanted to be treated."

His gut churned at her words. If he could slit their throats, he would do it. Torture would be better.

He placed his hand on her waist, thrilled she didn't flinch away from him. Instead she held herself still. Someday soon she would lean into him. Now he understood she simply wanted to keep the status quo because she didn't want to make him angry. She didn't want him to beat her or send her away. She had been willing to just do it, so she would get the sex with him done and over. He would never allow anything so preposterous.

He shuddered thinking about those two men who he considered less than human. "Very few words were exchanged between us. What he told Alistair might be a different story, but my friend has not divulged the gist of their conversation except that Perkins coveted Brenna last night." Which led to Brenna sleeping in the chamber with Alistair for her protection. He needed to remind himself and come to terms with that fact.

"My intended covets everyone in a skirt. I would be surprised if someone in your household was not in his bed last night."

"No one that I've heard of was forced. Perkins and your father would not have been allowed to leave this morning if anything like that had happened."

~ * ~

Wynnie wasn't sure how to proceed with Connal who seemed to be willing to wait forever to have sex with her. Not for one minute, now that she was getting to know him, did she think he would hurt her on purpose, but she didn't see any other end to sex.

He would have to prove it to her.

She turned to him then, "Truly I would like you to do what men do with their wives tonight. I don't want to put it off any longer than I have to, you know." She was plucking at her skirts and staring fixedly at her feet. "Even though a part of me is terrified, we must make sure there is a child growing in my womb when my father returns. We all know he will."

Connal let out a long slow breath of air, seeming to study her intently. "What about this? Tonight I let you do anything you want with my man's body. You can touch me and kiss me anywhere and anytime you would like. I won't complain and when or if you don't look at me with dazed eyes, perhaps we can take this one step further. It all depends on what I see in your eyes."

She grimaced and walked away, striding to the other side of the battlement, unsure of what all that would entail, touching his man's body. She certainly didn't think she could have sex without retreating to her pleasant place. When she stopped at the wall, he was beside her, leaning against the stones next to her, close to her, but barely touching. She felt a small shiver tease her as well as tiny wave of heat when he set his hand on her back.

"I wouldn't know how. Don't know what you would like. Never touched a man before." She closed her eyes, trying to imagine what he said, what he'd just given her permission to do.

He shrugged his broad shoulders then running his hand down her back, "I suppose we are at a stalemate. Either you make love to me, or nothing will happen between us. Do you want a baby?"

"I don't see why. It isn't as if you don't know how or what to do. You are experienced, I'm sure." Anger or perhaps frustration with this stubborn man seemed to simmer in deep dark places inside where she couldn't reach. His soft laughter irritated her even more.

"I'm sorry, lass. It seems I've laughed at your expense." He was gazing into her eyes and she his. Connal's brown eyes seemed to darken with some emotion she knew nothing about.

She wanted to learn though. She also wanted to learn to laugh.

Wynnie moistened her lips in expectation of something she wasn't sure of. His grin widened and it seemed he was enjoying the moment. "Look at me, Wynnie. Don't close your eyes."

"Why?" She held her breath, waiting and watching as his mouth slowly caressed hers. The touch was pleasant, something unexpected. She did remember the last time and it was also nice. He pulled away, leaving her gasping for a breath of air.

"Because I want you to always know I'm the man kissing you. If you keep your eyes open you will not be afraid."

"I dinna ken why it would be so important. No other man but you has kissed me." She realized she liked his kisses, perhaps even more than she cared to admit. "They seem to make me melt from the inside out and my stomach feels as if it has little butterflies flitting about inside."

"What makes you melt?" he queried, his voice husky and deliciously smooth, warming her.

She punched him on the shoulder wondering if he was purposely being daft. "Kisses, your kisses to be precise. No one else's kisses. Just yours, you horrid man." She crossed her arms in front of her. "Beast."

He moved away then, watching her intensely. "Perhaps this evening you can kiss me so I can feel the same way, melting from the inside out and the butterflies... you say they are flitting about in your stomach? Is that good or bad?"

Disappointed in his answer, she pushed that thought to the back of her head. "I thought you would kiss me again and yes the butterflies are good. You don't feel them?"

"I will kiss you every time you ask or you can kiss me anytime you like. Just say the word," he said, gently placing a tendril of her fiery red hair behind her ear. "But just not anymore right now. Would you like to go for a ride tomorrow? I'd take you today but until I hear from my people that your father and Perkins have left McKenna land, we should stay inside the castle walls."

"I'd rather not talk of them but of us, you. Do you change to your cat often?" She was curious about him. "I don't ken why but I wasn't afraid when you changed right in front of me. I didn't care if your cat saw me with no clothes on. It's different than when you look at me."

"Only when there is some sort of need. The other night I was restless so Alistair and my cousins and I went deep into the countryside so we could shift and run. I needed a cold swim in the loch and now I understand why the restlessness took over me. It was leading me to you."

"That's why you were out so late at night. Why you caught me, I guess. If I had known, I would have never fought you. As it was, I believed one of my father's minions had found me. I wanted to die right then. I knew I couldn't go back, but the way you captured me I understood I had no choice." She leaned into him, suddenly feeling more comfortable with the man.

He wrapped an arm around her, drawing her close, comforting and she understood from the way he held her, she could move away from him if she wanted. He would not hold her captive, would never do things she didn't want him to do.

"It was not well done of me."

"What? I'm not understanding." She blinked, confused as to what exactly he was speaking of.

"Tying you and taking you to the tower room. I'm not proud of myself but... Well, I guess there is no excuse." He let out a long heavy breath of air. "Tell me something about yourself."

"Like what?" She felt a smile growing in her heart, something she'd never experienced before.

"Well," he paused thoughtfully, touching the tip of her nose with a fingertip, his perfect white teeth gleaming in the sunlight. "I know the color of your eyes and your hair and that you must not weigh much over one hundred pounds. When were you born?"

"As my father tells me, it was a dark and evil night. My mother left not too many days after I was born. We dinna celebrate my birth. When the day would come around, it felt more as if a funeral was taking place rather than a celebration of the day I was born." The lightheartedness she'd felt only a few moments ago vanished in the wake of her memories.

"So you don't know?"

"I didn't say that exactly. I'm assuming it was the fifteenth of May. He would always disappear for the day, cursing my existence and me. I was left to fend for myself and many times..." She didn't want to finish her thoughts, didn't care to remember any of those days.

"Where did he go?"

"He never told me. In any case I never asked. He would usually come back in a better mood. Perhaps he had a woman he saw, a mistress or some poor soul who he would force."

"May fifteenth," he paused, seeming to think, "Do you want to celebrate your birth on that day or should we give you a new birth date, say October twenty-ninth. 'Twas the day I found you. The day could be considered a starting over for you as well as for me. At least I hope it is so."

"I'd like that." Truly she thought his idea was a fine one. "I've never had a real birthday before. When is yours?"

"October twenty-second, lass. I feel as if you were my gift for the year and I need nothing more."

"So, we are each a year older." A cold breeze seemed to sweep off the hills. "I'll be twenty next year." She never thought she would live that long.

He pulled her close, her back against his chest as he held her, his chin resting on the top of her head. She found she liked this man and wondered if this emotion could ever change to love. She'd never thought to like a man let alone love one. Mayhap she was living in a fantastical dream world one that would soon come crashing down around her. Guarding her emotions might be a prudent course of action for the days to come.

She closed her eyes, absorbing the warmth of this man, this very different man in the scope of her experiences. Warm, gentle and kind but in some ways he was a bit rough around the edges. Her father and Perkins were refined and always proper, not Connal. Yet the head of the McKenna clan was so much more a man that the others she'd known.

"We are indeed," he murmured, turning her in his arms and lifting her chin so she was peering into his eyes.

Hers were wide open now and she sensed he was going to kiss her again. She touched her top lip with the tip of her tongue, thinking she'd like to taste him. The thought sent a rush of heat to her cheeks. For a moment she looked away, not wanting him to see.

"My goodness..." She wasn't sure what to say as she felt the whispering warmth of his breath against her cheek. Yet is seemed he didn't miss the rush of color.

"You blush. What are you thinking that causes your cheeks to turn such a beautiful shade of pink?" He brushed his lips across her. His were so soft and moist, warm, tantalizing her senses. Her pulse pounded as she could barely catch a breath.

For a moment she lowered her lashes, swallowing and wishing she could tell him without blushing even more.

"Wynnie?" He touched his tongue to her lips, lightly then his lips slanted across hers for a quick kiss. "Tell me."

"If you promise not to laugh," she said, turning her head away for a second then deciding courage and the truth were the best way to proceed.

"Look at me, please." He sighed softly and she wanted to know what he was thinking. "I will never laugh at you, perhaps with you from time to time."

"I think I ken that but still..." she paused, plucking at his shirt, unsure why she was touching him and wishing for something more that he could give her but not knowing what that was. "I was thinking, wondering... I'd like to know what you taste like."

Gently, he ran his finger across her mouth. "After all you've been through in your short life, you unman me. I want to make the rest of your life one of happiness and pleasure yet I cannot promise there will be no difficult times for us. Can you accept that?"

"Don't expect promises or a lifetime of sunny weather. Just kiss me again. Let me taste you this time." She smiled at him, touching the cleft in his chin with the tip of her finger. "I like your kisses. They unravel me, make my knees weak."

"If you want to taste me, you'll have to open your sweet lips for me, give me your tongue. Can you do that?" Slowly he lowered his head.

She heard his groan and wondered at that. "Yes," she murmured as his lips closed over hers. She felt his tongue against her flesh, remembered his words and opened for him. The touch of his tongue inside her mouth, sweeping within amazed her and seemed to heighten all her senses as well as the butterflies in the pit of her stomach. She gripped his shoulders, her fingers tightening as his hands cupped her derriere and pulled her against him.

His arousal against her belly didn't frighten her even though she knew what it meant. The feel seemed to create sensations she didn't understand, never experienced before.

Then she found that his kiss deepened and her tongue was playing with his, touching and withdrawing, dancing and dueling. The taste of him swept through her as he tugged her bottom lip with his teeth. She found her knees did not want to function.

He lifted her in his arms, carrying her down the long steps to his chamber. She hoped he would have sex with her now, truly consummate their marriage. His arousal had pulsed against her and while fear should have been the overpowering emotion, it wasn't. For reasons she didn't understand, she wanted him.

She needed to cry out her distress when he sat down on the large chair and not the bed with her on his lap. He continued kissing her though, her face and neck then his teeth tugged on her ear. Little sounds escaped her, rippling from her lungs. She'd never felt anything so magical and enchanting before this kiss. Her hips seemed to be moving, arching upward as if searching for something and she kenned that only he could give it to her.

He stopped then, his breathing heavy as was hers. His head rested on her forehead. "We need to cease before I take this farther than you are ready. I can barely contain myself."

"I want you to kiss me again." Her voice was a thin wail that didn't sound at all like her. "And other things. The things men do."

"If I keep kissing you, we'll be on that bed and I'll be inside you, lass. I don't want to frighten or hurt you. I need for you to want me as much as I want you." He was refastening parts of her clothing that had somehow come undone.

Never before had a man set her clothes to rights. Usually they were in tatters when they finished. Truly she was beginning to understand just how different this man was from the others she'd known. He was even putting her hair back into the chignon that seemed to have been falling down around her shoulders.

"I do want you." Her voice cracked when she spoke, but when she looked at the bed, a small lump of dark fear and apprehension settled in her stomach rumbling around, replacing the sweet delicious butterflies.

"Maybe you'll want me more tomorrow," he said, finishing the last touches on her gown and hair. Then his voice husky, he asked, "Shall we have dinner?"

"Dinner?" She couldn't possibly eat. At the moment she was confused and stimulated to a point she didn't understand. It was a novel sensation but she was hot and felt so different.

"Yes, we didn't spend much time downstairs today. Food should be a priority if we want to keep up our strength."

Blindly, she was nodding her head, accepting whatever he said when she really wanted to continue to explore other possibilities between them. Then reluctantly, "I suppose we could go downstairs."

He set her off his lap, a too broad grin on his handsome face to suit her, thinking he was up to something. Her legs were wobbly. She was relieved when he offered his arm. She leaned on it for support.

In the hall, she saw the few people she did know: his cousins, Angus and Fergus, his sister and Alistair. They sat at a table, chatting together, laughing. A fire burned in the fireplace, a cheery glow encompassing the scene. A small dog lay by the fire soaking up the heat while a cat was curled next to his head.

All around children were, with the help of their parents, carving lanterns out of turnips for gaizin' on all hollows' eve. The children were preparing their masks and the lanterns for their visits to houses.

She smiled. All had been similar at her home near Glasgow.

He escorted her to his cousins and reintroduced her. They were with him the other night when he found her and brought her to the castle, as was Alistair. He led her around the keep presenting her to various people and as the list grew, she knew she would be unable to remember the names.

When he was done and she was thoroughly confused, he pulled up two chairs by his sister and Alistair. True to form he left her with his sister once more. It seemed he didn't feel like eating any more than she did. She watched his retreating back and wondered if he was going to shift and run again. She certainly wished she could do something to ease her frustration.

~ * ~

Oscar took his irritations out on Heather, Wynnie's mother. He always did. Whenever Wynnie escaped his plans by fleeing into the woods, he would come to this hovel where he kept her mother.

He fastened his pants, watching Heather. She was always stoic.

Had not been the first time he had sex with her. If Heather had ever shown a sign that she enjoyed his company, he might have kept her in a better place, somewhere she could live more easily.

From the first time, she fought him. He'd grown to like that side of her though, relished the few times he watched Wynnie try to fight the men he brought to her. It was always arousing. The resistance was part of the charm. When Wynnie began to withdraw from herself, that was when he decided to sell her to others besides Perkins.

The girl eluded him. While he told her he didn't know if she was his, those words had been a lie. Wynnie was his even though she looked just like her mother.

"Where is Wynnie?" she asked. "You always speak of her when you come, just to taunt me. I understand but..."

Anger simmered deep inside in the darkest places. He waved a hand. "She fled."

A smile formed on Heather's face. "Do you know where she is? Is she safe?"

"Safe enough. She took refuge at the McKenna's castle in northern Scotland. The McKenna says he is wed to her but the only proof of that was the fact she was in his bed."

"She is safe for now and my heart is glad."

"Perhaps I could hold your life over her head. She would come to me if she thought it would save her mother's life." He was pacing and rubbing his chin deep in thought.

"She won't believe you. The ruse you played with her was too true and thorough for her to think you lied all those years. She has believed I'm dead for a very long time."

"You might be right, but it won't stop me from trying."

~ * ~

"How long do I have to wait for my husband to believe I'm ready to be a wife in all ways?" Wynnie asked Brenna. "It's been over a month. He was the one who said I needed to be with child as soon as possible."

Brenna's heart went out to Wynnie. It seemed to her, Wynnie tried every way imaginable to convince Connal of that fact.

"I think I've a way he won't be able to resist you." Brenna said linking her arm through Wynnie's as they strolled in the garden. "But you will have to put aside your inhibitions. Courage, my dear."

Wynnie stopped, turning toward her, "Really? I've talked and talked. He won't listen to me. He will kiss me and make me feel hot and..." She was shaking her head, trying to tell Brenna everything, all the sensations.

"I ken what you're feeling."

"Do you? But," she paused, "Alistair makes love to you. He doesn't just kiss and make the butterflies dance in your belly."

"He does but I didn't come to him abused by people I should have been able to trust. Connal doesn't want to hurt you. He's afraid that if he does, you'll never trust him again."

"So, just what is this notion of yours? I'm ready to become his wife." She stopped to look over the yard. "He and Alistair have been fighting now almost daily. I do believe Alistair is getting tired of the battles."

"First of all, they do need to keep their battle skills sharpened. And second, if you want to make it impossible for your man to keep his hands to himself, all you need do is present yourself to him without a stitch of clothing on." Brenna took Wynnie's hands in hers, "I know it will seem awkward at first but you can do it. I know you can."

"How? He comes in late at night, dons his night shirt and crawls into the far side of that huge bed."

"He doesn't even give you a kiss goodnight?" Brenna asked, slowly dropping Wynnie's hands.

"He only kisses me when he knows it can't go any farther. We go to the parapets and he kisses me until I can't stand any longer. Then he will run any loose strands of my hair through his fingers. Sometimes he lets out a long-discontented sigh."

"That does not sound like the rumors that have always flourished about my brother. He has always been a lady's man, quick to bed a willing lass who might catch his fancy. He must really love you."

"Love? What is love? I certainly have never felt love from any human. Indeed, you and Connal are the only people who I even like." Wynnie hesitated for a second. "I did like the elderly woman who used to hide me from father. Her name was Berta."

"First, you need to stay awake until he comes to bed. Second, all you need do is wear, say a robe with nothing on beneath it. When Connal comes in and disrobes for bed, you should walk up to him and slip the robe off your shoulders. He will not be able to resist the temptation."

"You promise it will work." Wynnie's hands were shaking. "I would be mortified if he rejected me."

Brenna smiled, squeezing Wynnie's hands. "He will not reject you. I promise you, whenever you garner the courage to present yourself to your husband without a stitch of clothing on, he will make love to you. I promise. The act will tell him all that he's been waiting to hear from you."

It seemed to Brenna that Wynnie mulled her words over in her head for the longest time. "Courage, that is what I need."

"You can do it. I know you can," Brenna whispered. "Come, the day is growing late. We should get back inside. Do it tonight while you cannot come up with reasons to gainsay yourself."

Chapter Five

Connal finished the ale he was drinking before striding to the parapets to look over the land. It was the first snow of the season and the middle of December. He had yet to make love to Wynnie although he kenned she wanted him.

Yet he was afraid, terribly afraid he would hurt her and ruin everything.

The cowardice in him surfaced every time he thought of her eyes and the way they assumed a vague hue when he touched her. Granted it had been a month or more since he'd seen that vacant stare, but the memory haunted his soul and reminded him of the abuse she lived through at her father's hands, a man who should have protected her.

He looked up as the flakes touched his face and melted, wondering if Wynnie enjoyed the snow. In the morning he would have to find out. Perhaps they could go for a short ride into the hills. Would she even know how to play in the snow? Had she ever had the chance? So many questions and most of them he didn't ask not wanting to remind her of times better left in her memories.

His words about a quick pregnancy came back to haunt him. She was not, could not, unless he made love to her. Except for her sake and the status of their marriage, he didn't care. God willing, children would happen in their own time. He gritted his teeth, attempting to control his unruly body that seemed to harden every time he thought of her naked and in the bed waiting for him. That one glimpse of her was not enough.

This was not the way to go forward with this marriage. Perhaps he should make love to her in the dark so he wouldn't be able to see into her eyes. "You are a dimwitted fool, Connal McKenna, if you think you wouldn't feel her body stiffen in fear beneath you."

Inhaling a long and deep breath of air and tormented by his thoughts, he turned toward the stairway leading downward, determined to make it through another night of celibacy, lying beside her and wishing for so much more. At the door he paused, his hand on the latch. Closing his eyes, he drank heavily of the air he could absorb into him before entering. What he needed was a miracle.

A soft candle lit room presented itself to him, lights flickering all around. Gently, he closed the door, leaning against it, his gaze roamed the room, searching for the reasons. His stomach wrenched in sudden fear that something was very wrong.

"Wynnie? Is everything alright?" he asked as he stepped further inside wondering at the candles and the soft glow seeming to warm the room even while the fire had been built up. Perhaps nothing was wrong and mayhap she was just having trouble falling asleep.

"I'm fine." Her voice was soft, sounding different to his ears, almost compelling.

"Good then, you should go back to sleep." He slipped out of his shirt, his back muscles flexing when he felt her presence behind him.

"Connal?" Her hand rested on his back, caressed softly, enticed and he knew she didn't mean the gesture. A groan rumbled from deep inside. "You should go back to bed."

"Dinna want to."

He turned then, a gasp rasping from his lungs. "Wynnie..." She was standing in front of him with nothing covering her. Her hands were on the fastening of his kilt. He touched her trembling fingers, wishing he understood what she was about. Since that first night when they wed, he had not seen her naked. Now she stood in front of him with nothing on, not a stitch. She was the most beautiful sight in all his life. He couldn't swallow, couldn't breathe.

She moistened her lips, "Tonight, please... I want more than a kiss. I want you to make love to me. I want to ken what it feels like when you are deep inside me, loving me as only you can."

"Ach, but you're not ready, lass." His voice rasped from his lungs. He could barely speak let alone think. "My god but you're beautiful. I could never forgive myself if I hurt you."

"You won't."

"You don't know that."

The glow from the soft light of the candles seemed to highlight the rounded globes of her breasts as well as the gentle curve of her hips. "You should take the rest of your clothes off," she whispered. "I'll help if you like."

Had he really stayed away from her all of these weeks? She wanted him, had told him many times. Yet he continued to believe she would be terrified of him. This woman was not afraid, perhaps she only pretended, but he'd also told her there would be only pleasure. Her fingers fumbled with his clothing.

"Let me do that." He groaned again as her fingers brushed against aroused, pulsing flesh.

"You will have sex with me then?" Her smile was small and hesitant.

He guessed she wasn't entirely sure of what she was asking and it was now up to him to show her there was a difference between forced sex and making love. "I will." He was naked now. He scooped her into his arms, carrying her to the bed where the covers were already pulled back, waiting for them.

In his arms, he felt the hardening tips of her breasts as they pushed against him, rubbed temptingly. The weight of making this right for her pushed harshly on his shoulders. On the bed he came down beside her, tracing her collarbone with the tip of one finger, trying to figure out just how he should proceed.

She moistened her lips, her small pink tongue enticing him with the warmth it offered, yet he understood the delicacy of this situation. His lips brushed against hers, and she responded sweetly but with hesitation; still so much an innocent in this.

"Are you going to torture me first?" she asked, her hands resting on his chest. "I like the way you feel, Connal, but my body seems to be burning for you, for your touch. I've never known anything like this."

The groan rumbled up from deep in his chest. "I like the way you feel too, lass, *mo shiorghra*." *My eternal love*, he murmured. His mouth closed over hers, gently at first then the fire and the spirit of the night seemed to take over his heart. The inferno had been building since that day in October when he held her behind him on his horse and her body was flush against his.

She fought him then and he didn't understand why, couldn't comprehend why he acted the way he did. Perhaps there was a reason for everything.

When he pulled away, he needed to see into her eyes. They were wide open, a bit of awe and wonder in them but clear and cognizant of everything he was doing. She trusted him. He could read it in her eyes. He sensed the heat of her body against his, the curve of her thighs against him and knew she felt his arousal, pulsing against her.

Yet she didn't pull away from him.

Lightly he touched her breast, keeping his gaze upon her. He drew his fingers low over her ribs then against her belly, down her thighs. Her lashes fluttered lightly across her cheeks. "Are you sure, lass?" he asked her softly, and she lifted her gaze to his again as he invaded her more intimately. She drew her limbs together as the flames of his caress must be touching her. Yet her body surged against his caress. He laughed with sheer pleasure as his lips seized upon hers.

"I've never been more sure of anything," she sighed then the whisper of her breath stroked his cheek, "but you have to tell me what you want, what to do?"

"Candlelight," he told her. "Thank God that you craved the light, for whatever reason because I hunger for the sight of you and desire whatever you are willing to give this night. I'm so glad you chose to look at me too."

His lips covered hers again and again then growing bolder they traveled lower, in tempest and wild abandon to her breasts and ever lower to her belly. Brazenly, he touched her. She cried out loud, stunned by the intimacies he was taking with her. His touch like this was most likely nothing she'd ever felt before, and he prayed he was not hurting her.

He was determined in this to give her pleasure and vanquish the fears that possessed her for so many years. He teased her no longer but fell upon her with purpose, parting her thighs to his desire, cradling her

84

gently in his arms. He knew there would be no virgin's pain, but he didn't know how small and tight she was.

Easing inside her, he slowly stretched her, felt the heat and moisture that flowed for him, for the pleasure he was sure would follow. She was breathing heavily, her hips rising to meet him, drawing him ever deeper into her velvet warmth. She wanted him and it pleased him.

"It's alright. You won't hurt me." Her fingers were biting into his shoulders.

He continued to stroke her and kiss her until she was mindlessly moving against him. She closed her eyes. He allowed it for a moment. Then, "Open your eyes, sweet lass. I want to see you when I give you your first pleasure."

Tremors seemed to sweep from her and into him. "Connal!" she cried out his name as he surged ever deeper inside, harder and faster. All consuming tremors encompassed her.

He groaned and thrust one more time, feeling the release of his seed. "Wynnie." Exhausted, he whispered her name. The magic of the moment eclipsed him, seared into him as the darkness around his heart and soul lifted and was replaced with the light he'd always craved.

Rising above her, he brushed damp hair from her eyes, concern for her overriding all else. He braced his weight on his forearms but he still felt the tips of her breasts against his chest. He smiled, pleased with himself and what just happened between them.

"I had no idea," she spoke softly, touching his cheek, running a fingertip along his jaw. "I believe you now. Only pleasure."

His heart went out to her. Where lovemaking with Wynnie was concerned, he realized his goal by showing her it wasn't all about pain and domination. Now he prayed their lives would continue on a more even keel. Still, they needed to brace against the return of her father and intended. He had not claimed her. Had not wanted to inflict any pain tonight. Marking her in the way of the clan Chattan would wait for another time, a time when he could explain to her what would happen and how they would once again be joined for eternity.

He rolled to his side, pulling her close, her head and one hand resting on his chest. "I'd like to know what you are thinking."

"That you are not like the others. Your shoulders are broad and bronzed from the sun even though winter is nearly upon us. Everything about you is masculine and if I didn't know you so well, intimidating. When I first saw you, you stole my breath."

He laughed at her words, having never thought that way about himself. "It was snowing before I came to my room. Do you like the snow?"

She pushed away, her hair falling over her shoulders and tickling him. "It is always cold. Winter was a time when men were bored and it was harder for me to hide. Sometimes I could not get away. I always dreaded the first snow fall of the season."

"That is all done now. You should not think of those things again. Perhaps I can teach you how to enjoy the white stuff falling from the sky."

"What if father returns? What will we do?"

To his delight she was kissing him, light small caresses along his chest, sipping with her lips, teasing with her teeth. "You're playing with fire, lass." He was sure it was too soon to make love to her again but if she kept up the evocative and mercurial caresses, he wouldn't be able to control his unruly body.

"How so?" She smiled at him and by the expression in her eyes, he was sure she knew exactly what she was about.

He thought showing her might be easier than explaining. Bringing her hand to his heavy sex, he delighted in her small gasp of surprise before asking. "You ken now?"

"So soon?" She pushed against him, smiling at him. "If you want, I suppose... I would not say nay." Her teeth pulled her lip into her mouth as she stared at his heavy arousal.

When she turned her attention back to him, he groaned at her expression. "I can wait until..." He wasn't sure if he could wait until tomorrow or the day after that, not even the next ten minutes. He wanted her, needed her in so many ways. How he abstained for well over a month amazed him.

"Why should you postpone?" She kissed his chest lightly, swirling her tongue around a nipple. "Do you like that? You have to tell me, you know. I've no idea what a man likes and what he doesn't. I've never touched a man before you."

"Little minx, are you trying to seduce me? Of course I like what you are doing." He laughed softly, enjoying everything about her and willing to let her do anything she wanted to his man's body.

"I wouldn't know how but..."

"For not knowing you are doing an amazingly fine job." Her lips once more touched him, swept across his lips as she rose against him. Unable to resist, he cupped her breasts in his hands, loving the way they filled them. Then his hands were on her waist, lifting her to straddle him.

"Is this...?" She looked down, saw his rod nestled between her thighs. "Do you... what is it you want?"

"A way to make love," he prompted her, once more watching the ever changing expression on her face. "Any time you like you can put me inside you. It's your decision."

"Any time I like and what would I do?" she questioned even though he'd pretty much just told her and he was sure she was thinking and coming to some conclusions all on her own.

Answering her was not something he planned on doing. She was going to have to figure this one out by herself. His fingers rolled her taut pink nipples gently between them. Then he pulled her closer, sucking them into his mouth, worrying each one alternately with his teeth then tongue. He groaned, feeling the tempest rise within him faster than he ever thought possible. His hands circled her tiny waist then stroked over her hips before caressing her even more intimately. A little mew of pleasure filled her throat as she tossed her head behind her, arching her back, her hair tumbling gloriously around her, touching upon his chest.

It seemed she realized what he wanted and was slowly settling on him. She gazed down at him, her tangled red hair falling in disarray around him. The magic and the enchantment of the night seemed to increase. The tempest soared within him as she moved slowly at first.

"Ach, lass, you are in control. Let the sensations rise and grow until you can tolerate no more." She did and minutes later she lay against him, her skin damp with a fine sheen of moisture.

He ran his hands along her back, calming the storm that swept through them. The night would be short, he realized, because he could not get enough of his wife. She wove a web of fascination around him, his wife, his mate for eternity. His *mo shiorghra*.

"I dinna feel in control of anything," she sighed softly, still lying on top of him. "I cannot move and I do hope I'm not too heavy for you."

"No, it seems neither of us has any wits about us." He laughed again, pleased with the events of this night. He was a man well pleased by his wife and he hoped she was delighted as well.

He settled her close, listening to the soft cadence of her breaths as she slept. She was nestled against him, her back against his chest while he cupped her breast in a hand. With his wife he found heaven tonight.

On the morrow he should meet with Alistair and lay strategies for the spring. Her father would not come in the winter but when the sun began to shine and travel would not be life threatening. The pair would try to take back what they considered theirs.

They wouldn't succeed.

If his initial plans came to fruition, both Oscar and Perkins would vanish at the Kinnel stones just as Maurina had and just as all the enemies of the clan Chattan. He didn't know how or why, but the place was magical, and people didn't return after entering inside the circle.

When he came to bed this evening, he never expected his wife to seduce him. Brenna must have had something to do with this. He had been so caught up with his life he forgot about the urgent need for Alistair and Brenna to wed. He assumed they would have handfasted but he wanted her wed, the ceremony more binding these days. He would have to put the wedding in motion, assuming there would be no objections.

She pushed against him, seeming to want more warmth. He grinned. They made love three times before she finally fell asleep and perhaps they would again before he left the bedchamber. For the first time in years, he felt lighthearted. The weight he'd shouldered since Maurina showed her true self vanished.

He claimed Wynnie the last time they made love. The tiny marks on her shoulders would heal quickly and they caused her little pain. He told her what would happen and she agreed.

The banging on the door startled him and woke Wynnie. She sat up, covers falling to her waist and pushing her hair back, "What is it?"

"Cover up," He strode to the door and opened it before taking a long look at Wynnie. "This had better be important."

Alistair was in the hall with fist raised to knock again. "A visitor downstairs."

~ * ~

"One person?" Connal asked, raking his hands through his hair even while he dressed. "That's odd this time of year."

"Only one, and I believe it's a woman," Alistair said, grinning as he spoke and peering in the direction of the bed. "The men woke me first. For some reason they were loathe to bother you. Now I see why. The lady says she came to speak with Wynnie."

"Who do you think she is and why does she want to speak with me? I don't know anyone and except for your sister I don't have any friends," Wynnie asked, wishing she dared go with them and see for herself. "I don't know anyone save Father and Perkins who would want to talk to me. I certainly don't have any acquaintances." She was thinking of the elderly lady who used to help hide her from her father but the lady was far too fragile to make such a trip.

Connal turned to her, his eyes ablaze with emotions. She needed to see into his mind but she was afraid. "Get dressed and meet me in the keep. By the time you get there, we should know who is knocking at our door. Friend or foe, in any case."

She was nodding, her body trembling so hard she wasn't sure if she could move let alone dress herself. *It's a woman, not father or Perkins. I have no reason to be afraid.* "I will." She watched him leave, her fingers plucking at the covers, wishing nothing had come their way to disturb their morning.

Touching her lips, they had been well kissed and her muscles seemed to ache, she supposed, from the activity of last night that she wasn't used to. She needed his arms around her, sheltering her from the elements she understood were hurtling down upon her. This woman had to be the first of Oscar's ploys to take her away from the McKenna.

"May I come in?" Brenna poked her head around the corner of the door, smiling as if she knew something she shouldn't. "I've ordered a bath for you. I know Connal wanted you to come to the keep as soon as possible but I assumed," she paused and shrugged. "After our talk last night, I supposed perhaps you had the courage to go through with my brother's seduction and you would relish a few moments to think about last night and soak in some scented hot water."

"We've had that same talk every night for the last few weeks." Wynnie reminded her as she slipped into the tub. "What makes you think I carried through with your advice?"

"I understand that but you were different last eve, more determined and you seemed desperate to convince him you were ready to become his wife." Brenna busied herself with the breakfast scones that had been brought to the room then poured cups of tea. "I sensed you were afraid you might lose the stubborn man if you didn't do something desperate to keep him."

"You're right of course," Wynnie murmured. "I was desperate and I did take your advice."

"So, the two of you actually made love. I'm happy for you."

The bath was hot and steaming. Wynnie picked up the scented soap then uttered a small sigh as the heat of the water eased her muscles. "I'm tired, no exhausted. I think it would have been nice to sleep the morning away, just laze away beneath the warm covers while Connal held me close. If I'm not mistaken, Connal planned on just that."

Brenna sat on the hearth, her legs crossed, nibbling on a scone, her teacup close by. "So, it happened more than once?"

"Three times and I think he would have made love to me again if Alistair had not interrupted. I was wrapped in his arms and..." Wynnie would never forget the night, the tempest and the magic.

"No pain? Even when he put his mark on you?" Brenna asked. "I know it's not my business and of course you don't have to answer."

"Only when he claimed me. That was only for a second and that too vanished." She looked at one shoulder and saw the tiny marks. "Is it really true am I his mate for all time? Have we been wed before?"

"Aye, tis true. No man can separate the two of you, not your father or Perkins, not even death. The two of you will always find your way back to each other." Brenna stood, wandering the room, seeming restless.

"You need a wedding," Wynnie said, eyeing Brenna as she paced, picking up items then setting them back always in a different spot. "You and Alistair deserve a real wedding as well as a celebration of the nuptials. Winter is a wonderful time for just that sort of thing."

"You and Connal need a celebration also. He is the laird after all and head of the clan Chattan. Our people want him to be happy. They want to show their respect. It's not right the ceremony was done in such haste and the clan was not there to rejoice with the two of you."

"No, it was not," Wynnie sighed, rising from the water and wrapping a towel around her. "We must forget all that and see who has arrived and if this woman poses some kind of threat to me or your clan."

"Our clan," Brenna corrected.

"Yes, I suppose I am part of it now. Before last night I really didn't feel as if I belonged."

"I'm sure all will be fine with the woman. My brother should have made love to you sooner," Brenna said as she helped Wynnie dress. "If I had not shown up, I truly don't see how you could have put all this clothing on by yourself. Connal left in such a hurry with no concern for you, expecting you to arrive downstairs in an appropriate amount of time, properly dressed as well."

"If you had not come on your own, he might have sent you upstairs to help me," Wynnie said.

"If he passed me in the hall, mayhap. Truly the man should get you a ladies' maid. You need one with all your increasing duties. Now that you have a wardrobe you cannot possibly dress yourself. Connal, at times, is obviously too busy. I will not always be around to help. Although I'm sure he would rather undress you than dress you now that you two have solved your minor problem as husband and wife."

"Today, yes, of course you are right, but I don't want some lady I don't know helping me dress. It would be awkward." Wynnie smoothed her skirts thinking about all Brenna told her. "Even after a month I barely know anyone. In my home, I tried to stay away from people. Talking to people is just not something I ken how to do. It seems I'm always at a loss for words."

"You should pick her out yourself. Someone you feel comfortable around," Brenna said. "I'll introduce you to some suitable girls who would love to be given such an opportunity then you can spend time with them, perhaps have tea. I will tell them one of the qualifications for the job is putting you at ease."

"Someone my age?" Wynnie asked feeling for the first time that another person to talk with would be nice. "Conceivably someone I could confide in beside you."

"I'm not enough?" Brenna asked in a huff then chuckling. "It is always nice to have more than one confidant. I grew up here, have girlhood friends and we share most everything."

"Of course you are enough. It's just that so many times you are with Alistair. You do have a life and you are not someone who needs employment as a maid. However, I'm very grateful for your assistance today and all the other days that Connal left before he could help me."

"All the days you didn't want him to see you without clothing," Brenna laughed and Wynnie enjoyed the sound.

"After last night I no longer have that excuse. He, well, it seems." She was at a loss for the right words. "I still won't parade around the room without anything on."

"Touched and kissed every inch of you if my guesses are right. There is no need to blush. Alistair has done the same to me. He seems to like it when I lose control and scream his name when he gives me my woman's pleasure as he calls what he does to me. The scream strokes his manly sensibilities."

"Yes, well, I did the same with Connal and you say he must have liked that?" she queried, trying to remember his reaction, but it seemed only a few minutes later he was deep inside her again.

"Of course he did, a man likes that kind of thing. As I implied earlier, it makes them swell with manly pride," Brenna laughed, putting the finishing touches on her hair. "You are more than presentable but are you ready to meet your husband downstairs, understanding the entire clan will know what transpired between the two of you last night?"

Wynnie felt a wave of heat sweep through her to settle on her cheeks. "How would they know something like that? He wouldn't tell anyone would he?" Wynnie wasn't at all sure about what Brenna was saying to her.

"Because even though Alistair ripped him from his bed when he was about to make love to you for a third time or was it a fourth time, there was an undeniable grin on his face, the look of a man well satisfied," Brenna looked smug and too sure of herself. "My brother never grins."

"What does a grin have to do with anything?" Wynnie was more confused than ever.

"The man has been called a brooding monster for the last few years. If he comes downstairs grinning, it can only mean one thing. He's had a night of loving with his beautiful wife," Brenna laughed again, clearly enjoying herself and the wisdom she was imparting to Wynnie.

"Was that because of sex?" Wynnie truly needed explanations into her husband's behavior and the things that left him grinning versus brooding. He never really seemed to brood around her but neither did he grin.

Her husband. He was now her husband in every way. Was grinning. She felt suddenly very pleased with herself.

"Are you ready to see who this woman is?" Brenna asked.

Wynnie held her breath for a moment before letting it out in a soft whoosh. "I suppose I have to." Curiosity seemed to be overpowering the need to stay hidden away in this room.

"Then let's go." Brenna linked her arm through Wynnie's. "What possible harm could come of it?"

A few minutes later they entered the main hall and stopped. Wynnie saw Connal first. He'd been talking to Alistair and when he saw her, he strode toward her, a smile on his face.

"Ach, you look very beautiful today." He pulled her into his arms, kissing her full on the lips before deepening the kiss and lifting her off the ground. Connal had never done such a thing and it stole her breath. She wanted the sweet kiss to never end.

He set her on the ground, pushing a few strands of hair behind her ear, his grin heating her through to the core. "You are my wife and all of the clan's resources are available to you. Don't ever forget that," he whispered, his voice raw with emotion. "I suspect you will want to speak with the woman who arrived via an Adair coach, but I don't think she poses a threat to you. At least not at the moment, but you must proceed cautiously."

Wynnie didn't know how to reply and wondered at the urgency in his voice then the softness. He was preparing her for something and trying to give advice the best he could. "What is it you're not telling me?"

He nodded toward a slender redheaded woman. "She says she is your mother. Is it true?"

Wynnie gasped, startled by news she never expected. Then she looked in the direction Connal indicated. "I wouldn't know as she was supposed to be dead. She was taken from me before I have any memories of her. As I grew up, I was forbidden to speak of her. Even her name eludes me. Perhaps I never knew it."

"You look a lot like her," he told her, his voice soft. "Would you like to meet her? Perhaps if you talk to her, you will be able to ken if she is your mother or not. If you don't want to acknowledge her in any way, I'll send her back. Although I ken she is terrified of returning."

"I'm not in a hurry. If she could travel here in the beginning of winter, she has means. Why didn't she ever try to get me away from Father? Why didn't she help me or even inquire about my wellbeing?"

"That is something you can ask her. Besides, you only have your father's word she did not ask about you. Her name is Heather and yes, she arrived in a carriage. The driver left saying he wouldn't stay. His orders were to leave Heather here and return home."

"Who gave him those orders?" Wynnie was watching the woman sip her tea and delicately taste a scone. She was regal in her bearing and she couldn't be very old. perhaps late thirties. If that were true, it would mean she was very young when she gave birth. Her father had a penchant for younger women.

"He didn't say but I assume it was Adair since the coach had his shield on it." Connal held her hand in his, gently kissing the back. "I will stay by your side. Have courage, lass. The woman doesn't seem to mean you harm. Her health seems to be fragile as well."

"Yes, I would like that. I have so many questions if she is my mother. But I'm terrified to ask. What if she hated me? What if she knew what Oscar did to me?" Wynnie was sure though, Oscar had something if not all to do with her mother's disappearance and her young age spoke to her age when she was pregnant with her. It also spoke of her father's continuing treachery.

When she sat down across from the woman, there was no doubt in her mind that Heather was indeed her mother. She was looking at a mirror image of herself. She smiled then, thanking the stars above she had little of her father in her, especially his character.

Still, just because the woman was indeed her mother, didn't mean the lady didn't intend harm. Oscar might be holding some threat over the woman's head. Because of her absence, she had been through more than a little girl turned woman should be put through. Perhaps Heather's life had been no different.

"Why should I believe you're my mother?" She wanted to see into this woman's soul and hear why she left her daughter in the hands of Oscar Adair. Heather must have known what the man was like and the evil surrounding him.

"You shouldn't but I am. Your father sent me here to find out whatever I could about you and the stronghold. He wants me to betray you and if you want to send me home, then do so." When she set her teacup on the saucer, her hands where shaking.

"Are you going to do that? Give me back to Oscar who sold me to men to do whatever they pleased with me." Wynnie wasn't going to fall into this trap and neither would Connal.

Heather gasped, seeming startled by her revelation. She looked away and when she returned her gaze, there were tears in her eyes. "I dinna think he would do that to you, his daughter. I should have known better but in any case, there was nothing I could have done to stop him."

"You could have been there for me," Wynnie was breathing hard, her anger at this woman who abandoned her grew more intense with each second. She couldn't stand to look at her.

Heather reached out to her but Wynnie jerked her hands into her lap, looking away as she tried to keep the tears from turning to sobs.

"He locked me away," Heather blurted, her own tears sliding down her cheeks. "I was a prisoner in the very home where you lived.

Oscar never told me anything about you."

"The third floor room? I was forbidden to go there." She remembered the conversations at an early age. By the time she was older and might have defied him, she chose to hide other places, never venturing to the top floor.

"You would have found a locked door, nothing more. In any case, I would not have answered a knock. He kept me drugged most of the time, except when he wanted me then he wanted me wide-awake. Told me he didn't like making love to a corpse, but I never considered what he did as making love." Her bitterness was obvious.

"Did he force you too?" Wynnie blurted, wishing she had not asked when she saw the expression on Heather's face. "Never mind, I recognize that look of despair. Why would you help him bring me back?"

She slowly shrugged, a faraway expression on her face then inhaling deeply, "If Connal will not protect me, I will suffer Oscar's wrath as well as any man who wants me if I dinna do as he commands. Oscar is an evil man as well you must know."

Wynnie glanced at Connal who seemed distracted now by the children playing nearby. "I'm sure my husband will not send you back to Oscar. You must not betray us though."

"But will he protect me?" Heather asked, her eyes wide. "I would rather die than go back to that man and his friends."

"I understand all too well your fears, but I cannot speak for my husband. He will do what he thinks best. Which means he will probably shelter you." Wynnie prayed she was right but only time as well as Heather's actions would tell what he would do. A few tears did not mean the woman who claimed she was her mother was loyal to clan Chattan.

She felt Connal's presence behind her and wondered then what he overheard as well as his intentions. "As long as you are honest and true, the McKenna castle will be your home as well as your sanctuary. You need not fear the man. Is Oscar still your husband?"

She inhaled a swift deep breath, holding for a second, then, "He never was my husband. We didn't wed."

"Then I'm illegitimate, a bastard. Are you sure Oscar is my father? He told me many times he thought I was a bastard which was why I wasn't worthy of a respected place in his household, yet he sought to wed me to a wealthy laird. It never made sense to me."

"You are his but of course a bastard also. It wasn't until after I gave birth to you that he sold me to other men. Over the years he has not changed, will never change." Her voice was whisper thin and filled with emotion that tugged at Wynnie's heart.

Connal's hand settled on her shoulder, reassuring her, making her believe one day this would all be over.

~ * ~

Heather had never felt so alone and out of place. At first, he kept her in a small home near the castle. As time went by though, he decided she needed to live closer to him. Since then she'd been locked away for almost twenty years. Her only contact with the countryside was through a locked window three stories above ground. When she was younger, she harbored thoughts of escaping out that window but Oscar seeming to guess her intent had it painted shut. At the age of thirty-five she wondered what had happened to her life and how it had gone so terribly wrong.

Oscar Adair was what happened to her and she kenned she would never get those lost years back.

Now she looked across a table at a distrustful daughter, one she was never allowed to hold not even the first seconds after giving birth. Guessing now that Oscar had mapped out Wynnie's life the moment he saw her.

"I think Oscar had plans for you from the very moment he discovered you weren't a boy. He might have wed me if I'd given him a son." She tapped her fingers on the table, wondering about the hell he would have put her through if they were married and if it could have been any worse than the one she endured.

"Now at least he has no hold over you," Wynnie said, her voice soft, calming Heather's rattled nerves. "I need to speak with Connal. Will you be alright?" Wynnie asked as she stood.

"I'm fine. I've been given a room. Alistair told me once I spoke with you, I could retire there whenever I wanted. But I suppose I should stay here for the rest of the afternoon. What would I do alone in a room except brood? Maybe someone will be brave and talk with me. Not sure what I would say though..." She lifted her shoulders, searching the room.

"I'll send Brenna over if I see her. She's Connal's sister and she likes to talk to people."

"I certainly understand your reticence. You don't need to send anyone here for me or to keep me company. I'm used to listening to my thoughts," Heather murmured, understanding she'd spent the better part of twenty years entertaining herself. It seemed the present would be no different.

As the hours passed, she found she enjoyed watching the people; servants, children and the more prestigious members of the clan. Watching something other than the walls was new to her. Several of the servants stopped by from time to time to see if she needed anything.

Just time, all she needed was time with her daughter. Yet she knew the years she lost could never be regained. She prayed too that Wynnie would find a way in her heart to forgive her as well as what had been done to her when she had no mother to protect her.

Heather had always thought if she had done things differently or been better in some way, her life would have turned out differently. She sighed long and deep, knowing that wishing and praying would not solve any of her problems. All she could do was forge ahead and make her future better than her past.

"Hello, lass, it's a bonny good day today. I'm Elliott Frasier and I've brought you a pint and a basket of bread. More is on the way. I've a powerful hunger. Hope you like it. May I sit?"

She inhaled a deep breath, startled by the man seeming to appear from nowhere. "If you like." She had no idea how to respond to the man or his invitation. He was tall and broad of shoulders. His darkly stubbled chin did nothing to hide the broad smile on his face. His age eluded her though.

"I'd very much like to get to know you. You look familiar to me and I don't know why. Have you been here before?" He sat down, placing one of the pints of ale in front of her.

"My daughter looks like me." She spoke softly overwhelmed by this man who seemed to be friendly yet Oscar had acted that way the first time she met him. She would have to be careful not to fall into the same trap.

"The McKenna's wife," he paused, looking toward the couple who were visiting with Alistair and Brenna. "You are the spittin' image of her." He grinned at her showing a wealth of white teeth behind the dark beard.

"She's my daughter," Heather said. "Until today I haven't seen her since I gave birth." Strangely, at the thought moisture didn't pool in her eyes.

Elliott held her hands in his. For a second, she thought to pull away from him, but they were calloused from hard work, warm and she felt protected by him. An emotion no man had ever elicited in her.

"May I ask your name?" He didn't let go of her hands, but his dark blue eyes sparkled as if amused.

Heather's heart raced while she struggled to drag air into her lungs. She tugged and he let go, still grinning as if he understood the strange affect his presence had on her. "Heather Duffy."

"Heather, 'tis a nice name. So, you are visiting or here to stay?" he asked, holding his mug before drinking deeply. "Try the ale. If you don't like it, I'll bring you a tankard of mulled wine."

"I hope I'm here to stay," she said, trying the ale and coughing. "I've never had ale before."

"So you prefer wine." He started to leave the table and Heather assumed it would be to fetch the wine.

She reached out to him, her hand shaking. "Never had wine either, but I like this. Don't leave." Someone brought a platter of food to the table where they sat. "I like your company."

He leaned back in the chair, seeming relaxed and at ease. His long well-muscled legs were stretched out in front of him. "Tell me more about yourself."

"Not much to tell. Why don't you talk about yourself instead? I'm sure that would be much more interesting."

"I'm a crofter on McKenna land. The first part of my life, one might have called me a wanderer. Never found anywhere I felt at home until I walked onto this land owned by clan Chattan. Don't know how much you ken about the McKenna's but I'm like them."

"How is that? What are they like?" She was curious now, looking over the people in the room then her gaze settling once more on Connal. There was something about the clan that was different, and this man said he was like them, different, unique perhaps. She wasn't, but her daughter seemed to have a tiny bit of that air about her.

"I'm not at liberty to say," Elliott said, his voice gruff, "but sometime if the McKenna comes to trust you, I'll show you. That is if you are here to stay. I certainly hope you are."

"I want to stay and I want Connal McKenna's trust, but more than that I need my daughter to trust me." On her journey to the northern highlands she'd thought a long time about her daughter and the reception, terrified she might be immediately rejected. Her welcome had been hesitant, but she could tell Wynnie wanted to reach out to her.

She felt strange and apprehensive yet her thoughts flew back to the times when she was a young girl and dreamt of romantic love. How her thoughts ended up there she couldn't say. But this man was different and despite the years of abuse, she wanted to spend more time with him. Would like to feel the tender touch of a man's hand.

For a while, they ate in silence, simply because she had no idea what to say, and it didn't seem he wanted to talk either. He spent most of the time enjoying the food and laughing as he watched the room, his gaze always returning to her.

Then he stood and she was sure he would leave. "I'll show you around the castle if you like?" He extended a hand.

She was hesitant at first then remembered how secure she felt when his fingers closed around hers earlier in the day. "I think I'd like that. I know where my chambers are but not much else."

"If you'll go to the parapets with me, I'll show you my home. You can see it from the tower. Mayhap you'd like to visit me sometime."

Her knees were shaking. "Are we going to be alone?"

"Most likely. Do you have a problem with that?"

Then she blurted, her heart aching for something she'd never believed could come true. "I've never been alone with a man who didn't hurt me."

With her words she shocked him. His voice gruff and his eyes darkening, crease lines on his brow, "I would never harm you in anyway but if you don't want to go, I'll understand. We could walk where there are lots of people."

She laughed softly, amused, "Is there a place like that?"

"I was going to say the gardens, but this time of the day most likely we would find ourselves alone there also. What would you like, Heather? The choice is up to you."

She inhaled long and deep, believing this man could change her life for the better. Still, she could be wrong. She didn't have experience in deciphering the ways of men or their intentions.

Deciding courage should be her mantra, "To the parapets. I'd like to see where you live and the view of the countryside which I'm sure is spectacular." Her breaths were short and raspy and he grinned seeming to appreciate the affect he had on her body.

"If you like, we could ride there tomorrow, to my home."

She stopped midstride. Then, knowing she had to tell this man everything, "I haven't ridden since I was fifteen," *and my life changed for the worst.*

"Why is that?" his voice sounded concerned. "Why would you stop doing something that is so enjoyable?"

Once again, she inhaled a deep breath holding it for a few seconds before slowly letting it out. Then in a soft whisper, "Because I was held prisoner by a horrible man." She felt his fist tighten around her hand and she sensed he was angry but not at her.

"This is the man who hurt you." His voice was deep and gravely sounding.

"Yes, and others. You see, he sold me to his friends." He would not want to take that walk, would most likely not want anything more to do with her.

He stopped, turning to face her then lifting her chin, she looked into what seemed to be compelling and gentle eyes, "I would endeavor to change your impressions of men, but you have to learn to have confidence in me and ken that I would never do anything to cause you pain. Can you do that, lass?"

She was nodding her head, wishing she could form the words to tell him that for a reason she didn't understand she did trust him.

"I need to hear the one word."

She was still nodding, her body shaking. Then, "Yes. I want that, would like to trust someone."

"Good then, we'll proceed slowly." He offered his arm, which she accepted. "To the parapets."

Chapter Six

Spring rolled onto the Scottish countryside with elements of both rain and sunshine. It seemed everyday had a little of both. Brenna was with child now and Alistair seemed to dote on her, racing around the keep, trying to second-guess what she wanted or craved. She would reprimand him, telling her husband she was perfectly capable doing things for herself and that she wasn't an invalid.

Somehow the days between December and March got away from them and now the marriage of the two was planned for the next day. The clan had come in from the hills to celebrate the previous wedding of their laird as well as the upcoming nuptials of his sister and best friend. The cooks were busy in the kitchen creating all types of delicacies for the rest of the day as well as the feasting for the wedding day. Ale and wine flowed.

Connal stood with Wynnie on the parapets, his arm around her watching the road leading to the castle. He was always alert for incoming visitors, especially Oscar and Perkins.

"Are you happy, lass?" He turned toward her studying her profile before she shifted her full attention toward him. Her smile didn't seem sincere and he feared she thought along the same lines as he did. Their lives would be so much easier when they knew neither Oscar nor Perkins would arrive unannounced.

"Yes, and no," She touched his cheek with the palm of her hand, a tiny smile on her face. "Do you wonder when Oscar and Perkins are going to show up and if they do show up, I think Heather should stay in the castle instead of with Elliott as she has been doing. Oscar will want revenge when he discovers how happy she is and that she is wed to a good

103

strong man. He resents everyone and what they have even if it's as simple as joy."

"I'm praying he's lost interest in both of you." He turned his face toward her hand, kissing the palm. Trying to figure out some way to draw the two men to the McKenna land so they would arrive on his terms and when he was prepared.

She gasped at his touch. He grinned realizing months ago he would never grow tired of this woman and the way the smallest caress affected him. She was his moon and his stars as well as the source of all the sunshine in his life.

"But you don't think he has given up."

"I would be surprised if Oscar quit. He thinks of you as his possession. Perkins on the other hand seems to be easily diverted by anyone wearing a skirt." His hands bracketed her waist as he held her close. Wishing they were alone in the bedchamber, he softly brushed her lips with his once then twice.

When he looked at her again, her mouth was damp, the moisture left from the caress shimmering in the muted sunlight of the vanishing afternoon. He brushed his thumb across her soft full lips, delighting in the slight trembling of her body and the small noise from the back of her throat. He would never stop wanting and needing her.

"We should go downstairs. There is still much to be done before the wedding. Brenna, although the two of them have been handfasted since October, is a bundle of nerves. She's a mess. Every time I bring up something that needs to be done, she has this strange high-pitched laugh."

"What is it you need to do?" Connal asked, wondering why the women folk were so busy.

"To begin with, the finishing touches on her dress. Tomorrow morning we will have to pick the flowers. The cook will finish the cake in the morning then we will have to get Brenna ready for her soon to be legal husband, at least in the eyes of the British government."

"I see and all the men folk have to do is carry a basket of stones around the village until his soon to be bride takes pity on him and gives him a chaste kiss." Unable to help himself, he was chuckling softly, thankful he had not had that task presented to him.

"I suppose that's all besides showing up. Are you going to be Alistair's best man? If you are, I'm sure you will do a fine job making sure your sister does not run off before the nuptials."

Connal began to laugh harder realizing because of the haste of his marriage to Wynnie many traditions besides creeling were left undone. He pointed to the courtyard below, "Look, I say, Alistair is fortunate he only has to carry the creel around the courtyard instead of through the village too."

"Appears that someone filled it to the brim with stones. Even the mighty Alistair is staggering under its weight and having difficulty with the basket." Wynnie laughed at the site along with her husband. "Do you think Brenna will emerge any time soon to give him relief with a kiss?"

"I'm sure she plans on making him work a bit longer. See, she is over there watching for the right opportunity." Connal had turned Wynnie in his arms. She now leaned against his chest, his arm circling her just below her breasts, his hands slowly moving upward while she wriggled within his strong hold.

"And I'm sure admiring her bonny bridegroom while enjoying his kiss," Wynnie said. "I would that you..." she paused with a soft sigh, "Well, that is not to be." She waved a hand in the air. "Forget that."

"Would you like a real wedding? It could be arranged. I doubt if either Alistair or my sister would object to a double wedding tomorrow if I suggested something of that sort," Connal asked, refusing to forget anything. "I would give you everything you asked for if I had the power, a wedding is one of the simpler things."

"No, I never expected to have a life separate from Oscar and Perkins. Thought I would forever be at their mercy. I'm very lucky to have found you and would change nothing. A wedding is not something that I need to be happy. All I want is you."

"I'm glad of that, lass. I'm lucky to have found you also." He wondered if she loved him. True, she now understood he was her mate but did she love him?

She let out a long slow sigh, relaxing into him, her soft curves enticing him with wicked thoughts. They would have to put in an appearance to the festivities of the night but after that, he meant to spend the evening alone with his wife pleasuring her in any way she suggested. She would have to get up early to help with the bride, so he would have to put her to bed early.

"It seems Brenna doesn't have torture in mind for her new husband. She is already in his arms." Connal pointed below. "Should we join them? Looks as if your mother and Elliott are there also. We have much to talk about with them."

"Suppose we have no choice. Brenna will be disappointed if we don't show up and spend a few hours toasting the bride and groom."

"But Alistair would rather just proceed to the wedding bed. As would I," Connal said, trailing a line of kisses down her neck, enjoying the process even more when she lifted her chin giving him more access.

When they arrived below, it seemed the people of the clan were assembling for the celebrations, laughing and chatting, catching up with old friends and meeting new ones. Bagpipes played in the hall and the ale streamed non-stop. Connal held back no expenses for his sister's wedding. Now she was dancing with Alistair and he was twirling her around the main floor. There were tents outside with vendors selling their wares, beads, bobbles, cloth whatever a person might want. The wedding would be profitable for the surrounding merchants as well as most of the clan.

"Would you like to dance, lass?" Connal asked, hoping this time Wynnie would at least try.

She held back, her hands behind her anticipating him. "You know I've two left feet. No matter how hard I try, I trip and will probably bring you down with me."

"Well then, lass, you'd be on top of me and a slight roll..." He grinned wickedly, delighted with the slight blush on Wynnie's cheeks. "We will dance one dance. I promise you can step on my feet as much as it pleases you or is necessary for you to remain standing. I guarantee I will keep both of us upright."

She punched him on the chest and he laughed drawing her closer for a swift brush of his lips across hers. He felt her melt into him and was tempted to say goodbye for the moment to his clan and carry her upstairs to their bed. He held back though, beginning to dance with her, moving slowly at first before picking up speed. The bagpipes were lively. Their feet not so much.

From the last time she tried to dance she had improved. The tune lasted for a few more minutes, and he managed to dance with her until they reached the table where her mother and Elliott sat.

He pulled out a chair for her. "Thank you for the dance. Perhaps you would like to speak with Heather while I talk to her husband. There are some things we need to discuss. The pause will give time for you to catch your breath."

"If you insist," Wynnie laughed while she gulped air, sitting down and helping herself to the pint of ale that had been set in front of her while Elliott and Connal strode to a distant part of the room.

"They are going to guess what it is we are about," Elliott said, his attention riveted on his wife. "You're worried Oscar will show up here and Heather will tell me she has the right to know everything, will pester me until I divulge any current news so I'm not too sure what we are about, trying to keep secrets."

"Soon, I'm sure. The roads are passable and Oscar is a man who doesn't like to lose something he thinks is his." Connal's fingers tightened on his glass. "We need to figure out how to lure the two men here on our terms. I want to write the rules to the game that will play out as soon as they arrive."

"And the man believes both Wynnie and Heather are his." Elliott looked toward his wife, his fists tightening an eyebrow arching as he seemed to think. "I won't let him near her."

"For Heather's safety, you need to come into the castle until Oscar shows himself." Connal didn't really believe Elliott would agree to this but there was no other recourse.

Elliott lifted broad shoulders a look of chagrin on his face. "Could be all summer. Don't know when the man will make an appearance if he ever will. I've got crops to take care of and a growing family to feed. Don't think I can do that, run from a man who is less than a man. You well ken it is not my nature to flee from trouble."

"Couldn't help but overhear," Alistair slapped Elliott on the shoulder. "Sleep in the castle at night and work your land during the day.

I'll help and I'm sure there are others who will lend a hand. Keep Heather here where she will not constantly be looking over her shoulder. She won't complain too much with her daughter close by."

"Appreciate the offer but still don't like waiting around for something to happen," Elliott said.

"We don't have to wait. Confronting Oscar in his home makes some sense to me too," Alistair said.

"True, but what if he's put this all behind him and doesn't want anything to do with either Heather or Wynnie?" Connal asked, still thinking to bring the man here. "No, he's going to come. The only question is when and I want his appearance here on our terms."

Elliott ran his hands through his hair clearly distraught. "Don't like what my gut's telling me. It's not good."

Connal remained quiet while the men spoke. "Going to Oscar's home is not an option, and I understand the reticence in waiting. Don't like to feel as if I'm always on the defense but that is what we are going to have to do. Both Heather and Wynnie believe Oscar will come for them. They also believe he will be here sooner than later."

"I'll agree to Heather staying inside the walls of the castle but I need to guard our home. She needs to be protected but..." Once again he ran both hands through his hair, "I can't stay here every night. I need to safeguard my land and my crops. Even with help from the clan, Oscar could still do something to ruin me."

"What does Heather want?" Connal asked, thinking Wynnie would have an opinion if he decided to leave her one place while he stayed at another. If given the choice, he was sure she would to choose to stay with him.

"She's not liking my reasoning although I must confess, I haven't decided anything yet. Don't want to leave Heather alone even in the castle. Like to have her close by. That way I know what she is about and she is safe." Elliott sat down as a servant brought more drinks.

"Seems the women folk are talking. Think they are saying the same as us?" Connal asked as Wynnie turned her attention his way, motioning for him to join her and he assumed Alistair and Elliott as well.

"I'm sure Brenna has an opinion as does Wynnie," Alistair said, grinning. "Glad Brenna doesn't have anything to worry about unless Perkins comes along with Oscar. He had his gaze set on her last time. That's why we handfasted that night. Didn't want to make love to her unless there was some agreement between us. If she stayed in my room and my bed..." He didn't finish the sentence.

Connal knew what he stopped saying and he still, mate or not, didn't like the way Alistair went about seducing his sister. It wasn't well done of him. "You're right to not say anything more. While I ken it is far better you than Perkins seduce her that night, I still wish it had been done in a more proper or traditional way."

"But you would have done the same," Alistair said.

"Perhaps." Connal was unwilling to admit to that but if Wynnie had not been petrified that first night, he might have done the same and worried about the consequences later. Protecting her was all he could think about even then.

"So, nothing needs to be decided tonight. Both you and Heather will remain here through the revelry then you can make up your mind if you wish to return home," Alistair said.

"Don't know about the two of you, but I'm going to collect my wife. We need some time alone before chaos reigns tomorrow," Connal said as he headed toward Wynnie, thinking he would have an enjoyable night. Alistair and Elliott followed with the same intentions where their mates were concerned.

Connal stopped beside Wynnie, his gaze focused on her. "I've ordered wine and some of the delicacies the cooks have made for the rest of the evening to be sent to our room. I'd like to spend some time alone with my beautiful wife tonight, and I'm also going to pray nothing happens to tear me away from you." He extended his hand helping her to stand. Closing his eyes for a second, he enjoyed the moment and the small intimacy, knowing there would be more explorations this evening.

"I apologize for spending so much time away from you," she paused, "the wedding, you know." Then with a tiny lift to her shoulders, "Although it was you who insisted they have a big celebration. We've been working hard on Brenna's dress, but she continues to get larger." She leaned against his arm as they walked through the keep.

"Perhaps tonight we will make a little one," Connal said, wishing his wife was just as pregnant as her mother and Brenna. He couldn't help but wonder why not. Brenna had told him they were trying too hard but that didn't make a bit of sense to him.

They rarely spent a night apart and since December it had only been a handful of evenings when he didn't come to bed until early morning. Even some of those times, he would pull her into his arms and she would be more than warm and willing.

"I'm sorry," She pulled away from him, tears in her eyes. "I don't know what's wrong with me. I know you want children."

"Ach, lass, there is nothing wrong with you or me. God willing, we will have many children, as many as you want. Once everything settles down around us and we know we'll never see Oscar or Perkins again, perhaps then you will conceive," Connal tried to reassure her as well as himself. He knew of couples who never had children, and he did pray they would not be one of them. She had a child a long time ago when she was very young but she lost the babe. He didn't think that was the cause but he didn't really know. Wynnie was his mate. He would support and encourage her through any of their trials.

"I have been nervous particularly as spring grew closer," she admitted. "I never want to see those two men again, but I understand you need to make sure there is an end."

He opened the door to their room. Just as he ordered, a fire had been built up in the fireplace, candles lit around the room and an enormous array of food and drink sat on a platter on a table near the bed.

He poured them both a glass of wine, "Where would you like to sit?" His gaze was focused on the big bed. When she looked that way, she shook her head. "There will be time enough to explore the possibilities there. For now," she paused, "I just want to relax in your arms."

"What's on your mind, lass?" he asked, lounging back and trying to make himself comfortable when all he needed was his wife as well as the closeness he always felt when she was near.

"My mother, she doesn't think Elliott will run from Oscar. She says she won't leave him even to remain safe herself." Wynnie plucked at her skirt and Connal understood her nervousness. He needed to vanquish her fears yet he didn't know how.

"You're worried about Heather. I ken it but she is an adult as is Elliott. They will make decisions based on their needs not ours. You will have to trust in her choices. She spent too many years by herself, alone, and now that she has found her soul mate..." He shrugged, understanding, "She will not want to leave."

Wynnie inhaled a long deep breath of air. "He will kill her as he will me if given the chance. He has men who will follow him here just on the assumption they will be given the spoils of what is left over after he has had his fun."

"You believe he will come with men?" Connal was surprised yet nothing about Oscar Adair should shock him. Oscar was a cunning man and would understand Wynnie and Heather. He paused thinking and Wynnie would be well guarded but with the element of surprise he might well take what he wanted.

"Come, lass." He held her close. "Alistair and I along with Elliott will figure someway to bring the two men to the keep. For the rest of the night, I want to make love to my beautiful wife."

~ * ~

With the rising of the sun Connal woke Wynnie with a gentle kiss to the cheek. She sighed softly, snuggling into him and wishing she had a few more hours to sleep but there was so much to accomplish this day, Brenna's wedding day.

She rose and was surprised to see that Connal had ordered a bath for her and set out clothes for her to wear. The dress was one she had never seen and it was beautiful.

"When did you purchase this?" she asked holding the gown up to her.

He showed a row of even white teeth even while he was slipping on his kilt. "I had it made for you as a special surprise for today. The plaid is the McKenna dress plaid. I wanted our people to know how much you mean to me and that no other can take your place."

"Thank you." She wasn't at all sure what to say. The two words seemed so small to express how she felt. She smiled, wishing she had something to give him.

"You're quite welcome. The gesture is for me too. I want to show you off to our clan and let everyone know how proud I am to have you on my arm and next to me for the rest of our lives," Connal said, his voice gruff with emotions.

He always lightened her mood, not that today needed any help. "In any case, you will have to help me dress. So don't go very far. This morning you will not be able to get out of the ladies' maid duty by sending Brenna to me as she will be preoccupied as well." Wynnie enjoyed the play of emotions on her husband's face. She pointed a finger at him then shaking it at him with a grin, "Don't you dare leave or I will make you regret it. Don't you dare get any ideas about undressing me instead."

"In case you haven't noticed, you are quite undressed right now. Well, you know my preferences. Not safe for me to stay if we want to get to our duties on time," he muttered.

"Go on then. I will have to fend for myself," she said in a huff, waving her hand towards the door.

"I could send Heather to help you," he said as he slipped into a white shirt then a dark blue, velvet jacket before fastening his sporran. "It won't be a problem. I'm sure your mother would be pleased to come to your aide."

With her hands on her hips, devoid of clothing, she turned to him, "You could but you would regret it. This is your job today and you're shirking it." With a huge sigh, perhaps they should give up and go back to bed.

"You cannot say nay to me as well you ken. If I wanted to seduce you right this instant, you would melt in my arms, a pool of mush at my feet, just for me to have my manly way with you." He laughed as he stepped toward her. The raw passion in his eyes told her she should stop enticing him and settle into the hot water.

"I will only be a few minutes. You can wait that long for me." She hummed while she bathed and watched as he sat across the room staring at her. Perhaps it would have been better if he left and sent her mother to the room to help since she was feeling the heat of his gaze, her body responding to the silent invitation.

"Don't know if this is a good idea." Suddenly, he was kneeling beside the tub soaping a sponge. The glint in his eyes told her it was not something they should pursue.

"Go on with you. I give up. Send my mother or anyone else who is suitable that you run across. I should have found a ladies' maid months ago as both you and Brenna suggested and we would not be in this predicament. 'Tis all my fault. I'm sure of it."

He let out a heavy sigh but seemed to think what she suggested might be the best idea for everyone involved. Dropping the sponge into the liquid, he turned on a heel, but he didn't leave the room. He returned and stooped over the tub then holding her head between both hands, kissed her long and deep, his tongue finding entrance and seeming to devour her even as he wove a silken web of enchantment around her. Ribbons of heat swept through her. She changed her mind. Brenna could wait a few minutes. She met his tongue with hers, her hands sliding along his legs, discovering what was not beneath his kilt.

"Keep that in mind for tonight." Then he left as if nothing happened between them.

She heard his laughter and understood she'd been outmaneuvered just now. Closing her eyes, she inhaled long and deep feeling the need for her husband and his arms around her. She quickly finished the bath and was able to dry her hair before Heather knocked on her door. Wrapped in a towel, she stood and welcomed her mother with a quick hug.

"Connal told me he wasn't up to dressing you this morning." She waltzed into the room. "And I can see why. Even if I say so myself you are a verra beautiful woman. You would be quite difficult to resist for any man and your husband, well, it seems he can never resist your charms." She stopped suddenly. "I'm sorry, the words were meant only as a compliment not a reminder of times best forgotten."

"Thank you, I didn't take your words that way, but you wouldn't be prejudiced or anything, now would you?" Wynnie asked, her laughter light and infectious. She laughed some more.

Her mother started to laugh too, "Of course I am prejudiced. Now, let's see how quickly we can get you dressed in all this Scottish finery and into Brenna's room to help her out. She already has several of her friends there. They are washing her feet. I was never really sure why that tradition evolved unless some groom thought his new wife's feet were dirty and suggested to others that her feet should get washed before the ceremony and the bedding."

"I'm sure you are right. Dirty feet would be horrible in bed."

"Just hold still so we can get this done properly," Heather said, a beautiful smile on her face.

Wynnie was standing as Heather brought her one garment after the other and helped her with the fastenings. "Now, you understand that when Oscar comes you should not be staying at your husband's home. It is not safe. You must take care. We both know he will stop at nothing to get you back in his custody. I'm sure he is ruing the day he let you go."

Heather was pinning a broach, the luckenbooth that Connal had given her, on her shoulder. It was silver and engraved with two intertwined hearts topped with a crown.

"There, that is almost as beautiful as you," Heather said, gazing at her admiringly. "What I do understand is that where I decide to stay and what chances I'm willing to take are between Elliott and myself. I ken the danger though and am loathe to be taken back to my prison. Elliott will never let that occur and would join forces with the rest of the clan to keep that from happening to me, or you, for that matter."

Yet to Wynnie's ears her mother didn't sound too sure of herself. "You must be terrified of seeing Oscar again. Of course it is between you and your husband, but what does Elliott want you to do. He couldn't possibly want you to stay with him, could he?"

Heather stepped back letting out a rush of air as her body visibly shook. "Needless to say, we don't agree on this but even though I'm loath to do his bidding, I remember Oscar and the numerous assaults over the years. I don't want to be in that position again, at his mercy. Does not sit well with me even though I don't want to leave my husband. Perhaps he let me go because I'm too old for him. He did always have a penchant for younger women, young girls to be exact. And yet," she paused, "he does not like to lose anything he deems as his."

"Perhaps in this you should do Elliott's bidding. Connal has reassured me that he will send a message that is sure to bring the two men to the castle within their time frame." Wynnie hoped it was true. She didn't want to spend the next months looking over her shoulder or always going to the battlements to peer down the road.

"What we should do is stop worrying and find Brenna. We need to enjoy the day. When I left, the servants were bringing in food and drink. Are you hungry?" Heather asked, stepping towards the door and seeming to want a change of subject.

She also needed for the conversation to go in a different direction. It was after all Brenna's wedding day. "Starving, Connal kept me up most of the night doing the most..." Wynnie stopped then putting her hand over her mouth. One just didn't speak to their mother of such things.

"As did Elliott with me. Our men are an incorrigible lot and when they are in bed, they have one thing in common as well as one thing on their mind. I've grown used to my husband's touch and the pleasure he gives to me."

"I'm not with child though," Wynnie touched her belly, pushing back the threatening tears. "It seems of the three of us, I'm the only one."

"You will be as soon as Perkins and Oscar are gone from our lives. It is the tension and the fears that keep you from conceiving," Heather said, her smile brightening the morning for Wynnie. "We just don't know what or when anything is going to happen."

"But you carry Elliott's baron. Aren't you stressed too?" It was a puzzling question to Wynnie.

Heather reached with a small lift to her shoulders. "Women react in different ways to different situations. Of course I'm worried, but I've spent years more terrified than I am now. With every footstep outside my door, I found myself shaking in terror. Elliott gives me a reason to love and enjoy life. I try not to look to the past or the future. I'm living in the present and enjoying every second."

"I suppose I should feel the same but..."

"You're young and terrified of losing what you have. While I feel the same to some degree, I want to live each day loving my husband and enjoy his tenderness. While he is a huge and powerful man, I do believe he is the gentlest sole on this earth."

"I'm glad for you and perhaps I should feel the same. I did spend six long years under Oscar's power, but after the first few assaults I was able to escape. Father rarely found me. I usually hid deep in the woods in a small cave I found where I stashed blankets and fire wood for the long winter days and nights. Even when there were no men to pay for my body, I kept to myself in fear of my father who rarely let a day go by without giving me to someone."

"Come, let's not speak of the past when our futures are so promising." Heather stepped back. "I do believe you are perfect in every way. The gown will tell everyone how much you mean to your husband."

Arm and arm they strode through the hallways until they reached Brenna's room. As Heather predicted the women just finished washing Brenna's feet and one young lady found the ring in the small tub. Tradition said she would be the next to wed.

"We are finally here," Wynnie said as she was handed a glass of wine.

"And it's about time too," Brenna said laughing, as she waited for the next layer of clothing.

"I really need something to eat before I start drinking," Wynnie said, sipping the beverage and enjoying the taste even while her stomach growled its displeasure.

When finished, Brenna was dressed in the Stuart dress tartan. "Well, you are about to become a Stuart. Any reservations?" Heather asked. Once again, she was standing back and admiring the young woman in front of her.

"None at all," Brenna said, smoothing her skirts before accepting a glass of wine. "I've been his wife in every way since the end of October. This just makes everything that much more special."

"You should eat something," Wynnie said. "It's probably going to be a long day then Alistair will whisk you off to his chambers for a long night of lovemaking. You will need sustenance if you want to make it through the night."

"I believe he is going to whisk me off to his ship. We would like some time alone and away from everyone else. Since we can't leave McKenna land until all of this is finished with Oscar Adair and Perkins, we decided to spend some time on his ship even though it is not going anywhere. Connal assured me the cooks made sure we had plenty of food onboard."

Wynnie felt a bit of jealousy. She had spent no time away from the castle with her husband. This was something she didn't know about Alistair Stuart. She wondered if her husband owned a ship too.

"An entire fleet of them." Brenna seemed to guess the question before it was asked. "Well, the McKenna's have four ships. We mostly send goods to France in exchange for their fine French brandy, the wine and champagne as well. They like the wool from our sheep among other things. The trade has been quite lucrative for the clan."

"I see," Wynnie plucked at her skirts, feeling more than a little insecure and jealous as well, "Why wouldn't Connal tell me something like that?"

"It's no secret. You didn't ask and he didn't think about telling you. Men are like that, a bit obtuse. If they can't see a reason for you knowing something unless you ask, they usually don't bring it up," Brenna said. "In any case, if things get really bad with your father, Connal can take you for an extended voyage and a visit in Paris. Do you speak French?"

"A little," she said a bit distracted at the moment.

"Perhaps the two of you can go on a belated honeymoon when all this business with your father is finished."

"That would be nice but at the moment all I would relish is peace and quiet and the knowledge we will be left alone to live our lives without worrying about what might happen the next day or even the next second." Wynnie finished her wine. "Are you ready to say your vows?"

The women left the room, still chatting. Stepping outside, the sun was warm and if there had been clouds in the sky, they vanished. Alistair and Connal stood in front of the Kirk doors. They were both grinning and watching them as they approached. At least one hundred guests stood outside waiting for the bride to appear and the vows to be said.

For a moment Wynnie had a bout with jealousy again. Saying vows to Connal was important to her. Maybe she could find a time tonight to tell him how she felt and that she would pledge her life to him. She needed to tell him her personal vow and how she felt. The first wedding had been necessarily brief and held few tender moments to hang onto, as they grew older.

Wynnie was one of the bridesmaids in respect for her position as sister in law. Brenna had two others who were escorted by Fergus and Angus McKenna, cousins to Brenna.

When the vows were finished, they headed inside for the Nuptial communion and blessing of the food.

Wynnie now stood beside her husband, leaning into him as she watched the happy couple. There had been weddings where she grew up, but she only attended a few. Fear for her wellbeing always accompanied celebrations of any sort. Her father would give her to any man attending the festivities who voiced they might want her.

The revelers sent the happy couple off to the ship amidst a flurry of rice and ribald comments. Wynnie felt Connal's hand creeping higher on her ribcage and pushed it down, laughing.

"Not here. You ken I'll give you whatever you want in the privacy of our room. Don't you dare seduce me here and now."

"Then I believe we've come full circle. We spent the day at the wedding of my sister and best friend, now we shall spend the evening celebrating our life together."

He swooped her into his arms, twirling her around a couple of times before carrying her into the castle and up the steps to the battlement. Where he set her down, they could see Brenna and Alistair riding toward the sea.

He pulled her close, brushing his lips across hers, his hand cupping her breast, his thumb rubbing across her nipple. "That was nice but I'm an impatient man."

"Why did you bring me here then?"

"I believe this was the place of our first kiss." He smiled at her tenderly pushing hair from her face. "I didn't know it would happen at the time I first saw you, but you have changed my life for the better."

"I've put the castle at risk."

"You are my mate and I as well as the clan don't care about any danger you might have brought with you. We will defend you without hesitation. I don't know what it was but that first evening, I behaved badly. Did things I'm ashamed of. It didn't seem as I could help myself. To me you were ravishing, still are."

"Truth be told, I could have fought harder. I think I wanted you to catch me but would never admit it even to myself. I was furious you brought me to the tower room and sought to leave me there along with the rats."

"It was only a ploy so you would willingly accept my chambers over the other possibilities. I wanted you from the moment I first saw you. I wasn't about to give you a chance to get away," Connal laughed, running his hands down her back. "Shall we move on to the master chamber and more pleasant endeavors?"

She could never refuse him. He was her eternal love.

~ * ~

Oscar read the message from Connal McKenna for the second time. Pacing the room, he realized the power now was not in his hands. Connal threatened him subtly but nonetheless his words were a threat not a warning. He wanted to see him and Perkins by the end of the month.

This was not how he planned the next meeting with Wynnie and Heather. He didn't like the summons. Quickly, he penned a message to Perkins expecting the man to show up when he felt like it. Since Wynnie escaped him last October, Perkins spent little time here. Almost a year had passed and he believed the McKenna had forgotten.

He resumed his pacing, looking out the window from time to time and watching the rain slip from the sky. Leaving the room for any reason this time of year was abhorrent to him. His limbs ached when he rode in a carriage for too many hours. He liked his meals on time and served at his dinner table along with his French brandy afterwards. And, to replace Heather and Wynnie, he found two whores who actually enjoyed his proclivities of force or at least they put up with him for the money he paid. That fact bit at him. He would have to figure out a way to sell their services to his friends so he could reap the multiple rewards.

Oscar poured himself a brandy, setting the message to Perkins aside and planning on sending it in the morning. Ringing the bell on the end table, he waited for Summer Nectar to arrive. She was a much better lover than either Heather or Wynnie. She actually knew what to do with her body and didn't fade away into another world when he took her.

Closing his eyes, he waited for her, thinking of all the delightful things she would do with his man parts, things no one else had done. He must have fallen asleep because when he woke, Perkins was standing over him.

"When were you going to tell me?" Perkins asked, his voice shaking with venom.

Oscar sat up quickly, adjusting his pants, "Tell you what?"

"That we were summoned to McKenna land. You realize it could be a trap." Perkins poured himself a drink, downed it in one gulp before pouring another.

"Of course I realize that and of course it's a trap. Where is Summer? I summoned her hours ago." He stood, striding to the door before looking out to see if she was in the hall. Perkins would have stopped her if he arrived before her.

"I sent her back to her room. Told her she could come back in an hour and she was to bring Autumn Rain with her. Right now we need to talk."

"About what?" Oscar drummed his fingers on the table. His impatience was eating at him. He wanted Summer and he didn't want to talk to Perkins about the McKenna summons. He just wanted it to go away.

"About what we are going to do," Perkins insisted, gazing out the window.

"And what would that be? We don't really have a choice now do we? The McKenna holds the upper hand and we will have to comply in some way, whether we like it or not."

"He just wants a truce between us and I, for one, am willing to agree to anything he suggests. I don't fight." He dusted off his waistcoat, pulling it down to cover his sagging belly. "So, if that is their wish, they'll be disappointed.

"No, and neither do I. The only fight I enjoy is one a woman will give me when we're having sex. Summer is perfect. She actually enjoys what we do. Never thought I'd find one woman like that let alone two."

"Don't delude yourself, both women like the money. If we'd paid Heather and Wynnie, they most likely would not have run off."

"You might have a point." Oscar was beginning to slur his words. He sat up straight, shaking his head to clear his vision. He didn't want to fall asleep before he could entertain Summer.

"You realize of course he wants to meet us at the Kinnel Stone Circle."

"Of course I do. What does it matter?"

"There are rumors about those stones," Perkins said.

"And what are those rumors?" Oscar had about as much as he wanted tonight from Perkins.

"People disappear there."

Chapter Seven

It was All Hallows' Eve. The slight breeze whispered of the evil coming their way. This year Connal knew the source of that evil. He shielded his eyes from the sunshine glinting off the mountains beyond, praying this would end soon. He and his men arrived at the circle of stones earlier than prearranged to make sure there were no surprises. The land was flat and one could see anyone coming at least a few miles across the grazing pasture before the hills rose high to break the view.

God, but he missed his wife. He kissed her goodbye two days ago, leaving her with strict instructions just in case Oscar decided to go to the castle instead of the Kinnel Stone Circle. He smiled, thinking of Wynnie, his *mo shiorghra*. The months away from her father changed her. When she first arrived, she was strong and resilient in some ways but also afraid of her shadow and terrified when anyone new visited. She didn't trust easily and seemed to jump at every sound. Now she was making friends and joining with the other women. Often, he found her head close with many of the clan, gossiping.

"You think they will come?" Alistair asked, leaning on his saddle horn, his brows furrowed together. "Not so sure myself. Why should they put themselves at risk doing our bidding?"

"They will be here. I didn't give them a choice. There are laws against raping women in Scotland. Exposure would put him in jail as well as create a scandal that would initiate more scandal. He would lose everything. While that scenario would give me pleasure, it would not give me as much satisfaction as watching the two of them disappear from my life forever."

"And you will persuade the pair the same way as you persuaded

Maurina?" Angus asked while he looked across the grazing field. No roads led to this special place, just foraging animals, grass and some heather. The grass undulated in waves as the breeze sifted through the blades.

"It's a convincing argument. Life somewhere else, at least that's what we assume, or certain death." Connal stretched upward to see further, his fingers tense on the reins. While he gave the others and appearance of confidence and patience, he felt little of either.

"Whatever waits beyond those stones might be terrifying. I'm sure it is better than living in a British prison," Angus said.

"Anything is better," Fergus agreed with his brother. "Would never want to rot in prison. I'd take my chances with the unknown. Always did believe in the magic of life and all the possibilities. There are forces, natural and unnatural, out there that none of us can understand."

"It might be our word against theirs," Alistair offered, sitting up taller as if that might give him a better look into the distance.

"It would be except there is a certain British lieutenant whose daughter somehow found herself trapped with these two men. They forced her and took her virginity without her consent. The lieutenant has wanted revenge for some time now. It seems she has never been the same since it happened. Refuses to see people, especially men and keeps herself in her room."

"But he would have to be here," Alistair argued.

Connal nodded to the south. Three redcoats were riding toward them across the grazing land. "They will be here sooner than Wynnie's father and once intended."

"And Perkins and Oscar will be presented once more with the choice in front of them," Alistair said. "If they don't choose the stones, what then?"

"We fight to the death. They've also been told that was a choice," Connal said. "Told them if they didn't make an appearance we would find them."

"What if they walk into the circle and nothing happens?" Angus always the pessimist asked.

"Never happened before but if it does, then I suppose neither man will have a choice. They will be taken into custody if they refuse to fight," Connal said.

The soldiers drew closer and Connal was rewarded with the look of determination in the lieutenant's eyes. This would all turn out the way he expected.

"Where are the men?" he asked with noted impatience. "Thought you said they would be here."

"They will be." Connal spoke with an assurance he didn't' quiet feel. "In any case, they've been told we will hunt them down if they don't appear. Their fate will be much better if they come of their own accord."

"A buffer between them and me," the lieutenant agreed. "Personally, for what they did to my daughter, I'd string them up by their man parts if I had my way in this."

"Or castrate them," another soldier offered.

Connal thought either scenario would be fitting but if they lived through the ordeal, he and Wynnie would still find themselves looking over their shoulders. He didn't want that for her or her mother. No, the Kinnel stones were the answer that he hoped would please everyone involved.

"I prefer them to disappear. I don't ever need to wonder if they are lurking around some corner waiting for me, or if somehow they escaped the prison they were confined in," Connal said with a heavy sigh and apprehension. "My wife and her mother need to live in peace."

"Perkins has an eye for my wife too and I feel the same," Alistair said. "They either disappear or they die."

Elliott spoke up then. "Couldn't we castrate them before they walk through the stones to disappear? That way they won't be able to hurt another woman in any other place or time. People never change their true colors."

"That is a lovely thought," The lieutenant offered, sporting a broad grin. "Very appealing."

"We promised no violence if they came of their own accord. I'm a man of my word," Connal said, wishing he hadn't sworn such a thing. Castration would set some of his fears at bay.

"They wouldn't have come without the assurance," Alistair said, still searching the landscape.

"They still might not come. Don't see any indication of them yet," Elliott said seeming to search the horizon for any sign of people.

"It's still early," Connal spoke, realizing he had every confidence the pair would show up. "Patience."

The sun was nearly past its zenith when the two men were spotted riding toward them. Rain began spitting from the dark clouds that were scattered, giving an eerie feeling to the scene. Connal knew before the end of the day they would be soaked through to the skin and would need to take shelter for the night. They would not be able to ride home as planned until the next morning.

Perkins and Oscar stopped in front of Connal, grim expressions on their faces. They seemed to notice the lieutenant and his men. Their actions had finally gone full circle. They would indeed pay for their crimes.

"I see you came and I'm assuming a fight is not your first choice," Connal said, smiling inside for the first time since penning the letter to these two men.

"We would not win in that case," Perkins said speaking for both of them. "We are not fighters."

"No, you wouldn't but it would be against me and the lieutenant. The fight would be fair if you choose to reconsider," Connal said, understanding these two men needed to make the decision without being coerced.

"You must pay for your crimes against our women," the lieutenant spoke up, his voice harsh. "Me, I'd just as soon kill you or castrate you. It is what you deserve."

Oscar dismounted and walked toward the stones before he entered. He inhaled long and deep, looking backwards to Perkins expecting him to follow. "I've packed a satchel. I'm assuming I can take it with me."

Connal lifted his shoulders, "Take anything of yours you want."

He nodded, walking back to his horse then taking the reins into his hands. Only Oscar walked toward the circle and into the middle. In a blink he was seen then he was not.

At the sight a shiver snaked down Connal's spine. The same happened when Maurina walked into the circle of stones.

"Where did he go?" Perkins asked, his voice shaking as he started to turn his horse around.

"No you don't." The lieutenant and his men blocked Perkins.

Connal grinned, leaning on his saddle horn. "No one knows. You going to take your chances with the unknown or do you want to clash swords with the lieutenant here? If you kill the lieutenant, I will be next. For you there is no escaping your fate. You will die today if you make the choice to fight."

Connal watched the man's Adam's apple bob up and down in his neck. He delighted in Perkins' fear. The man had never thought about the terror and pain he evoked with the women he forced. Castration should have been the punishment.

"He would never vanquish me so... what is it you want?" the lieutenant asked. "Life or death?"

Perkins' finger ran around the collar of his shirt as if he tried to loosen it. "Suppose I'll take my chances in the circle."

"You best hope you disappear," the lieutenant said.

"Or you'll follow me?" Perkins challenged.

"No, just wait until you get hungry enough to come out and meet your fate."

"Under the circumstances we've been more than generous with your lives," Alistair spoke up.

"Go on," Connal said, his grin wide now that he knew Perkins would vanish from this part of Scotland yet he prayed that wherever he showed up, he would be a wiser man.

"Very well," Perkins said then rode into the kinnel circle of stones and disappeared.

~ * ~

Wynnie smiled happily, knowing Connal was everything to her, her life, her mate through all eternity. Another year had passed since Oscar and Perkins vanished through the stones. Once more it was All

126

Hallows' Eve. From the parapets they could see the bonfires on the horizon. It was their second year together.

Heather had been right. As soon as the tension and stress from knowing her father could show up any time vanished, she conceived. Now she sat in the solar, Connal beside her, watching her baby wave his arms excitedly in the air.

Brady was laughing and cooing at his father's antics. If Connal was nay careful, the baby would toss the contents of his stomach right in Connal's face. She laughed with them as Connal lay beside the infant, tickling his stomach.

"Do you think he'll be a shifter like you?" Wynnie asked, hoping the little boy would grow up to be just like his father.

"I think he will be," Connal spoke, still watching the child. "He has shown some subtle signs."

"Truly there was a time I didn't think I would have a child." She sat down on the floor next to her husband.

"I'm glad we have the babe, but it would not have mattered to me," he told her, holding his hand out to her suggesting she join him on the floor.

"And why is that?" She bent over and with her hands on either side of his head, kissed him, her tongue slipping over his lips in a silent quest.

"Because I'm a sucker for you, my darling Wynnie. You are my eternal love as well. Was the first time I saw you racing away from me in the darkness. I knew I had to find a way to make you mine."

"You didn't proceed as a gentleman." She pushed away from him, but he wouldn't have the distance. He pulled her on top of him as he lay back on the floor."

"Who's to say I didn't let you have your way because we will be together through eternity?" she asked, as he rolled over and was now bracing himself above her. His gaze was raw with breathtaking passion and her body seemed to melt beneath his.

"Don't you think it's time for Brady to take a nap?" he asked, kissing her softly across her collarbone then lower.

"He just woke," she told him, moving so he had better access to her neck while she arched toward him and he placed gentle kisses on her exposed skin.

"Where is the nanny?" He rose to look out the door then called out.

A woman appeared so quickly, she must have been waiting for the summons. Without direction, she seemed to know what to do and scooped Brady into her arms, leaving them alone.

Connal closed and bolted the door. Leaning against it he stared at her. "I'm thinking I'd like to see you with nothing on."

He began to undress, quickly slipping from his clothing then striding toward her. He was adept at women's clothing and despite the layers, she was suddenly naked beneath him.

"Should we work on a second child?" he asked as his lips explored her.

"I think we should wait until Brady is a bit older." She could barely breathe as his hands found all the magical and enchanting spots he knew so well.

"Don't know if I can do that." He slipped inside her, holding still. "But I'll try."

She ran her hands along his back. "How did I get so lucky to wander onto McKenna land?"

"Everything happens for a reason," he murmured as his lips found hers again and again. "God, I can't resist you. I'm such a sucker for you. Yes, you are my eternal love, Wynnie, my beloved, *mo shiorghra*. I love you, you know."

"I love you too," she murmured as she reveled in the magic and mystery that Connal so easily created in her. "All I ever wanted was to love and be loved."

"And so you are."

Sorceress' Secret
C. L. Kraemer

Chapter One

Twenty-first Century
Eugene, Oregon

Gwynedd slipped the key into the front door. Surprisingly, the wooden closure swung freely and offered no noisy resistance. She sensed a bit of magic about the place as she was driving up the entry road. The earth around a location kissed with magic hums sweetly if the magic is white or screams dissonantly if the magic is black. This acreage hummed.

The smell of ink on parchment tickled her nose. Books in all shapes and forms lined every imaginable space. The real estate agent had warned her about the interior's condition, but seeing it first-hand made all the difference in the world. Seating, in various configurations, infused the front room with a welcoming atmosphere. Gwyn wandered past the books to the back of the building noting a well set up kitchen, public restrooms, and tucked into a corner of the house, a bedroom with private bath.

As she meandered from room to room, she was aware of the whisper of tiny wings. She didn't wish to frighten the Fae checking her out, so she feigned ignorance of their presence. She moved into the kitchen. Opening a cupboard, she located cups and saucers, tea infusers, and loose tea. Going through the motions, Gwyn prepared a cup of tea which she carried to a table in the front of the library. As was custom, she poured a bit of the brew into her saucer and pulled out a sugar packet she'd snagged from the restaurant where she'd eaten lunch. She opened the sweetener for little hands to grasp.

Sitting at the table and gazing around her new home, she issued an invitation. "Please join me." She could sense disruption in the air.

Quiet voices tested her hearing.

"You—you can see us?"

The voice felt... disembodied.

"Yes. I mean no harm to any magical creature."

"Even the night elves?" There was a tremor in the question.

"It will depend on many things."

"What?"

"I'll have to wait until I meet them."

More shuffling ensued before Gwyn found herself face-to-face with two wee folk: one small female, blonde of hair and green of eyes, and a medium sized male, blonde and brown-eyed.

He backed up and sized up this new human. "Where is the Librarian?"

"As I understand it, she married and moved to Ireland near the Giant's Causeway." Gwyn leaned back in her chair to give the small Fae enough space to 'wace'. It was the Fae version of pacing done with wings.

The little female moved within her direct vision but held enough distance not to be captured. "Are you sure she isn't coming back?" The tiny wings trembled.

"I'm sure. She signed the papers that sold the library to me. I'll be living here." Gwyn knew the magic folk were not going to be happy. They intensely disliked change in their world. "I have every intention of opening the library to all. Maybe, I'll open the coffee shop again. I'm not sure yet."

The buzzing whir of tiny wings zipped past her into the kitchen. "Where is she?" A medium sized wood nymph swooped to the front of Gwyn's face and hovered, tiny hands fisted on her waist.

"And you are?" Gwyn pulled back a bit, the fury presented in her face giving her pause.

"I'm Chrissy. Who the hell are you?" She leaned forward and pushed toward Gwynedd.

"I am Gwynedd Summers, the new owner of this property."

"Since when?" This wood nymph was not like any Gwynedd had bumped into previously. She was not shy nor was she hesitant to confront a human. She pushed forward, a scowl covering her face. Her deep violet eyes narrowed.

Gwyn sighed. "I'd hoped not to do this so soon." With a quick movement, she held up her index finger and murmured, "Still."

Two Faeries and one wood nymph were frozen in place. Their eyes wide in surprise.

"I wanted to meet my magical neighbors under congenial circumstances... not in a confrontation. I am Gwynedd Drucilla Summers; 12th generation sorceress. My family dates to a time before these lands knew people. I–sensed–a great deal of sorcery and magic folk in this area, so I wanted to be where I wouldn't have to fear constant intrusions should I slip.

"I understand you were great admirers of the Librarian, but when she joined with her night elf mate, he gave her the gift of long living. They chose to reside in the lands of Ireland. She contacted the local Other person to sell her home, and I bought it.

"If you promise not to attack me, I'll remove the spell. Blink once for yes." She looked at each of the wee folk and received a positive answer. Lifting the same finger, she whispered, "Free."

Whirring of wings and Fae swearing filled her ears.

Chrissy flew to face her. "Why didn't you just say so in the beginning?"

Gwyn shrugged. "Even magical folk fear the sorcerer. I've no desire to bump heads with anyone looking for a fight. I figured enough time had passed so the major rifts within the community would have been healed."

"Well, maybe for the Others, but we are Fae. We live long and remember even longer. If you allow the Night Elves back into the Library, I'll never come back." She turned her back and winged to the kitchen.

Gwyn could see she needed to get the full story. "Would you three be willing to tell me what happened here?"

Chrissy floated back in and landed on the table in front of Gwyn. The little Fae were conversing between themselves. They turned to the wood nymph and nodded.

"We'll tell you. About..."

Gwyn held up a hand. "I don't wish to be rude, but I don't want to have any interference while you fill me in. Please give me a moment to guarantee our privacy." She stood up and walked to the front door, locking the handset. She did the same to the door in the kitchen. Then she walked to the middle of the Library and began to murmur lowly.

"Mother Earth, our words don't share,
With any who think they will dare,
To eavesdrop on what we say here.
A wall of silence this place will cover,
No one to hear a single word uttered."

She turned to each compass direction and evoked the incantation again. When she finished, the building and land around the Library wore a wall of magic keeping others out and the foursome inside safely in. "Okay. If anyone comes to the house, what they will see if they stare in the window is–nothing. It will appear as if no one is home. We are covered until I lift the spell."

The three little visitors grinned at each other.

Gwyn moved to the center of the library and the comfortable seating provided. "To whom am I speaking?"

The little blonde Fae with green eyes spoke first. "I am Ailidh, and this is my mate, Kayne." He nodded. "She," the tiny blonde pointed a small finger at the wood nymph, "is Chrissy. So, we've exchanged names. Do you want us all to tell you the story?"

Gwynedd nodded. "You all will have different versions, and I'd like to hear what you have to say so I can see a couple sides. Who wants to begin?"

Chrissy winged to the arm of the chair and took a seat. "I guess I will since I was the first to meet the Librarian."

For several hours, the Fae of the forest relayed the history and events which led to her becoming the new owner.

Gwyn rose from the seat and stretched. "It's been a very, long day. I believe I shall fix myself something to eat. You are welcome to share my food and, if you are too tired to wing your way home, please stay where you like except my bed."

Chapter Two

Gitty wrapped her hands around the steaming mug, walking to the picture window that overlooked the valley. Dusk was creeping across the meadow and painting the sky in soft pastel shades. However, the Night Elf on the hill saw none of the beauty through her anger. What she had been seeing was a light in a building she thought long abandoned. An utterance escaped her lips. "There can be no way that traitor would *dare* to show his face in this valley."

She closed her eyes but could sense no familiar magic. She did feel vibrations of an old—very old—sorcery.

Morgan, Gitty's brother, meandered through the living room oblivious to his sister's agitated form. "Nice sunset, don't you think?"

Gitty turned and growled. "What has that to do with–anything?"

He looked at the snarling entity he knows to be his sister. "What has your knickers in a twist?"

She faced him. "You truly are the biggest idiot I know."

"What?"

"Have you not noticed the spike of magic in the valley?" She arched a brow.

"Why should I? I'm unable to use it anymore. Keeping track of the level of magic in the valley would just be a constant reminder of my situation."

She huffed an impatient breath and shoved past him. "Bog slug."

Morgan watched his sister stomp from the room. "And she wonders why she's alone." The real reason, he knew from direct experience, was a heart turned to stone was incapable of loving. "I don't know who is worse. She with her cold, stone heart or me with my hollow,

5

love-starved one."

Deciding this line of thinking would require too much concentration, he retired to his room and a night of mindless television entertainment.

Gitty was unable to stand still. She needed to get to the valley floor and check things out first-hand. She bolted to her room and changed to jeans and a shirt. Grabbing a jacket on her way to the garage, she stuck a hand in the pocket and found crumpled paper. Pulling out the bar napkin with name and phone number written on it, she tossed the rubbish to the ground. "Ignite."

Opting to use the pickup truck for discretion's sake, when she backed from the garage, she glanced at the gas gauge and swore. "Damn it, Morgan. You're as capable of filling the gas tank as I am." She spied the paper still lying on the ground. "Double damn. I hate being without my magic!"

She pushed the accelerator to the floor of the vehicle, sending dirt and gravel skittering across the driveway. "There has got to be a way to retrieve my magical abilities. This life without it will kill me. No wonder the Others die so young." She slowed the truck, observing the posted speed limit. A speeding ticket couldn't be magicked away when one didn't have the ability to use the arts. Executing a left turn into the long driveway of the Library, Gitty suffered a moment of doubt. The lane to the building was barren save a few wayward leaves.

The house in the distance was dark. Was it possible she imagined the light?

"No. I'm driving to the front and parking. Walking around the place will tell me what I need to know." Having made her mind up, Gitty gave the accelerator gas and parked the truck in front of the Library. She stepped out of the truck, struck by the unnerving silence. Glancing skyward, she noted branches being moved by an invisible wind, however, they were making no noise. Bushes nearby shook slightly, and the grass blades shivered. The quiet was unnatural.

"Gah! I've become a frightened child without my powers." She strode to the front of the porch and peered into the windows finding only darkness. Furniture near the glass appeared pushed aside and forgotten,

6

showing decades of collected dust. The results were the same in all the windows she could peer through. The house, for all intents and purposes, was empty. The back and sides offered further proof of decades of deterioration. The forest was moving to retake the land.

"There's nothing here. Maybe I should visit the old country to see if I can find a way to restore my abilities."

Climbing into the truck, she failed to note the slight movement behind the window curtains. Her appearance had been noted, and her actions were being tracked.

~ * ~

Gwyn moved the curtain slightly to observe the stranger peeking in the windows. The fear in the room was palpable. Rustling of wings gave away the small guests. "Don't worry. She can't see or hear us. All she sees is a dark room with lots of dusty furniture."

Skepticism hung in the air until they heard the door to the vehicle slam, and the truck barrel down the driveway.

~ * ~

The hair on Gitty's arms prickled. "There is magic being used in or around the old Lending Library. I'd stake my reputation on it." She arrived at the house on the hill more agitated than when she'd left.

Morgan watched the force that was his sister storm in from the garage. She made a direct line to her office, the one that had been their father's, slamming the door behind her. "Hello to you, too." Of one thing he could be certain, Gitty would be shut in the room until she'd exorcised whatever demons she was battling. His evening just entered a more enjoyable phase.

Chapter Three

Oscar Adair and Perkins, no first name–just Perkins—stood transfixed. "Where the bloody hell are we?"

Perkins, in a rare moment of clarity, shrugged his shoulders but spoke not a word. The braying of a very loud animal nearby jolted them to the extremely large wagon moving directly at them. They jumped out of the way swearing when they hit the embankment and tumbled into the small stream.

"What the..." Oscar scrambled up the small hillock and watched the wagon moving away from him at a rapid pace. "There na be horses. How can that wagon move? Witchcraft?" He turned to Perkins. The man's face was near see through.

"Witchcraft?" He was visibly shaking.

Oscar scowled. "Stop actin' like a lass. How else would ya explain the movement of the wagon?"

"Steam?"

Oscar narrowed his eyes. "You be daft."

Perkins seemed to be regaining the color in his face. "Nay. There be a bloke experimenting with steam ta make wagons move fast without horses."

"Who told you"

"I heard it in the pub."

Oscar rolled his eyes. "They were having one on you. Canna make wagons faster lessen you get bigger, stronger horses."

The pair bickered as they stood on the hillock.

"Wherever we be, we need be thinkin' bout shelter. I've no plan on bein' some beastie's dinner." Oscar surveyed the area not spotting any obvious dwellings. He moved to the black path. "Seems this path be the best way to move across the land, though, we best keep an eye out for the wagons. Not lookin' to be run over by one."

Perkins grunted his agreement. The pair trudged along the hard wagon track looking at buildings and greenery unlike any in the Highlands. The sun lowered in the sky, taking the temperature with it, and reminding them both, they were wet to the bone. Luck was elusive and lodgings sparse. Fact was, they'd not seen many buildings during their trek. As hope for a night out of the elements dwindled, sitting back from the road, nearly invisible under the tangle of blackberries and ivy was a hut. The question of inhabitants answered by the darkness within.

Oscar left the track and poked about. "Well, it not be Inverness Castle, but it might keep out the cold and beasties."

Perkins balked. "I will nae go into a hovel with but dirt on the ground for sleeping."

Oscar levelled a poisonous glare his direction. "If you woulda kept ma lass for yourself, and not farmed her out like a common trollop, we wouldnae be having this talk. But suit yerself. I'm nae sleepin' out of doors." He burrowed beneath the vines and explored the hut. It appeared to have served as a home. There was a table, wobbly and sporting chipped paint, with two attending chairs of dubious reliability nearby. Ragged material fluttered in the breeze wafting through the broken windows. He maneuvered around debris on the floor discovering an adjoining area to the dining table. A door led to an area with the remains of a sleeping cot. There was another room with a porcelain tub, *must've been a Lord,* and a porcelain chamber pot, but he couldn't fathom how to empty the thing. He re-entered the room with the cot as Perkins appeared.

"You'll nae be sleepin' on the cot. Tis mine. But you can keep ye arse from the cold by sleepin' on the table."

Perkins opened his mouth to object but found he was looking at Oscar's back on the cot. He trudged to the front area and tested the table. It was spindly but, taking in the floor, a sight better than sleeping on the boards.

The setting sun brought a chill that crept through the windows and over the warped boards making up the floor. Perkins looked about and noted a strange metal box against the wall in the other room. He made his way to the container, placing a hand on the cold iron. When he ran his hand over the exterior, recognition set in. If he could locate some dry wood nearby, there was a possibility of creating heat. It might stop Oscar from his mocking comments.

He stumbled to the door and pushed. Nothing. Grabbing a piece of metal sticking out about waist height, he pulled. Again, nothing. Frustration pushed at him. He wiggled and turned the metal knob. A snick sound alerted him something was happening. He turned the knob and pushed to no avail. Perkins sighed. *One more time.* He turned and pulled the door feeling the opening swing in his hands. So as not to enter into the irritating game again, he left the opening wide as he scouted for burnable wood. He filled his arms and shuffled inside, setting his find on the table.

One more trip to find a long, slender stick, and he attempted to clean the flue. Who knew how long it had been since the thing had been cleaned? Best to warn the birds nesting there about the impending end to their home. Moving the wood from the table and placing it next to the box, he put a few pieces inside and threw in bits that had fallen off. Perkins stood and rummaged in his sporran for the flint he knew to be there. Squatting, he smacked the flint and created a spark within the belly of the wood box. Fire grew in the box exuding heat into the room. He pulled the table near the wood stove and opened the door of the belly. Once he succumbed to the siren song of slumber, the hovel fell silent.

Sunlight poked at his eye. Exhaling a breath, Perkins pried open an eyelid spying the cloud of condensation. He rolled off the table and fumbled his way to the stove. Placing wood and kindling into the cooled interior, he struck his flint and reignited a blaze.

Grumbling and swear words filled the sleeping room. "I've nae hurt this bad since… I canna remember." Oscar slogged from the room, his *feileadh mhor* clinging to his behind. He scooted said backside to the stove and breathed a sigh. "Ah, warmth." It took a moment before his statement registered in his foggy brain. He turned and stared at the stove as it quickly warmed. Looking back at Perkins, he asked, "How, when…?"

Perkins could see a barrage of questions forming. "Last eve when you lay down, I thought I spied a beastie against the wall. I decided I may as well check it. Once I got close, one touch proved it nae to be a beastie but metal. I realized it were a stove, so I went out and gathered wood and kindlin'. If'n I was ta sleep in this here room, I was nae wantin' to die of the cold."

Oscar picked up a chunk of wood and chucked it into the belly. "Maybe we can be stayin' here til we find a way home."

"What if the Lord of the manor rides by? We be thrown in gaol and kilt."

Oscar looked around. "I be thinkin' he dinna much care about this hovel. He's not put much care into it now, has he?"

Perkins couldn't argue. It had been many a year since any type of effort had been expended on the small abode. "Aye. Your words ring true."

Oscar scratched his stomach which had begun growling. "This be good fur sleepin', but what are we to do about food?"

Perkins swiveled about and stared out the window at the barren land. Indeed, there were more trees than around his village, but he knew nothing of the beasties of the land. What might kill him and what could he eat? His own stomach complained loudly. "Aye. I'll be cursing Connal McKenna and all his seed for takin' my betrothed and banishing us to this Goddess-forsaken place. What are we to do indeed?"

Chapter Four

Gwyn rolled her neck. Ever since the night elf had come poking around, she couldn't shake the sensation of close observation. Per the Fae stories, the elves weren't a factor. They had lost their magic due to their greed. So, what was the ripple in magic that set her hair on end?

She paced. Unsettling sensations bounced off the walls of the library. To try and combat the heebee jeebees, she picked up a duster and set to work cleaning years of dust from the surfaces. What she succeeded in doing was stirring up a massive cloud. She opened the door off the kitchen. "Out!" A storm of particles large enough to rival anything in the Sahara whooshed out the side of the building. That's when she heard it… coughing, uncontrollable coughing.

She sent tendrils of magic to touch her forest friends. They were safe and far from her location. She stepped toward the door. "Disappear." Fading into a blanket of invisibility, she moved out of the library into the back yard. A figure emerged from behind an overgrown bush near the back door. Dirty, disheveled hair and torn clothing, the female appeared out of place.

Eighteenth century by the style of the clothing. Gwyn trailed the figure as it ventured into the house. The first stop was the kitchen to rummage through the cupboards grabbing food items which were consumed immediately. She went out back. "Appear." She brushed dust from her clothes and headed to the Library's interior making as much noise as she could.

The figure jumped and turned to face her.

Gwyn stood blocking the exit. "Who are you, and what are you doing in my home eating my food?"

The anemic face lost all color. "I—I be Maurina." She backed up to the wall and slid to the floor. Her eyes, wide with fear, rolled up into her skull. She slumped over on her side.

Gwynedd pushed out a breath. "Darn it." She ventured to the inert form on the floor and checked for a pulse. It was faint but there. Standing, she closed her eyes and pulled energy from the surrounding area. "Heal." Wavering, Gwyn walked to a chair in the main room of the Library and slumped down. Healing spells were very draining. She would need to meditate for a day and find a suitable offering she could use to thank the Goddess for gifting her the power to help this young woman.

Gwyn needed light on her face and fresh air in her lungs, the stench of 18th century hygiene leaving her eyes watering. She wasn't sure where her visitor stood in the scheme of things, upper or lower class, but her guest's journey was taking its toll on any freshness acquired prior to the trip. Pulling to a standing position, she strolled out the front door. After her discussion with the Fae, she'd opted to keep a safety spell over the property at all times. When the tall, blonde night elf came visiting, she was thankful for her diligence.

Stepping from the porch to the sidewalk area, she noted the cooling temperature. Just a small bite in the air whispered of the approaching All Hallows' Eve. Gwyn toyed with the idea of a small gathering of magical folk in the Library. Her meandering thoughts followed her circuitous path leading her to an area at the side of the building. She stood looking at what had once been a well-tended, thriving garden. Now, the ratio of weeds to food items was about even. Leaning over, she plucked a large orange pumpkin from the ground. Knocking on the skin, she smiled at the sound. "Perfect for the Goddess."

Arms wrapped about the smooth gourd, she soaked up the positive essence of the plant. She entered the kitchen and placed the pumpkin on the counter. A moan across the room reminded her there was an out-of-time visitor on her floor. She ventured to the limp Maurina noting the color of her face, what there was of it, had returned.

"Maurina?" Gwyn wasn't entirely sure of the reaction she would receive.

"Oh, me head. Did you catch the scoundrel who hit me?" She was clutching the sides of her head and rocking.

"I have something that might help." Gwynedd retrieved the aspirin she'd put over the stove for emergencies and a glass of water.

Upon her return, Maurina had her knees pulled to her chest and was resting her head on the caps.

"This is willow bark pressed into little buttons. Don't chew as they are very bitter. Put them in your mouth, take a swig of water, and wash them down your throat."

Gwyn stepped back and watched as Maurina examined the aspirin tabs.

Maurina looked up at her. "Be ye sure these tiny dots can help my pain?"

"Aye."

"Okay, but if these be poison, I shall haunt you forever."

"Duly noted."

The furrow of her brow let Gwyn know her guest hadn't understood the response.

She put the pills on her tongue, wrinkling her nose at the bitterness. Gwyn pushed the water her direction indicating she should drink.

Maurina choked the pills down, coughing and making a sour face. "That has the taste of the devil."

Gwyn withheld the urge to smile. "Aye. But you will soon reap the benefits of its healing properties."

"Do you mean I won't hurt anymore?"

"Exactly."

"That would be a blessing. Where am I? This does nae look to be the highlands."

Gwyn helped her to a chair at the front of the library. "Would you like a cup of tea?"

"I'd *like* a wee dram of whiskey, but tea will do fine."

The sorceress proceeded to set the kettle to heating on the stove. She grabbed a couple mugs from the kitchen cupboard, placing teabags in each. When the kettle whistled, she filled each mug, then carried them to the table, setting one in front of her visitor and the other in front of the place where she was to sit. Back to the kitchen for sugar and milk. When she stepped out the kitchen door, Maurina was holding the teabag out of the water, looking perplexed.

"What be this–thing you put in the water?" The wrinkles in her forehead deepened.

Gwyn gently pushed her hand down so the bag was immersed in the hot water. "This is a tea bag. It is a special thin cloth bag that holds the leaves so there aren't bits and bobs of the tea floating in your drink. Sugar or milk?"

Maurina had become fascinated with dipping the bag in and out of the cup. "What does one do when finished dipping?"

Gwyn smiled. The question was legitimate for a person out of their time element. "You can squeeze the bag dry…"

"With your hands?" The look of horror was authentic.

"… or leave the bag in the cup and finish drinking."

Maurina stared at Gwyn. "You jest. You expect me to soil my hands?"

Gwyn stared at the woman. Her outer wear showed quality. It was evident to the sorceress this female was of the upper class, whatever century she'd inhabited. "Do not take out the bag if you don't wish to soil your hands."

Maurina sipped the brew. "Quite tasty."

Waiting until the visitor had relaxed and imbibed some tea, Gwyn realized it was time to explain to her the current situation. "Lady Maurina?"

"Yes?"

The response was automatic. The sorceress had figured correctly. "You are not in the highlands any longer."

"Piffle. There be a bite in the air that speaks to the coming of winter, as always."

"No. You are in a place that has just been discovered in your time. It's called America."

"Aye, I've heard speak of the land. They tell of half-dressed heathens that kill the men and ravish the women."

"Not any longer. Those days have long since passed."

"Wait… you spoke of *my* time? What be the year now?"

"Two thousand and twenty."

Maurina jumped from her chair. "YOU LIE! Tis a trick to gain access to the wealth of my kin. You've taken me from my land and will seek payment for my release."

Gwyn could see reasoning with this woman was not going to work. She slowly touched the arm of the traveler while invoking a calming spell.

The woman stilled, her eyes fluttering, and she pulled in deep draughts of air. "It canna be. How could this happen?"

Intoning more vocally, the sorceress walked the woman through the years, helping her to accept the many changes. She manipulated her back into the chair, sliding her hand from Maurina's arm, which she set across her lap.

"There be much change from this time to mine. I feel quite tired of recent. Might there be a place to lie my head?"

Gwyn led her to a divan in the main area of the library. She lay the woman on the couch and took the afghan from the back, covering her. Before she left the room, the sounds of gentle snoring filled the air.

Chapter Five

Gitty paced her room. The trip to the Lending Library was unsatisfactory, at best. She knew there was magic being applied in the valley. Granted, it wasn't as prolific or sophisticated as in earlier years, but the light buzzing on the top of her skin indicated its current use. She needed to move, and pacing wasn't enough.

"A good long ride will serve to ease my nerves." She changed into riding gear fit for the cool season and headed to the stables. Saddling her mare, she sensed the animal's excitement.

"Yes, love. We're going for a long ride today. I think we should look over our kingdom, don't you?"

The animal snorted and pawed the ground. Gitty swung up into the saddle, settling in for the long tour of the family's holdings around the valley. The years had slipped by with such rapidity, the properties could be in any shape. The pair cantered past the library and made way toward the eastern mountains.

Coming into view was a home that's location seemed familiar but Gitty couldn't recall the last time she or Morgan had surveyed it. Blackberry vines and ivy wrapped the walls in green, thorny webs. Even so, there appeared to be smoke rising from a space near the top of the mound.

"Squatters. I'd better start policing these places more often." She reined her mare to a halt near some sweet grass. A quick looping of the reins over the branch of a tree was a failsafe to keep her from wandering away in search of more to eat. It was times like these she could really use magic. She was having to learn how to be stealthy. At six foot, five inches tall, with long, white hair, hiding was not as easy for the Night Elf as it might be for others.

There were voices from the interior... male. By the different pitches, she surmised two people were using the abode.

She calculated the layout of this building: small and functional. The door to the kitchen swung open easily. *Must be how they got inside.* A figure squat in front of the old woodstove. There was another voice coming from a different area out of her line of sight.

"Well, ya better start thinkin' on it. Not sure there be a king, but I'm bettin' he's not going to be happy if we hunt on his land."

"Aye, that be truth. First, we need to find out where we be."

Gitty could hear the accents and determined the pair were from the British Isles. Probably Scotland if the burring of the 'rs' was any indication.

"Oscar?"

"Aye?"

"There be a fine lookin' steed out by the tree. Think we been found?"

"Go look, you dolt."

Perkins turned from the window with the partial view to face the white-haired, tall night elf. "AAHHH!" His eyes rolled back in his head right before he passed out.

Oscar appeared upon hearing Perkins yell. His mouth opened but sounds failed to emerge. He, too, dropped to the floor. Gitty peered at the pair. "Gits." She did a quick reconnoiter of the small cabin noting a pair of old lamps left by renters or squatters. Didn't matter. She would utilize them, anyway. Pulling a dirk from her boot, she cut the electrical wire from both lights. Grabbing the chubbier of the two, she set them back-to-back and bound their wrists. Waiting for the interlopers to revive, she poked about the place retrieving a wobbly chair from the area she surmised was the kitchen. *How do people live like this?*

Moaning interrupted further investigation. She hauled the chair back to the living area and set it to face her captives.

"Oh, me head." The one called dolt tried to put his hands to his head, discovering his inability to move. "What the...?"

Oscar's eyes fluttered, and he began showing signs of life. "Where the bloody hell are we?"

Gitty, sitting with the one leg crossed atop the other and tapping her boot with the dirk, replied. "That is the question you should have asked before anything else. You are in Oregon, in the United States of America, in one of my houses."

Oscar scowled. "You're lyin'. Tis' no place called Or-ee-gone or United States of A-mare-ee-ka in the Highlands."

Perkins nodded. Oscar was the smarter of the two. He'd know the truth.

Gitty let a slow smile cover her lips. "You're right. You know this land as British America. The part where we are was mostly Indian land until the early 1800s." She watched the faces of the two men drain of color.

Oscar swallowed, licked his lips, and asked, "What be the time now?"

"Two thousand and twenty." Gitty smirked. "Welcome to the 21st century, gents."

It was evident the men didn't believe her. Distrust and skepticism showed in their expressions. Perkins was the first to speak.

"You be lyin' like Oscar said. Someone kidnaped us and left us to die on the moor. They know not that we be Highlanders and made of stronger stuff."

"I don't have time to try and make you believe me. I don't really give a damn. What I do care about is, what am I to do with you? Technically, I can have you arrested and thrown in the gaol until you die."

"No! We've not stolen but time and wood for the fire. Point us in the direction of the Highlands and we'll leave." Perkins was starting to speak with more courage. Oscar appeared to be trying to wrap his mind around the century difference.

Gitty broke into laughter. The harsh sound echoing through the small cabin. "It would take you a month or longer on foot to reach the Eastern shore, then you'd have to find a way to make enough money to secure passage across the Atlantic Ocean to Scotland. I believe you're stuck."

Perkins face turned a strange shade of white tinged with blue.

"Oscar? What are we to do? I've not enough in my Sporran for such a trip."

Oscar emitted a growl. "We're stuck, you git. We'll be lookin' at spendin' time in gaol. We can only hope they have bread that not be moldy."

The night elf stood and walked around the bundled pair. "I *might* be able to offer a solution."

The chubbier of the two flashed a glance toward her ice blue eyes. "And that would be?"

"I'm in need of some help. I'm too well known around here for the–project–I have in mind. All I can offer is use of this," she waved a hand around the room, "and food. I'll school you on how to use the modern conveniences in the house, but you'll answer to me whenever I desire."

Oscar spoke lowly. "This is naught but magic, and you are a witch. I'll not be damning my soul to everlasting purgatory for a bite to eat."

Perkins wiggled against the man. "Think, man, think. My stomach does bid me eat, and I'd much rather face purgatory to freezing, right now."

Gitty could see this was going to take a bit more persuasion. "Well, gents. I've other things to do. I'll be on my way. Maybe I'll stop in tomorrow, maybe not. Have a nice day." She turned on her heel and tromped out the back door, slamming it as she left. *That ought to give them something to think about.* She untethered the reins, swung into the saddle, and kicked the horse to a gallop, ignoring the yelling permeating the air. Tomorrow, she was certain she'd have full cooperation from the pair.

Chapter Six

Dawn stretched a gentle fog across the meadow in front of the library, turning the land into a golden sight. Gwynedd sighed over her cup of tea and allowed her mind to meander through the most recent events. It was evident her guest had been pushed through a time portal, but where? She would need to investigate and put a protection spell around this end of the tunnel. Wouldn't do to have 18th century folk popping in all the time. Shuffling sounds in the library proper alerted her to the fact her wayward guest was moving about.

"Where am I?"

The question is one that would arise each time Maurina would wake.

"This not be the Highlands." The statement ended on a high note.

"No, Maurina, this is *not* the Highlands. Sit back on the divan and take a deep breath. Your situation will come to you." Gwyn murmured a memory spell to nudge the information she'd given the woman.

"Right. What might I do about, well, my personal needs?" Maurina's face colored.

"Follow me." Gwyn waited for the young woman to stand. She wound her way through the library area to the public restroom. Once the pair entered the room, Gwyn gave her a quick explanation of the workings of the modern bathroom. She opted to wait for the time traveler to emerge from the stall.

"How does the water disappear?"

"You press the silver protrusion on the side of the porcelain chair."

"I think not! I shan't dirty my hands." The comment was followed by a foot stomp.

21

"Then you'll be locked in the stall for the rest of the day."

There was some unintelligible muttering followed by the sound of the toilet flushing. Maurina exited the stall and held her hands before her.

"I feel soiled. Where may I clean?"

The sorceress moved her to the sink. She turned the faucet, testing to ensure the water was warm, and put the traveler's hands beneath the flow. She watched as Maurina's eyes widened in amazement. She then placed the palms of the traveler's hands under the soap dispenser, rubbing them together to work up a lather much as one would do for a small child. When all was said and done, she provided a paper towel for the woman to dry her hands.

"That is the way we relieve ourselves in the 21st century. Now... the time has come for you to bathe. Your clothing is in dire need of mending and cleaning, also. It stinks."

Maurina faced the sorceress. "I bathed several days ago. I be not sure what ye have heard about us, but cleanliness is a virtue in the Highlands." She stomped from the bathroom to the kitchen area.

Gwyn followed and turned her toward the small room serving as her bedroom. "March." The pair entered the room where Maurina was guided to a small bathroom with shower, sink and toilet. "This," Gwyn pointed to the shower stall, "is where you will bathe. I'll give you directions and you'll follow them precisely. You have twenty minutes to wash your body and hair. Here," she pointed to the clean bath sheet on the rack, "is your drying sheet." She showed Maurina how to turn on the water, adjust the temperature setting, and turn it off. "Please remove your clothing and hand it to me."

With back to the visitor, she waited, listening for the rustle of clothing. She held a hand behind her to hold the items. Maurina was in the shower with water turned on and moaning in delight before Gwyn had left the room with the laundry. Placing the items on top of the washer, she muttered, "Repair". The clothing knit together. Once repaired, she tossed all the items into the tub followed by a generous amount of detergent. A careful listen let her know the shower had ceased to run so Gwyn started the machine. She went to the bedroom and, out of courtesy, knocked on the door.

"Enter." Maurina stood wrapped in the bath sheet, hair dripping on the floor.

"Did you not dry your hair with the towel?" Gwyn frowned.

"Yes. But there be too much hair and nae enough towel." Petulance oozed from the visitor.

"I don't have time for this," Gwyn muttered. "Freeze." She pointed at the woman's hair. "Dry." A breeze wafted through the room. The time traveler's dry reddish hair fell to below her waist.

"Free." Maurina stood, hair fluttering in the breeze, chill bumps rising on her alabaster skin.

"Do ye have a robe I might use til my clothing is ready?" She turned to Gwyn.

"Yes. However, I have a better idea. Why don't you don the clothing of this century and see if it suits you?" She rummaged through her drawers and pulled out a pair of jeans and a t-shirt for the traveler to wear. Underclothing would have to wait.

"Ye would have me dress as a lad? Nay." Maurina crossed arms over an impressive bosom.

Gwyn realized a bra would be necessary if her uninvited guest were to wear a t-shirt. She'd have to magic one specifically for the lady. "Then you'll just have to sit naked in this cold room until your clothing can be cleaned. That could take a day... maybe a week."

The lady plopped herself on the bed. "Tis a nice room, small, but comfortable. I believe I shall stay here until my things are ready."

Gwyn snapped around. "Oh, no. This is my room, and you'll not be taking it over. In this century, you have no title. You are just another woman in a land where women outnumber men. Up," she pulled the traveler to her feet. "Clothing." A bra and underwear appeared on Maurina. Gwynn grabbed the jeans and pointed at the legs. "Put these on, NOW." She snatched the t-shirt from the bed, handing it to the lass after she wiggled into the jeans. "Slip this over your head and down your body."

Once the t-shirt was in place, Gwyn instructed Maurina on securing the jeans. She stepped back and took a look. Damned if the traveler didn't wear her clothes better than she.

"This is *my* room. I will not give it up to anyone. You will stay on the divan in the Library main until we can find a way to send you back to your own time. Do you understand?"

Maurina nodded. "I have to admit, these lad garments are comfortable. I'm still a bit chilled. Might there be a shawl I could wrap about my shoulders?"

Gwyn opened her closet door and pulled out a sweater that she handed to the lady. "Try this."

Shrugging into the new item, Maurina's fingers lingered over the woven material. "Tis a fine item made from Scottish sheep."

Gwyn frowned and moved to read the label at the back of the collar. Maurina was correct. This was one of her grandmother's sweaters. It'd been a gift from her when she traveled the highlands.

Shoes would be integral to keeping the visitor well. Gwyn rummaged in her shoe closet and found a pair of runners she'd bought only to discover the sizing was incorrect. They would have to do. She indicated Maurina to sit on the bed and placed socks and the tennis shoes on her feet. When Maurina stood she wobbled a bit but hesitantly stepped toward the door.

"I be not sure if I wants to go back to me time. These shoes are ugly, but me feet donna hurt." She turned her foot in the shoes and wiggled them back and forth.

Gywn groaned. All she needed was a time traveler living in the house. *Why not? I have two Fae and a wood nymph as companions.* "I'm hungry. Let's get something to eat."

The pair headed to the kitchen to quiet the rumbling of their bellies.

Chapter Seven

Drool meandered down the rubbled face of Oscar to his shirt. He snorted and snapped his head back, smacking Perkins awake.

"Bloody, hell, Oscar. Dinna need a cracked skull." Perkins tried to lift a hand to rub the spot. He was cinched into place. "I be starving. Couldna you lied to the wench, eh? A bit of food would sure go a long way, now."

Oscar groaned. "Shut up, Perkins. Yer always thinkin' bout yer stomach. We need ta find a way out of here. Kin you free yerself from the ropes?"

The pair strained against the bindings unsuccessful in their attempt to liberate limbs.

Perkins slumped against Oscar. "We be screwed, ole' man."

"Who ye be callin' old?"

Perkins couldn't see the growing scowl covering Oscar's face.

"Ye be right, though. We be screwed."

~ * ~

Gitty tap closed her phone. "Maybe a bit of food and water will get me what I want." She entered the room once used by her father as an office and opened the niche behind a picture sheltering a safe. The dwindling stash of money made her situation precarious.

With her magic, she was able to bend the will of anyone who dared to block her way. Basics such as electricity and water flowed freely. This torment of living as an 'other' constantly reminded her of how much she hated non-magical folk. *So needy.* She grabbed a stack of bills and closed

25

the safe, spun the dial, and shut the painting. Turning, she found Morgan glaring at her, arms crossed over his chest.

"Just when were you going to tell me about that?" He pointed at the wall.

"Never. It has nothing to do with you." She shoved past him.

"Like hell it doesn't. Everything in this house is to be evenly split between us. Father said so."

Gitty stopped at the doorway into the hall and pivoted to face him. "If you are referring to the traitor that exchanged a perfectly good life for a sawed off, gnome wife, he lost any authority over his *things* the moment he walked out the door to join her.

"What is in that safe is mine. If you think you can take it from me... I dare you to try."

It had been a long time since Morgan had seen Gitty so riled. He shook his head.

"I didn't think so. That would require backbone; something you lost ages ago." She executed a sharp turn and left Morgan standing in the office.

"I need to go for a ride." He stomped to his bedroom and changed into his riding habit. Being on his horse had the effect of soothing away his tensions. The way he currently felt, he'd be riding a fortnight before the muscles in his neck relaxed enough to fully turn his head.

Slamming the door with as much might as he could muster, Morgan loped to the stables and saddled his steed, Tristan. He stepped into the saddle and tapped the animal to a cantor, reveling in the wind whipping past. The bite of air against his skin had him urging the beast to a gallop. Realizing he wanted this journey to last more than half an hour, Morgan reined back the horse allowing Tristan to set his own pace. The surrounding terrain was unfamiliar to the night elf. The horse plodded along a narrow path through a tightly populated forest. He was really confused. The trees appeared to be old growth, and if memory served, the previous year forest fires destroyed much of the landscape around his home and the surrounding valleys.

The path meandered through the trees and opened to a large meadow bordered on one side by swift-moving rill. Tristan halted by the brook and dropped his head to drink.

"Good idea." Morgan dismounted and stretched his limbs. The pale green stalks undulating next to the clear water offered a quiet respite. He gazed at the spot picturing a nap with boots off and sunshine caressing his face. As he strolled toward the inviting spot, he caught a blur from the corner of his right eye. Before he could identify said blur, Morgan was flipping through the air, arms and legs floundering in opposite directions. At that point, he realized this was not going to end well–for him. "Uh-h-h." Lying on his back, he struggled to breathe. "What the…?"

A fuzzy face appeared over his; wet, long tongue licking his face then woofing at him. The creature darted away.

Morgan pushed up from the ground. He snatched the reins and leapt into the saddle urging Tristan to a gallop. Pounding hooves broke the peace of the meadow and punctuated the intensity of the chase. Just as Morgan rode up to the side of the little mutt, it would zig-zag away.

Swear words tumbled from his lips. He reined in the horse and jumped from its back to the ground, giving chase on foot. He'd get close to the little dog and blasted creature would apply a burst of speed. Several times, he thought he'd lost the animal. He'd stop, put his hands on his knees, and bend over to catch his breath. A short woof would find the little animal standing before him, ears forward and tail wagging.

"You beggar! You think this is a game, don't you?"

"WOOF!" and off the beast would dart.

Morgan reached his point of no return. Plodding back toward the field with inviting, undulating, tall grass, he hoped his steed would still be grazing in said grass. He was.

So was the irritating, little dog and Tristan was nuzzling the mutt. "Traitor."

The steed snorted and flicked his tail, just missing the end of Morgan's nose. The little dog darted away to a large, two-story, bright red fire hydrant Morgan could not remember seeing previously. Knowing where the small beastie had gone gave him the inclination to amble, not dash, to the—building. He walked the perimeter but was unable to locate an entry. Pounding on the outside proved the covering was metal and, judging by the echoing, the interior appeared to be hollow.

"Miserable mutt. Okay. You win." A panel next to him slid up. He looked around the field to see if he could spot the person trying to trick him. The low burbling of the stream and his horse gorging on the sweet meadow grass were the only changes from five minutes earlier. He inched forward and peered into the opening. The interior of the structure was lined with metal counters holding various panels of blinking lights, numerous levers, and rows of buttons, some red, some green. One button had the form of a paw print.

Curiosity won over common sense, and Morgan fully entered the hydrant. He jerked around when a shushing sound punctuated in his ears. Darting toward the closing entry, he slammed his fists on the wall only succeeding in creating a dissonant racket. He turned and slid down the wall to the floor. "Bugger. I just wish I could go back to 16th century Britain where being a male held more weight."

A disembodied, velvety voice spoke, causing Morgan to start in surprise. "Year?"

He smiled. *Okay, I can play along with the joke.* "Take me to Rockfleet Castle."

"Year?"

This game was grating on Morgan's nerves. "1575, alright?"

"Done."

A high-pitched whine pierced his ear, and his stomach rolled. *Where the bloody hell is that mutt?*

A fuzzy nose peeked around the corner of a metal wall. The ball of fur inched its way toward Morgan, stopping before him, and plopping his hindquarters down. He offered a paw.

"Oh, so we're friends now?" Morgan couldn't help but chuckle. This little guy had provided more entertainment than he'd experienced in a while. He took the proffered paw. "Truce. I'm Morgan. You?"

The mutt woofed. The sultry voice intoned, "Batzy."

"Pleased to meet you, Batzy." The room shuddered causing the unlikely pair to brace against what they could. A sudden bone-jarring drop then silence. Dog and man exchanged looks.

"Guess we've arrived, eh?"

Batzy woofed his agreement. The outside wall silently slid open.

28

A rush of chilled air filled the room. Morgan strained to identify the familiar sound. "Waves?"

The air smelled, and tasted, of salt–sea salt. Belly crawling to the opening, he peeked outside. He turned to look at the dog. "I don't think we're in Oregon, Batzy."

~ * ~

Gitty stopped the truck next to the ivy-covered house. *Have to hire someone to trim back those plants–later.* For the time being, the camouflage would keep her captives hidden until she could get them to complete her mission. She grabbed items she'd purchased at a local drive-through, household items the men would need, as well as raiding Morgan's closet. As she neared the door, the cacophony of snores assaulted her ears. She quietly opened the door then slammed it shut. Carrying the bag with hot food in front of her, Gitty put the aromatic prize on the table.

"Morning, gents. Sleep well?"

The night elf ventured into the kitchen and turned on the faucet. Screeching, followed by a ghastly rumble, announced the arrival of water in pipes unused to the liquid for many a year. The initial color was nearly black, lightening to a brown and, finally, running clear. She checked cupboards for anything to use as cups or glasses and found nothing. Having figured there would be a need for a few things, Gitty put together a small care package at home for the unusual visitors.

She went to her pickup and unloaded a couple boxes from the back, carrying them inside the house. In the kitchen, she set up dishes, drinking vessels, and utensils. There were a couple pots, but she doubted these two would have any knowledge of cooking.

Strolling to the bathroom, she opened the sink faucet, leaned down and turned on the water beneath the toilet, finally, turning on the shower. Again, the screeching and burbling of unused pipes. She opened a closet just off the kitchen to find an old, but useable, broom.

"Good. They can start by cleaning this pigsty."

Finally, with two pair of wide eyes noting her actions, she put sleeping bags on the table and turned to face the men.

"Morning. I'm guessing by now you have figured out I've brought food." She waved a hand over the bag to send the aroma wafting their direction. Her action was met with groaning and muffled swearing.

"I will untie you so you can eat and use the facilities. If you need directions on how to use the toilet, just ask. I do need to warn you, I'm deadly with a dirk, so any untoward movement may end in your demise." She pulled the blade from a wrist holster and twirled it before stepping over to free the men.

"Bloody hell. I canna feel me hands. Or me damn legs." Oscar continued his rampage under his breath.

"You spoke to food?" Perkins was rubbing his hands and wiggling his fingers. "Dinna smell like anythin' I know."

Gitty dropped the bag on the floor. "It's called a hamburger and French fries. The potatoes have been cut in thin slices and fried. The burger is just a big sandwich. There are two burgers for each of you." She investigated the bedroom portion of the house. The old cot was threadbare and stability wasn't a guarantee. She sighed. If she were expecting cooperation from these two, she would have to cloth them somehow, making certain they had sufficient bedding and food, until the task was accomplished.

She returned to the pair. Standing in front of them, she pulled out her phone and lined up Perkins in the camera sight. She snapped a shot of his face then did the same to Oscar.

"When you've finished eating, there are bathing items in the bathroom. Clean up: hair, body, as much of everything else as you can." Gitty looked at their outfits and wrinkled her nose. "You need to find a way to wash your clothes. They smell. In the meantime, I've brought temporary clothing for you to wear until you can clean your garments."

The pair looked at their attire, wrinkled and sporting crumbs and spots of unknown origins.

Oscar spoke. "Yours would be, too, if you'd been, whatever it is we've been, and wanderin' in a new place. We were freshly washed before all of this …" he waved his hand, making certain he didn't drop a single crumb from the food to the floor, "happened. We're not rabble from the far north. We're Highlanders and proud of it. Just so you don't go thinkin' yerself better than we, I am Laird of my clan. Perkins, there, is just a Baron; but all the same, we're not common."

Gitty stifled the urge to laugh. *Guess you can take everything from a man but his pride.*

"What was that you dun with the black box?" Oscar's suspicion of everything might prove a deterrent in the future endeavor.

She pulled up pictures of the two. "Took your picture. Just in case you decide to cross me, I'll have something to give the Sheriff." She turned the face of the instrument to him. "There's your face, in all its unshaven glory."

Color drained from the blustery one's face. "Tis bad magic." He squinted at the phone. "That not be me. That fellow is wicked ugly and foul looking."

Perkins peeked over his shoulder. "Aye, Oscar. That be your ugly face. We been tryin' to tell you for years, but you dinna listen."

Gitty flipped the screen to the shot of Perkins. He tilted his head from side to side. "Not a bad lookin' sort. Face the ladies love." He winked at Gitty.

She scowled his direction. Stepping outside the small home, she pulled deeply of the air. The house bore the stench of years of neglect. *Best check our other properties. If I need to provide income, being a landlord can't be that difficult.* The two inside needed something to inspire their allegiance. Maybe the promise of a return to home? She couldn't provide it, but they didn't need that information. She walked the property line as indicated by a very dubious fence of unknown age. The land was populated by wildflowers and trees someone had planted in the past. It wasn't unattractive but would require some work to be presentable for renting. Gitty sighed.

"Best get back inside and see what's happening." She trod to the back door and was struck by the silence. Peeking in, she noted one of the travelers with a pair of Morgan's jeans and a puzzled look on his face. "What seems to be the issue?"

"I know what to do with the button, but the metal strip below puzzles me. Leaves me man parts in the breeze." Perkins looked at the zipper then up to Gitty, his eyebrows raised in question.

"See the little piece hanging down at the bottom?"

Perkins nodded.

"Pull upward toward the button." Gitty crossed her arms. "When you need to use the facilities, you just unzip it, do your business, and zip it up."

Oscar rounded the doorway, a thunderous look covering his face. "What the hell is this bloody thing?"

Gitty looked at Perkins who stepped over and ran Oscar through a quick tutorial of zipping up his trousers. The legs were quite long on both men. Morgan, like Gitty, was well over six feet tall. Neither Perkins nor Oscar were much taller than five foot ten. Both men looked at their pant legs then Gitty.

"May I suggest rolling the material?" She motioned to move toward them and stooped, turning up the excess material. "This should suffice until your clothing has been cleaned. Now, I have a task requiring two gentlemen not known to the locals."

Oscar took a defensive stance. "That would be?" Perkins had moved behind the older gent.

"I am Lord of all the land around here. Recently, I've heard tell there is a rabble-rouser who has moved into a building beyond the golden meadow. She is riling up the neighbors and causing a great deal of trouble on my estate. I need someone to capture her and bring her to me so I may deal with her on my own terms."

"And what be the reason we would dabble in another Laird's problems?" Oscar asked.

"There is a reward of 5,000 Sterling pounds for her capture and delivery to me."

Perkins pushed Oscar, who glowered at his partner, and whispered, "Five thousand!"

"I believe with her capture, there will be a way to send you back to your own time." That brought a swift light to the eyes of the visitors.

Oscar turned to Perkins. They both bobbed their heads in unison. "We'll do it. I'm guessin' you'll tell us where this problem is located and how we might approach her."

"I'll give you full details tomorrow." Gitty allowed a corner of her mouth to turn up.

"Good. Can you explain how we're supposed to put on these–things?" The man held up a T-shirt.

"Same as a night shirt."

Both men wiggled into the clothing. Perkins looked at the logo on the front of his shirt and frowned. "Why are there markings on this?"

Gitty allowed a sigh to escape. "It is what the people of this time do. Like wearing your family crest. Okay, gents, we're going for a ride in my pickup truck."

The men swapped startled looks. "You mean the horseless wagon?" Oscar's rough voice was quiet and subdued.

Gitty smiled. "Yes. I think it's time to get some dinner and give you a quick tour of my lands." She herded the two out to the truck and hustled them inside, strapping the seatbelts around them.

This is going to be interesting. "If you gentlemen know how to pray, I'd start now."

She turned over the engine and put the truck in reverse. Once she was able to enter the highway, she shifted to drive and hit the gas. The screams from the cab could be heard all over the valley.

Chapter Eight

The flurry of wings inside the Library stirred up a small tornado of dust. Gwynn stepped from her room to three angry faces at her eye level. "What is the problem, wee ones?"

"Her." The answer was given in unison.

Gwynn decided to feign innocence. "She, who?"

"That time traveling bi—"

Gwynn held up a hand to stem the vile flow of insults she thought were about to be hurled. "What has *she* done now?"

The flood of answers filled the air, wings batting as fast as the words fell from the mouths.

"And she is seated in the library, at a table, as if she expects to be waited upon." Chrissy rolled her eyes and winged away. Ailidh and Kayne took her lead and left the doorway to allow the sorceress to move into the kitchen.

"Hmm. Doesn't look as if any preparations have been made for the morning meal." Gwynn strolled into the main portion of the building and, just as the wee ones had spoken, the unexpected visitor was sitting with her hands clasped in her lap, gazing out the window.

She walked to the table and looked at Maurina. "Morning."

Maurina dipped her head in acknowledgement. "And to you. Can you let me know when the morning meal will be served? I find myself quite hungry this morning."

"Have you coin to pay for your meal?" Gwynn asked.

"Of course, I don't. You know that." Color blossomed in Maurina's cheeks and down the back of her neck.

"Well, then. No money, no service. You'll need to fix the food for

34

yourself if you won't be paying. That is the way this century's women do it. I can show you where everything is located in the kitchen and show you how to clean your dishes when you are finished."

The visitor exploded from the chair, knocking it to the ground. "I'm not a cook, nor a maid, nor any other type of house servant. I am a *Lady*. And as such, it is my expectation things will be done for me at my desire." She stomped from the small table and out the back door slamming it so hard Gwynn was afraid the glass would break.

"I believe we have a communication gap." She sighed as she walked to the kitchen. She retrieved the bread from a cupboard and put two pieces in the toaster. Stepping to the stove, she set the kettle to heating for tea. Opening the refrigerator, she pulled out the butter and marmalade. For some unknown reason, this morning she was craving marmalade. The click of the door caught her attention, and she turned to see the petulant time traveler standing against the closed door.

"I, uh, I apologize."

Must be killing her to say that or she really is hungrier than she is mad.

Gwyn moved to the counter in time to catch the toasted bread as it popped from the machine. She spread butter and marmalade on the two slices and placed them on small plates. In the makeshift area she used for her meals, she put the plates on the table. The kettle whistled and tea was concocted. The pair sat down.

"If there were any way I could return you to your home, I would. Since that isn't about to happen, I think you need to accept your situation. You are welcome to stay here until other arrangements can be made that will suit you. In the meantime, I would ask you to contribute what you can to the running of this place. Make an effort." She moved to the toaster and put two more pieces of bread into the machine. When they were done, she prepared them and brought them to the table.

There was silence as the pair of women ate the light meal.

"I am so far from all I know that I canna make sense of it. But you have been kind and shared with me what you have. If you'll show me, I'll try to do my part."

"Thank you." Gwynn picked up the dishes. She rinsed them off and set them in the dishwasher. Going through the ritual of putting in soap and starting the machine, she turned to see Maurina with mouth open and eyes wide.

"What is that?"

"I guess you could say it is a mechanical scullery maid. It washes and dries the dishes. It doesn't put them away but considering how much work it saves me, I have no problem stacking clean, dry dishes back into the cupboard."

Gwynn moved to the back door and indicated Maurina should follow. The pair walked around the building to the garden on the side. Maurina was handed a hoe and asked to get rid of the weeds in the rows. She glared at Gwynn but nodded. Going back inside, Gwynn stopped midway. A sensation of wind through a tunnel turned her to look at the huge oak tree. She was under the impression this was Chrissy's home, but the odd feeling persisted. She moved away. Turning around, she caught Maurina staring at her hands and brushing dirt from them.

This is going to be a very difficult day. She entered the kitchen and, once again, was face to faces with the Fae.

"Are you going to make her go away?" Ailidh fisted tiny hands on her hips. She bobbed up and down slightly making Gwynn feel just the slightest seasick.

"Let's sit and talk. Trying to watch you while you wing to keep at my level makes me feel nauseous." She pulled out the chair at her kitchen eating spot. Three Fae landed nearby and stood impatiently tapping their toes and exhibiting fearsome expressions.

"I get you aren't happy with the unexpected visitor, but I can't just send her back. First, I have no idea where she came from, and second, that type of spell would put me in bed for a week. It takes a long time to create and a long time to recover. If you have a better suggestion, I'm up for it."

Kayne looked at the sorceress. "You aren't at all like any of the wizards we've seen before. None of them would hesitate to cast a spell on someone. Why do you?"

Gwynn took a moment. "You all have lived a very long time, right?"

There was a murmur of agreement.

36

"Then you are aware every action has a reaction."

"Uh, what?" Chrissy hitched a hip.

"If I cast a spell to send her back, there would be consequences to what I have done; at the other end, she might land in the middle of a war and be killed before her time. All her children, grandchildren, and so forth wouldn't be born. Maybe she would land *before* she was born. The consequences are too great to contemplate just *'poof'* sending her away."

"Then what are we to do? We like being seen by you. It's nice to move around with you knowing we're here and having you watch out for us. She just barrels through and has nearly knocked Kayne off a shelf, slammed a book so close to Ailidh her skirt blew off, and she is constantly in the cupboards and refrigerator in the kitchen looking for food. You have to do something!" The Fae all nodded their heads.

Gwynn sympathized with her small friends. This female from another dimension was becoming a royal pain. "Let me do some research. I have some books handed down through my family which might have an alternative. In a day or two, something might pop up." She stood and waited for the wee ones to decide where they would move.

"We're going to sit here and talk a bit." Chrissy said.

"Okay. I'll be in the back of the library researching."

Once Gwynn left the room, the Fae started planning.

"I sense the Sorceress is as kind as the Librarian was. I doubt she'll willingly banish the Other." Kayne folded his arms across his chest.

Ailidh nodded in agreement. "If she were inclined to do it, she would have done so by now. That female is a pain. Almost as bad as the Night Elf."

"She's definitely as self-centered and obnoxious," Chrissy said. "I think we need to make the move to push her into the vortex."

"I agree." Ailidh said.

Kayne asked, "Why didn't you tell the Sorceress about the vortex? It would have taken care of the problem, and she wouldn't have to worry."

Chrissy shrugged her shoulders. "She didn't ask."

"Let's see if we can make this monstrous pain in our home disappear." Ailidh winged to the door. "Open."

The portal swung open allowing the three Fae to exit. They drifted around the back of the house to the garden area, not seeing the time traveler. A quick reconnaissance of the yard proved her to be looking down the road in front of the house.

"If I take off down the road, she won't see me, and I can go... where?" Maurina yanked a leaf from the nearest bush and threw it to the ground. "I hate not having the ability to make a choice. I am a *Lady*, not a scullery maid, or cook, or gardener. I don't want to live in this horrible time. I *like* having people wait on me. I deserve it. I'm from nobility, after all." She stomped a foot then meandered back to the pumpkin patch. Kicking at the dirt rows, she continued muttering and stabbing in the air with a finger, feebly pulling the hoe across weeds and melons alike.

Chrissy motioned the others over to her location. "Look." She pointed to the ground. "There is a good-sized rope on the ground. If we pool our energy and use a bit of magic, we can trip her into the tunnel. It won't actually be our fault if she gets sucked into the spinning vortex, will it?"

Kayne smirked. "We can move the rope to the front of the maelstrom. We'll go back, appear in front of her, and scare her into backing up, then, what was it the Sorceress said? Oh, yeah, 'poof', disappear while we pull the rope tight. She'll trip backwards and," he snapped his fingers, "be gone and out of our lives."

Ailidh and Chrissy looked at each other and back at Kayne. The three agreed the plan was a good one. They flew to the rope and, in unison, moved it to the location they desired.

Maurina continued to grumble and pout, pushing the dirt back and forth on the ground. Something buzzed around her face and she swiped a hand to chase the bug away. The animal continued to pester her. She looked up to glare at the insect, screaming when she spotted three tiny beings with wings directly in front of her eyes. "What are you? Sweet Jesus!" Backing away, she tripped on a pumpkin, smashing it, and getting seeds and pulp all over her clothing. Springing up from the ground, she threw down the hoe, trying to push away from the beings coming at her. She'd passed the back edge of the house and the shade from the large oak tree was creating a chill over her pumpkin-spattered clothing. Wind grabbed at her sweater and tossed her hair around her face. She clawed at

38

the unruly mess.

The three-winged creatures disappeared. Maurina took one more step back and tripped over an object, falling into an abyss. The vortex closed. Wind died down and the Fae flew back into the house.

Once inside, they congratulated each other on a job well done.

Gwynn entered the kitchen and put the kettle on the stove to heat up. "What has the three of you so happy?"

"The unwelcome guest is gone." Chrissy flew toward the stove and gathered the small cups for the Fae.

"What?" The kettle whistled and Gwynn made a pot of tea for the party of four. She took the teapot, sugar, and milk to the table. Once she made a cup for herself, she helped the others prepare their tea. "Now what is this all about?"

Kayne took a sip from the cup he'd just been blowing air over to cool the liquid. "We sent the time travel lady away." He slurped his tea.

Gwynn smiled. "Of course."

Ailidh and Chrissy exchanged looks. Chrissy spoke up. "Yes, we did. We sent her into the vortex. She's gone back to wherever it is she came from–or not."

Gwynn's cup clattered to the table. "How? Where? Why didn't you tell me?"

"You didn't ask."

Gwynn closed her eyes and counted to ten. "Do you suppose you could show me where this vortex is?"

The three Fae spread their wings and flew to the back door. Gwynn accommodated them and opened the door following the trio to a spot in front of the ancient oak. "This is it?"

Chrissy pointed directly at the tree. "If you focus on the trunk, you'll see the opening waiver."

Gwynn looked at the spot the Nymph was pointing and, sure enough, the air waivered slightly, dipping inward. "We need to find a way to close it or block it. I don't particularly want visitors from who-knows-what century popping into my house."

Ailidh and Kayne glanced at each other and lowered their heads. Ailidh spoke. "We, the three of us, usually conjure a spell to block the opening for about a month. It's a ritual we do at the full moon. We kind of got caught up in you being here, and the Lending Library being open again. We forgot."

"Hmm. I think the four of us need to conjure a spell right now to close this for now. After a week or so, we'll close it for good. We don't need any other *lost* souls wandering into our time, do we. What do you think?"

Three little, winged bodies bobbed up and down. Gwynn gathered around her and spoke the words very slowly so they would remember them. On the count of three, the foursome concentrated on the spot and murmured the words in unison. Three rounds of the chanting and the soft whisper of wind ceased.

"That should do it for now." Gwynn breathed easier. "What say we go inside and finish our tea?"

They promenaded back to the house and closed the door to finish afternoon tea.

Chapter Nine

Several days passed where the 18th century travelers only saw the white-haired Laird at mealtimes. She would hand Perkins a list of chores she wanted accomplished. If they dared to complain, she threatened to call the Sheriff. On the fourth day, she brought a bucket of chicken emitting spicy, warm smells, mashed potatoes in quantities fit for Henry VIII, and enough gravy to cover a mountain. She placed the feast on the table.

Oscar examined the containers. "What be this?"

"What does it smell like?" Gitty opened the lids.

"Smells like food." He stepped closer and peered into the bucket. "Fowl if I be not mistaken. And this?" He pointed to the other boxes.

Gitty was quickly losing what little patience she had. "Have you cleaned your platter?"

"Aye. You threatened us if we didn't." He muttered lowly, "As if we were wee lads."

She directed a blistering glare his direction. "Good." Going to the kitchen cupboard, she retrieved a plate and silverware from a drawer. Back at the table, a large spoon helped to place a considerable amount of potatoes on the plate and helped to cover them with gravy. She picked up a couple pieces of chicken and sat down to eat. "Serve yourselves; eat, don't eat. I don't care. Just thought I'd provide a bit of a treat for all your hard work."

Perkins didn't have to be invited twice. He followed Gitty's example and was soon digging into the mashed potatoes smothered in gravy and devouring the chicken. Oscar opted to join the pair.

When all had been sated, Gitty crossed arms over her chest and

41

cleared her throat. "Gentlemen. It is time to discuss the task I wish you to complete for me."

The men exchanged nervous glances, Oscar finally speaking. "Ah, the lass with a price on her head."

She pushed back on the chair, rocking on two legs. "Yes. That's the one."

Oscar scowled. "Why canna you fetch her without us?"

"In your time, would *you* have searched out a neighbor telling lies about you?" She lifted a brow.

He bristled. "I have lads to do that for me."

"Exactly. Driving the mechanical beastie is a bit different than riding a steed or handling a team of horses and a wagon. To keep from crashing, your attention needs to be on the roadway. As Laird, I need lieutenants to assist me in the more," she pursed her lips and frowned slightly, "distasteful duties I'm required to carry out. You will be those lieutenants this time. The act of assisting me will win you the bounty set upon her head, and I'll have the opportunity to clear up my business with this tenant."

Oscar's eyebrows met in the middle of his forehead. He was not inclined to trust females in general and this one in particular. "How are we to know who she is, and the means to bring her to you?"

"As I said, I will drive you to the tenant's business. That will be our task for the day."

Perkins groaned. "Not that. Turns me bowels quite inside out."

"Get over it. This tenant is female and small."

Perkins looked to Oscar. "Makes it a bit easier, eh?"

Oscar grunted.

"Then let's go. The sooner you accomplish this task; the closer you'll be to home."

The group trudged to the truck, Perkins slowing his pace with each step forward.

"What is your problem?" Gitty stood holding open the driver's door.

"Be there no other way?" Perkins face had taken on a tinge of green.

"No. Get in."

Oscar grabbed his arm and shoved him into the seat. "Blighter."

The vehicle rumbled down the highway at sixty miles an hour, both traveler's eyes wide, hands white from clutching the upholstery. Gitty observed the longer Perkins sat in the cab of the truck, the more his face developed a puce hue. When the truck slowed and turned onto the driveway, he released an audible sigh. She parked in front of the building.

"What in bloody blue blazes are you doin'?" Oscar asked. "We've lost the element of surprise. Do you not have any battle sense at all?"

Gitty clenched the steering wheel. "The tenant calls this place a library, open to all. Would you hesitate to tie your horse up front of a public house?"

He gave her a beady stare. "And how are we to get this lass to come with us?" He cocked his head to the side.

Gitty rolled her eyes. "Ask. If that doesn't work, well, use your imagination."

The pair exited the truck, Perkins pulling deeply of the fresh air. "I'll be bloody glad when we get back home. Canna say I be too fond of livin' in this time."

"For once, I agree."

They tested the door and swung it open. Inside, the building fragrances tickled their noses; some familiar, some new.

"I smell tea." Perkins sniffed.

Oscar shook his head. "Always thinkin' with your stomach." He glanced about and when he couldn't locate a person, he spoke. "Hello?" They'd reached the area of the kitchen. A note was taped on a wall facing the open library.

Perkins looked at Oscar. "Do you read?"

"Of course."

"What does it say?"

The note read, "Out in the garden at the side of the house if you need help. G."

Oscar squinted at the scratchings on the paper. "Outside. Let's go."

They exited through the front door and met Gitty sitting at one of

43

the tables set up on the porch. "Why are you here–alone?"

Perkins popped up. "Oscar read a sign inside which says she is outside. So, we came outside."

She stared at the two before going into the library. Her recollection of the last time she was here still rested on the top of her memory. The drain of magic from her body had left her exhausted and weak for several days. She shivered with the thought. A note on the wall caught her attention. She read it and groaned. Maybe using these two dolts wasn't such a good idea. She returned to the porch where the pair of travelers were sitting.

"Will we be going now?" Oscar asked.

"No."

"Why not?"

"The sign says she is outside in the garden… at the side of the house. Go there. Should be much easier to convince her to come along with you. There are no neighbors for a mile or so. If she kicks up a fuss, no one will hear."

The men rose from their seats and went down the porch stairs. Oscar guided Perkins to the right. A small fence enclosed the area of the garden, so they went around the fence. When they reached the end, a small person was using a hoe to attack weeds.

Perkins whispered to Oscar. "We dinna have a weapon. What if she attacks us?"

"We're bigger, and there be two of us. I think we kin handle the lass."

They were in the midst of whispering when the lass turned around. "Hello. Can I help you?"

"Yes. We'd like you to accompany us." Perkins smiled.

Gwynn was taken back. "Why would I do that?"

"We been asked to bring you to the Laird. She said there would be no fuss if we asked." Perkins smile was fading.

"She who?" Gwynn had an idea but wondered if this pair knew.

Perkins turned to Oscar. "Did she tell you her name?"

"No. Just said she was Laird of this valley. That be all I needed to know."

Gwynn suspected the identity of the perpetrator of this request. Unbeknownst to the two men, Ailidh was quietly observing over Gwynn's right shoulder. She spoke up. "The night elf is out front on the porch. What are we going to do?"

"Watch."

The pair stopped. Oscar speaking. "Watch, what?"

Gwynn dropped the hoe and held her arms in front of her. "Freeze."

The travelers were rooted to the spots where they'd stopped.

Gwynn strode to them. "The Laird, as she calls herself, is a Night Elf. I'll bet she didn't tell you that, did she? Whatever she has offered you, she has no intention of paying or giving. I'll bet she didn't let you know I'm a Sorceress, did she?"

Both men's eyes were opening wider and wider. Fear exuded from their bodies.

"Now. I'm not sure where you landed, but a comrade of yours ended up in my garden damaging my pumpkins. Might as well make it a win for all." She pushed each man on top of a ripe pumpkin watching as the melon burst seeds and grist over the visitors. She lifted them with a muttered spell. "Free."

"Look, lass. We dinna know any of that stuff you said about the Laird. She offered us 5,000 Sterling to bring you to her. Told us it would help us get back home." As Perkins nattered away, he and Oscar were backing up toward the old oak tree.

Gwynn watched as they closed the distance to the vortex opening. When they were at the threshold, she stopped her forward motion. "I'm not sure why you ended up here, but you don't belong in this century. Go home." She raised on her toes and yelled. "GO!"

The men leaned back, wind-milling their arms. As the wind sucked them into the opening, Gwynn heard the one called Perkins yell, "We're goin' home!"

She smiled, "Sorry, mate. No guarantees." She had another problem planted on her front porch, a Night Elf. What did this dirge want with her? Only one way to find out. Gwynn walked to the front porch and sat next to a startled Elf.

"What is it that you want from me, Elf?"

Gitty rose from her chair. "Uh, I, uh, I really need to get home."

Gwynn let the corners of her mouth curl in a smile. "Not so fast. Freeze." The Elf was locked standing in a defensive pose. "What is it you want from me that you would endanger the lives of two unwilling travelers?"

The Night Elf's eyes were wide with surprise–at first. Now, they took on a steely glare.

"I can only surmise your intentions. You think I could be intimidated into conjuring your magic back. Even in the Wizarding community, we heard about the Night Elves who were stripped of their abilities AND the consequences of anyone who was unwise enough to help them steal it back. I think it best if you leave this property and never return. I will be informing the high council of your actions. Not going to look very good on a resume."

She walked up to the tall intruder. "Free."

Gitty's body loosened. "You've not heard the last of this."

"For your own sanity and safety, I would suggest you give this course of action a rest." Gwynn watched as the visitor stomped to her vehicle and roared out the driveway. "I need a glass of wine, but I'll get ice water instead."

Chapter Ten

Lending Library, All Hallows' Eve

The front porch sported smiling pumpkins and flickering electric candles. Cornstalks were stacked together in a teepee fashion and colored lights twinkled in the windows and around the doorsill. A banner announcing, "Happy Halloween all Ghosties and Goblins", hung on the front of the porch. Inside the library, the sound of laughing children wafted out the door.

Ailidh and Kayne looked in the windows.

"Why do they play all those games?" Ailidh turned to her partner.

"I don't know. Maybe they want to scare away bad spirits. Laughter is the best way, don't you know?" He shrugged his shoulders.

"Maybe so. I'm glad Gwynn is here. I feel safe knowing she can handle the Night Elves, and she can see us. It's so good to have our valley back."

Kayne smiled as he put his arm around his lifemate. "So it is. Happy Halloween, Ailidh."

Thirteen Magic Pumpkin Seeds
Genie Gabriel

Chapter One

"You're not my dad!" the words of his eight-year-old niece echoed in Finn Dagdaman's mind as he walked behind Chloe, her mother, and her mischievous little white dog along the narrow country lane toward the castle next door.

Overhead, the naked branches of oak trees rattled in the stiff breeze, promising a chilly Halloween day and perhaps spooky times this evening. To Finn, the trees seemed to watch him. Waiting for him to trip over their gnarly roots or slip on the leaves that had been shed onto the spongy ground beneath his feet. Providing proof he could never be as good as his brother or live up to Ethan's example. Unless he agreed to the military's proposal.

Then maybe even his niece would admire him. In the time he had been staying with them since his brother left for his current military assignment, Chloe had not been impressed with the human Uncle Finn.

But he didn't have to decide until tonight–at the stroke of midnight on Halloween.

As they approached the driveway of Aunt Maddie's castle, the driver of an old wooden wagon pulled by what seemed to be a sway-backed, bony horse came to "life."

"Climb aboard, my pretties," a robotic voice invited. "If you dare. Bwahahaha!"

As soon as they boarded the wagon and sat down, seat belts in the form of snakes slithered over their laps. The old nag whinnied and clattered up the driveway. The wagon slid onto the drawbridge just as it started to raise and made it across in record time.

At the heavy wooden door of the castle, the wagon halted, and the snake seat belts retracted.

"Welcome to Aunt Maddie's Castle," the driver's robotic voice intoned. Then he and the horse went back to "sleep."

Madelaine Ainsworth herself swung open the massive wooden door, dressed as the artist she was in a paint-spattered shirt and a beret perched at a rakish angle on her head rather than one of her larger, more audacious hats.

"I thought Uncle Horace was going to have a hologram of a ghost open the door." The wings on Chloe's fairy-witch costume seemed to sag with disappointment.

"He was waiting for you to help him finish it," Maddie said. "Go on down to his workshop. He'll be expecting you."

"I get to go to Uncle Horace's workshop? Squeezy peaches!" With her wings once more perky, Chloe and her little dog trotted toward the basement stairs.

Maddie greeted Chloe's mom with a hug and winked at Finn over her shoulder.

"Thank you for making this night special for Chloe," Adalie said. "She's really missing her dad and has been giving her uncle Finn a pretty hard time."

"Not having a beloved parent around can be devastating for a child," Maddie said. "My niece and nephew were about Chloe's age when they came to stay with us. That's why we built this castle. To bring some magic back into their lives. Halloween was one of our favorite times. Everyone else is in the kitchen. Come and say hello."

I don't even have a costume. Finn forced himself to smile in spite of feeling like a misfit as he greeted the costumed characters who made up Aunt Maddie's household. Would agreeing to the military's proposal to become fully bionic make him feel more comfortable? An old television show had lauded the abilities of a bionic man, but the robotics that rebuilt his right side and saved his six-year-old life after a vehicle accident only made his growing body seem more klutzy. He fumbled physically and socially all through his adolescence and teen years, and well into his twenties.

Maddie's nephew, Ryan, wore chef's whites, complete with a tall

2

toque blanche on his head. He handed Finn a sampler plate loaded with breakfast food. "Pumpkin spice pancakes and waffles with warm caramel syrup, plus pumpkin Dutch baby with caramelized apples. There's also pumpkin spice oatmeal in the slow cooker and pumpkin spice granola to sprinkle on top or eat plain. Coming up later today will be pretzels, cookies with cinnamon cream cheese frosting, pudding shots, cheesecake bites and much more. All pumpkin spice or apple, of course."

Finn carefully took the plate with his left hand rather than risk gripping too hard with the bionic fingers of his right hand and shattering the plate.

"Don't forget your pumpkin spice latte or cider." Dressed as bird watchers as they had been during their misadventure when they met, Maddie's niece, Rissa, and her military husband ran the latte machine this morning.

Seeing Ian's buzzed haircut reminded Finn of the decision he had avoided until today and he gripped the cup too hard, crushing it and spilling hot liquid down his arm.

"Omigosh!" Rissa pulled Finn toward the kitchen sink and turned on the faucet. "Put your hand under cold water so it doesn't burn."

She turned his hand over and looked at him strangely. "No cuts and your hand isn't even red."

"Been that way since I was a kid. Guess my body had to develop an immunity to my clutziness." Finn set the plate of food on the counter to tear off a paper towel and dry his hand. Ian didn't say anything but watched him closely as he handed Finn another latte. "Thanks."

Finn picked up his plate of food–carefully–and sat at the far end of the table, wishing he could disappear into the faux gray stone wall.

"Today is open house for everyone in the neighborhood," Maddie said. "We'll have trick-or-treaters all day. Some will stay to party. Others will gather their candy and move on. The person who gets the orange straw in their latte will pull the first shift with the ghost hologram at the door to hand out candy while everyone else gets to eat and party."

Seeing his chance to escape the party crowd, Finn said, "I'm not much for parties. So I'll volunteer to pull the first shift to hand out candy."

"Any trick-or-treaters who come to the door will expect a

performance, even if they aren't staying for the party," Ryan said.

"What kind of a performance?" Finn wondered if he had made a mistake with his offer. He could follow up his cup crushing by taking selfies with the trick-or-treaters using the camera in his robotic eye or leaping onto the roof with the help of his bionic leg. But that would be breaking his personal vow not to use his bionic prowess like a party gimmick in hopes others would like him.

"Well, with the hologram being a ghost, you'd be expected to wear a sheet and make eerie sounds. Singing in three-part harmony is optional."

"That might be something Chloe would enjoy," her mom suggested. "Since she refused to go trick-or-treating without her dad."

And I'm not her dad, as Chloe often reminds me, Finn thought. *Even with bionic vocal cords I can't much stay in key, unlike my brother who was a soloist with the high school choir.* "I'm not much of a singer."

"Not to worry," Aunt Maddie said. "Horace will pipe music through the castle audio system and you can lip sync. We'll even come up with a costume for you."

Later that day Finn found himself wearing a sheet and stationed near the massive wooden door of the castle with a not-so-enthusiastic Chloe, who looked down the hallway toward the kitchen and the laughter of the party about every thirty seconds. "When can we go back to the party with everyone else?"

"Half an hour until the next shift comes on." Finn injected cheerfulness into his voice. "Here comes another little witch."

"And a cat. Where's my dog? Batzy loves to chase cats."

As Chloe turned to look for her little white dog, Batzy spotted the orange cat and zoomed out the door after her, catching a black and orange table cloth over his head as he clipped a small table set in the hallway with a bowl of candy corn on top of it.

Finn grabbed for the bowl, juggling it from one hand to another as packets of candy corn bounced up and down.

"Batzy! Come back!" Chloe ran after her little dog and Finn awkwardly chased after them both, still clutching the bowl of candy, his sheet costume flapping as he ran.

4

Chapter Two

From outside, the three-story Victorian house looked like any other haunted house. Shutters hung askew by one hinge, framing several broken windows where lights flickered off and on.

Tall, gaunt trees surrounded the house, their bare branches scraping against the second story windows as if trying to get inside. Within the rickety picket fence, a black iron cauldron the size of a small car bubbled with a green liquid, steam rising into the darkening clouds.

While the storm built and wolves howled outside, the inside of the Victorian house glowed with warmth from a fire burning in the fireplace and the soft flicker of candles.

"Mom, have you seen Sherbet?" A red-haired little witch with a patch of freckles across her nose peered under the table, looking for her cat.

"She knows to stay close by. Use the magic mirror to scan the neighborhood."

"We don't have a magic mirror, Mom. A computer monitor relays video from a drone."

"I liked the Magic Mirror better," Asteria muttered.

As Shabina Louise scanned the area via the computer monitor, she was horrified to see Sherbet being chased through their pumpkin patch by an orange and black...something. "Omigosh!"

Asteria came up behind her daughter. "Oh, dear. What is that?"

As they watched, the little cat and whatever was chasing her serpentined among the pumpkins.

"They're in the enchanted pumpkin patch," Shabina Louise whispered. "Is that woman another witch? Maybe she'll help Sherbet!"

5

But as the little cat ran between the woman's legs, her arms cartwheeled as she tried to keep her balance...teetering...teetering...then the chaser dashed on the scene and the woman went down. Ker-splat! Fanny first onto a pumpkin.

The cloth slid off the chaser, revealing a little white dog, who paused long enough to taste the splattered pumpkin. He chewed for a moment, scrunched up his face and licked his lips. Then Sherbet hissed at a passing trick-or-treater and the little dog was off again, chasing the cat.

"Can't you turn him into a statue or something so he doesn't chase Sherbet?"

"A spell is underway and the darn computer in charge of tracking has a glitch so it can't be interrupted. I'm sure Sherbet will run fast and come home. After all, she is a witch's cat and knows a few things."

"Pleeeease. We have to do something."

Asteria frowned. Her daughter had grown too reliant on technology and others to fix her problems. Time for her to realize she was quite capable of casting a spell. "You'll have to do this yourself. Why don't you give Sherbet rocket shoes so she can run faster? And don't forget to gather thirteen pumpkin seeds from the thirteenth pumpkin in the thirteenth row. I need them for a spell to turn our house back to normal or we'll be spending all year doing repairs."

"Right." Shabina Louise nodded uncertainly. *Save Sherbet first, then gather the pumpkin seeds.* "Rockets on shoes, that's what I choose. To bring Sherbet home, no more to roam."

But Sherbet wasn't prepared for the sudden surge in speed and tumbled ears over tail, landing with a ker-thump right in front of Batzy.

Chapter Three

Maurina sat in pumpkin gunk, every belief she ever had turned upside-down, shaken, and covered with pumpkin innards. If she ever had the chance to apologize to her ex-fiancé, she would fall down on her knees and beg his forgiveness for calling him a "freak of nature." He was simply a shapeshifter, but the creatures she had met since being catapulted from the 1700s to wherever she had landed today were so many times more unusual.

When she spotted the castle after this last transport, she thought perhaps she was at least near someone who would give her a carriage ride back to her own suite of rooms so her servants could fill her copper bathtub with steaming water and she could forget all of this happened. Even the little orange kitten twining among the pumpkins gave Maurina hope her world was back to normal.

Then the door of the castle flew open and out raced a black and orange ghost-like thing, followed by a little witch with fairy wings and a man covered with a flapping sheet carrying a bowl of...something.

Leery of what other creatures might be lurking in the castle, Maurina sought a hiding place to gather her wits and try to make sense of yet another strange world.

She looked around and saw a barn in the distance. Certainly not up to her usual standards, but perhaps shelter for a short time.

Maurina cautiously pushed open the door of the barn. The squeal of rusty hinges shivered up her spine. She stepped inside and waited a few moments for her eyes to adjust to the dusty twilight darkness. As the smell of old hay settled around her, she looked for a hiding place.

She didn't care to climb into the loft where spiders were sure to be lurking, but perhaps one of the stalls contained clean hay. Maurina stepped forward and emitted a shivery screech. Spider web! She hated spiders and swatted at the sticky stuff that clung to her face and hair. Instead of getting rid of the offending web, it seemed to grab her more tenaciously, wrapping around her entire head.

Lifting a corner of her skirt, Maurina wiped at her face and hair. The substance seemed thick as honey. Not like any spider web she had encountered in the few unfortunate times she had assignations in shadowy places. This barn was obviously not suitable for a hiding place.

Maurina backed away, hoping to find a source of water to clean herself. A task for which she should have only had to ring a bell. But that was in a previous life. Now it seemed she had no life at all–only misadventures. She shook her head, trying to think clearly. She felt funny. Twitchy. With a craving for flies. With or without wings. Ugh. Why would she think that? Her body itched. She rubbed her ribs and felt bumps, two on each side. That were growing! Maurina rubbed them more vigorously, and the bumps grew faster. What in tarnation was happening?

Maurina crouched low. Flexed her arms and legs. And legs. And legs.

Eek!

She was terrified of spiders and now she had turned into one! How could she get away from herself?

Caught in the web, she ended up dangling by her legs. She opened her mouth to scream in outrage and a bug flew inside! Spitting and sputtering, Maurina used her front two legs to extract the wings. Definitely not in the same class as the desserts prepared by her cook for special occasions.

Maurina closed her eight eyes and sighed. Now what?

Chapter Four

Batzy skidded to a stop, watching the orange cat tumble over and over toward him until she thumped into him–with more power than any little cat should have–and knocked Batzy down.

The shoes revved one more time, then turned off, leaving Batzy and Sherbet staring at each other.

"Aren't you supposed to run from me?" Batzy asked.

The little cat pulled in a dramatic sigh. "Go ahead and eat me. No one will even notice I'm gone."

Taking a step back, Batzy thought now might be a good time to go home. Then he noticed the little orange cat was wearing rather strange footwear. His curiosity made him stay. "I'm not really sure what dogs do when they catch cats. I just chase them. I didn't realize cats had such cool shoes either."

"Rocket shoes. You never know what will happen when you're a witch's cat."

"Aren't witches' cats black?"

"All the others are. I'm the odd cat out at our house. So I'm not going home."

"Oh." Batzy sat down again and stared at the little cat. "Won't you get hungry and cold?"

"That's why I'm going to find a new home. Will you help me?"

"Well, don't you think your witches will miss you? What if they turn me into a toad or, bones forbid, a cat? Sorry, nothing personal."

"My little girl's magic doesn't work too well yet. She's still practicing. You'd probably end up being a lion or something."

"That's still a cat. I don't think I'd like being chased."

9

"I don't like it either. So don't chase me anymore, okay?"

Not chase cats? That was one of life's pleasures. But Batzy guessed he could make an exception for this particular cat.

"Okay." Batzy fell into step beside the orange cat as she stood up and started walking down the country lane. The bare branches of trees rustled overhead, a subtle accompaniment to the occasional howl of a wolf. "What's your name?"

"Sherbet. What's yours?"

"Batzy." They walked a short distance before Batzy asked, "Where are you going to look for a new home?"

"I'm not sure. Maybe I'll just stay in that old barn."

Batzy eyed the old building that seemed to lean further sideways with each gust of the blowing wind. "There probably won't be anyone to take care of you."

"My witches say it's enchanted, so maybe I'll only have to wish for food and a can of tuna will appear. Tuna is my favorite. As long as I don't have to catch my own dinner." Sherbet shivered at the thought. "Let's go check out the barn."

As Sherbet strutted toward the weathered gray barn, Batzy sniffed all around. Interesting scents but probably not safe. Just his kind of misadventure!

When they arrived at the old plank structure, Sherbet pushed open the door and whispered, "Do you scent anything dangerous?"

"Smells like that human from the pumpkin patch, except her scent just disappears–whoa!" Batzy shook his head. "I'm stuck in something."

"Looks like a giant spider's web. Wow! It stretches all across the barn."

Batzy pushed at the web with his front feet, trying to unstick it from his head. "I've never seen a spider's web this strong. Now I know what a fly feels like when they get caught."

"It can't be that bad. Let me help you." Sherbet put her back feet against the web and yanked with all her might at Batzy's legs. "I can't get you out either."

Sherbet let go of Batzy's leg and flopped upside-down, her feet stuck to the web. "Now I know what you mean. I'm stuck too. And here comes the spider!"

"Use your rocket shoes to blast us free!"

"Oh, yeah. I forgot about those. Hang on tight!" Sherbet grabbed Batzy's paws, squeezed her eyes closed and chanted as she had heard her little girl do, "Rocket, sprocket, blast us free, flying out of here over the trees."

Chapter Five

"Moooooom! That didn't work. Sherbet isn't coming home. She's walking away with that dog."

"Take Argyle and go get your cat. Remember, all you have to do is tap his hat and he'll turn into a gargoyle to protect you."

Shabina Louise scratched under the chin of the grinning Corgi dog. "I remember. Will you save some eye-of-newt punch for me?"

"Newts are an endangered species. We switched to licorice drops that look like eyes. But I'll save you a cup of brew." Asteria drew a deep breath. So many changes coming down from Spell Central–computer programs and being politically correct. She'd rather just ride her broom and cast spells. "And don't forget the thirteen pumpkin seeds. I need those before midnight to reverse the spell on our house."

As Shabina Louise approached the gate in front of their Victorian house, a man wearing a sheet with large eyeholes paused, breathing hard from running. "Did you see a little white dog wearing a black and orange table cloth run by here?"

"That's your dog chasing my cat?"

"Batzy won't hurt your cat." Chloe adjusted the fairy wings on what was otherwise a witch's costume. "He only chases them. When they stop running, he has to find his way home and sometimes he gets distracted. So we're going to find him."

"I'll go with you. That way, Argyle won't have to turn into a gargoyle to protect me. That always gives him a headache. He'd rather nap by the fire anyway." With a pat on his head, Shabina Louise sent Argyle back into the house.

Then the little witch looked more closely at Chloe's costume.

12

"Wish I had wings. Such pretty things. Let's make them pink, I think."

Shabina Louise tapped her shoulder blades three times.

"Whoa! Pink dragon wings and they are huge!" Chloe's eyes rounded in awe.

"Moooooom! My wings didn't work right. I wanted pink fairy wings like hers." Shabina Louise pointed at Chloe with her wand.

"Hey, watch that thing," Chloe said, then added hopefully, "Unless you can bring my dad home."

"I'm not allowed to do things to other people, 'cause I'm still learning."

Asteria came out of the house and took in the scene at a glance. "Try again. It can take practice for a spell to work."

The little witch rolled her eyes in silent protest, then chanted, "Little wings. Fairy wings. Pink please for Shabina Louise–that's me!"

Instantly, delicate pink fairy wings appeared on her back. "Got it this time. Thanks, Mom. Now I'm going with–"

"Chloe and her uncle. I know. You don't think I'd let you take off with just anyone, do you? Your wings disappear at eight o'clock, young lady, so you need to be home and getting ready for bed. And bring me the pumpkin seeds before you go."

"Oh, Mooooom, it's Halloween. Can't I stay up late?"

"Even witches need their beauty sleep." Asteria eyed Finn in his sheet-as-ghost costume closely, then winked at him. "If you don't have her home by eight, I'll turn you into an egotistical jock. And I much prefer a man with enough character and integrity to wear a costume to make a little girl happy."

Finn stammered out, "Y-yes, ma'am."

Fascinated with this man's reaction to her teasing, Asteria held out her hand. "I'm Asteria."

Without taking her eyes off Finn or releasing his hand, Asteria said to her daughter, "Bring the pumpkin seeds so I can finish this spell and I'll fly out to join you."

"Your hand feels different than most men's." Asteria caressed Finn's bionic hand and a small smile froze on his face as the electronic computer implanted at the same time as his bionics relayed messages to his brain. *Attractive woman, though not like a normal mortal. Smells mysterious. Elevated pulse and slightly dilated eyes indicate she is attracted and perhaps sexually interested in you. Too soon to make a move on this one. She is powerful and would shut you down in an instant.*

The unsolicited romantic advice from this computer doused Finn's wayward thoughts before they even gained traction. Not for the first time, he figured this software had been programmed by an independent, smart-mouthed female.

"I'll bring your daughter home safely before eight o'clock...Asteria." *Just her name rolling off his tongue seemed sexy.* Finn quickly checked his out-of-character thoughts. He was not prone to lust at first sight like some other males and definitely not toward this strongly self-confident woman. Her teasing about turning him into a jock might be just a Halloween jest. On the other hand, there was definitely something that set her apart from the average woman.

~ * ~

As the girls walked toward the pumpkin patch, Chloe said, "Your name is cool."

"I don't like the Louise part, but mom says it makes spells work better because I'm named after one of her witch friends and it adds her power when I use my full name." The little witch dragged her pointy-toed purple shoes in the dirt as she walked toward the pumpkin patch.

"My dad chose my name. But he's not home so Uncle Finn is supposed to be the man in our house." Chloe lowered her voice and whispered to the little witch. "But he's not like my dad at all."

"My dad's not home either," Shabina Louise said. "I'm not even sure I have a dad. My mom says she got me from a pumpkin patch."

"That just a story parents tell kids 'cause they don't want to explain how babies are made."

"I already know that stuff. Help me count. Thirteenth row." Shabina Louise counted as she walked. "Then the thirteenth pumpkin."

Again, she counted, but her nose crinkled in dismay as she stood

14

in front of the thirteenth pumpkin. "Oh no. It's the pumpkin the lady fell on."

"Won't any old pumpkin work?"

Shabina Louise shook her head. "Has to be the thirteenth pumpkin in the thirteenth row. We'll have to dig through the smushed stuff and hope there are thirteen seeds left."

The two girls carefully dug through the smushed pumpkin innards and came up with...twelve seeds.

"One short." Shabina Louise frowned. "Wonder where that lady went. Bet she has seeds stuck to her fanny."

"We can look for her while we look for your cat and Batzy," Chloe said.

"Good idea. I'll give these seeds to my mom."

Shabina Louise ran into the old Victorian house and soon reappeared, her mother's reminder fading as the screen door slammed shut. "Be home by eight and I need that thirteenth pumpkin seed!"

Though Finn told his mind to keep a bionic eye on the girls searching the pumpkin patch, his thoughts and gaze returned repeatedly to the house where the sexy witch named Asteria had disappeared.

Was she really a witch? She and her daughter talked quite casually of spells. And, with his own eyes, he had seen huge pink wings appear on Shabina Louise then a few moments later turn into delicate fairy wings with just a simple rhyme. He could do an instant replay with his bionic eye if he chose to. He could also run an instant replay of the sway of Asteria's hips as she walked away, and he didn't need any robotic technology to do that.

So if she was a certified, spell-casting witch, could she turn him into something he wasn't? Like the egotistical jock she mentioned? Why did the thought of becoming someone different bother him? Robotic technology had done that when he was six years old to save his life.

And that was a problem, Finn realized. The bionics that replaced most of the right side of his body that had been crushed in the car accident made him something he wasn't comfortable with. Gave him superhuman strength in one arm and hand. Transformed one leg into a high-jumping, fast-as-lightning machine. Provided one eye that could see great distances in light or darkness, as well as snap photos and provide instant replays of whatever was in his line of vision. And somewhere in his brain had been implanted a GPS that allowed him to tap into satellites to always know his geographic location.

He might always know where he was physically, but he had not yet found his way emotionally. Had not come to terms with the part man, part machine he had become with what was then experimental technology. How could he have spent twenty-some years floundering?

Chloe and Shabina Louise returned, interrupting Finn's thoughts.

"Mission accomplished?" he asked.

"Um, not quite," Shabina Louise said. "Besides needing to find my cat and Chloe's dog, we need a thirteenth pumpkin seed."

"Well, I see a chunk of orange on that barn door. Maybe it's pumpkin innards." As Finn strode in the direction of a big old barn, the girls fell into step behind him.

When they pushed open the door, Chloe shrieked. "Spider!"

Chapter Six

"Do you really think it was wise to let your daughter go with that strange man?" Louise was an experienced witch of indeterminate age who had mentored Asteria from the time she had learned of her gifts–about the same time teenaged hormones kicked in. Asteria credited Louise with saving her sanity and definitely encouraging her outspoken personality.

"Not a strange man. I went to college with Adalie––she's Chloe's mom–and have been hearing about her husband and his brother, Finn, for years. She's the one who suggested we move here when this house came up for sale."

"Was she trying to match-make you with a mortal?"

Asteria smiled. "Perhaps. But mostly she wanted a friend nearby. She also knew I was ready to move out of the big city. She didn't tell me her brother-in-law was geeky hot, though."

"He's a mortal, Asteria, and that means trouble. It's better to conjure up a man, then break the spell when you tire of him."

"I think there's more to Finn than what he appears on the surface. How many mortal men would dress up in a sheet to make a little girl happy? But I'll see what my daughter thinks of him before I decide for sure. Besides, I can watch them with the magic mirror–"

"Computer monitor," Louise interrupted with a smirk.

"Magic computer mirrotor..." Asteria rolled her eyes. "And be there in an instant if something goes wrong."

Asteria adjusted the computer monitor to track Finn and the two girls on their search, then turned her attention back to her fellow witch, who was scrolling through the description of souls who had been banished to the enchanted pumpkin patch to be given another chance to redeem their offenses against others.

"Is the woman who fell on the pumpkin one of our assignments?" Asteria asked.

"Yes," Louise said. "Came from the 1700s via a stop with the faeries and night elves. She insulted a shapeshifter, but I think she will redeem herself. She's low risk, so let's monitor her remotely."

"How many more offenders to review?"

"A lot. Last year was a busy one for dirty deeds." Louise scrolled farther down the list. "Here are two very nasty ones. Raped a young woman–actually still a girl. Do we really have to give them another chance?"

"Those are the rules." Asteria frowned. "But we can safeguard all the young girls by making certain parts of their anatomy dysfunctional."

The other witch cackled. "I'm betting they don't make it."

A deep sigh rippled through Asteria. "I agree, but the rules–"

"Say everyone gets a chance–I know. Uncle Werey will personally monitor them."

"In wolf form or as a man?"

"Depends on how much motivation they need to change." Louise continued to scan the computer monitor. "Let's deal with the others to make sure they can't cause too much mischief before midnight."

Chapter Seven

Finn stopped dead in his tracks. A massive web stretched across the barn, and moving rapidly toward them was the largest spider he had ever seen. "Just stand still. In spite of their eight eyes, spiders don't see very well. They use their other senses to locate prey."

"Well, she seems to have located us." Chloe huddled closer to her uncle and squeezed her eyes closed. "I just want to find my dog and go home. Do something, Uncle Finn!"

With Chloe clinging to his leg in fear, thoughts of his allergic reaction to spider bites dissolved in the face of finally being an uncle that Chloe could be proud of. Glancing around for a weapon to save them from the spider, Finn realized he still carried the bowl of candy corn he had saved from certain destruction when Batzy knocked over the table.

Hope this works! Finn narrowed his eyes in concentration and threw the bowl of candy corn at the spider. Using the keen sight from his bionic eye and the strength of his robotic arm, his aim was spot-on accurate—kind of. The bowl hit the web right where the spider would have been if she hadn't started scrambling after packets of candy as they flew through the air.

Gathering as many as she could carry, the spider scurried off to stash them in one of the rafters.

"Look at that," Finn whispered. "I think she likes candy. Let's get out of here while she's busy."

As they carefully back-stepped toward the door of the barn, the spider dropped suddenly in front of them. Chloe shrieked again. With no more candy to throw to the spider, Finn considered grabbing up both of the girls to make a run for the door.

However, the spider didn't seem threatening. She simply held out a packet of the candy and, from the pleading look in her eight eyes, Finn could have sworn she was asking for him to open it. Slowly, he reached out and took the packet, tore it open, and emptied the candy onto the palm of his hand. When he held the candy out to the spider, she daintily reached out with one of her legs and took a piece.

With a noise that sounded suspiciously like "Nom, nom," she repeated the gesture until all the pieces of candy corn were gone. Then she disappeared, only to drop down on a thread of web a few seconds later with another packet. Finn repeated the process.

When the spider disappeared yet again, then reappeared with another packet, Chloe whispered, "What will happen when the candy is gone?"

"Don't know." Finn shook his head slightly.

"We still need to find Batzy and go home. My mom is going to be worried."

"And my wings disappear at eight," Shabina Louise added.

"Ms. Spider, we need to be going," Finn called out. "Enjoy the candy."

But when they stepped through the door out of the barn, the spider was there again, her legs full of packets of candy.

"I think she wants to go with us," Shabina Louise said.

The spider appeared to nod her head.

"Ohhhh-kay." Not really believing what was happening, Finn went back into the barn to pick up the bowl the candy had been in, then went back outside. "You can ride in this with your candy."

The spider crawled into the bowl and held up a packet of candy to be opened. Finn opened several packets and dropped the candy loose in the bowl. The spider settled down happily to munch on the sweets.

"Her name is Maurina and she doesn't want to live in a barn with other spiders and eat bugs," Shabina Louise announced.

"But–never mind." Finn laughed at himself for relating to a spider who didn't feel like she belonged. All his life he had felt like a misfit. Still did, but had finally realized he needed to find the positive aspects in his difference. "We'll sort this out after we find Batzy and Sherbet and get home. Where shall we look now?"

Still munching on the candy, the spider pointed one of her legs down the shadowy road.

Chapter Eight

"Wow! We're flying!" The hair on Batzy's face flattened against his skull as he and Sherbet shot up in the air and over the treetops.

"I don't like heights!" Sherbet's voice trembled as she and Batzy clung to each other. "And I don't know how to turn off these rocket shoes."

"Can you at least make them turn left?" Batzy asked. "Or we're going to crash into those—"

Squeals of alarm erupted all around them as a colony of bats scattered to avoid being hit by the flying dog and cat. Only one unfortunate little bat thumped into Batzy's stomach and the three of them tumbled onto the soft moss-covered ground under bare-limbed trees that rattled as the wind moaned through them.

"That was fun!" Batzy grinned.

Sherbet kissed the ground, and the little bat held his head with his front feet. "I have a headache."

"Sorry," Sherbet said. "I've never had rocket shoes before. Can you still fly?"

"Don't think so. Feel dizzy."

"My witches could fix that," Sherbet said.

"Climb on my back and you can go home with us. You are ready to go home now, aren't you, Sherbet?" Batzy asked hopefully.

"Well, maybe just to help our bat friend. What's your name?"

"I'm usually called Batzy."

"That's my name too!" Batzy the dog was delighted.

"That could be confusing," the bat said. "I can be Batram instead. I've always wanted to be called Batram."

"Why?"

"It sounds dignified, don't you think?" Batzy and Sherbet thought about this for a moment, then both nodded.

"So which way is home?" Sherbet asked.

Batzy shrugged. "I don't know. My little girl, Chloe, usually comes to find me when I run off on a misadventure."

"My echolocation is offline. Sorry, no help from me either." The little bat rubbed his head.

"Okay." Sherbet closed her eyes and spun in a circle with one paw pointing out in front of her. When she stopped and opened her eyes, she said, "The paw points this way. Let's go."

Chapter Nine

Howls echoed off the bare branches of trees outlined in black against the orange-yellow of a full moon. As Finn and the two girls trudged down the narrow road looking for Sherbet and Batzy, gathering clouds played peek-a-boo with the moon, warning of a coming storm.

"What's that shrieking sound?" Chloe sidled closer to her uncle Finn.

"The cat high danger alert," Shabina Louise said. "I've heard it from my mom's cat, Ebony."

"Danger from a cat or to a cat?" Finn asked.

"Like cats are being attacked. Come on, we have to help!" Shabina Louise started to run in the direction of the howls, and almost stumbled over Sherbet and Batzy as they huddled in the shadows by a tree.

"Hooray! We found you." Shabina Louise scooped up Sherbet and hugged her tight as Chloe squealed in delight at finding her dog, Batzy.

"Did you hear the howls?" Sherbet asked.

"That's why we were running," Shabina Louise said. "We have to help!"

"Wait!" As the girls raced in the direction of the howls, Finn struggled to keep the flapping sheet from tangling in his legs. How could he keep the girls safe and rescue the cats without using his bionic strength, as he had vowed years ago not to do after several disastrous incidents?

Check things out first, then come up with a plan, Finn told himself.

"I see them!" Shabina Louise said.

"Not a good idea to just charge into the middle of this," Finn said. "Let's get out of sight behind this tree and come up with a plan."

As they crouched behind a crooked tree, they listened to taunting

24

voices amid the howls.

"First we'll dunk 'em in this water–"

"Yeah, let's do it."

"Then cover them with glue and glitter."

"Then what?"

"Well, I dunno...just...let's do that."

"Yeah. Okay. Yeah."

"I see my mom's cat, Ebony!" Shabina Louise pointed toward the silhouettes of a man holding a cat by the scruff of the neck while another man urged him on. "Little cat become big cat! Scat! Scat!"

The cat let out a roar like a lion.

"Whoa!" The man dropped the cat.

When he kicked at it, the cat let out another roar and climbed up his leg. The man swatted at it and the cat dug its claws into his arm to climb higher. With a howl of pain, the man yelled, "Get it offa me!"

Instead of helping his cohort, the other man took off running.

"Tree, tree, don't let him go free!" Shabina Louise chanted.

Tree roots erupted from the ground, tripping the man as he tried to escape. He stumbled and fell, but scrambled to his feet.

Letting out another roar that ended in a squeak, the cat named Ebony had now climbed on the man's head. He finally managed to dislodge her and stumbled after his partner.

The girls and Finn rushed to make sure the black cats were not hurt.

"Are we glad to see you!" the cats chorused.

Except Ebony, who pointed to her throat and mouthed, "I can't make a sound now. What was that noise that came out of me?"

"You were supposed to turn into a black panther," Shabina Louise said. "And the trees were supposed to wrap their branches around those nasty men so they couldn't run away."

"It might not have turned out the way you intended," Finn said. "But it was brilliant."

Shabina Louise looked sideways at Chloe's uncle. "You think so?"

"High five?" Finn held up his hand.

"We bump fists now," Shabina Louise said.

"Oh. Sorry. I'm not really up on the latest fad."

"My spells don't always work the way I want them to, so guess we're alike in being out of step." Shabina Louise slapped Finn's hand in an answering high five, then fisted her hand. He bumped her hand and they grinned at each other.

"Can we go home now?" One of the other black cats looked around nervously. "It's not really safe to be a black cat out on Halloween."

"Then why are you out?" Sherbet asked.

"Those creeps snuck into our house and stole us," one of the cats said.

"Cats are usually pretty good at hiding," the little witch said.

The two cats looked at each other. "We're actually stuffed cats. No claws to defend ourselves."

"Why would these guys steal you?"

"Jewels woven into our collars, and gold dust to weight our feet."

"That seems odd."

"It happened a long time ago. An evil witch put a spell on us–well, it was supposed to be on our master but we protected her. So we get one chance, every Halloween, to look for our beautiful master."

"How long ago?" the spider named Maurina spoke up.

"We have no sense of time when we are stuffed cats, but we have searched for over two hundred Halloweens."

"People only live just over seventy-eight years in the United States. Slightly more in the United Kingdom and Canada," Finn said. "So your person most likely is not alive."

"Well, maybe a great-grandchild or great-great-great..."

"Wait a minute," the spider said. "When my grandmother was dying, she kept muttering something about cats and spells and witches that took her jewelry. We thought she was just a crazy old woman, but...just maybe. She had a brooch with the family crest–ruby in the center–and a diamond and emerald necklace that disappeared."

"That describes our collars," one of the cats exclaimed. "We've been looking for you! Now we don't have to be stuffed cats any more. We can live!"

"Even if I'm a spider?"

The cats looked confused. "Not sure about that."

"My mom can figure that out," Shabina Louise said. "As soon as we get home. But Mom is not going to be happy with Ebony. Unless you have a good reason for leaving our yard."

Without a voice right now, the cat simply frowned.

"She said those two men escaped from the enchanted pumpkin patch and she had to help her friends," Sherbet said.

Ebony nodded.

"Oh, no!" Shabina Louise said. "We can't let them get away."

"Why not?" Chloe said. "The cats are safe."

"There are rules..."

Chloe and Finn looked at Shabina Louise, waiting for more of an explanation.

"I don't think I'm supposed to tell anyone who's not a witch."

"I need to get all of you home safely. Your moms will worry," Finn said. *And Chloe's dad should be at Aunt Maddie's castle tonight–if their mission was a success.*

"Mom said everyone from our pumpkin patch has to be monitored."

"That pumpkin patch story is just about babies," Chloe said. "And it's not true."

"Actually, there's a different story about our pumpkin patch." Shabina Louise stared at the pointed toes of her purple shoes.

"You have to give me a really good reason not to take all of you home right now," Finn said.

With a deep sigh, Shabina Louise finally said, "People who have done bad things go to the pumpkin patch. Sometimes it's just naughty, but other times it's really, really bad."

"And these two did something really, really bad?" Finn asked.

"I've seen these men before, back in the 1700s where they–" Maurina the spider glanced at the girls. "Let's just say they are really bad men."

"Seventeen-hundreds?" Finn asked.

"Yes," the spider said. "That's where I'm from. But I wasn't a spider. I was a woman. A lady in a wealthy family, actually."

Finn looked at the spider, disbelief plain on his face.

"It may sound a bit unreal. In fact, I'm having a hard time believing this myself, and I'm not really sure how I got here. I made the mistake of insulting a shapeshifter, so one minute I was in this stone circle in Scotland, the next minute I was seeing faeries and night elves...you don't believe this, do you?"

"Let's just say I'm skeptical."

"I want to go home," Chloe said.

"I think that's a really good idea." Finn took Chloe's hand.

"I can't go home until we catch those really bad men. What if they hurt someone else?" Shabina Louise crossed her arms and stared at Finn. "Besides, I want to do this. To show I can do something right for a change. My spells don't work. I can't even make a decent eye-of-newt punch on my own. I'm a failure as a witch."

A failure. Finn knew that feeling far too well. From as far back as being a first-grader staring up at the jungle gym and knowing his skinny little arms were not strong enough to swing all the way across.

Betcha can't do it, one of his classmates taunted. And he couldn't. Only three bars across and his arms gave way and he collapsed on the sawdust beneath the play structure. Their laughter echoed in his mind as clearly as it had so many years ago. Of course, that was before the bionic arm.

Could that taunt really have held him back from adapting to his bionic body parts and becoming someone strong and special? Someone who could do a lot of good for others? It wasn't too late. He could start now. "Well..."

"How many talking spiders have you met?" Maurina asked. "Doesn't that make you question what you thought you knew? Maybe if we catch these bad men, that will show I'm trying to atone for what I've done in the past. Then some magic will change me back into a woman, so my cat friends won't have to go back to being stuffed."

"I say we vote." Shabina Louise stood up extra straight.

"I'm always up for a misadventure." Batzy wagged his tail. The cats nodded in agreement, as did Maurina the spider.

"Chloe, what do you say?" Finn asked his niece.

"As long as Batzy stays with us so he doesn't get lost again."

"Yes!" Shabina Louise pumped her fist. "We can save the world from evil!"

"After we let your moms know what we're going to do," Finn said.

Both Chloe and Shabina Louise looked crestfallen.

"Can't we wait another half hour?" Shabina Louise slid a sideways look at Finn. "Those bad guys already have a head start. Maybe if we hurry we can catch them and still be home by eight o'clock."

"Against my better judgment, we'll wait another fifteen minutes."

Shabina Louise made a discreet fist pump and fast-walked in the direction the men had gone, not noticing the shadowy wolf standing still as a statue nearby.

Unfortunately, just past the trees lay a cemetery.

Chapter Ten

"Are you sure they went this way?" Chloe stared at the rusted metal arch proclaiming this was indeed a place for those who had passed on. Beyond the archway, several dozen headstones discolored with age leaned crookedly against each other.

"There's no other way to go without swinging through the trees like the man of the apes."

"Looks really creepy," Chloe said.

"Maybe the lady who fell in the pumpkin patch went this way too. I can't go home without that thirteenth pumpkin seed for my mom," Shabina Louise said.

"Why?" Batzy asked.

Shabina Louise explained about needing thirteen seeds from the thirteenth pumpkin in the thirteenth row.

"Um, that lady would be me," Maurina the spider said hesitantly. "I was going to hide in the barn but got tangled in a web and turned into a spider. That's why I wanted to come with you. I was hoping one of you could help me be a person again. Besides, I like your candy."

Shabina Louise moaned. "Nothing seems to be going right. We have to help our bat friend, turn Maurina back into a person so the cats don't become toys, come up with a thirteenth pumpkin seed from that thirteenth pumpkin that Maurina squashed...AND find the bad guys."

"I think I swallowed one of those seeds." Batzy burped.

"Can you spit it up?"

Batzy hacked a few times like a cat with a hairball. "I think it might have to go out the back way."

"Oh." Shabina Louise wrinkled her nose.

"Walking is supposed to be good to get things moving," Finn said. "We have a lot to do to get home by curfew, so let's make it a fast trip through the cemetery."

"If we see any ghosts, I'm gonna shriek like a little girl," Chloe whispered.

"You are a little girl," Shabina Louise said drily. "Besides, you're walking with your uncle who is dressed like a ghost."

"Then maybe other ghosts won't bother us. You get to lead, Uncle Finn."

"Not ladies first this time, huh?" Taking a deep breath, Finn stepped under the rusted metal arch.

"Ahwooooooo."

Finn froze and Chloe said, "What was that?"

Batzy doggie-chuckled. "Just trying to break the tension."

Chloe slipped her hand into Uncle Finn's on one side and Shabina Louise took his other hand.

"Stay close together and we'll soon be out of here." Finn quick-stepped around headstones within the wrought iron fencing, leading the girls and band of animals on a respectful serpentine route, trying not to offend any of the dearly departed who might be hovering nearby.

They had nearly reached the gate on the opposite side of the cemetery when they heard another eerie, "Ahwoooooo."

"Not funny, Batzy." Chloe clenched her teeth as she scolded her little dog.

"Not me this time." Batzy and the cats twined around the legs of the humans as they turned as one unit toward the sound of the moan.

A pink woman with blue hair stood nearby, swaying, perhaps to music heard only by her.

"Let's keep moving," Finn whispered as they backed toward the exit.

They almost made it when a cool breeze whooshed behind them, blocking their way. "Just a small favor, please. As one ghost who loves children to another."

"Oh, hello," Finn said. "Sorry to bother you. We were just leaving."

He pointed at the arched exit and the pink ghost said, "I'll go with you. I won't be any trouble. And I'll leave you to go on your way when I find my children."

"Find your children?"

"They should be out trick or treating. That's what we did–do, I mean do–on Halloween every year."

"But you don't know where your children are?" Finn asked.

"Um, nearby. I think they moved last year. I couldn't find them."

"Last year. You haven't seen your children for a year?"

"Or maybe it's been longer. A mom should see her children more often, right?" Sadness seemed to fade the ghost's pink color. "But once a year is all I get. When I died...they said only until my children didn't miss me anymore. Do you think they have forgotten me?"

"I'll never forget my mom," Chloe said.

"Me either," Shabina Louise chimed in.

"There, you see? They will be expecting me. I just–that's the favor...I can't leave here without a live person. And only on Halloween so I don't scare other live ones. So if I could just, you know, go with you for a bit. Just until I find my children..."

The girls tugged on Uncle Finn's hands.

"Only on Halloween? That seems to be a theme today."

"Let's help her. I'd want to see my mom," Chloe said.

"We're already looking for pumpkin seeds and bad guys before we can get you home to see if your mom can help with the spells," Uncle Finn said.

"Bad guys?" the pink ghost asked. "A couple of pudgy guys dressed a bit oddly? I think they might be easy to find. You see, they were trying to tip over headstones and I, um, may have been a bit mischievous."

The group looked at the ghost, waiting for the rest of the story.

"Well, I was upset at what they were doing and kinda came up out of my headstone like a ghost making spooky sounds. Think they were a bit flustered, like to the point of making brown stains in their pants, which they shucked off as they ran out of here." The ghost pointed to a couple pairs of pants and several shoes strewn over the ground leading to the exit of the cemetery. "Ran right into the blackberry patch, they did. Shrieking

32

and yiking like, well, like walking barefoot and bare-bottomed through stickers. May have brought me bad karma, but I kinda giggled..."

Another whoosh of wind swirled around the group and materialized into Shabina Louise's mother.

"Mom! I, um, might be a little late getting home."

"The magic computer mirrotor sent me a red flag about that." Asteria gave her daughter a wry look, then turned to the pink ghost. "Considering what those bad men did to end up here, you actually generated several high fives among us less-than-saintly witches. So we thought it only fair that we help locate your children."

"Are they going trick or treating? This is the only night..." The pink ghost faded to white, which made her blue hair seem more bright as the moon emerged from behind the clouds.

"Why don't you see for yourself? I have an address. Hop on my broom and I'll take you there. Shabina Louise, do you think you can make it home by curfew?"

Finn looked at his watch and shook his head. Shabina Louise gulped. "Can I have an extra half hour? Because it's Halloween, you know."

"This one time."

Shabina Louise hid a smile. That's what her mom said every Halloween.

"And don't forget the thirteenth pumpkin seed..."

"So how did you die?" Asteria asked as she and the pink ghost rode her broom to the house where her children lived.

"I don't remember."

"Dying is pretty important not to remember what happened."

"It was...odd. We were trick or treating as usual on Halloween, and a van came out of nowhere going way too fast. I pushed my kids out of the way but, before I could run, it crashed into me. I didn't feel any pain, then I was floating about twenty feet off the ground. But I could also see me–at least my body–walking on down the street with my kids as if

33

nothing had happened."

The pink ghost paused. "How could I have died if I could still see me alive? But why was I floating above everything? And when I tried to get to my kids and go home, something kept pulling me farther up and away.

"Then there were angels and I tried to explain what happened and I shouldn't be there. They said something I didn't understand and finally allowed me one day a year–Halloween–to be with my kids. But only until they didn't need me anymore.

"I worry it won't be much longer until they forget about me. I want to watch them find love and have kids of their own..."

Silence stretched for a few heartbeats before Asteria asked, "Why are you pink?"

"It's the costume I was wearing that Halloween."

"But why would you stay in costume? This could be a spell."

"Why would someone put a spell on me?"

"Not all witches have the highest of integrity. Occasionally, we hear of one who takes over the body of a mortal. Doesn't make sense to me, but it usually involves being obsessed with a man." Asteria tried to shake off the niggling thought that being obsessed might happen with her growing desire for Finn. That's what it was–just desire. She hadn't indulged in physical pleasures for quite a while and her body was getting cranky.

"You mean it's possible this witch wanted my husband and switched bodies with me to get him?"

"I'm not saying that's what happened, but it's possible."

"Can you reverse this spell?"

"I'd have to know what specific spell she used."

"Oh." Disappointment tugged the pink ghost's mouth downward.

"There are other ways you could be with your children again." Asteria's broom gently landed in the shadows of a tree whose bare branches spread above the entire front yard of a house on the edge of town. An older home, well-settled in a neighborhood of similar homes.

"The angel said I was only allowed one night a year."

"I don't follow the same rules as angels."

"You mean you could...wiggle your nose or pull your ear or..."

Asteria laughed. "I'm not a television witch. Much more sophisticated. I use rhymes."

At the ghost's confused look, Asteria laughed again. "I'm teasing. When my Shabina Louise was a baby, I started rhyming my spells to amuse her. It's been a bond between us."

"Oh." Hope turned the ghost a lovely lavender color. "Do you think you could rhyme a spell for me to be with my kids more often? Now they are facing the temptations of being a teenager, they may need me more than ever but not realize it."

"I think maybe I could, especially if a spell caused you to pass over."

The ghost glowed a vibrant violet.

"Your children might not know who you are," Asteria cautioned.

"That might be better anyway," the ghost said. "At least for now."

"OK. Look in this magic computer mirrotor and tell me what you see."

Inside the house, a woman talked to her children. "Trick or treating was our favorite night of the year. Even my mom would dress up and go trick or treating with us. This is her last costume..."

"That's me in the picture!" the ghost whispered. "But the woman telling the story is...I'm younger than she is. How can she..."

"What year did you die?" Asteria asked.

"I-I'm not sure."

"Well, your children are grown and have children of their own. Those are your grandchildren."

The ghost shook her head so adamantly her hair swung like a blue halo around her head. "My children cannot be grown. We always went trick or treating together. This is our night...the only night..."

"There might be another way to be with your grown children and grandchildren if you're willing."

"I'll do it."

Asteria laughed. "You should probably hear what I have to say before you agree to this."

"Okay. But I'll say yes any way."

"Well, your daughter has been looking for a kitten for her children. Would you like to be that kitten?"

The pink ghost didn't even pause before replying, "Yes."

Chapter Eleven

So if I was a guy with a bare butt full of stickers, where would I go? Finn thought as he and the girls and their group of critters skirted around the blackberry bushes.

"Where do we look now?" Chloe glanced expectantly at her uncle Finn.

"I was just thinking about that." Finn was pleased. At least Chloe was trusting him on something. Even if he wasn't quite sure how he would deliver. "I think the bad guys would look for a place they could pick the stickers out of their bare...um, body parts."

Both girls giggled.

"There's an old house not too far from here." Finn could see the sagging roofline with his bionic eye. "Let's check it out."

As they approached the house, Finn commented, "Well, it looks deserted, but let's be careful so the bad guys don't see us if they are inside."

Everyone nodded, except Batzy, who was sniffing his way along the rickety old fence surrounding the darkened house.

"Batzy, stay with the rest of us," Chloe said sternly.

The little dog looked at Chloe, then his eyes sparkled with mischief and he wiggled under the fence and ran straight toward the house.

"No!" Chloe turned her anguished gaze toward Finn. "Do something, Uncle Finn!"

Finn stared at the house, which looked like something out of a horror film. Dark with missing shingles, shutters that banged against the house, and a porch that slanted at an odd angle. Finn swallowed. Horror

37

movies always gave him nightmares. Still, to make his niece proud of him and save Batzy, he would go into this creepy looking place.

"You scared?" Chloe asked.

"Just figuring out the best approach," Finn lied. He reached for the gate and pulled it open. The rusty hinges screeched and a shiver ran down his spine.

"Needs a bit of oil." He tried to smile in reassurance, but the girls made sure to stand behind him as they cautiously proceeded up the cracked sidewalk.

Halfway up the walkway, a colony of bats swooped low over their heads.

"Renegade bats!" Batram exclaimed. "Take cover."

The girls grabbed Sherbet and the other cats, then Finn scooped up the girls as the group raced around the corner of the house, with Batram and Maurina in spider form clinging to his collar.

They huddled in darkness for a few moments as black clouds covered the moon and thunder rumbled in the distance.

"Maybe Batzy didn't really go into this house," Chloe whispered as she clung to her uncle.

Then a loud "boom!" exploded from inside the house, followed by a shriek and a bark.

"That was my Batzy!" As her fear dissolved in the need to help her little dog, Chloe ran toward the door, followed closely by her uncle and the rest of the group.

When they reached the house, the door was slightly open. Finn held a finger to his lips and they cautiously stepped inside. Eerie organ music filled the air, as if announcing them as intruders. Chloe and Shabina Louise, with the cats cuddled in their arms, stepped closer to Finn.

"What's that?" Chloe pointed toward a long, narrow box sitting among the dusty furniture in the darkened parlor.

"Looks like a coffin," Shabina Louise said.

"Do you think a vampire lives here?" Chloe whispered.

"It's night time. He'd be out sucking someone's blood."

"Ew." Chloe wrinkled her nose, then shrieked when an old man in a tuxedo appeared beside the coffin.

38

"I was kidding," Shabina Louise whispered. "Make him go away, Finn."

"Um, good evening, sir. We're sorry to bother you, but the door was open and our little dog ran in here–"

"Did he knock over my corpse?" Beet red with displeasure, the old man waved toward the coffin.

As one stiffened unit, Finn and the girls stepped backward.

"It only blooms once every decade and your dog ruined that!"

"A corpse? That blooms...every decade?" Finn wondered if they could escape this crazy old vampire with their blood still in their veins.

"Yes." The old man turned on a soft lamp that spotlighted the remains of a plant tilted sideways in the coffin. "Amorphophallus titanium, otherwise known as the corpse flower."

A vase-shaped plant, green on the outside with a throat of deep purple, rose about three feet above an over-sized flower pot. A tapered, soft green growth in the shape of a candle had started to emerge from the center, but was indeed broken.

Shabina Louise took a cautious step toward the exotic-looking plant. "A friend of my mom has one of these. It blooms every year."

"That's not possible," the old man said. "Once every decade if you are lucky and now it's ruined."

"Witches have ways." Shabina Louise circled the plant. *What were the words of the chant the old witch had used? Pretty, pretty, before you die. Open your bloom now don't be shy. The smell might make some run away, but it will be gone in a couple days.*

"Careful! Don't make it worse." The old man watched the little witch closely. Then sniffed. "Faith and begorrah, it's going to bloom. What magic did you do?"

Shabina Louise shook her head. She hadn't even said the words of the chant out loud. With the others, she watched in fascination as the vase-shaped growth opened and a second tapered stalk in the middle grew and grew until it nearly reached the ceiling of the parlor.

"I must have a picture of this!" the old man exclaimed. "Where's my camera? Can never find that confounded thing when I need it."

"The camera in my eye is pretty good," Finn said.

"Camera in your eye?" the old man looked at Finn blankly and the girls stared at him.

"Um, I mean on my 'eye' phone. Yeah. Those have been around for a number of years."

"Well, I must have a photo, so that will have to do."

"We could all do a selfie with the flower," Shabina Louise suggested.

"A selfie?" Bewilderment deepened on the old man's face.

"We'll just show you."

They all gathered around the coffin with its flower and tried to say "cheese" while Finn snapped the photo, but the picture showed scrunched up faces and noses plugged because of the horrendous smell that brought to mind rotten meat emanating from the flower.

They quickly moved to another room, even the old man, though he continued to admire the flower from an almost smell-free distance.

"Do you have internet so I can send you the photos?" Finn asked.

Bewilderment once again returned to the old man's face.

"Guess not. I'll just print these out after we get Batzy home safely, then bring them over to you."

"Thank you." The old man smiled, making him seem less sinister. "Do you mind if I go with you? I could use some fresh air, if you know what I mean."

"So where is Batzy?" Chloe asked.

Chapter Twelve

As they searched the house for the mischievous little dog, they discovered the back door open.

"What lies behind your property?" With his bionic eye, Finn could see acres and acres of cornstalks. But no little white dog. Was Batzy hidden among the corn? Or had he made another detour?

"A farm where they have planted corn for as long as I remember," the old man replied, then chuckled. "Though sometimes I don't remember things very long."

"Let's start searching there."

When they approached the cornfield, they were greeted by a scarecrow who shook his arms to chase away the crows sitting on him.

"Oh. Oh. Visitors." The scarecrow pulled a tuft of straw out of his ear, frowned, and added it to a pile of straw in a wheelbarrow. "Might need this some day."

Then he turned to Finn and the girls. "What would you like to see first?"

"We're looking for my little white dog," Chloe said.

"Dog? I don't remember a dog being in the corn maze."

"He just ran out of that big house and came this direction."

"There's a house over there? Sorry, I don't see very well with these button eyes."

"Did you happen to see two men without pants?" Finn asked.

"Oh, no, that couldn't be. No shoes, no shirt, no service. Hmm, well maybe. Those signs don't say anything about pants. I'll just have to think about that."

"And the dog? Did you see a little white dog?"

"Well, I must have if you say he came this way. I just don't recall. Perhaps we can tour the maze and look for your little dog." The scarecrow set off through the maze with a stiff-legged gait, perhaps due to the sticks that poked out of the straw-filled jeans of his legs. "To the right we have cornstalks. And to the left we have...more cornstalks."

The group looked at each other uncertainly. Finn shrugged, then followed the scarecrow. The girls and the old man from the haunted house fell into step behind him.

"Batzy! Batzy!" Chloe called as they walked.

"Oh, did you find him?" the scarecrow asked.

"Um, no," Chloe said. "I was just hoping he would come to me like he does when dinner is ready–dinner! If I had Batzy's dinner, he would come in an instant."

"Good idea. According to the GPS implanted in my brain..." Finn paused as the girls and the old man stared at him again. "Ah, in my watch...we're heading in the right direction to get back to Aunt Maddie's castle. Oops! Not now, we turned a corner. Now we're back on the right track...Mr. Scarecrow, how long is this maze?"

"I'm really not sure. I've never found the end of it. I just wander around a bit and enjoy the cornstalks, then go back to my post."

"We'll never find Batzy," Chloe lamented.

"Or those bad men," Shabina Louise added.

"I rather like the corn maze," the old man said. "I've rarely been out of my house the last decade, waiting and watching for my corpse flower to bloom. So this is a nice outing."

"I think it's time we ask for some help." Much as Finn wanted to be a hero, wandering around with two young girls looking for a mischievous little dog and a couple of bad guys while a storm threatened to rain down on them any time wasn't really safe. "My GPS says this is the way back to Aunt Maddie's castle. So, let's make our own pathway. Thank you, Mr. Scarecrow!"

"I think I'll just walk with my new friend," the corpse flower man said. "We both seem to enjoy the cornstalks."

So, the group waved to the scarecrow and the old man, then blazed their own trail through the cornstalks, hoping they were going in the right direction.

Chapter Thirteen

"I hear sirens," Chloe said as they emerged from the cornfield.

"That was a fast response to our request for help."

"Or the neighbors calling the police." Uncle Werey slunk up beside them as a wolf and shifted into a man.

Finn and Chloe gaped in amazement, but Shabina Louise simply took this as an ordinary occurrence. "What happened?"

"Unfortunately, these two hooligans sent to the enchanted pumpkin patch keep racking up more crimes instead of trying to redeem themselves. They broke into a house where the owners were on vacation, and found some booze and a hot tub to soothe their wounds from the blackberry thicket. The neighbors heard all their noise and called the cops."

"Is jail better for the bad guys than the enchanted pumpkin patch?" Shabina Louise asked.

A swirling cool wind ruffled the bare branches of a tree nearby and the little witch's mom materialized beside them. "Magic sent them to us to deal with, so mortal means weren't working to change these two."

"What do you have in mind?" Uncle Werey asked.

"Truly starting over," Asteria said. "If only this darn computer would let me pause the enchanted pumpkin spell so I could use old-fashioned magic."

"I, um, might be able to help with that," Finn said.

"You know computers?"

"Been programming them for years." Finn didn't think it wise to admit he also had been paid to hack into some of the most top secret systems in the world for the military and had lived most of his life as part robot.

She might think it's pretty cool. Of course the computer implanted in his brain would choose this moment to comment.

"Be my guest." Asteria handed Finn her computer tablet. "I'm pretty disgusted with all technology right now."

Finn stared at the beautiful witch for long moments. *Wonder if that means she wouldn't be interested in a guy who has computer parts for almost half his body?* "I'll see what I can do."

As he turned his attention to the tablet, he didn't notice Asteria staring at him thoughtfully. But he did hear his internal computer comment, *Stay open to possibilities. You aren't getting any younger and you haven't had any action for a while...or ever.*

Keeping his head lowered to hopefully cover his blush, Finn stared resolutely at the keyboard. As soon as he accessed the programming, he knew this was no ordinary computer. "Where did you get this?"

Asteria shrugged. "Some computer geek my friend, Louise, knows."

A computer geek with a high-level government security clearance, Finn thought as he rapidly hacked into the military system he had been banned from accessing in the midst of his brother's assignment. *Better warn my brother they may have some dark magic in their midst.*

It's Halloween. Are you going trick or treating? Finn keyed in the message.

While he waited for a response, Finn searched for the code that would allow Asteria to pause the spell in progress. Oddly, it seemed linked to the military channel being used by his brother's unit.

No treats tonight, his brother's response came back. *Can't find the candy.*

Finn frowned. The coordinates for the target his brother's unit was seeking had been sent hours ago–before he had been banned from accessing the channel. It should have been easy to send out the drone and be back in plenty of time to meet Chloe at Aunt Maddie's Halloween party.

"Are you having any luck?" Asteria interrupted Finn's thoughts of his brother.

"Um, some odd programming. Just give me a couple more minutes."

So what were the chances of a witch's spell to redeem bad guys being crossed with a military channel? Finn wondered. Not likely unless someone was intentionally interfering with the messages. "What kind of bad guys show up in your enchanted pumpkin patch?"

"All kinds." Asteria shrugged. "Murderers and rapists as well as those who simply offended someone who had magic."

"How about a deposed dictator looking for a return to power?"

Asteria's brow crinkled as she looked at Finn oddly. "Not in recent recall. Why do you ask about that specific kind of offender?"

"Putting two and two together, and coming up with something other than four." Finn returned his attention to the computer. His brother's unit was supposed to be taking out a dictator who had been overthrown about a year ago but disappeared before he could be jailed or executed. Then intelligence recently discovered he was trying to rally forces to stage a counter coup.

The country was small but in a strategic location for defending several allies. If the mission of Ethan's unit was screwed up, this might be the first country to topple to enemy forces, with others following like dominos.

I need to send the true coordinates to Ethan with a warning, Finn thought.

So he sent a message of his own over the channel, posing as a geeky video guy with a cult following who liked to twist holidays. "When I was four years old, my older brother accidentally let slip that Santa Claus wasn't real and I was crushed. So I fired back with 'I suppose you don't believe in the Easter Bunny either.' The look on my brother's face gave away that lie too and I burst into tears. 'But the Great Pumpkin is real'. Yep, the only one who never showed up. That's the one he assured me was real."

With the transmission sent, Finn quickly backed out of the channel, covering his cyber-tracks as he went so the location of the computer he used could not be traced and put Asteria in danger. Then he

46

blocked the channel to remove the glitch from the witch's spell so Asteria could add her own magic to dealing with the rapists.

And he just had to hope the message reached his brother and Ethan remembered the private code they used when they were kids to keep secrets from their parents.

"You should be good to go." Finn handed the computer tablet back to Asteria.

The suspicious look in her eyes told Finn she would question him later about exactly what he did.

"You said something about making these rapists truly start over?" Uncle Werey's comment returned Asteria's attention to the task at hand. "The old ashes to ashes, dust to dust atonement perhaps?"

As the red and blue lights of police cars flashed in strobe-light effect against the house where the two men had taken refuge, Asteria glanced up at the tree in the yard as thunder rumbled once again. "That's a good idea."

Several officers emerged from the back yard of the house with two handcuffed men. As they passed under the tree, Asteria began to chant, "Ashes to ashes, dust to dust, to pay for their crimes is indeed a must. Not in a jail where they could make bail, but back to nature where, without fail, they will do good instead of cause travail."

Lightning crackled across the sky and one of the men stumbled, then the other, as their feet and legs disintegrated. Inch by inch, their bodies transformed into a fluttering of leaves, drifting down, down, down onto the ground beneath the tree.

Then from the branches above, two remaining walnuts fell to the ground.

One of the stunned officers reached over to pick up the handcuffs, the only thing left that suggested something more than a pile of leaves might have existed. "How are we gonna write this in a report?"

Uncle Werey slid a glance at Asteria. "Well played, my dear. What better fate for a couple of rapists than to become compost for a tree that loses its nuts every year?"

With another glance at Finn, Asteria nodded in response to Uncle Werey's comment. "Creativity counts."

"How are the other offenders doing on atonement?" Uncle Werey asked.

Chapter Fourteen

"Let me check the computer." Asteria accessed the tracking log. "Which is working perfectly now thanks to Finn. Offenders are at about fifty percent redeeming themselves and outcome unknown for the rest with four hours left until midnight."

"Can we find Batzy and go home?" Chloe's woeful look tugged at Finn's guilt.

"We also need to help Batram regain his sonar and turn Maurina back into a human," Shabina Louise said. "All before midnight."

The adults shared a look. "Okay, girls, let's head back to the party at Aunt Maddie's."

As the two girls set out slightly ahead of the adults, Finn asked, "Are all the offenders from the past?"

"Many are because the shock of traveling to a different era can make them more open to changing their ways, and they aren't in a familiar environment with their usual connections," Asteria said. "But we also get modern-day politicians and lawyers–anyone who thinks they don't have to comply with the laws and agreed upon behaviors of their time. Again, shock value can be good therapy. If an offender comes face to face with a power they can't manipulate or control, it shocks them into changing. However, some offenders like these two are good at adapting their crimes to fit any time period or circumstance. That's when more drastic measures are taken to make sure they don't harm others."

Asteria paused, then pinned Finn with a direct look. "Now, tell me about this deposed dictator."

Finn knew Asteria would see through anything less than the truth. Yet his agreement with the military bound him not to reveal some information. "Much of the details are classified military information. But the basics are this dictator was overthrown about a year ago, then disappeared, and has been gathering support to regain his power. My brother's unit is charged with making him disappear permanently."

"Wait a minute." A frown of concentration wrinkled Asteria's brow. "There was a kerfluffle in the magic community at the same time about witches mixing too closely with mortals in a little country named Hallowoden. That's when Spell Central was established and witches were given computers to control their spells. Supposedly to keep dark magic from growing too powerful. Didn't set right with me at the time, so I've kept up my own magic the old-fashioned way with spells and potions."

Finn keyed the country name into his computer. "Looks like another kerfluffle–a news flash about a zombie apocalypse happening now. Think it's fake news?"

"Well, many things are possible with dark magic."

With a few more keystrokes, Finn said, "Thought I remembered a scientific possibility for zombies. A neurotoxin found in some sea creatures can cause problems walking and breathing as well as a confused mental state. Says high doses could also cause paralysis and coma, which makes some people seem dead. I would think a doctor could tell the difference, but generations ago doctors weren't always available. So if relatives thought someone was dead and buried them...waking up and trying to dig out would be a real challenge. Unless grave robbers were prying open coffins and someone sat up to have a chat."

A corner of Asteria's mouth kicked up in a half smile. "There really is more to you than you appear. And, as I recall, a potion made with the corpse flower can turn people into zombies also."

"We met an old man who had one in a coffin," Finn said.

"It must be carefully combined with other ingredients under specific conditions. Otherwise, the one casting the spell could succumb to a coma. Older witches knew this well, but it became used for dark magic and was forbidden by Spell Central. Only a few witches, like my friend, Louise, retain this knowledge."

"Witches who use dark magic wouldn't care what was forbidden, would they?"

"No, they wouldn't. These times of great world chaos have affected witches also, bringing up issues buried long ago to be vanquished. Just as with humans, there has long been the conflict between dark and light magic among witches, and where to draw the line between."

"Sometimes more than a line. More like a very blurry no man's land between the two."

"You have been there."

"Most of my life, it seems." Finn looked at Asteria. *Would she understand? Would she consider him a freak? One of dark ones?* When declared clinically dead at six years old, Finn had no choice in his father's decision to revive him with experimental bionic body parts.

Now he faced his own decision: whether or not to become fully bionic and a tool of the military. Was this a choice between dark and light?

From what his brother shared about military operations, much was kept secret, even from those involved in a mission. The need to keep information out of enemy hands if someone was captured? Or the selfish desire for power by dark forces in charge?

He would become a hero, they said in trying to sell him on their scheme. A pathfinder in a new generation of soldiers that used technology coupled with brains and physical might beyond that of a mere human to keep peace in the world.

Yet, Finn wondered, *could a super-warrior designed for conquering, war and violence really be content with peace?* All his life Finn's desire for a sanctuary where he could feel he truly belonged had eluded him. Becoming a super-soldier sounded like it would take him farther away from contentment, and certainly would further set him apart from all other people.

"Finn?" Asteria's voice pulled him from his musings. "Was there something you wanted to tell me?"

Yes, tell her, his internal computer urged.

This time, Finn pushed the voice aside. "Ah, sorry. My mind went off-rail for a moment. You think dark magic may be interfering with the atonement of souls sent to the enchanted pumpkin patch?"

Asteria considered this mortal man named Finn. He was indeed more than he appeared, and she did not for a minute buy the excuse about his mind wandering. This man had something deep and serious going on.

"Hey, what's taking you two so long to catch up?" Uncle Werey reappeared as Chloe and Shabina Louise waited impatiently a short distance ahead.

"We've come up with a mystery." Asteria briefly outlined what she and Finn had discovered.

"If a deposed dictator and someone with dark magic were working together to gain power, staging a zombie apocalypse, then saving the panicked masses by defeating the zombies would be a creative way to do that."

"Does anyone who appeared in the enchanted pumpkin patch for atonement hold that much dark magic?" Asteria scrolled through the list of offenders.

"They wouldn't really need much power if the mortals were predisposed to believe in zombies," Uncle Werey said.

"I agree," Finn said. "They could run old zombie movies to set people thinking about the possibility of a zombie apocalypse, and run footage on the news, along with the information about the neurotoxin that can cause zombie-like symptoms..."

"And the imagination of mortals could do the rest." Asteria shook her head. "They would be out digging up great-aunt Hilda to make sure she was already dead."

"Depending on whether or not they had spent all the inheritance she left them." Finn's teasing remark earned a smile from Asteria.

"Well, I can transport to Hallowoden and deal with anyone using dark magic," Uncle Werey said.

"While my brother's military unit takes out the deposed dictator, now that they have the correct coordinates of his location," Finn said.

"And we can find Batzy, as well as help Batram and Maurina."

"Great! Let's meet at Aunt Maddie's party afterward."

Chapter Fifteen

With a swirl of a spell cast by Asteria, the group returned to the meadow where Batram had collided with Batzy and Sherbet when they were escaping the spider web using the power of Sherbet's rocket shoes. The wind rattled the bare branches of the trees surrounding them, reminding them the storm still had more power to unleash.

"I've been researching what could go wrong with sonar." Because it was faster, Finn accessed the internet with his bionic eye while he faked scrolling on his phone.

You wouldn't have to do that if you were just honest with the people you love, his internal computer stated. *But Asteria is smart. She knows something doesn't correlate.*

No time for that internal debate right now, Finn said to himself. *Maybe after we set things right from this misadventure.*

"It could be a matter of adjusting the range of the sound waves. In which case, Batram might have received a slight concussion and everything will be fine when that heals. Or..." Finn looked at Batram. "Have your ears always been slightly bent?"

"Slightly bent?" Confusion crinkled Batram's brow.

"Folded backward a bit at the tips?"

"I don't know. That sounds like one of my uncle's ears when he hit a window after eating fermented blackberries from a human's wine making."

"If you collided with Sherbet and Batzy when they were rocketing over the trees, maybe your ears got bent in the collision. So it might not be sending the sound waves that's the problem, but in receiving the signals you get back."

"So how could we straighten them?" Shabina Louise asked.

"Hair gel," Chloe stated. "That's how my mom made my hair stand on end to go with my costume."

Batram looked at Chloe's hair closely. "Your hair glows and is sparkly."

"Florescent hair gel with sparkles," Chloe said. "Special for Halloween."

"Well, if it helps correct my sonar, I'll try it. Maybe I'll start a new trend among the other bats."

"Where's your hair gel?" Shabina Louise asked.

"On the bathroom counter at my house, I think."

"You think?"

"Well, I tossed a bunch of stuff on my bed, but Mom did my hair in the bathroom, so she probably put it back where it belongs."

Shabina Louise turned to Asteria. "Could you make the hair gel appear here?"

Asteria raised an eyebrow. "I think that would be good practice for you. Just have Chloe picture her bathroom in her mind and command the hair gel to materialize here."

The little witch pushed out a frustrated sigh. *Why did her mother make her do everything for herself? Asteria's spells always worked and Shabina Louise had to try several times.*

As if reading her mind, Asteria said, "When I was a girl, my spells didn't always work first time either. It may seem frustrating to try over and over, but that's the way your spells become really good."

Shabina Louise pursed her mouth in concentration for a moment, then held out her hand and said, "Gel so sparkly, gel so bright, come to us tonight."

With just a slight hesitation, a tube of toothpaste appeared in her hand. "You have florescent toothpaste with sparkles too?"

Chloe shrugged. "The hair gel should be on the other side of the sink."

Once again, Shabina Louise held out her hand. "Tube on the left, not the right, make an appearance, colorful and bright."

"That's it!" Chloe squealed in delight.

54

"Good job, my girl. Now let's see what we can do with Batram's ears."

"You hold Batram," Chloe said to Shabina Louise. "And I'll put the gel on like Mom did with my hair."

The girls set to work and soon had Batram's ears standing straight up again.

"Ready for a test flight?"

Slowly, Batram nodded his head. Shabina Louise held her hand up. "High in the sky, straight and true, may your sonar work perfectly for you."

Batram flew in a practice circle around the tree, then tilted his face upward and soared higher. Above the trees, then toward the moon, he looped back down and shouted, "Just call the bat hotline if you need me. And thank you, my friends. Happy Halloween!"

The humans waved and the animals wagged their tails in fond farewell to their little friend.

"What's the bat hotline?" Chloe asked.

"Probably just a joke." Finn did not want to confess that with the acute hearing on his right or bionic side he could hear the signals sent out by bats to echolocate, as well as mimic bat "clicks" to tune into the bat hotline that linked bat colonies all around the world. "Okay, next stop?"

"Well, I'd like to be human again." Maurina stared at her eight legs, one at a time. "I've learned that words can be hurtful, so think before speaking. After seeing how all of you try to help others, I realize the life I had back in the 1700s was very selfish and shallow. I wasn't making a positive difference in anyone's life, including my own."

"Bravo, my dear." Asteria took off her pointed witch's hat and bowed to Maurina. "You have done what the enchanted pumpkin patch is meant to do: change a person's thinking to make a better life. But this darned computer has another glitch that won't let me access my spell book to look up a potion to help you become human again."

Thought I fixed that too. Finn frowned as Asteria handed him the computer tablet. "Let me make one more tweak to the programming to let you access your spell book while the tracking program also keeps tabs on those transported to the enchanted pumpkin patch."

"I want to access everything Spell Central decreed we should automate," Asteria said. "I think Bruney was taken in by the pretty face of a con man masquerading as a computer expert. This will bring witches into the modern world, he said. Will make magic much easier, he insisted. Dolion just wanted to her magic to increase his own power."

As Finn accessed the programming, the wind began swirling around them.

"What's happening?"

Grateful for the strength of the bionic side of his body, Finn locked his arms around the girls and Asteria, who clung to the cats and Batzy. Maurina in spider form dropped into Finn's pocket to ride out the storm.

Faster and faster. Around and around they spun. When the wind stopped abruptly and they fell toward the ground, Chloe screamed.

Chapter Sixteen

Ethan Dagdaman watched in disbelief as a werewolf appeared in the midst of the zombies attacking the capitol city of the small country of Hallowoden.

Their original mission had been to assassinate the deposed dictator of the country, but their commanding officer changed that focus when a group of what appeared to be zombies were spotted advancing on the capital city.

Zombies are not real, Ethan told himself. *We need to complete our original mission and let someone else deal with the Halloween characters. Probably a bunch of role players on a Halloween prank.*

But their CO had been adamant about the change in orders. Unusual in itself, as he was generally the first to question any deviation from the original plan.

"Hey, bro, it's almost the witching hour of midnight."

Irritation crackled through Ethan when he heard his brother's voice. His CO had also banned Finn from using military channels with some flimsy excuse about a new regulation regarding civilians. They could sort all that out later–after their mission was complete. Besides, Finn was supposed to be keeping his daughter occupied so she wouldn't mind as much he was missing their favorite night of the year. "I'm kind of busy right now. Don't you have enough girls in your life to keep you out of my hair?"

"Got things covered on this end. Did you see that earlier video of the zombie geek? Reminded me of how we used to role play those cheesy movies about zombies versus werewolves. Remember how Mom would tell us they were all fake and we should return to the reality of doing our

57

chores or Dad would beat us with a belt when he got home?"

"I don't have time for a trip down memory lane, bro. Just take care of what you need to do. Out."

His brother was usually pretty sharp, but today he seemed to be off his game, like the CO. Both obsessed with zombies and... wait a minute. If Finn had been blocked from military channels, how did he know about that geeky video guy? And how did he know about the zombies and the werewolf that just appeared? The zombies could have been shared on the Internet, but the werewolf just arrived. Finn couldn't know that unless...

Crap! They didn't role play zombies and werewolves when they were kids. And their mom never threatened them with stuff like, "Wait till your father gets home." She took care of discipline herself because their dad spoiled them rotten when he was home. And no way would either of their parents beat them. The entire message was fake. Just like the zombies attacking the capitol? A ruse to draw them away from their original mission?

Ethan hadn't paid any attention to the earlier video that had come through. Figured it was just another idiot with too much time on his hands. But maybe it was his brother trying to get a message to him.

So Ethan searched for that corny video. It seemed the geeker was taking a trip down holiday memory lane, just as his brother had done. *How could I have been so dense?* Ethan derided himself. Finn was much too serious about life to make up stories about holidays and interrupt a military mission by sharing them. So what was the message?

"Dagdaman!" the CO shouted. "Program that drone to take out the zombies."

His brother sending nonsense messages. A CO acting out of character. If Ethan was wrong about this, he would be court-martialed and perhaps risk the lives of untold civilians by not wiping out the zombies or whatever those creatures were.

Watching what appeared to be a nonsense video, Ethan hoped he remembered the code he and Finn used when they were kids to send secret messages to each other that their parents didn't understand. But what the hell had possessed the CO today? He was indeed acting like a witch with a hole in her favorite cauldron.

"Programming now," Ethan replied.

The CO rubbed his hands with glee–something he'd never done before. Ethan watched the CO's face intently as he directed the drone toward their original target using the coordinates in his brother's geeky message.

As news of a direct hit reached their unit, the CO turned toward Ethan and shrieked like a banshee. His face contorted and the man fell to his knees, vomiting a green sticky substance that oozed across the ground.

"Suit up in protective gear and contain that!" Ethan shouted. "Don't let it touch your bare skin!"

As several members of his unit responded, the CO pushed to his feet in a shaky stance. "What the freaking hell possessed me?"

"Not sure, sir," Ethan responded. "But we have it contained and will send it to the lab for analysis."

"Let's just nuke it instead."

Ethan smiled to himself. That sounded more like the crusty old CO he had known for years.

"Holy jumping zombies, look at that!"

Ethan glanced at the computer monitor and heard his daughter's terrified scream.

Chapter Seventeen

The breath whooshed out of Finn's lungs as they landed with a harsh thud on the hard-packed dirt. His next breath caught in his throat with the sight of a staggering mass of zombies lumbering toward them.

Without thinking, Finn stumbled to his feet and once again swept the entire group up in his arms and sprinted to a slight rise where he had caught sight of Uncle Werey.

"You are strong for a mortal," Asteria said as Finn set them on their feet.

Finn's slight smile held no humor as he ignored Asteria's comment. "How do you kill zombies?"

"Decapitation," Uncle Werey said.

"Cut their heads off?" Even Shabina Louise made an "ew" face at this statement.

"These are no ordinary zombies." Asteria was rapidly scrolling through the tracking log. "These are offenders sent to the enchanted pumpkin patch for atonement."

"If they just arrived today, how did they become zombies so fast?"

"Rapidly spreading virus." Finn was also researching on his computer.

"Moooooom, they're getting too close."

Asteria glanced up from the tracking log and frowned. "How are we going to decapitate that many at once?"

"My research says zombies can't swim."

"Well, I can buy us some time with a spell. Give us a boat, so we can float. Then add water, water, to fill a lake to the brim, because zombies cannot swim."

60

Instantly, they were riding in a boat, and the first line of zombies was knocked down by the rising water. But the ones behind simply lumbered a different way and rose up out of the water.

"How are we supposed to steer this thing?" Uncle Werey asked. "There's no motor or steering wheel."

"I'm a spell caster, not a boat builder." Asteria spared a frown toward Uncle Werey before she chanted, "Add an oar or two; that will give Werey something to do."

An oar appeared in each of Uncle Werey's hands. "Not exactly what I had in mind."

"Quit whining and just row, row, row our boat." Asteria turned her attention back to the tracking log. "Who would have something to gain by infecting the pumpkin patch offenders with a zombie virus?"

"Oh, Asteria, my dear, you should know the answer to that question." An oily-charming face appeared on the computer monitor.

"Dolion."

"I told you I would be back. We will take over the world one little dictatorship at a time. Killing with those silly drones simply gives me more human fodder for my zombie army."

"My brother's mission." Finn tried to hack into the military channel to reach his brother. "Blocked. And again."

"Use my computer." Asteria handed Finn her tablet.

In a nanosecond, Finn was on the channel, replacing the oily Dolion with his own geeky broadcaster meandering down memory lane again. But this time communicating directly with the zombies. "Remember when we were human? Our clothes were new and our bodies were buff. We didn't have to chase humans to survive. Those beach babes came to us. All we had to do was lie next to the water and look cool."

"Look at the zombies!" Uncle Werey said. "They're lying down at the edge of the water where they will drown. This is ridiculous, but it's working. Keep talking, Finn."

But Dolion intercepted Finn's broadcast on the channel. "Get up, you fools! It's a human trick. You must hunt the humans."

"Crap! They're getting up again. And the water is receding."

"Dolion pulled the plug on our lake. Wish my witchy friend,

Louise, was here."

"Darling, all you had to do was ask." Louise materialized in the boat. "Why are you not enlisting help from your daughter? It's time our little sorceress earned her broom."

"Aunt Louise, my spells don't even work most of the time." Shabina Louise's eyes grew wide as she shook her head.

"Nonsense. What better way to practice than on the undead? No messy feuds with mortals that way. We'll be doing them a favor."

Shabina Louise swallowed and whispered. "What should I do first?"

"A spell, my dear, to conjure a weapon. What do we have to work with?" Louise looked around the boat. "A bit limited on resources here. Why ever did you not conjure a yacht or a gunboat, Asteria?"

"I was a bit under the gun and multitasking."

"Haha. Good pun. But no excuse for slacking in creativity. Let's start with those silly oars. I think they could nicely turn into spears."

"Just two spears?" Shabina Louise asked. "There are more than two zombies."

Louise laughed. "Use the power of multiplication, my girl, and make two thousand spears. Go on, give it a try."

Shabina Louise took a deep breath and began to chant, "Wooden oars, splinter apart, turn into spears, pointy and sharp."

With an explosive poof! the oars did indeed turn into spears. But tiny ones, the size of toothpicks.

"Oops! Moooooom! The zombies are getting closer again!"

"Deep breath, Shabina Louise, and try again."

With wide eyes and a jerky, shallow breath, Shabina Louise chanted, "Bigger, bigger, like a tree, stop those zombies from eating me...er, we...er, us.

In an instant, the tiny spears became large as logs, stabbing into the ground to surround the mass of zombies.

"Not exactly what I had in mind." Shabina Louise shrugged.

"But the zombies are now contained in a jail made of spears," Asteria said. "That gives us time, once again, to come up with a way to destroy them."

"Ashes to ashes again?" Uncle Werey asked.

"Not with Dolion in the picture. I think he could use dark magic to have the zombies rise from the ashes."

"With Dolion the source of the dark magic, we must also eliminate him." Louise tapped a long, red-polished fingernail against her chin.

"Spell Central would never approve of that. He has too many friends there."

"I didn't say we would ask Spell Central." Louise's gaze met Asteria's without blinking. "His demise would merely be collateral damage in saving the world from zombies."

"Um, I have an idea." Maurina in spider form tentatively raised one of her legs. "Since getting tangled in a spider web in the barn turned me from a human into a spider, could wrapping the zombies in a web also turn them into spiders?"

The group looked at each other.

"Possible," Asteria said.

"Definitely worth a try." Louise nodded her head.

"That's a pretty big area to cover with web," Asteria said. "And Maurina could get eaten or swatted by a zombie if she gets too close."

"I could toss her back and forth around the spears," Finn said. The others looked at him oddly. *Ah, well, he might as well confess.* "Bionic parts on the right side. Makes me really fast. I could toss her across the spear jail and race around to the other side to catch her. Then toss her back and race around. Over and over until we cover the entire area."

"Bionic parts?" Asteria asked. "That allow you to move that fast?"

With a nod, Finn said, "Handy to get away from bullies."

"Why didn't you just hit them with a bionic fist...never mind. You're not that kind of guy."

Finn definitely wanted to ask Asteria if she thought that was a good thing or not, but he wasn't sure he wanted to know her answer. Besides, they had a small country–and perhaps the entire world–to save from a zombie apocalypse.

Doing what Finn had described to the others, he and Maurina wove a web across the zombies. As the zombies swatted the web in their stumbling attempt to get out of their jail and find more human victims, they indeed began transforming into spiders. A few at a time at first. The rotting flesh of their legs turned into hairy spider legs. Then their arms. As they hunched over to crawl, four more legs emerged from their sides. As their torsos and heads morphed into spider form, the transformation was complete.

By this time, zombies were transforming into spiders like a tidal wave spreading throughout the jail of spears.

The group of humans and witches and others stood in awe.

"What if they bite humans?" Chloe whispered. "Will those humans become zombies?"

"Good question. Maybe something could eat the spiders before they scurry out of their jail."

"I know! Batram and his relatives. Bats eat spiders, don't they?"

"Well, my research shows some of them do," Finn said.

"Let's invite them to dinner! You can do that by tapping into the bat hotline like Batram said, right?" Chloe look at her uncle Finn expectantly.

~ * ~

So much for Finn's intent to win Chloe over without using his bionics. But pride was a small price to pay to save the world–or at least this little country.

Putting to use his bionic vocal cords that could emit sounds higher than most humans can hear, Finn hoped he could imitate Batram's distress call to tap into the bat hotline and explain what they needed.

After a few fumbled attempts, a colony of Batram's relatives appeared nearby. Curious but wary, they settled in the lush foliage of nearby trees. With Maurina hidden once again in Finn's pocket so the bats wouldn't eat her, Finn offered what he hoped was a plausible explanation of what they wanted.

"Bats get blamed for carrying viruses anyway. Once word spreads that bats may be carrying a zombie virus, that would really keep predators away from us, including humans."

"There would probably be a horror movie filmed about you,"

Shabina Louise said. "Bats would be famous!"

"Or infamous," Uncle Werey commented.

"Seems ridiculous we strike fear in people much bigger than us, but a lot of humans are afraid of bats."

"Maybe mortals will learn and be grateful you helped save them from a zombie apocalypse."

"Perhaps a few humans. I'm guessing most of them won't look up from their cell phones long enough to bother," the bat spokes-critter said. "But these spiders will provide a feast for us, so bon appétit!"

When the bats had eaten all the zombie spiders, they gave a collective colony burp of thanks and flew off to rest in a nearby cave.

"Great. One major problem solved. Now to deal with Dolion," Asteria said.

"We have an idea." The former stuffed cats spoke up. "Since dark magic turned us into stuffed cats, can't we turn dark magic into a stuffed...something?"

"Dolion would make a pretty ugly stuffed doll."

"How about something else? Something useful?"

"Our scarecrow guide in the cornfield maze was stuffed. How about turning Dolion into a scarecrow?"

"He will fight any attempt to weaken his power," Louise said. "We'll have to trick him. Make him think he's getting something he wants."

"Like a corpse flower with the power to make people seem like zombies to add to his zombie army," Asteria suggested.

"Brilliant! Our friend in the haunted house has a corpse flower."

"How convenient it's right next door to Dolion's proposed new home in the cornfield."

"Dolion won't fall for anything from the three of us." Asteria indicated herself, Louise and Uncle Werey. "Who is going to convince him traveling to our neighborhood to steal the corpse flower is a good idea?"

Chapter Eighteen

"Are you sure, Maurina?"

Drawing a deep breath to stop her spider legs from shivering, Maurina nodded.

"Okay, let's turn you back into human form and start the next step of our plan," Asteria said. "Finn, I believe you were fixing the glitch in my computer that allowed me to access my spell book without shutting down the tracking log for the enchanted pumpkin patch."

"Hopefully without getting caught up in a zombie apocalypse this time." Finn once again accessed the programming. "I think I've found the problem. Easy fix in the code and now you should have access."

"You are my hero!" Asteria kissed Finn on the cheek as he handed her the computer tablet. "In spite of being a computer geek."

Finn forced a smile as he sighed inwardly. *Now that she knew about his bionics, he had ruined a beautiful relationship before it even began.*

Don't write this woman off so easily. The darn internal computer sounded smug, as if she knew something Finn didn't.

Asteria looked at him speculatively, then turned her attention to the tablet. "Maurina, there are a couple ways to turn you back into a human. The easiest is to return to the place where you changed into a spider and, if we had a piece of the clothing you were wearing or something from when you were human, that would be excellent."

"I don't know what happened to the clothes." Maurina frowned. "I went into the old barn and got tangled in the spider web. All my clothing seemed to disappear when I changed into a spider."

"We can at least go back to the barn and try to find something

66

there." With a spell cast by Asteria, the return transport to the barn was much less harrowing than the storm that spun them to the little country overrun by zombies.

As they alit near the barn, Finn scanned the area, spotting a piece of cloth on a sticker bush.

"Sharp eyes," Asteria said. "That was pretty much hidden."

Finn forced a smile. He had been doing that a lot around Asteria. Since she hated computers, he had no chance of a relationship with her, so what did it matter if she knew the truth. "Just call me robo-nerd."

"Look! There's a pumpkin seed attached to this cloth." Shabina Louise triumphantly held up the seed. "The thirteenth seed from the thirteenth pumpkin in the thirteenth row. We can have our house back the way it was!"

"Or we can help Maurina become human again." Asteria plucked the seed from her daughter's fingers and tucked it into a small velvet pouch that disappeared under Asteria's cloak.

"Oh." Shabina Louise's face fell.

"What do you mean?" Maurina asked.

Asteria explained the spell that made their old Victorian house look abandoned for Halloween. "With thirteen seeds from the thirteenth pumpkin in the thirteenth row of the enchanted pumpkin patch, we reverse the spell so the house is once again just a beautiful historical house on the day after Halloween."

"And without the pumpkin seed?"

Asteria shrugged. "We get to fix up and paint the house the old-fashioned way–with elbow grease and paint brushes."

"Oh." Maurina echoed Shabina Louise's disappointed comment. "Isn't there another way?"

"All the spells have to be completed by midnight," Asteria said. "That includes turning you back into a human, which will keep your cats from becoming stuffed ones again. That's more important than the house."

"I can help with the house." As soon as the words were out of his mouth, Finn regretted them. Why torture himself with being around Asteria and her daughter when "Uncle Finn" was all he would ever be?

But with his bionic parts, he could paint faster than ten humans combined. If Asteria was going to sacrifice an instantly beautiful house to help Maurina, the least he could was give up a week or two of his time. "With my bionic arm I can have your entire house painted before a normal human would even have the can of paint opened and stirred."

"Why would you do that? You barely know us."

Fake an answer or tell the truth? Finn decided telling Asteria he was more than half in love with her was not a good idea, so he side-stepped the real truth. "My sister-in-law has known you for a long time and I have a few weeks before I need to be anywhere. Might as well be useful."

As before, Asteria pinned him with a look that said she knew there was more that he wasn't saying, but let it pass.

"Maurina, let's get you back in human form, then we'll sort out the rest of the spells." Asteria held the scrap of cloth and pumpkin seed in her hands, then took a deep breath and chanted, "Spider, spider, spin your web. Round and round, flow and ebb. With the enchantment of this pumpkin seed, let Maurina once again a human be."

Maurina's eyes grew round as two of her spider legs once again became human legs, and two more became arms, and the four that had grown out of her sides dissolved into mere bumps on her ribs.

"Oh, my." Maurina stretched to a full stand. She patted her arms and torso and looked down at her human legs and feet. "I'm me again. How can I ever thank you?"

"By shutting down Dolion and his dark magic," Asteria said.

Maurina took a deep breath. "Right."

"You can still change your mind and we'll find another way. You've done more than enough for atonement of the offense that sent you to the enchanted pumpkin patch."

"Nah. I think this saving the world stuff could become addictive."

"Dolion can be dangerous," Louise cautioned. "We'll all be here for support, but if he spots us, he will realize it's a trick."

"I can do this," Maurina said, as much to reassure herself as the others.

~ * ~

In spite of her brave words, Maurina wasn't sure she could pull off fooling Dolion into thinking she had decided to join him in dark magic. She truly regretted her shallow life in the 1700s, and feared if she pretended to still be that person she would slip back into her selfish ways.

"We'll be with you, Maurina." The two black cats rubbed against her legs as she crept toward the haunted-looking house where the corpse flower stood blooming in all its stinky splendor.

Though the old man had agreed with their plan to stage a "break-in" to steal pollen from the vase-shaped part of the plant for the zombie potion, so much could go wrong to tip Dolion off. Then his anger and dark magic would be focused on her.

Thunder rumbled as Maurina crept toward the house. At least the dark clouds amassing low in the sky crowded out most of the moonlight and allowed her to blend with the shadows. She stayed next to the overgrown hedge along the side of the house so she could push open one of the windows into the parlor. The old man promised he would unstick that particular window so it would open easily.

As she reached toward the window, lightning flashed nearby, seeming to spotlight Maurina's presence. She gasped and ducked down, once more seeking the shadows.

She huddled there for long moments, her cats purring soft reassurance, blending with the rumble of the thunder.

You can do this, Maurina coached herself. *Everything has been planned. Easy in, easy out with the pollen. Hand it over to Dolion and the witches will take care of the rest.*

With a deep breath, she pushed open the window and hoisted herself into the house. Her cats scrambled after her. She paused to get her bearings and focused on the corpse flower sitting in a coffin.

"So nice of you to join us, my dear." As Dolion laughed, thunder crashed right overhead and lightning flared, glinting off the syringe he held at the old man's throat.

Maurina's gaze met the terrified look in the old man's eyes.

"Did you and your good little witch friends seriously think I would leave something as important as the zombie potion to a floozie rich girl from three centuries ago? You all underestimated me and now your friend here pays the price. I'm going to inject him with the potion to be sure it works. Then you will be his first victim." Dolion's evil laughter cackled again as thunder shook the house.

The noise of the storm muffled the thud of the back door opening and Batzy's barking as he dashed into the house, heading for Maurina's two black cats.

They hissed and dashed across the room, straight for Dolion and the old man he still held in a headlock. Batzy raced after them, barking with glee at the chase, and upended both men.

"Ungh!" Dolion uttered a cry of strangled surprise as the old man fell on top of him, knocking him breathless.

The old man scrambled away on his hands and knees, and Maurina rushed to help him up. "Let's get out of here before Dolion recovers his breath."

But Dolion didn't rise quickly. In fact, when he staggered to his feet and slowly turned their way, the flesh on his face was sagging and rotting away.

"Oh my heavens," Maurina whispered. "He must have fallen on the syringe with the zombie potion."

The front door crashed open, and Finn, Asteria and Uncle Werey ran inside, with Louise following a few steps behind.

They all watched as Dolion stumbled, the bones of his legs disintegrating under the weight of his body. Within minutes, all that was left of the dark magic master was a few shreds of clothing.

"A zombie potion made from the corpse flower is a very delicate blend that must be aged at least a year or the virus acts so quickly it destroys itself before there is time to transfer to a new host." Louise stared at Dolion's remains. "Fire cleansing and bright, reclaim all that is dark tonight."

As lightning crackled across the sky once again, lavender flames burst briefly inside the house, consuming all sign of what had once been

Dolion.

"Nothing left to even make a scarecrow," Finn said. "Guess our buddy in the cornfield will have to save his straw for someone else. Let's go enjoy what's left of Aunt Maddie's party."

Chapter Nineteen

The weary group brightened as they approached Aunt Maddie's castle. Batzy ran ahead and was waiting by the buffet tables for the humans to share snacks with him.

In addition to a few breakfast yummies from earlier, Aunt Maddie's nephew, Ryan, had continued to cook and bake and sauté all things apple and pumpkin spice throughout the day. So the buffet tables were still loaded, offering breads, cookies, pies, cakes and cupcakes, scones, cheesecakes and more.

After the costumed guests loaded their plates with food, a gaoler offered them a hot drink and led them to the basement dungeon. A fire burned in the huge stone fireplace that filled one end of the recreation room.

Finn listened quietly as Chloe, Shabina Louise and others shared stories of their misadventures.

"We started out in the enchanted pumpkin patch," Chloe said. "That's where Batzy chased Sherbet–"

"She's my cat. I named her for my favorite dessert of my favorite season, sherbet in the summer," Shabina Louise added.

Asteria shook her head. "Hard to believe a witch doesn't like Halloween as the best holiday."

"Maybe I'm not all witch," Shabina Louise said. "You never have told me who my dad is. Just that you got me out of a pumpkin patch."

"That's a tale for another day," Asteria said mysteriously.

"Well, if I was all witch my spells would work the first time, all the time." Shabina Louise frowned.

"My inventions don't always work the first time," Uncle Horace said. "Sometimes I have to adjust them a half dozen times or more."

"You do?" Shabina Louise asked. "So my mom is right that practice makes perfect spells?"

"Works for inventions."

The sound of the trick or treat wagon coming alive caught the attention of the partiers.

"It's later than normal for tricker or treaters." Aunt Maddie frowned at the security monitor that showed a large, fuzzy blue monster with one eye in the center of its head riding alone in the wagon.

Relief stirred in Finn's gut. He hoped this meant his brother's mission had been a success. "Hey, Chloe, didn't one of your favorite movies have a monster like that? Let's check it out."

"Okay." Chloe cheerfully stood up. As she and Finn walked toward the heavy wooden door of Aunt Maddie's castle, she slipped her hand in her uncle's. "I'm sorry I was so awful to you, Uncle Finn. You helped us find Batzy and we had a great adventure–even if it was kinda scary sometimes. I was just missing my dad and..."

Chloe swiped at her eyes with a fist.

"Hey, I understand. Your dad has always been my hero too."

"Yeah?"

Finn nodded.

"Well, you're pretty special too."

Finn's heart nearly burst with joy at his niece's praise. Finally, he felt like he truly belonged in his family.

"Ahwoooooo!" The ghost hologram activated as the old wagon clattered up the driveway.

Finn and Chloe waited in the doorway as the fuzzy, blue monster climbed out of the wagon and stared at the Chloe.

She sidled closer to Finn and whispered, "Why is that monster staring at me?"

"Why don't you ask him?"

Chloe put her hands on her hips and scowled at the man in the monster costume. "Why are you staring at me?"

"Because I can't believe how beautiful you are and how much you've grown and how much I love you." The man took the monster head off.

"Daddy!" Chloe launched herself into her father's arms, burying her face in the fuzzy blue costume.

"Ethan? Is it really you?" Chloe's mother ran down the hallway, the cape of her costume flowing behind her. In a heartbeat, she was also engulfed in the arms of the fuzzy blue costume.

Eventually, Chloe, her mom and her beloved daddy made their way to the buffet tables, which still boasted an abundance of pumpkin spice and apple delicacies.

"Finn, you knew and didn't say a word about Ethan coming home?" Chloe's mom half-scolded her brother-in-law.

"It wasn't a sure thing and I asked Finn not to say anything," Ethan defended his brother. "I knew how disappointed you and Chloe would be if things didn't work out. So it was better to keep what I hoped would be a pleasant surprise."

"I'm delighted and grateful you are home and safe." Chloe's mom kissed her husband again. "It's past Chloe's bed time, so I think we will move this celebration to our own home. Maddie and Horace, thank you as always for your generous hospitality. Chloe, call your dog and let's go home."

"Batzy, let's go home!" Chloe looked around for the little white dog. "He was here just a minute ago."

"Probably stopped by the time machine–"

"Horace means the giant fire hydrant in the back yard," Maddie interrupted.

"You're right, my dear. We keep dog treats out there for Batzy. Then he tunnels under the fence to go home."

"He's probably curled up in his bed with a snack," Chloe's mom said.

But Batzy had one more stop before he went home.

Chapter Twenty

Finn walked Asteria and Shabina Louise home, wishing...

Well, wishing for something that couldn't be: a relationship with this beautiful witch and her daughter. At least he would be able to hang out near them for a while helping to repair their house.

You're giving up before you even try, his internal computer said.

Finn ignored the voice and continued the argument in his own mind. Unless he chose to become fully bionic. A super-soldier as the military was pressuring him to do. A role model for the greater good of society. Then he would be undergoing surgery and perhaps months of recovery before more months of training and a lifetime of military missions.

Pah. Doesn't fit you, the computer said.

Finn started to listen to the internal voice. *Well, I don't want the spotlight. Today's misadventures had been more than enough action and excitement for a lifetime. But am I being selfish to want a quiet life and, yeah, a woman and family to love?*

The military will just use you and dump you when new technology comes along, the voice said. *Or if there are budget cuts. Or a new administration. Or new priorities. You know how they just dump the old stuff.*

Finn knew that. For years, they had ignored him. Until someone had been purging old files and found record of his surgeries and thought he could be useful.

You said it yourself, the voice said. *Can a super-warrior designed for conquering, war and violence really be content with peace? You don't want to fight. What will you do when they tell you to kill someone?*

75

"You're very quiet." Asteria stepped closer to Finn and took his hand as they walked.

Frowning, Finn wondered, *Tell her or not?* "I have a decision to make with no clear answer of what would be best."

"I hope whatever you decide means you'll be nearby...to help paint like you said you would."

As they paused on the walkway, Batzy trotted around the corner of the Victorian house and grinned.

"Or maybe just be nearby since I'm hoping Batzy's grin means he just passed that thirteenth pumpkin seed."

"Saved from painting the house by a little white dog who started out by chasing my cat." Shabina Louise smiled. "I think I'll take Sherbet and go to bed."

"I'll be up in a few minutes." Asteria watched her daughter disappear inside. "So, tell me how you got the bionic arm. That's not standard issue for mortals now, is it?"

Tinged with painful memories, Finn's smile came out rueful. "A drunk driver plowed into our car when I was six. Crushed the side of the car where I was riding and I was declared dead. My military dad pulled some strings to use this experimental technology to save my life and my geeky awkward little self became part robot."

"That must have been tough."

Finn looked at Asteria to gauge what she really felt, and met the sincerity in her gaze.

"I suppose most boys would think it was really cool. But I had one arm that could throw a baseball several blocks while the other had trouble holding a pencil some days. One leg that ran faster than a racecar and one that still tripped going up stairs. My body seemed to be at war with itself."

"Like not knowing who you are." A faraway look drifted into Asteria's eyes. "I went through a time when I didn't want to be a witch. Wanted desperately to be mortal."

They walked the short distance to the porch before she continued. "That's when I met Shabina Louise's father. I want to marry you, he said. Have a family. Unfortunately, sex came first, then a baby, but no marriage. He neglected to tell me he already had a wife. But I wanted so badly to believe him..."

Asteria drew in a deep breath. "Of course, my friend, Louise, welcomed me back. Welcomed my baby. And I've never told my daughter she's half mortal. There never seems to be the right time. But I know she has the right to know. The longer I wait, the more I fear she will hate me. And I love her fiercely. What will I do if she hates me?"

Finn touched Asteria's cheek. "You will hurt. Then you will find a way through it."

Asteria nodded against Finn's hand. "I'm going to tell her tonight. Will you stay...for a while? In case I need a bionic shoulder to cry on?"

"Moooooom, I'm getting cold and I want to go to bed." Shabina Louise peered out the door of the old Victorian.

"You can sit by the fire while I help Shabina Louise get ready for bed."

~ * ~

"Chloe's lucky to have a dad who loves her," Shabina Louise said as she and her mother walked down the hallway past portraits of their witch ancestors mixed among framed artwork Shabina Louise had created as she grew from preschooler to the budding young lady witch she was today. "Why don't you conjure up a dad who loves me?"

As their voices faded down the hallway, Finn stared into the fire. A feeling of rightness–of belonging–settled over him. Wise or not, Finn decided to take a chance on a relationship with Asteria. Considering their misadventures today, there was plenty he could do as a civilian. So, he sent a text message to his contact in the military. *Am honored by your offer to become a super-soldier, but the military life isn't for me. Perhaps some wounded, returning vets would gladly volunteer to be a super-soldier and regain their mobility.*

Knew you'd make the right decision, his internal computer said.

He tucked his cell phone into his pocket as Asteria returned to the room.

"Ah, I love that little girl." Asteria handed Finn a cup of brew and sat on the love seat beside him with a cup of her own. "She didn't seem surprised when I told her about her dad. Said the right dad would come along."

Asteria took a sip of her brew, then stared at Finn. "A lot of witches conjure up a man to please them. Then just break the spell when they are tired of him. But I think I've found a man who pleases me and I don't want to break the spell. I think that man could also be good to my little girl. Are you up for being that man?"

Looking at this sexy, beautiful witch, Finn drew a deep breath. "Are you sure?"

"Yes. You're intelligent, kind, courageous, responsible. Perfect father material." She dropped her voice to a whisper. "You are also sexy as a hex. I think we could fly high together."

"Um, am I under some sort of spell?" Finn held up a hand. "Don't answer that, because I'm going to say yes anyway."

Asteria's laughter tinkled like silver bells as the clock struck midnight and the Victorian house began transforming back to its original beauty. "It's the spell of love."

~ The End of Another Misadventure ~

Coming Soon by Christine Young
at
Rogue Phoenix Press

Sweet Dreams

Chapter One

Cactus Junction

Guy McKenna negligently leaned against the bar in the Red Neck Saloon, a beer in hand, watching the line dancing. He was bored and tired of waiting for something he didn't think would ever come his way. In the pub the air was stagnant and the music boisterous. For the time he relished the noise as well as the crowds that filled the small bar on Saturday nights. It took his mind away from the fact he was nearing twenty-seven and he still had not found his mate. His brothers and sisters were happy, content in their lives with children.

After returning from Iraq, he needed the familiar sights and sounds. So much that happened over there had been out of his control and the visions he had terrified him, would cause him to wake in a cold sweat. They were nightmares that taunted him mocking his very existence.

Now his dreams and visions had changed.

Needing to forget the dreams haunting him night after night for the last month, he stayed at the bar when he would have usually gone home. His soul mate permeated his thoughts but he'd never seen her, didn't know where to find her, certainly not in the Red Neck Saloon in Cactus Junction. He supposed stranger things could happen. When he closed his eyes at night, falling into a deep sleep, her face was central to the entire dream. The sight of her was etched in his head, seared through all eternity.

If he saw her, he would know her.

He watched a young couple kissing in the corner of the bar, the young man's hands roaming in too many places they shouldn't. He shrugged to himself, knowing if the opportunity with his soul mate presented itself, he'd be doing the same, but in private. He wasn't about to share her with anyone. He almost walked over to the couple to tell them there were rooms upstairs they could rent for the night or a few hours.

The McKennas were too well known in this territory to let anyone see them share intimacies with a soul mate or any woman for the matter. The gossip would spread quicker than a man could blink. He had his share of women over his lifetime, but he needed to move on and find meaning in this world. His siblings had found their mates. Now it was his turn, but where was she?

Well hell, if not in Cactus Junction, where then?

His beer glass drained he turned at the bar, taking his gaze from the doorway for only a moment to request a second beer. Dipping his hand in the bowl of peanuts, he was surprised by the sensation scurrying down his spine. The hair on the back of his neck prickled, stood on end. A fine sheen of sweat formed on his forehead. Unnerved, unsettled, excited for something. He knew not what.

The soft fresh scent of oranges waffled through the air. For a moment he couldn't think, couldn't breathe. When the moment finally passed, he sucked in a huge draft of air.

"What are you drinking, cowboy?" Her body pressed against his, luscious curves that would fill his hands seemed to be the focus of all the sensations coursing through him, a primal heat filling his soul. He was afraid to look at her, terrified he might do something incredibly foolish.

The lady's voice was a sultry purr sending his body quivering with need, titillating shock waves pulsing through him. A woman's body let alone the sound of her voice had never affected him like this. He paused a moment as tension mounted, radiated through him from toes to head, stopping momentarily in his groin. Slowly, he turned to look at the face possessing the amazing voice and the full curves he wanted to wrap his hands around. His breath stopped for a few seconds at the vision smiling at him. He was staring into the face that he dreamed of.

His mate.

His woman for life and into all eternity. His mouth went dry while his gut churned in anticipation.

He cleared his throat, but his words still came out in a feeble croak, nothing like his normal husky timber. "Beer." The bartender handed him the bottle he for asked for earlier.

"Pinot Gris," she told the bartender, leaning casually on the bar. Half turned toward him, her body was as sultry as her voice. The blouse she wore was unbuttoned so far he could see the lace of her bra and it was tucked into a tight fitting pair of short shorts. She didn't seem to care she was half dressed while he was lusting after her. He could barely keep his tongue in his mouth.

"Drinks on me," he told her then nodded to the bartender. "Keep them coming. I think we're going to be here for a little while." Long enough so he could ask her to come home with him tonight or find out where she lived. He couldn't let this one go without getting vital information.

"Yes, sir, Mr. McKenna," the man said. "Let me know if you need anything else. Obviously, drinks are on the house."

She held the glass by the stem and slowly sipped seeming to keep her gaze on him. "Thank you," she murmured, licking her lips while she slowly twirled the contents of the glass, her eyes seeming to be focused on the liquid, no longer on him. He needed to change that, needing her full attention. Nothing less would do.

"What brings you to Cactus Junction?" he asked politely, needing to know everything about this lady. Besides the basics such as what's your name, this seemed the simplest place to start.

She looked at the bar, her long blond hair falling in front of her face. When she looked up, "Guess one could say I'm looking for something and I'm running from something." She pushed the hair behind her ears, her blouse parting provocatively with the gesture.

Unable to keep his eyes from the view she presented, he decided not to try. He wanted to reach out and touch the strands just to see how soft they were. "A riddle?" he asked, "Would you like to find a table?" Preferably a table in a dark corner where no one would see them.

She was shaking her head, lips smushed together provocatively. "No riddle, just the truth." She offered a tiny smile and slight shrug of slim shoulders. "And yes, a table would be nice. I don't usually talk to strangers," she mumbled, staring into her glass before turning his attention to his mouth. "For some reason I find odd, you don't seem to be a stranger."

He wasn't a stranger. He needed to tell her the truth but understood she'd have to figure it all out for herself. "Follow me." He leaned forward then waved his hand at the bartender, "Have Jan bring us some fries." Then to the lady who had yet to introduce herself, guess he hadn't introduced himself either, "You hungry."

"I could eat a few fries." She admitted as she followed him, her smile a bit hesitant. "As long as we've ketchup."

At the table, he held out his hand in greeting, "I'm Guy McKenna." He paused waiting for her to reciprocate. He was acting like a love-struck fool, knew it. Didn't care.

"No names between us is so much easier. However, if you insist, I'm Cas Doyle."

"Irish, I see."

"Scottish?" she asked.

The fries arrived while they stared at each other. Guy, for the first time since he could remember, was tongue-tied. He thought when he met his mate none of this first date stuff would be happening. *This wasn't even a first date.* "Okay..." he paused, "Yes, Scottish once, now American. I could tell you the story of my clan, but it would probably bore you to tears."

"You really don't have to make idle conversation. I like you and if you must know, I think silence," she paused, staring at him with her summer sky blue eyes, "is refreshing."

Her glass of pinot was almost empty so he ordered a second. Sometimes silence was refreshing, but he needed to know more about her. Everything about her, he amended. If he had to close the bar with her tonight to learn a few things, he would. He wanted the answers to the riddle. "Where do you live?"

She shrugged her delicately slim shoulders again before smiling at him. "Here and there. Mostly there. Never stayed in one place very long. I'd like that to change though."

"That's mighty vague," he told her, looking for something more relevant. If she was running from someone or something the more he knew the easier it would be to find her if she left here without a word. That thought sent a cold chill down his spine in the heated atmosphere and called him back to the very reality that they were just meeting. He had no hold over her.

"I'm guessing you live here, in Cactus Junction." She reached out to touch his hand, effectively changing the subject from her to him.

The sensation sent a jolt of sexual longing straight to his groin. He wanted to pull that beautiful hand to his mouth and kiss her fingers, suck them into his mouth but realized prudently it was too soon. Scaring her away was not a good ploy. "Just down the road then off it to the right. Can't get to my house unless you walk or ride a horse. Well, a Harley would get you there too."

"See, you like your privacy and perhaps silence too. We are much the same in that," she told him while she held her glass of wine to her lips. "I don't get along well with very many people. I'm a bit of a recluse I've been told, but I like you."

The second glass arrived. The waiter took the first away. He wondered how many he should let her drink or if she would stop herself. He did mean to take her home tonight if she was agreeable. He really wasn't a drink em up take em home kind of guy. Yet that was exactly what he was doing.

For the greater good, he told himself.

He had an excuse or better, a reason. She was, after all his soul mate. She would be willing without too much to drink. Maybe not tonight. He wanted her tonight.

"I like my privacy but I wouldn't call myself a recluse," he agreed, his voice soft. "Only because I haven't found anyone to share my home with. Perhaps if I do find someone I'll build a road to my house. Wouldn't want my special person to get lost trying to find her way home."

"Me too," she said, moistening her lips, her small pink tongue sweeping erotically across her bottom lip, "like privacy and my laptop more than people."

He wondered if she knew how provocative that tiny gesture was.

Anything she did would arouse him he admitted. Absolutely anything. "So, you come from here and there. Where was the last place you called home?" he asked, needing to back up to the first question which wasn't really the first question. Eventually, he'd find out what she was running from.

"I was in graduate school. Stanford." She pursed her lips then finished the glass of wine. "So," she tapped her fingers on the base of the glass, "I guess you could call that the last place I called home."

He ordered both of them another. Clearly distraught, it seemed she didn't want to open up to him. Yet he craved knowledge about her.

"And you left. Why?" He drummed his fingers on the table, waiting for a response, impatient yet trying to understand her hesitancy because they didn't know each other. "I guess that's none of my business."

"You're right, it's not but I don't think you'll hurt me. I feel safe with you and I don't understand the reasons. Don't feel that way around men very often. Don't talk to men." Another glass of wine was set in front of her. She stared at it for a moment before looking to him again. "Are you trying to get me drunk? I should slow down."

"No and whatever you want."

Her lashes lowered then, "I guess it is up to me to say no."

Lord, but he didn't want her to say no anything. "What were you studying?" Perhaps that would be an easier question and might give him some insight into his recalcitrant soul mate. She obviously felt some attraction but didn't appear to understand exactly just how potent and raw that magnetism was.

"Paranormal abnormalities in the southwest. There have been plausible sightings, you know, shapeshifters, mostly big cats but there was a wolf sighting a few years ago. I left my studies because something terrified me. I started running but whatever it was it followed me. For some reason I ended up here."

His heart caught in his throat. He wasn't sure where to go with this but knew she wasn't telling him the entire story. "Do you think shapeshifters exist?" Slowly, he sipped keeping his gaze focused on her over the rim of the glass.

She smiled at him again. This smile was somehow different. One eyebrow rose a fraction. Then, "I know they exist. I know something else too."

He finished his beer before ordering another round for both of them. Then after minutes of thought, "How? How do you know something so strange or is it just speculation?"

She shrugged those delicate shoulders again, ones he wanted to kiss from one side to the other, "Just my gut. No, actually I've seen one, a coal black jaguar shapeshifter in my dreams. I've seen all of him except his face. I've seen him take his clothes off and shift then in another dream I've seen him change from the jaguar back to a human."

Cas had seen him... naked. Or had she seen one of his brothers or sisters? No, he was sure she was speaking about him. She said him. "What do you mean?" he asked, suddenly feeling out of his element and a bit at a disadvantage. She'd seen him naked and... strangely he didn't feel at all violated. He had this unthinkable need to ask her if she liked what she saw. He drug in a slow breath of air.

"I think I've had a bit too much to drink." She finished the glass in front of her then changing the subject, "Should be getting back to my room before I fall asleep right here."

"At the hotel?" he asked, "I'll walk you back, unless you'd like to come home with me." Where did that come from? He didn't want her to think all he wanted from her was a one nightstand when he craved a lifetime. If she was truly running from something dangerous though, he wasn't about to leave her alone and unprotected in the hotel. If she refused to come home with him, he'd stand guard outside her room.

Or inside.

"You said," she paused, "a person had to walk. Don't know if I can make it that far in these shoes." Cas looked at her feet before she let him help her to stand then leaned on him. "I'm feeling a wee bit tipsy. I think I drank too much." Her words began to slur a bit. She was adorable, endearing.

"You don't have to walk. I rode my horse." He chuckled thinking of holding his mate in his arms while riding his horse, taking her home, to what would be there home soon, he hoped.

"Then you're going to walk." She wrapped an arm around him, steadying herself. "Should I tell you now or later that I don't know how to ride a horse? Terrified of them really. I could fly..." she gasped, putting a hand over her mouth, her eyes wide as saucers.

He stared at her a moment trying to understand then calked it up as too much wine. "Neither of us is going to walk. We're both riding my horse. Come on, I'll show you." His eagerness came through all too clear, but she didn't seem to notice.

A few minutes later they stood in front of his horse. "Names Sam. He always sees me home even when I've had a few too many. Knows his way with his eyes closed. Don't even have to use the reins. He's as gentle as a kitten."

She stepped back a few feet, her hands outstretched as if she warded him off. Then repeated an earlier statement. "Don't know how to ride a horse. Never been this close to one either. How the devil am I going to stay on? How am I going to get on?"

"Easy enough, I'll ride the horse and you can sit on my lap. I'll make sure nothing happens to you. I promise." He almost said and you can ride me but stopped himself just in time, but he might explore with his hands, just a little. The last thing he wanted was to send her running away from him before they even got to know each other. He didn't want to be the one she was running and hiding from.

"How do we accomplish this then." Her words slurred even more now. She wavered slightly, her hands reaching out to grab him for support. "I doubt if I can mount that thing."

"I'll mount Sam and you can give me your hand then I'll pull you onto my lap." He said as he proceeded to do just that.

"Don't know..." She was backing away from him, her head tilted slightly, her eyes squinting as if she tried to see what was in front of her.

"You can do it. Besides I know you don't want to stay at the hotel by yourself. Whatever you're running from might find you there." He watched her face pale while she swallowed hard.

"I never thought of that."

A few minutes later, Cas sat his lap, her body trembling as he slowly let Sam take the lead. He held onto her, praying something wouldn't spook her or his horse. He was sure he just died and was in heaven. Her feminine curves fit soundly against the hard planes of his body.

"You have to trust me," he told her, his whisper close to her ear. He lightly touched the lobe with his tongue. "I'm not going to let anything happen to you. I've got you. All you have to do is relax."

"So you say," she murmured softly, leaning against him doing as he asked. "I wish..."

"Do you trust me?" he asked, hoping she'd say yes, his hands running up then down her arms.

"I want to," again a whisper.

He began to chant a song his great grandfather, an Apache medicine man, taught him when he was a child. The chant always soothed his nerves when he was upset or frightened as a child as well as during the skirmishes, the endless nightmare of Iraq. He felt Cas slowly relax into his body. She could be falling asleep she had so much wine, but her body didn't relax totally. Her hand rested on his forearm. He felt the curve of one breast push against his chest. This was good. It was all so very good. He would find out more about her when the time was right.

A full moon appeared in the sky just as he reached his home. A slight breeze cooled the hot summer air. His house was built in a small grove of trees, some he planted years ago some more recently. In times of draught, he had to haul water yet they survived just as his clan survived, lived and prospered in these barren lands.

He bent close to her ear and whispered. For a moment he was tempted to touch the shell of her ear with his tongue but held back this time. He wanted her to be the aggressor this first time with here, "We're here."

She placed her hand on his chest, her fingers kneading his skin through his shirt. "I think we've stopped. Told you Sam knew his way home."

"Umm..."

"I'll let you down. All you have to do is land on your feet. Do you think you can do that?"

"Maybe, I'm like a cat. I always land on my feet."

Her words sent a shiver down his spine. *Like a cat.* "Here you go. There's a bale of hay beneath your feet so you don't have so far to go. Be careful. Don't fall."

She slid through his arms and while she didn't exactly land on her feet, she didn't fall either. Looking up at him, she sat on top the bale of hay, smiling. "I'm okay."

He dismounted. "I have to take care of Sam. You wait here and I'll be back in a few minutes then we can go to the house."

"I'll just lie down here. Wake me up when you're done." She curled into a ball, her hands beneath her cheeks.

Also by C. L. Kraemer
at
Rogue Phoenix Press

The Lending Library

Chapter One

Ailidh wobbled precariously on her high heels.

Kayne smirked. "Having problems, dear?"

"Shut up!" she snapped. "I need to practice this until I get it right. We don't really have many options left open to us, Kayne. You had better practice, too."

He stopped and steadied himself on the railing of the porch. He wriggled his feet out of the closed leather shoes that encased them.

"I don't know why you insist we wear these ridiculous articles of clothing. This long-sleeved shirt cuts off the circulation to my hands not to mention the lack of space for my wings and these long pants chap my legs.

"Worst of all, are these horrendous leather shoes. They pinch and make my feet swell. Why do we have to go through all of this? I don't understand." Kayne grumbled.

Ailidh sighed and slowly, *patiently* explained to him, once again, why they were practicing.

"Remember last Wednesday when Keegan and Connal lost their dwelling? The sound of their tree crashing to the ground was deafening. The Others are moving out more and more. We will lose our home if we don't act first. Now, put your shoes back on and walk for just five more minutes."

Kayne wrestled his shirt off and threw it to the porch's deck. He pulled the long pants off his body and left them in a heap next to the shirt. Bending forward, he touched his toes gingerly as he gradually unfurled his lacey wings. Slowly, he pulled himself to an upright position. Shoulders back, wings completely expanded, he lifted his 18-inch form to its full height and looked at Ailidh defiantly.

"I don't need to fit into the Others' world. They need to adjust themselves to my world and leave us alone."

Ailidh, teetering, grabbed the lower railing of the porch and shook her head.

"Kayne, most of the Others don't even know we exist. How can they adjust to something they don't even believe?"

"They adjust to animals, don't they?"

"The animals chose to be seen. We did not. Remember? Our great, great grandfathers took a vote and decided we would endanger ourselves more if we continued to be visible to the Others. At that time, they didn't have all the machinery they have now. They moved into our lands at a slower pace. Now, put on the clothes and try to adjust."

"No." Kayne kicked at the clothing on the porch. "I'm going to get a magazine and a cup of coffee. You can stand here and practice day and night for all I care."

He turned on his heels and lifted himself off the ground with his delicate appendages. He lazily winged his way into the open window of the building marked *Lending Library*.

Hovering until he landed on the balls of his feet, he folded the wings tight to his torso and walked to the corner of the building signed Coffee Shop. He sat in a small chair snugged close to the matching table. Sliding the Newsweek someone had tossed on the table toward him, he flipped through the pages. Minimized for easier handling, the magazine was still large enough to require both of his hands to turn the pages. A diminutive nymph in a waitress uniform with a "Chrissy" nametag took his order for a latte. Ten minutes later, she returned with the steaming liquid in a cup.

"Thanks, Chrissy." Kayne picked up the cup carefully and took a sip.

"No problem, Kayne," she had a surprisingly deep voice for a nymph. "Where's Ailidh?"

Kayne jerked a thumb over his shoulder toward the front porch.

"Practicing," he grunted.

"Oh," Chrissy mopped the table next to Kayne's with a wet rag then flew daintily to the kitchen with the dirty cups and saucers she'd picked up. One of the resident dryads of the valley, Chrissy was living in the tree behind the Lending Library. Her home across the meadow had been one of the first destroyed.

Ailidh is right. Kayne frowned at the silent admission. The Others were invading his world with frightening, swift, uncaring swaths into the forestlands. Soon there wouldn't be an Ancient tree left. While, at a glance, their movements seemed random, even careless, Kayne had noted a pattern, albeit haphazard, to their actions. Months earlier he'd watched from a safe distance as the huge screeching yellow machines ripped up his ancient wood friends and squashed their bodies beneath armored tracks. He could never be sure whether the squealing had been the old trees or the vicious yellow machines. After the first occasion of watching as they destroyed a sea of Ancients, Kayne had left on shaky wings and flown home. Ailidh was furious at him, thinking he'd been with his friends drinking honeysuckle wine. He couldn't stop throwing up long enough to tell her what he'd seen.

When the thunder and growl of the angry yellow tree destroyers rumbled over their living room ceiling several months later, Kayne sat Ailidh down and explained what had happened that fateful night.

He took her soft, dainty hand in his and looked into her sparkling moss green eyes.

"We must be prepared to move from our home."

Ailidh's exquisite wings trembled. "Why?"

The earth near the entrance to their home groaned and bits of dirt drizzled from around the doorway.

Kayne pointed up. "That—that—monster will reach into our home and pluck us up with no regard whatsoever. I've seen it rip out the Ancient trees in the glen over by Drystan's home.

"The night you thought me so drunk I could not speak, I was ill from watching The Others kill the Ancient trees and destroy homes of our friends. I couldn't stop being sick long enough to explain to you. When I finally got the horror of that picture out of my mind and stopped throwing up, you'd gone to bed—angry. I didn't want to disturb you."

Ailidh's face blanched and she slumped to the cloth-covered chair Kayne had so carefully carved from a branch the Ancient tree had gifted them.

"Wh-wh-why? We've not harmed them. Why do they want to rip out our homes and make us move?"

"I don't know my love, but we've got to find a way to fight back or we'll be next."

Kayne had soothed Ailidh's fears that night, but she began a campaign to move to Faetown and get out of the meadow and woods they called home.

Kayne sighed. She'd get her way and they'd move, but he wasn't going without a fight.

He felt a soft rush of air caress his cheek and looked up to find Ailidh alighting gently on her bare feet, her toes inflamed and angry looking.

He nodded to her. "Better get the Librarian to wrap those before they swell too much. Wouldn't want to put your *shoes* in the rubbish bin." Licking several fingers, he turned the page, the crinkle of the slick paper echoing off the wall of books.

When his smarmy comment met with silence, Kayne looked up to see a large tear meandering down Ailidh's cheek. He dropped the magazine to the table and hung his head, pushing out air between his lips. He'd done it again. He'd hurt the one woman who put up with his attitude and still loved him. Most women of the Fae would have kicked out his boastful self long ago not tolerating his pride and pomposity. Not Ailidh. She'd just look at him with those enormous sparkling moss green eyes, pat his hand and kiss his cheek. Kayne, unlike most Fae men, preferred one mate and one mate only. He never had understood the need to wing from inviting mossy bed to inviting mossy bed.

He reached out and grabbed the wayward drop heading toward the fine line of Ailidh's jaw.

"I'm sorry, my love. Let's see if the Librarian has something to ease the pain." Kayne lifted himself from the chair and fluttered to the back of the building.

On the door was a sign. It read: "Rap loudly. Human hearing."

Kayne pounded on the door, settled himself on the floor, and waited.

Slowly the big door opened; before him stood a giant of a person. He sucked in a deep breath and felt his wings tremble.

Pulling up a stool, the giant Librarian sat. She was nearly at his eye level. A gentle smile touched her lips and crinkled her gray eyes. The essence of wild roses swirled lightly on the air.

"Kayne. How can I help you?"

Her soft voice purred quietly to his keen hearing.

Kayne opened his mouth but nothing came out. He coughed, stepped back then winged himself up a foot. At this level, he was looking in to the kind eyes.

"Ailidh... Ailidh has been practicing with those high heel shoes, and now her feet are swollen and hurting. Do you have something that would help?"

Linda thought for a moment. "I do believe I have something to ease her pain. I also have some Epson salts you can take with you so she can use them tonight. Wait here."

Rising from the step stool slowly, she walked to the back of the small room and opened a cupboard on the wall. Taking out a box and a bottle, the Librarian returned to the doorway.

"May I come out and administer to her?" Gray eyes questioned as she stood with the medicine in her hands.

Kayne hesitated. Ailidh liked the Librarian, but he still didn't trust her. After all, she was one of the Others. He turned his head and saw his mate trying to stifle the large tears meandering down her cheeks by swiping at them with the back of her hand.

"Yes. Please. She's in such pain."

Linda was surprised. Very few of the wee folk had become comfortable with her presence. Ailidh was the exception, so getting their permission to move about her own home was necessary if she was to keep them coming into her library.

"Lead the way, Kayne." She wasn't above playing to his male vanity.

As they got closer to the tiny faerie, Ailidh straightened in her chair and sipped from her coffee drink. She was a bit startled to see the Librarian out in the building. She didn't come out in the daytime for fear of scaring away the wee folk that gathered. Something must really be wrong for her to take such measures.

"Librarian." The sweet sound of Ailidh's voice carried to the odd pair approaching her.

"Ailidh. How are you today?"

"I'm well, thank you. What brings you out of your room?"

"Kayne asked me to see to your feet. He mentioned you were suffering and asked if I could help."

Ailidh shot Kayne a glare. "My toes are swollen and hurt a bit, but they will heal without help, thank you."

Linda could sense a fight brewing and opted to take the diplomatic way out.

"Well, let me give you some of my healing helpers. Use them if you like and if not, hang on to them. At some point in the future, they might come in handy. These little orange pills here relieve pain from the inside out, small dose aspirin. I believe you have this remedy in a leaf you brew; this is just easier to take and not quite so bitter. Just swallow them, don't chew, and in about 20 minutes you should feel some relief from the aching."

Linda gently shook the box of Epsom salts.

"These salts work if you place them in hot water and soak your feet. They're called Epsom salts and can be quite handy for those days when you've trekked too far. I'd be more than happy to get a tub so you could start the healing now."

Ailidh looked at Kayne's worried face and the concern on the Librarian's face. She pushed out a sigh.

"All right. If it will make both of you happy..." She watched relief flood the faces of the two people she cared about the most. If this would stop her feet from throbbing... she'd try anything.

"I'll get Chrissy to give you a hand." Linda took a step and hesitated. Turning, she asked, "Is that all right with you?"

Ailidh nodded.

Linda trod lightly on the old oaken floor. As she came close to the kitchen, she stopped, waiting until all her clothing had stopped rustling. She cleared her throat and closed her eyes. She'd made an agreement with the small ones to ask permission before peering directly at them—it was considered polite in their realm.

"Chrissy?" Linda whispered.

"Yes, Librarian?"

"May I speak with you?"

"Of, course, Librarian. Let me dry my hands and I'll join you.

Linda sighed quietly. These wee ones had taught her to slow her world down. It was a lesson she greatly valued.

The whirl of wings wisped past her face and she scrunched her eyes tight.

"Please, Librarian. I thought we had agreed we would not stand on the formalities. Open your eyes. I wish to see your storm-cloud colored eyes."

Chrissy maneuvered herself to sit on the hand railing that separated the kitchen from the main floor.

Linda relaxed her features and allowed her eyes to open; before her sat the tiny nymph. She had clad herself in a fifties-style, carhop uniform, ingeniously made from the petals of daisies and roses.

Linda allowed a smile to touch her lips. "You're looking very… official today. Any particular reason?"

Chrissy shifted her position. "Yes, I was reading on the Internet that servers used to get something called tips. Every server I saw had a uniform so I decided I like this style best and put it together. Maybe I'll get some tips."

Linda was finding it very hard not to laugh aloud. "Well, Chrissy, I don't really think you have a need for tips."

Chrissy pushed her lower lip out and furrowed her brow into a thunderous frown. "Why?"

Linda caught herself before a grin covered her face. "Because tips are paper money customers leave if they think the server has done a good job. Since you live here in the forest and most of your housing, food, and needs are met without having to buy anything, paper money doesn't really have any value, does it?"

Chrissy's lip pulled in and she smoothed her brow. Her face took on a quizzical look and she tilted her head. "I think you're right. Well, this uniform would be wilted by the end of the day, anyway. I'll just wear my regular clothes tomorrow. Was there something you needed, Librarian?"

Linda allowed herself a small chuckle. "Yes. Ailidh has injured her feet, and I wish to get a pan large enough for her to fit in both her feet. I'll need to have water warm enough to melt these salt crystals and then a towel available for her to dry her feet."

The little nymph narrowed her eyes and puzzled the situation. "I know there are some large pans in the very back of the cupboard. Will you come in and pull them out?"

Linda hid her surprise. She never entered the kitchen when Chrissy was working. Her size terrified the little nymph and it was, again, one of the agreements they had made. Moving very slowly, Linda entered the tiny room. She crouched on her knees and opened a very tiny door. In the back was a small, quart size, sauté pan which she was sure was the pot the little nymph meant. Using two fingers to slide out the pan, she pulled it from cupboard and placed it on the top.

"Is this the one you meant?"

Chrissy buzzed into the room and looked at the pan. "Yes. I'll warm some water in it in the microwave…"

"Uh, don't do that. The one thing that won't work in the microwave is metal. If you'll allow me, I'll find something plastic…"

Chrissy smacked her forehead. "Librarian, don't worry. I'll just have to use my magic. How silly of me to forget heating water is one of the first things we're taught. So, if you'll leave?"

Linda rose slowly from the floor and feeling somewhat like a pretzel, backed out of the small space. She rolled up to her full 4 ft. 8 in. height. It felt good to stretch her cramped muscles.

"I'll leave this to you, Chrissy."

Turning she noted Ailidh and Kayne deep in conversation. Something about the body language of the two wee ones was very wrong. It made Linda think. These two were not the only faeries to come into the library and whisper in frightened, muted tones. Linda was determined to find out what was causing such consternation among the Fae community. From the trembling of their wings, she needed to move fast or her tiny folk would be gone, and Linda would be alone with her library full of books.

Also by Genie Gabriel
at
Rogue Phoenix Press

More Than Just a Dog

Chapter One

Horace Ainsworth patted the side of the giant red fire hydrant towering two stories above him then addressed the terrier mix dog staring at him curiously. "It's finished. Now don't you dig in my Maddie's roses any more or potty on the pansies."

Batzy stared at Horace's retreating back for a moment before he hiked his leg on the nearest flowering plant.

Then he turned his attention to the odd-looking structure the Big Human had erected. Not like any fire hydrant he'd ever sniffed. A canine would have to be the size of King Kong to give this thing a proper marking.

Though it did smell like the water that sprayed out of the hose when the human across the street yelled at him. Batzy grinned and lifted his leg, imagining he was returning the spray of the yelling human.

As he circled this mysterious structure, the smell of fresh paint and overturned earth drifted into his nostrils. It was bigger than the merry-go-round at the park where his human, Chloe, sometimes took him.

Wonder what's inside?

Batzy scratched at the side of the structure then trotted another few steps and scratched again. About halfway around he found an opening. Not tall enough for the Big Human, but just about perfect for his little girl, Chloe. Batzy darted inside and lifted his face to sample the aromas.

No scents of danger but much to explore. Like this box of dirt. Odd. Big humans usually didn't appreciate the joys of digging. Hadn't he just been told not to dig in the rose bushes? A sniff and a poke with his paw uncovered a bone. Fresh out of the package. Batzy looked around. What game was the Big Human playing?

"Batzy!" his little girl was calling him.

Batzy stepped out of the digging pit. *Hmm. I smell peanut butter.*

He put a front paw on a cabinet for balance and nosed a button. A bone-shaped treat fell into a bowl below. Also fresh out of a package. The Big Human was definitely up to something. Batzy gobbled it down quickly before looking around again.

"Batzy!"

Drat! He had to go. On his way out, Batzy stepped back into the digging box and snatched up the bone. Outside once again, he pushed the bone through the gap under the fence, and squeezed through after it.

He popped up on the other side with only a few more streaks of mud on the white of his belly and wagged his tail at Chloe. He'd go back to explore the Big Human's structure later.

~ * ~

Satisfied he had neutralized the threat to Maddie's rose bushes, Horace returned to the workshop in the basement of their castle-shaped home. In King Arthur's time, the sorcerer Merlin might have worked his magic in similar surroundings. Had Merlin simply been a scientist with an observing eye and a searching mind?

That's how Horace saw himself: open to possibilities and what others might consider impossibilities. He loved to explore "what if" and took delight in disproving "facts." Edison did it with the light bulb. The Wright brothers did it with airplanes. Horace continued that tradition with a flying car and a robot that served dinner, as well as a play structure made out of a water tower and painted like a giant fire hydrant for the dog next door. After all, who said inventions had to be serious?

Horace scanned the stone walls lined with tables and shelves stacked with high-tech inventions and mechanical gadgets in various stages of development. What should he work on next?

He nearly set aside the recipe card propped on the computer keyboard, except he hadn't seen the word "urgent" on a recipe before. Horace realized it was a phone message from his cousin, Clement. "Will arrive tomorrow with submarine."

Horace scratched his chin. What would his space engineer relative be doing with a submarine?

Suddenly, the alarm for the garages began wailing. A glance at the security monitor showed a truck pulling a trailer painted in vivid red and orange careening around the castle had clipped the gutter downspout and set off the alarm.

A net dropped over the trailer, tangling in a wheel and jerking it sideways. Unfortunately, the truck continued its forward momentum until it also lurched to a stop, now sitting almost side by side with the trailer.

If Horace didn't know his wife was safely painting in her studio, he would have sworn she was driving the truck.

He hurried out of his workshop to be sure both truck and driver were okay.

A tall, lanky man wearing a white shirt and black slacks jumped down from the driver's seat as the truck shuddered to a stop, grinning at Horace. "Hi, Cuz."

A frown creased Horace's forehead as he stared at the argyle suspenders that kept Clement Ainsworth's slacks pulled up into a permanent wedgie. The same suspenders Clement bragged had garnered him a date with the prettiest sorority girl at college some thirty-odd years ago. "But your message said you'd be here tomorrow."

Clement waved away Horace's confusion. "I called yesterday. You need a new secretary."

"My nephew took the message—"

"Like I said, you need a new secretary."

Horace made a mental note to come up with a more efficient way to deliver messages. "Why are you here? This doesn't look like a submarine."

Clement frowned. "Paperwork hold-up. But we can start work without it."

"Work on what?"

After a suspicious look around, Clement dropped his voice to a whisper. "A probe to explore black holes."

Horace also looked around, seeing nothing of danger except his cousin's lack of driving skills. "You mean black holes in space caused by stars burning out?"

"Well, that's the generally accepted theory."

"And do you have a probe in the trailer?"

"Nah. This is a mobile fabrication laboratory." Clement walked to the back of the trailer, stepping over the tangled netting that had captured one of the wheels. "This will make us a working prototype of the probe."

Horace stepped inside the trailer behind his cousin. "What is all this?"

"Laser cutter, CNC machine tools, robotic water jet, a rapid prototyping device—just to name a few. All run by cutting edge computer software."

Horace's hands tingled with the desire to pry open the metal casings on the equipment and see how the machines really worked. "Don't you make anything by hand?"

"You're still living in the dark ages, Horace." Clement laughed again. "No one makes things manually anymore."

Horace squared his shoulders, determined not to let his older, city slicker cousin make him feel inferior the way he had in college. "I do."

Clement's expression turned immediately apologetic, something Horace had rarely seen. "That's why I need you."

With a deep breath and a frown, Clement looked Horace squarely in the eye. "You're the detail man. You make visions a reality. Others know the theories, but you know how to make them work."

"Um...right." Horace was still a bit off balance and definitely wary of his cousin's change in attitude. For the first time Horace could recall, Clement seemed to appreciate his skills rather than denigrating them. Surely Horace could give the man a chance to explain—and examine these intriguing machines—before Maddie threw Clement off their property. "Tell me what you have in mind."

"Saving the world."

Buy these books and check out all the books by these authors at:

http://www.roguephoenixpress.com

Rogue Phoenix Press

Representing Excellence in Publishing

Quality trade paperbacks and downloads

in multiple formats,

in genres ranging from historical to contemporary romance, mystery and science fiction.

Visit the website then bookmark it.

We add new titles each month!

www.ingramcontent.com/pod-product-compliance
Lightning Source LLC
Chambersburg PA
CBHW071450170626
46811CB00007B/2534